He Knew He W
Vol. II

He Knew He Was Right
Vol. II

by

Anthony Trollope

He Knew He Was Right vol. II, by Anthony Trollope

This book in its current typographical format first published 2008 by

Cambridge Scholars Publishing

12 Back Chapman Street, Newcastle upon Tyne, NE6 2XX, UK

British Library Cataloguing in Publication Data
A catalogue record for this book is available from the British Library

ISBN (10): 1-84718-706-4, ISBN (13): 9781847187062

CONTENTS

CHAPTER L. CAMILLA TRIUMPHANT

It was now New Year's day, and there was some grief and perhaps more excitement in Exeter for it was rumoured that Miss Stanbury lay very ill at her house in the Close. But in order that our somewhat uneven story may run as smoothly as it may be made to do, the little history of the French family for the intervening months shall be told in this chapter, in order that it may be understood how matters were with them when the tidings of Miss Stanbury's severe illness first reached their house at Heavitree.

After that terrible scene in which Miss Stanbury had so dreadfully confounded Mr Gibson by declaring the manner in which he had been rebuffed by Dorothy, the unfortunate clergyman had endeavoured to make his peace with the French family by assuring the mother that in very truth it was the dearest wish of his heart to make her daughter Camilla his wife. Mrs French, who had ever been disposed to favour Arabella's ambition, well knowing its priority and ancient right, and who of late had been taught to consider that even Camilla had consented to waive any claim that she might have once possessed, could not refrain from the expression of some surprise. That he should be recovered at all out of the Stanbury clutches was very much to Mrs French—was so much that, had time been given her for consideration, she would have acknowledged to herself readily that the property had best be secured at once to the family, without incurring that amount of risk, which must unquestionably attend any attempt on her part to direct Mr Gibson's purpose hither or thither. But the proposition came so suddenly, that time was not allowed to her to be altogether wise. 'I thought it was poor Bella,' she said, with something of a piteous whine in her voice. At the moment Mr Gibson was so humble, that he was half inclined to give way even on that head. He felt himself to have been brought so low in the market by that terrible story of Miss Stanbury's which he had been unable either to contradict or to explain that there was but little power of fighting left in him. He was, however, just able to speak a word for himself, and that sufficed, 'I hope there has been no mistake,' he said; 'but really it is Camilla that has my heart.' Mrs French made no rejoinder to this. It was so much to her to know that Mr Gibson's heart was among them at all after what had occurred in the Close, that she acknowledged to herself after that moment of reflection that Arabella must be sacrificed for the good of the family interests. Poor, dear, loving, misguided, and spiritless mother! She would have given the blood out of her bosom to get husbands for her daughters, though it was not of her own experience that she had learned that of all worldly goods a husband is the best. But it was the possession which they had from their earliest years thought of acquiring, which they first expected, for which they had then hoped, and afterwards worked and schemed and striven with every energy and as to which they had at last almost despaired. And now Arabella's fire had been rekindled with a new spark, which, alas, was to be quenched so suddenly! 'And am I to tell them?' asked Mrs French, 'with a tremor in her voice. To this, however, Mr Gibson demurred. He said that for certain reasons he should like a fortnight's grace; and that at the end of the fortnight he would be prepared to speak. The interval was granted without further questions, and Mr Gibson was allowed to leave the house.

After that Mrs French was not very comfortable at home. As soon as Mr Gibson had departed, Camilla at once returned to her mother and desired to know what had taken place. Was it true that the perjured man had proposed to that young woman in the Close? Mrs French was not clever at keeping a secret, and she could not keep this by her own aid. She told all that happened to Camilla, and between them they agreed that Arabella should be kept in ignorance till the fatal fortnight should have passed. When Camilla was interrogated as to her own purpose, she said she should like a day to think of it. She took the twenty-four hours, and then made the following confession of her passion to her mother. 'You see, mamma, I always liked Mr Gibson, always.'

'So did Arabella, 'my dear before you thought of such things.'

'I dare say that may be true, mamma; but that is not my fault. He came here among us on such sweetly intimate terms that the feeling grew up with me before I knew what it meant. As to any idea of cutting out Arabella, my conscience is quite clear. If I thought there had been anything really between them. I would have gone anywhere, to the top of a mountain, rather than rob my sister of a heart that belonged to her.'

'He has been so slow about it,' said Mrs French.

'I don't know about that,' said Camilla. 'Gentlemen have to be slow, I suppose, when they think of their incomes. He only got St. Peter's-cum-Pumpkin three years ago, and didn't know for the first year whether he could hold that and the minor canonry together. Of course a gentleman has to think of these things before he comes forward.'

'My dear, he has been very backward.'

'If I'm to be Mrs Gibson, mamma, I beg that I mayn't hear anything said against him. Then there came all this about that young woman; and when I saw that Arabella took on so, which I must say was very absurd, I'm sure I put myself out of the way entirely. If I'd buried myself under the ground I couldn't have done it more.

And it's my belief that what I've said, all for Arabella's sake, has put the old woman into such a rage that it has made a quarrel between him and the niece; otherwise that wouldn't be off. I don't believe a word of her refusing him, and never shall. Is it in the course of things, mamma?' Mrs French shook her head. 'Of course not. Then when you question him very properly he says that he's devoted to poor me. If I was to refuse him, he wouldn't put up with Bella.'

'I suppose not,' said Mrs French.

'He hates Bella. I've known it all along, though I wouldn't say so. If I were to sacrifice myself ever so it wouldn't be of any good and I shan't do it.' In this way the matter was arranged.

At the end of the fortnight, however, Mr Gibson did not come, nor at the end of three weeks. Inquiries had of course been made, and it was ascertained that he had gone into Cornwall for a parson's holiday of thirteen days. That might be all very well. A man might want the recruiting vigour of some change of air after such scenes as those Mr Gibson had gone through with the Stanburys, and before his proposed encounter with new perils. And he was a man so tied by the leg that his escape could not be for any long time. He was back on the appointed Sunday, and on the Wednesday Mrs French, under Camilla's instruction, wrote to him a pretty little note. He replied that he would be with her on the Saturday. It would then be nearly four weeks after the great day with Miss Stanbury, but no one would be inclined to quarrel with so short a delay as that. Arabella in the meantime had become fidgety and unhappy. She seemed to understand that something was expected, being quite unable to guess what that something might be. She was true throughout these days to the simplicity of head-gear which Mr Gibson had recommended to her, and seemed in her questions to her mother and to Camilla to be more fearful of Dorothy Stanbury than of any other enemy. 'Mamma, I think you ought to tell her,' said Camilla more than once. But she had not been told when Mr Gibson came on the Saturday. It may truly be said that the poor mother's pleasure in the prospects of one daughter was altogether destroyed by the anticipation of the other daughter's misery. Had Mr Gibson made Dorothy Stanbury his wife they could have all comforted themselves together by the heat of their joint animosity.

He came on the Saturday, and it was so managed that he was closeted with Camilla before Arabella knew that he was in the house. There was a quarter of an hour during which his work was easy, and perhaps pleasant. When he began to explain his intention, Camilla, with the utmost frankness, informed him that her mother had told her all about it. Then she turned her face on one side and put her hand in his; he got his arm round her waist, gave her a kiss, and the thing was done. Camilla was fully resolved that after such a betrothal it should not be undone. She had behaved with sisterly forbearance, and would not now lose the reward of virtue. Not a word was said of Arabella at this interview till he was pressed to come and drink tea with them all that night. He hesitated a moment; and then Camilla declared, with something perhaps of imperious roughness in her manner, that he had better face it all at once. 'Mamma will tell her, and she will understand,' said Camilla. He hesitated again, but at last promised that he would come.

Whilst he was yet in the house Mrs French had told the whole story to her poor elder daughter. 'What is he doing with Camilla?' Arabella had asked with feverish excitement.

'Bella, darling don't you know?' said the mother.

'I know nothing. Everybody keeps me in the dark, and I am badly used. What is it that he is doing?' Then Mrs French tried to take the poor young woman in her arms, but Arabella would not submit to be embraced. 'Don't!' she exclaimed. 'Leave me alone. Nobody likes me, or cares a bit about me! Why is Cammy with him there, all alone?'

'I suppose he is asking her to be his wife.' Then Arabella threw herself in despair upon the bed, and wept without any further attempt at control over her feelings. It was a death-blow to her last hope, and all the world, as she looked upon the world then, was over for her. 'If I could have arranged it the other way, you know that I would,' said the mother.

'Mamma,' said Arabella jumping up, 'he shan't do it. He hasn't a right. And as for her Oh, that she should treat me in this way! Didn't he tell me the other night, when he drank tea here with me alone—'

'What did he tell you, Bella?'

'Never mind. Nothing shall ever make me speak to him again, not if he married her three times over; nor to her. She is a nasty, sly, good-for-nothing thing!'

'But, Bella—'

'Don't talk to me, mamma. There never was such a thing done before since people were people at all. She has been doing it all the time. I know she has.'

Nevertheless Arabella did sit down to tea with the two lovers that night. There was a terrible scene between her and Camilla; but Camilla held her own; and Arabella, being the weaker of the two, was vanquished by the expenditure of her own small energies. Camilla argued that as her sister's chance was gone, and as the prize had come in her own way, there was no good reason why it should be lost to the family altogether, because Arabella could not win it. When Arabella called her a treacherous vixen and a heartless, profligate hussy, she spoke out freely, and said that she wasn't going to be abused. A gentleman to whom she was attached had asked her for her hand, and she had given it. If Arabella chose to make herself a fool she might but what would be the effect? Simply that all the world would know that she, Arabella, was disappointed. Poor Bella at last gave way, put on her discarded chignon, and came down to tea. Mr Gibson was already in the room when she entered it. 'Arabella,' he said, getting up to greet her, 'I hope you will congratulate me.' He had planned his little speech and his manner of making it, and had wisely decided that in this way might he best get over the difficulty.

'Oh yes of course,' she said, with a little giggle, and then a sob, and then a flood of tears.

'Dear Bella feels these things so strongly,' said Mrs French.

'We have never been parted yet,' said Camilla. Then Arabella tapped the head of the sofa three or four times sharply with her knuckles. It was the only protest against the reading of the scene which Camilla had given of which she was capable at that moment. After that Mrs French gave out the tea, Arabella curled herself upon the sofa as though she were asleep, and the two lovers settled down to proper lover-like conversation.

The reader may be sure that Camilla was not slow in making the fact of her engagement notorious through the city. It was not probably true that the tidings of her success had anything to do with Miss Stanbury's illness; but it was reported by many that such was the case. It was in November that the arrangement was made, and it certainly was true that Miss Stanbury was rather ill about the same time. 'You know, you naughty Lothario, that you did give her some ground to hope that she might dispose of her unfortunate niece,' said Camilla playfully to her own one, when this illness was discussed between them. 'But you are caught now, and your wings are clipped, and you are never to be a naughty Lothario again.' The clerical Don Juan bore it all, awkwardly indeed, but with good humour, and declared that all his troubles of that sort were over, now and for ever. Nevertheless he did not name the day, and Camilla began to feel that there might be occasion for a little more of that imperious roughness which she had at her command.

November was nearly over and nothing had been fixed about the day. Arabella never condescended to speak to her sister on the subject; but on more than one occasion made some inquiry of her mother. And she came to perceive, or to think that she perceived, that her mother was still anxious on the subject. 'I shouldn't wonder if he wasn't off some day now,' she said at last to her mother.

'Don't say anything so dreadful, Bella.'

'It would serve Cammy quite right, and it's just what he's likely to do.'

'It would kill me,' said the mother.

'I don't know about killing,' said Arabella; 'it's nothing to what I've had to go through. I shouldn't pretend to be sorry if he were to go to Hong-Kong tomorrow.'

But Mr Gibson had no idea of going to Hong-Kong. He was simply carrying out his little scheme for securing the advantages of a 'long day'. He was fully resolved to be married, and was contented to think that his engagement was the best thing for him. To one or two male friends he spoke of Camilla as the perfection of female virtue, and entertained no smallest idea of ultimate escape. But a 'long day' is often a convenience. A bill at three months sits easier on a man than one at sixty days; and a bill at six months is almost as little of a burden as no bill at all.

But Camilla was resolved that some day should be fixed. 'Thomas,' she said to her lover one morning, as they were walking home together after service at the cathedral, 'isn't this rather a fool's Paradise of ours?'

'How a fool's Paradise?' asked the happy Thomas.

'What I mean is, dearest, that we ought to fix something. Mamma is getting uneasy about her own plans.'

'In what way, dearest?'

'About a thousand things. She can't arrange anything till our plans are made. Of course there are little troubles about money when people ain't rich.' Then it occurred to her that this might seem to be a plea for postponing rather than for hurrying the marriage, and she mended her argument. 'The truth is, Thomas, she wants to know when the day is to be fixed, and I've promised to ask. She said she'd ask you herself, but I wouldn't let her do that.'

'We must think about it, of course,' said Thomas.

'But, my dear, there has been plenty of time for thinking. What do you say to January?' This was on the last day of November.

'January!' exclaimed Thomas, in a tone that betrayed no triumph. 'I couldn't get my services arranged for in January.'

'I thought a clergyman could always manage that for his marriage,' said Camilla.

'Not in January. Besides, I was thinking you would like to be away in warmer weather.'

They were still in November, and he was thinking of postponing it till the summer! Camilla immediately perceived how necessary it was that she should be plain with him. 'We shall not have warm weather, as you call it, for a very long time, Thomas and I don't think that it would be wise to wait for the weather at all. Indeed, I've begun to get my things for doing it in the winter. Mamma said that she was sure January would be the very latest. And it isn't as though we had to get furniture or anything of that kind. Of course a lady shouldn't be pressing.' She smiled sweetly and leaned on his arm as she said this. 'But I hate all girlish nonsense and that kind of thing. It is such a bore to be kept waiting. I'm sure there's nothing to prevent it coming off in February.'

The 31st of March was fixed before they reached Heavitree, and Camilla went into her mother's house a happy woman. But Mr Gibson, as he went home, thought that he had been hardly used. Here was a girl who hadn't a shilling of money, not a shilling till her mother died, and who already talked about his house, and his furniture, and his income as if it were all her own! Circumstanced as she was, what right had she to press for an early day? He was quite sure that Arabella would have been more discreet and less exacting. He was very angry with his dear Cammy as he went across the Close to his house.

CHAPTER LI. SHEWING WHAT HAPPENED DURING MISS STANBURY'S ILLNESS

It was on Christmas-day that Sir Peter Mancrudy, the highest authority on such matters in the west of England, was sent for to see Miss Stanbury; and Sir Peter had acknowledged that things were very serious. He took Dorothy on one side, and told her that Mr Martin, the ordinary practitioner, had treated the case, no doubt, quite wisely throughout; that there was not a word to be said against Mr Martin, whose experience was great, and whose discretion was undeniable; but, nevertheless, at least it seemed to Dorothy, that this was the only meaning to be attributed to Sir Peter's words: Mr Martin had in this case taken one line of treatment, when he ought to have taken another. The plan of action was undoubtedly changed, and Mr Martin became very fidgety, and ordered nothing without Sir Peter's sanction. Miss Stanbury was suffering from bronchitis, and a complication of diseases about her throat and chest. Barty Burgess declared to more than one acquaintance in the little parlour behind the bank, that she would go on drinking four or five glasses of new port wine every day, in direct opposition to Martin's request. Camilla French heard the report, and repeated it to her lover, and perhaps another person or two, with an expression of her assured conviction that it must be false at any rate, as regarded the fifth glass. Mrs MacHugh, who saw Martha daily, was much frightened. The peril of such a friend disturbed equally the repose and the pleasures of her life. Mrs Clifford was often at Miss Stanbury's bedside and would have sat there reading for hours together, had she not been made to understand by Martha that Miss Stanbury preferred that Miss Dorothy should read to her. The sick woman received the Sacrament weekly not from Mr Gibson, but from the hands of another minor canon; and, though she never would admit her own danger, or allow others to talk to her of it, it was known to them all that she admitted it to herself because she had, with much personal annoyance, caused a codicil to be added to her will. 'As you didn't marry that man,' she said to Dorothy, 'I must change it again.' It was in vain that Dorothy begged her not to trouble herself with such thoughts. 'That's trash,' said Miss Stanbury, angrily. 'A person who has it is bound to trouble himself about it. You don't suppose I'm afraid of dying do you?' she added. Dorothy answered her with some commonplace declaring how strongly they all expected to see her as well as ever. 'I'm not a bit afraid to die,' said the old woman, wheezing, struggling with such voice as she possessed; 'I'm not afraid of it, and I don't think I shall die this time; but I'm not going to have mistakes when I'm gone.' This was on the eve of the new year, and on the same night she asked Dorothy to write to Brooke Burgess, and request him to come to Exeter. This was Dorothy's letter:

Exeter,
31st December, 186—.

MY DEAR MR BURGESS,

Perhaps I ought to have written before, to say that Aunt Stanbury is not as well as we could wish her; but, as I know that you cannot very well leave your office, I have thought it best not to say anything to frighten you. But tonight Aunt herself has desired me to tell you that she thinks you ought to know that she is ill, and that she wishes you to come to Exeter for a day or two, if it is possible. Sir Peter Mancrudy has been here every day since Christmas-day, and I believe he thinks she may get over it. It is chiefly in the throat what they call bronchitis and she has got to be very weak with it, and at the same time very liable to inflammation. So I know that you will come if you can.

Yours very truly,   DOROTHY STANBURY.

Perhaps I ought to tell you that she had her lawyer here with her the day before yesterday; but she does not seem to think that she herself is in danger. I read to her a good deal, and I think she is generally asleep; when I stop she wakes, and I don't believe she gets any other rest at all.'

When it was known in Exeter that Brooke Burgess had been sent for, then the opinion became general that Miss Stanbury's days were numbered. Questions were asked of Sir Peter at every corner of the street; but Sir Peter was a discreet man, who could answer such questions without giving any information. If it so pleased God, his patient would die; but it was quite possible that she might live. That was the tenor of Sir Peter's replies and they were read in any light, according to the idiosyncrasies of the reader. Mrs MacHugh was quite sure that the danger was over, and had a little game of cribbage on the sly with old Miss Wright for, during the severity of Miss Stanbury's illness, whist was put on one side in the vicinity of the Close. Barty Burgess was still obdurate, and shook his head. He was of opinion that they might soon gratify their curiosity, and see the last crowning iniquity of this wickedest of old women. Mrs Clifford declared that it was all in the hands of God; but that she saw no reason why Miss Stanbury should not get about again. Mr Gibson thought that it was all up with his late friend; and Camilla wished that at their last interview there had been more of charity on the part of one whom she had regarded in past days with respect and esteem. Mrs French, despondent about everything, was quite despondent in this case. Martha almost despaired, and already was burdened with the cares of a whole wardrobe of solemn funereal clothing. She was seen peering in for half-an-hour at the windows and doorway of a large warehouse for the sale of mourning. Giles Hickbody would not speak above his breath, and took his beer standing; but Dorothy was hopeful, and really believed that her aunt would recover. Perhaps Sir Peter had spoken to her in terms less oracular than those which he used towards the public.

Brooke Burgess came, and had an interview with Sir Peter, and to him Sir Peter was under some obligation to speak plainly, as being the person whom Miss Stanbury recognised as her heir. So Sir Peter declared that his patient might perhaps live, and perhaps might die. 'The truth is, Mr Burgess,' said Sir Peter, 'a doctor doesn't know so very much more about these things than other people.' It was understood that Brooke was to remain three days in Exeter, and then return to London. He would, of course, come again if if anything should happen. Sir Peter had been quite clear in his opinion, that no immediate result was to be anticipated either in the one direction or the other. His patient was doomed to a long illness; she might get over it, or she might succumb to it.

Dorothy and Brooke were thus thrown much together during these three days. Dorothy, indeed, spent most of her hours beside her aunt's bed, instigating sleep by the reading of a certain series of sermons in which Miss Stanbury had great faith; but nevertheless, there were some minutes in which she and Brooke were necessarily together. They eat their meals in each other's company, and there was a period in the evening, before Dorothy began her night-watch in her aunt's room, at which she took her tea while Martha was nurse in the room above. At this time of the day she would remain an hour or more with Brooke; and a great deal may be said between a man and a woman in an hour when the will to say it is there. Brooke Burgess had by no means changed his mind since he had declared it to Hugh Stanbury under the midnight lamps of Long Acre, when warmed by the influence of oysters and whisky toddy. The whisky toddy had in that instance brought out truth and not falsehood as is ever the nature of whisky toddy and similar dangerous provocatives. There is no saying truer than that which declares that there is truth in wine. Wine is a dangerous thing, and should not be made the exponent of truth, let the truth be good as it may; but it has the merit of forcing a man to show his true colours. A man who is a gentleman in his cups may be trusted to be a gentleman at all times. I trust that the severe censor will not turn upon me, and tell me that no gentleman in these days is ever to be seen in his cups. There are cups of different degrees of depth; and cups do exist, even among gentlemen, and seem disposed to hold their own let the censor be ever so severe. The gentleman in his cups is a gentleman always; and the man who tells his friend in his cups that he is in love, does so because the fact has been very present to himself in his cooler and calmer moments. Brooke Burgess, who had seen Hugh Stanbury on two or three occasions since that of the oysters and toddy, had not spoken again of his regard for Hugh's sister; but not the less was he determined to carry out his plan and make Dorothy his wife if she would accept him. But could he ask her while the old lady was, as it might be, dying in the house? He put this question to himself as he travelled down to Exeter, and had told himself that he must be guided for an answer by circumstances as they might occur. Hugh had met him at the station as he started for Exeter, and there had been a consultation between them as to the propriety of bringing about, or of attempting to bring about, an interview between Hugh and his aunt. 'Do whatever you like,' Hugh had said. 'I would go down to her at a moment's warning, if she should express a desire to see me.'

On the first night of Brooke's arrival this question had been discussed between him and Dorothy. Dorothy had declared herself unable to give advice. If any message were given to her she would deliver it to her aunt; but she thought that anything said to her aunt on the subject had better come from Brooke himself. 'You evidently are the person most important to her,' Dorothy said, 'and she would listen to you when she would not let any one else say a word.' Brooke promised that he would think of it; and then Dorothy tripped up to relieve Martha, dreaming nothing at all of that other doubt to which the important personage downstairs was now subject. Dorothy was, in truth, very fond of the new friend she had made; but it had never occurred to her that he might be a possible suitor to her. Her old conception of herself that she was beneath the notice of any man had only been partly disturbed by the absolute fact of Mr Gibson's courtship. She had now heard of his engagement with Camilla French, and saw in that complete proof that the foolish man had been induced to offer his hand to her by the promise of her aunt's money. If there had been a moment of exaltation, a period in which she had allowed herself to think that she was, as other women, capable of making herself dear to a man, it had been but a moment. And now she rejoiced greatly that she had not acceded to the wishes of one to whom it was so manifest that she had not made herself in the least dear.

On the second day of his visit, Brooke was summoned to Miss Stanbury's room at noon. She was forbidden to talk, and during a great portion of the day could hardly speak without an effort; but there would be half hours now and again in which she would become stronger than usual, at which time nothing that Martha and Dorothy could say would induce her to hold her tongue. When Brooke came to her on this occasion he found her sitting up in bed with a great shawl round her; and he at once perceived she was much more like her own self than on the former day. She told him that she had been an old fool for sending for him, that she had nothing special to say to him, that she had made no alteration in her will in regard to him 'except that I have done something for Dolly that will have to come out of your pocket, Brooke.' Brooke declared that too much could not be done for a person so good, and dear, and excellent as Dorothy Stanbury, let it come out of whose pocket it might. 'She is nothing to you, you know,' said Miss Stanbury.

'She is a great deal to me,' said Brooke.

'What is she?' asked Miss Stanbury.

'Oh a friend; a great friend.'

'Well; yes. I hope it may be so. But she won't have anything that I haven't saved,' said Miss Stanbury. 'There are two houses at St. Thomas's; but I bought them myself, Brooke out of the income.' Brooke could only declare that as the whole property was hers, to do what she liked with it as completely as though she had inherited it from her own father, no one could have any right to ask questions as to when or how this or that portion of the property had accrued. 'But I don't think I'm going to die yet, Brooke,' she said. 'If it is God's will, I am ready. Not that I'm fit, Brooke. God forbid that I should ever think that. But I doubt whether I shall ever be fitter. I can go without repining if He thinks best to take me.' Then he stood up by her bedside, with his hand upon hers, and after some hesitation asked her whether she would wish to see her nephew Hugh. 'No,' said she, sharply. Brooke went on to say how pleased Hugh would have been to come to her. 'I don't think much of death-bed reconciliations,' said the old woman grimly. 'I loved him dearly, but he didn't love me, and I don't know what good we should do each other.' Brooke declared that Hugh did love her; but he could not press the matter, and it was dropped.

On that evening at eight Dorothy came down to her tea. She had dined at the same table with Brooke that afternoon, but a servant had been in the room all the time and nothing had been said between them. As soon as Brooke had got his tea he began to tell the story of his failure about Hugh. He was sorry, he said, that he had spoken on the subject as it had moved Miss Stanbury to an acrimony which he had not expected.

'She always declares that he never loved her,' said Dorothy.'she has told me so twenty times.'

'There are people who fancy that nobody cares for them,' said Brooke.

'Indeed there are, Mr Burgess; and it is so natural.'

'Why natural?'

'Just as it is natural that there should be dogs and cats that are petted and loved and made much of, and others that have to crawl through life as they can, cuffed and kicked and starved.'

'That depends on the accident of possession,' said Brooke.

'So does the other. How many people there are that don't seem to belong to anybody and if they do, they're no good to anybody. They're not cuffed exactly, or starved; but—'

'You mean that they don't get their share of affection?'

'They get perhaps as much as they deserve,' said Dorothy.

'Because they're cross-grained, or ill-tempered, or disagreeable?'

'Not exactly that.'

'What then?' asked Brooke.

'Because they're just nobodies. They are not anything particular to anybody, and so they go on living till they die. You know what I mean, Mr Burgess. A man who is a nobody can perhaps make himself somebody or, at any rate, he can try; but a woman has no means of trying. She is a nobody and a nobody she must remain. She has her clothes and her food, but she isn't wanted anywhere. People put up with her, and that is about the best of her luck. If she were to die somebody perhaps would be sorry for her, but nobody would be worse off. She doesn't earn anything or do any good. She is just there and that's all.'

Brooke had never heard her speak after this fashion before, had never known her to utter so many consecutive words, or to put forward any opinion of her own with so much vigour. And Dorothy herself, when she had concluded her speech, was frightened by her own energy and grew red in the face, and shewed very plainly that she was half ashamed of herself. Brooke thought that he had never seen her look so pretty before, and was pleased by her enthusiasm. He understood perfectly that she was thinking of her own position, though she had entertained no idea that he would so read her meaning; and he felt that it was incumbent on him to undeceive her, and make her know that she was not one of those women who are 'just there and that's all.' 'One does see such a woman as that now and again,' he said.

'There are hundreds of them,' said Dorothy. 'And of course it can't be helped.'

'Such as Arabella French,' said he, laughing.

'Well yes; if she is one. It is very easy to see the difference. Some people are of use and are always doing things. There are others, generally women, who have nothing to do, but who can't be got rid of. It is a melancholy sort of feeling.'

'You at least are not one of them.'

'I didn't mean to complain about myself,' she said. 'I have got a great deal to make me happy.'

'I don't suppose you regard yourself as an Arabella French,' said he.

'How angry Miss French would be if she heard you.. She considers herself to be one of the reigning beauties of Exeter.'

'She has had a very long reign, and dominion of that sort to be successful ought to be short.'

'That is spiteful, Mr Burgess.'

'I don't feel spiteful against her, poor woman. I own I do not love Camilla. Not that I begrudge Camilla her present prosperity.'

'Nor I either, Mr Burgess.'

'She and Mr Gibson will do very well together, I dare say.'

'I hope they will,' said Dorothy, 'and I do not see any reason against it. They have known each other a long time.'

'A very long time,' said Brooke. Then he paused for a minute, thinking how he might best tell her that which he had now resolved should be told on this occasion. Dorothy finished her tea and got up as though she were about to go to her duty upstairs. She had been as yet hardly an hour in the room, and the period of her relief was not fairly over. But there had come something of a personal flavour in their conversation which prompted her, unconsciously, to leave him. She had, without any special indication of herself, included herself among that company of old maids who are born and live and die without that vital interest in the affairs of life which nothing but family duties, the care of children, or at least of a husband, will give to a woman. If she had not meant this she had felt it. He had understood her meaning, or at least her feeling, and had taken upon himself to assure her that she was not one of the company whose privations she had endeavoured to describe. Her instinct rather than her reason put her at once upon her guard, and she prepared to leave the room. 'You are not going yet,' he said.

'I think I might as well. Martha has so much to do, and she comes to me again at five in the morning.'

'Don't go quite yet,' he said, pulling out his watch. 'I know all about the hours, and it wants twenty minutes to the proper time.'

'There is no proper time, Mr Burgess.'

'Then you can remain a few minutes longer. The fact is, I've got something I want to say to you.'

He was now standing between her and the door, so that she could not get away from him; but at this moment she was absolutely ignorant of his purpose, expecting nothing of love from him more than she would from Sir Peter Mancrudy. Her face had become flushed when she made her long speech, but there was no blush on it as she answered him now. 'Of course, I can wait,' she said, 'if you have anything to say to me.'

'Well I have. I should have said it before, only that that other man was here.' He was blushing now up to the roots of his hair, and felt that he was in a difficulty. There are men, to whom such moments of their lives are pleasurable, but Brooke Burgess was not one of them. He would have been glad to have had it done and over so that then he might take pleasure in it.

'What man?' asked Dorothy, in perfect innocence.

'Mr Gibson, to be sure. I don't know that there is anybody else.'

'Oh, Mr Gibson. He never comes here now, and I don't suppose he will again. Aunt Stanbury is so very angry with him.'

'I don't care whether he comes or not. What I mean is this. When I was here before, I was told that you were going to marry him.'

'But I wasn't.'

'How was I to know that, when you didn't tell me? I certainly did know it after I came back from Dartmoor.' He paused a moment, as though she might have a word to say. She had no word to say, and did not in the least know what was coming. She was so far from anticipating the truth, that she was composed and easy in her mind. 'But all that is of no use at all,' he continued. 'When I was here before Miss Stanbury wanted you to marry Mr Gibson; and, of course, I had nothing to say about it. Now I want you to marry me.'

'Mr Burgess!'

'Dorothy, my darling, I love you better than all the world. I do, indeed.' As soon as he had commenced his protestations he became profuse enough with them, and made a strong attempt to support them by the action of his hands. But she retreated from him step by step, till she had regained her chair by the tea-table, and there she seated herself safely, as she thought; but he was close to her, over her shoulder, still continuing his protestations, offering up his vows, and imploring her to reply to him. She, as yet, had not answered him by a word, save by that one half-terrified exclamation of his name. 'Tell me, at any rate, that you believe me, when I assure you that I love you,' he said. The room was going round with Dorothy, and the world was going round, and there had come upon her so strong a feeling of the disruption of things in general, that she was at the moment anything but happy.

Had it been possible for her to find that the last ten minutes had been a dream, she would at this moment have wished that it might become one. A trouble had come upon her, out of which she did not see her way. To dive among the waters in warm weather is very pleasant; there is nothing pleasanter. But when the young swimmer first feels the thorough immersion of his plunge, there comes upon him a strong desire to be quickly out again. He will remember afterwards how joyous it was; but now, at this moment, the dry land is everything to him. So it was with Dorothy. She had thought of Brooke Burgess as one of those bright ones of the world, with whom everything is happy and pleasant, whom everybody loves, who may have whatever they please, whose lines have been laid in pleasant places. She thought of him as a man who might some day make some woman very happy as his wife. To be the wife of such a man was, in Dorothy's estimation, one of those blessed chances which come to some women, but which she never regarded as being within her own reach. Though she had thought much about him, she had never thought of him as a possible possession for herself; and now that he was offering himself to her, she was not at once made happy by his love. Her ideas of herself and of her life were all dislocated for the moment, and she required to be alone, that she might set herself in order, and try herself all over, and find whether her bones were broken.'say that you believe me,' he repeated.

'I don't know what to say,' she whispered.

'I'll tell you what to say. Say at once that you will be my wife.'

'I can't say that, Mr Burgess.'

'Why not? Do you mean that you cannot love me?'

'I think, if you please, I'll go up to Aunt Stanbury. It is time for me; indeed it is; and she will be wondering, and Martha will be put out. Indeed I must go up.'

'And will you not answer me?'

'I don't know what to say. You must give me a little time to consider. I don't quite think you're serious.'

'Heaven and earth!' began Brooke.

'And I'm sure it would never do. At any rate, I must go now. I must, indeed.'

And so she escaped, and went up to her aunt's room, which she reached at ten minutes after her usual time, and before Martha had begun to be put out. She was very civil to Martha, as though Martha had been injured; and she put her hand on her aunt's arm, with a soft, caressing, apologetic touch, feeling conscious that she had given cause for offence. 'What has he been saying to you?' said her aunt, as soon as Martha had closed the door. This was a question which Dorothy, certainly, could not answer. Miss Stanbury meant nothing by it nothing beyond a sick woman's desire that something of the conversation of those who were not sick should be retailed to her; but to Dorothy the question meant so much! How should her aunt have known that he had said anything? She sat herself down and waited, giving no answer to the question. 'I hope he gets his meals comfortably,' said Miss Stanbury.

'I am sure he does,' said Dorothy, infinitely relieved. Then, knowing how important it was that her aunt should sleep, she took up the volume of Jeremy Taylor, and, with so great a burden on her mind, she went on painfully and distinctly with the second sermon on the Marriage Ring. She strove valiantly to keep her mind to the godliness of the discourse, so that it might be of some possible service to herself; and to keep her voice to the tone that might be of service to her aunt. Presently she heard the grateful sound which indicated her aunt's repose, but she knew of experience that were she to stop, the sound and the sleep would come to an end also. For a whole hour she persevered, reading the sermon of the Marriage Ring with such attention to the godly principles of the teaching as she could give with that terrible burden upon her mind.

'Thank you thank you; that will do, my dear. Shut it up,' said the sick woman. 'It's time now for the draught.' Then Dorothy moved quietly about the room, and did her nurse's work with soft hand, and soft touch, and soft tread. After that her aunt kissed her, and bade her sit down and sleep.

'I'll go on reading, aunt, if you'll let me,' said Dorothy. But Miss Stanbury, who was not a cruel woman, would have no more of the reading, and Dorothy's mind was left at liberty to think of the proposition that had been made to her. To one resolution she came very quickly. The period of her aunt's illness could not be a proper time for marriage vows, or the amenities of love-making. She did not feel that he, being a man, had offended; but she was quite sure that were she, a woman, the niece of so kind an aunt, the nurse at the bedside of such an invalid were she at such a time to consent to talk of love, she would never deserve to have a lover. And from this resolve she got great comfort. It would give her an excuse for making no more assured answer at present, and would enable her to reflect at leisure as to the reply she would give him, should he ever, by any chance, renew his offer. If he did not, and probably he would not, then it would have been very well that he should not have been made the victim of a momentary generosity. She had complained of the dullness of her life, and that complaint from her had produced his noble, kind, generous, dear, enthusiastic benevolence towards her. As she thought of it all, and by degrees she took great pleasure in thinking of it, her mind bestowed upon him all manner of eulogies. She could not persuade herself that he really loved her, and yet she was full at heart of gratitude to him for the expression of his love. And as for herself, could she love him? We who are looking on of course know that she loved him; that from this moment there was nothing belonging to him, down to his shoe-tie, that would not be dear to her heart and an emblem so tender as to force a tear from her. He had already become her god, though she did not know it. She made comparisons between him and Mr Gibson, and tried to convince herself that the judgment, which was always pronounced very clearly in Brooke's favour, came from anything but her heart. And thus through the long watches of the night she became very happy, feeling but not knowing that the whole aspect of the world was changed to her by those few words which her lover had spoken to her. She thought now that it would be consolation enough to her in future to know that such a man as Brooke Burgess had once asked her to be the partner of his life, and that it would be almost ungenerous in her to push her advantage further and attempt to take him at his word. Besides, there would be obstacles. Her aunt would dislike such a marriage for him, and he would be bound to obey her aunt in such a matter. She would not allow herself to think that she could ever become Brooke's wife, but nothing could rob her of the treasure of the offer which he had made her. Then Martha came to her at five o'clock, and she went to her bed to dream for an hour or two of Brooke Burgess and her future life.

On the next morning she met him at breakfast. She went down stairs later than usual, not till ten, having hung about her aunt's room, thinking that thus she would escape him for the present. She would wait till he was gone out, and then she would go down. She did wait; but she could not hear the front door, and then her aunt murmured something about Brooke's breakfast. She was told to go down, and she went. But when on the stairs she slunk back to her own room, and stood there for awhile, aimless, motionless, not knowing what to do. Then one of the girls came to her, and told her that Mr Burgess was waiting breakfast for her. She knew not what excuse to make, and at last descended slowly to the parlour. She was very happy, but had it been possible for her to have run away she would have gone.

'Dear Dorothy,' he said at once. 'I may call you so, may I not?'

'Oh yes.'

'And you will love me and be my own, own wife?'

'No, Mr Burgess.'

'No?'

'I mean that is to say—'

'Do you love me, Dorothy?'

'Only think how ill Aunt Stanbury is, Mr Burgess; perhaps dying! How can I have any thought now except about her? It wouldn't be right would it?'

'You may say that you love me.'

'Mr Burgess, pray, pray don't speak of it now. If you do I must go away.'

'But do you love me?'

'Pray, pray don't, Mr Burgess!'

There was nothing more to be got from her during the whole day than that. He told her in the evening that as soon as Miss Stanbury was well, he would come again, that in any case he would come again. She sat quite still as he said this, with a solemn face but smiling at heart, laughing at heart, so happy! When she got up to leave him, and was forced to give him her hand, he seized her in his arms and kissed her. 'That is very, very wrong,' she said, sobbing, and then ran to her room the happiest girl in all Exeter. He was to start early on the following morning, and she knew that she would not be forced to see him again. Thinking of him was so much pleasanter than seeing him!

CHAPTER LII. MR OUTHOUSE COMPLAINS THAT IT'S HARD

Life had gone on during the winter at St Diddulph's Parsonage in a dull, weary, painful manner. There had come a letter in November from Trevelyan to his wife, saying that as he could trust neither her nor her uncle with the custody of his child, he should send a person armed with due legal authority, addressed to Mr Outhouse, for the recovery of the boy, and desiring that little Louis might be at once surrendered to the messenger. Then of course there had arisen great trouble in the house. Both Mrs Trevelyan and Nora Rowley had learned by this time that, as regarded the master of the house, they were not welcome guests at St Diddulph's. When the threat was shewn to Mr Outhouse, he did not say a word to indicate that the child should be given up. He muttered something, indeed, about impotent nonsense, which seemed to imply that the threat could be of no avail; but there was none of that reassurance to be obtained from him which a positive promise on his part to hold the bairn against all corners would have given. Mrs Outhouse told her niece more than once that the child would be given to no messenger whatever; but even she did not give the assurance with that energy which the mother would have liked. 'They shall drag him away from me by force if they do take him!' said the mother, gnashing her teeth. Oh, if her father would but come! For some weeks she did not let the boy out of her sight; but when no messenger had presented himself by Christmas time, they all began to believe that the threat had in truth meant nothing, that it had been part of the ravings of a madman.

But the threat had meant something. Early on one morning in January Mr Outhouse was told that a person in the hall wanted to see him, and Mrs Trevelyan, who was sitting at breakfast, the child being at the moment upstairs, started from her seat. The maid described the man as being 'All as one as a gentleman,' though she would not go so far as to say that he was a gentleman in fact. Mr Outhouse slowly rose from his breakfast, went out to the man in the passage, and bade him follow into the little closet that was now used as a study. It is needless perhaps to say that the man was Bozzle.

'I dare say, Mr Houthouse, you don't know me,' said Bozzle. Mr Outhouse, disdaining all complimentary language, said that he certainly did not. 'My name, Mr Houthouse, is Samuel Bozzle, and I live at No. 55, Stony Walk, Union Street, Borough. I was in the Force once, but I work on my own 'ook now.'

'What do you want with me, Mr Bozzle?'

'It isn't so much with you, sir, as it is with a lady as is under your protection; and it isn't so much with the lady as it is with her infant.'

'Then you may go away, Mr Bozzle,' said Mr Outhouse, impatiently. 'You may as well go away at once.'

'Will you please read them few lines, sir,' said Mr Bozzle. 'They is in Mr Trewilyan's handwriting, which will no doubt be familiar characters leastways to Mrs T., if you don't know the gent's fist.' Mr Outhouse, after looking at the paper for a minute, and considering deeply what in this emergency he had better do, did take the paper and read it. The words ran as follows: 'I hereby give full authority to Mr Samuel Bozzle, of 55, Stony Walk, Union Street, Borough, to claim and to enforce possession of the body of my child, Louis Trevelyan; and I require that any person whatsoever who may now have the custody of the said child, whether it be my wife or any of her friends, shall at once deliver him up to Mr Bozzle on the production of this authority, LOUIS TREVELYAN.' It may be explained that before this document had been written there had been much correspondence on the subject between Bozzle and his employer. To give the ex-policeman his due, he had not at first wished to meddle in the matter of the child. He had a wife at home who expressed an opinion with much vigour that the boy should be left with its mother, and that he, Bozzle, should he succeed in getting hold of the child, would not know what to do with it. Bozzle was aware, moreover, that it was his business to find out facts, and not to perform actions. But his employer had become very urgent with him. Mr Bideawhile had positively refused to move in the matter; and Trevelyan, mad as he was, had felt a disinclination to throw his affairs into the hands of a certain Mr Skint, of Stamford Street, whom Bozzle had recommended to him as a lawyer. Trevelyan had hinted, moreover, that if Bozzle would make the application in person, that application, if not obeyed, would act with usefulness as a preliminary step for further personal measures to be taken by himself. He intended to return to England for the purpose, but he desired that the order for the child's rendition should be made at once. Therefore Bozzle had come. He was an earnest man, and had now worked himself up to a certain degree of energy in the matter. He was a man loving power, and specially anxious to enforce obedience from those with whom he came in contact by the production of the law's mysterious authority. In his heart he was ever tapping people on the shoulder, and telling them that they were wanted. Thus, when he displayed his document to Mr Outhouse, he had taught himself at least to desire that that document should be obeyed.

Mr Outhouse read the paper and turned up his nose at it. 'You had better go away,' said he, as he thrust it back into Bozzle's hand.

'Of course I shall go away when I have the child.'

'Psha!' said Mr Outhouse.

'What does that mean, Mr Houthouse? I presume you'll not dispute the paternal parent's legal authority?'

'Go away, sir,' said Mr Outhouse.

'Go away!'

'Yes out of this house. It's my belief that you're a knave.'

'A knave, Mr Houthouse?'

'Yes a knave. No one who was not a knave would lend a hand towards separating a little child from its mother. I think you are a knave, but I don't think you are fool enough to suppose that the child will he given up to you.'

'It's my belief that knave is hactionable,' said Bozzle whose respect, however, for the clergyman was rising fast. 'Would you mind ringing the bell, Mr Houthouse, and calling me a knave again before the young woman?'

'Go away,' said Mr Outhouse.

'If you have no objection, sir, I should be glad to see the lady before I goes.'

'You won't see any lady here; and if you don't get out of my house when I tell you, I'll send for a real policeman.' Then was Bozzle conquered; and, as he went, he admitted to himself that he had sinned against all the rules of his life in attempting to go beyond the legitimate line of his profession. As long as he confined himself to the getting up of facts nobody could threaten him with 'a real policeman.' But one fact he had learned to-day. The clergyman of St Diddulph's, who had been represented to him as a weak, foolish man, was anything but that. Bozzle was much impressed in favour of Mr Outhouse, and would have been glad to have done that gentleman a kindness had an opportunity come in his way.

'What does he want, Uncle Oliphant?' said Mrs Trevelyan at the foot of the stairs, guarding the way up to the nursery. At this moment the front door had just been closed behind the back of Mr Bozzle.

'You had better ask no questions,' said Mr Outhouse.

'But is it about Louis?'

'Yes, he came about him.'

'Well? Of course you must tell me, Uncle Oliphant. Think of my condition.'

'He had some stupid paper in his hand from your husband, but it meant nothing.'

'He was the messenger, then?'

'Yes, he was the messenger. But I don't suppose he expected to get anything. Never mind. Go up and look after the child.' Then Mrs Trevelyan returned to her boy, and Mr Outhouse went back to his papers.

It was very hard upon him, Mr Outhouse thought, very hard. He was threatened with an action now, and most probably would become subject to one. Though he had been spirited enough in presence of the enemy, he was very much out of spirits at this moment. Though he had admitted to himself that his duty required him to protect his wife's niece, he had never taken the poor woman to his heart with a loving, generous feeling of true guardianship. Though he would not give up the child to Bozzle, he thoroughly wished that the child was out of his house. Though he called Bozzle a knave and Trevelyan a madman, still he considered that Colonel Osborne was the chief sinner, and that Emily Trevelyan had behaved badly. He constantly repeated to himself the old adage, that there was no smoke without fire; and lamented the misfortune that had brought him into close relation with things and people that were so little to his taste. He sat for awhile, with a pen in his hand, at the miserable little substitute for a library table which had been provided for him, and strove to collect his thoughts and go on with his work. But the effort was in vain. Bozzle would be there, presenting his document, and begging that the maid might be rung for, in order that she might hear him called a knave. And then he knew that on this very day his niece intended to hand him money, which he could not refuse. Of what use would it be to refuse it now, after it had been once taken? As he could not write a word, he rose and went away to his wife.

'If this goes on much longer,' said he, 'I shall be in Bedlam.'

'My dear, don't speak of it in that way!'

'That's all very well. I suppose I ought to say that I like it. There has been a policeman here who is going to bring an action against me.'

'A policeman!'

'Some one that her husband has sent for the child.'

'The boy must not be given up, Oliphant.'

'It's all very well to say that, but I suppose we must obey the law. The Parsonage of St Diddulph's isn't a castle in the Apennines. When it comes to this, that a policeman is sent here to fetch any man's child, and threatens me with an action because I tell him to leave my house, it is very hard upon me, seeing how very little I've had to do with it. It's all over the parish now that my niece is kept here away from her husband, and that a lover comes to see her. This about a policeman will be known now, of course. I only say it is hard; that's all.' The wife did all that she could to comfort him, reminding him that Sir Marmaduke would be home soon, and that then the burden would be taken from his shoulders. But she was forced to admit that it was very hard.

CHAPTER LIII. HUGH STANBURY IS SHEWN TO BE NO CONJUROR

Many weeks had now passed since Hugh Stanbury had paid his visit to St Diddulph's, and Nora Rowley was beginning to believe that her rejection of her lover had been so firm and decided that she would never see him or hear from him more, and she had long since confessed to herself that if she did not see him or hear from him soon, life would not be worth a straw to her. To all of us a single treasure counts for much more when the outward circumstances of our life are dull, unvaried, and melancholy, than it does when our days are full of pleasure, or excitement, or even of business. With Nora Rowley at St Diddulph's life at present was very melancholy. There was little or no society to enliven her. Her sister was sick at heart, and becoming ill in health under the burden of her troubles. Mr Outhouse was moody and wretched; and Mrs Outhouse, though she did her best to make her house comfortable to her unwelcome inmates, could not make it appear that their presence there was a pleasure to her. Nora understood better than did her sister how distasteful the present arrangement was to their uncle, and was consequently very uncomfortable on that score. And in the midst of that unhappiness, she of course told herself that she was a young woman miserable and unfortunate altogether. It is always so with us. The heart when it is burdened, though it may have ample strength to bear the burden, loses its buoyancy and doubts its own power. It is like the springs of a carriage which are pressed flat by the superincumbent weight. But, because the springs are good, the weight is carried safely, and they are the better afterwards for their required purposes because of the trial to which they have been subjected.

Nora had sent her lover away, and now at the end of three months from the day of his dismissal she had taught herself to believe that he would never come again. Amidst the sadness of her life at St Diddulph's some confidence in a lover expected to come again would have done much to cheer her. The more she thought of Hugh Stanbury, the more fully she became convinced that he was the man who as a lover, as a husband, and as a companion, would just suit all her tastes. She endowed him liberally with a hundred good gifts in the disposal of which Nature had been much more sparing. She made for herself a mental portrait of him more gracious in its flattery than ever was canvas coming from the hand of a Court limner. She gave him all gifts of manliness, honesty, truth, and energy, and felt regarding him that he was a Paladin such as Paladins are in this age, that he was indomitable, sure of success, and fitted in all respects to take the high position which he would certainly win for himself. But she did not presume him to be endowed with such a constancy as would make him come to seek her hand again. Had Nora at this time of her life been living at the West-end of London, and going out to parties three or four times a week, she would have been quite easy about his coming. The springs would not have been weighted so heavily, and her heart would have been elastic.

No doubt she had forgotten many of the circumstances of his visit and of his departure. Immediately on his going she had told her sister that he would certainly come again, but had said at the same time that his coming could be of no use. He was so poor a man; and she, though poorer than he, had been so little accustomed to poverty of life, that she had then acknowledged to herself that she was not fit to be his wife. Gradually, as the slow weeks went by her, there had come a change in her ideas. She now thought that he never would come again; but that if he did she would confess to him that her own views about life were changed. 'I would tell him frankly that I could eat a crust with him in any garret in London.' But this was said to herself, never to her sister. Emily and Mrs Outhouse had determined together that it would be wise to abstain from all mention of Hugh Stanbury's name. Nora had felt that her sister had so abstained, and this reticence had assisted in producing the despair which had come upon her. Hugh, when he had left her, had certainly given her encouragement to expect that he would return. She had been sure then that he would return. She had been sure of it, though she had told him that it would be useless. But now, when these sad weeks had slowly crept over her head, when during the long hours of the long days she had thought of him continually, telling herself that it was impossible that she should ever become the wife of any man if she did not become his, she assured herself that she had seen and heard the last of him. She must surely have forgotten his hot words and that daring embrace.

Then there came a letter to her. The question of the management of letters for young ladies is handled very differently in different houses. In some establishments the post is as free to young ladies as it is to the reverend seniors of the household. In others it is considered to be quite a matter of course that some experienced discretion should sit in judgment on the correspondence of the daughters of the family. When Nora Rowley was living with her sister in Curzon Street, she would have been very indignant indeed had it been suggested to her that there was any authority over her letters vested in her sister. But now, circumstanced as she was at St Diddulph's, she did understand that no letter would reach her without her aunt knowing that it had come. All this was distasteful to her, as were indeed all the details of her life at St Diddulph's, but she could not help herself. Had her aunt told her that she should never be allowed to receive a letter at all, she must have submitted till her mother had come to her relief. The letter which reached her now was put into her hands by her sister, but it had been given to Mrs Trevelyan by Mrs Outhouse. 'Nora,' said Mrs Trevelyan, 'here is a letter for you. I think it is from Mr Stanbury.'

'Give it me,' said Nora greedily.

'Of course I will give it you. But I hope you do not intend to correspond with him.'

'If he has written to me I shall answer him of course,' said Nora, holding her treasure.

'Aunt Mary thinks that you should not do so till papa and mamma have arrived.'

'If Aunt Mary is afraid of me let her tell me so, and I will contrive to go somewhere else.' Poor Nora knew that this threat was futile. There was no house to which she could take herself.

'She is not afraid of you at all, Nora. She only says that she thinks you should not write to Mr Stanbury.' Then Nora escaped to the cold but solitary seclusion of her bed-room and there she read her letter.

The reader may remember that Hugh Stanbury when he last left St Diddulph's had not been oppressed by any of the gloomy reveries of a despairing lover. He had spoken his mind freely to Nora, and had felt himself justified in believing that he had not spoken in vain. He had had her in his arms, and she had found it impossible to say that she did not love him. But then she had been quite firm in her purpose to give him no encouragement that she could avoid. She had said no word that would justify him in considering that there was any engagement between them; and, moreover, he had been warned not to come to the house by its mistress. From day to day he thought of it all, now telling himself that there was nothing to be done but to trust in her fidelity till he should be in a position to offer her a fitting home, and then reflecting that he could not expect such a girl as Nora Rowley to wait for him, unless he could succeed in making her understand that he at any rate intended to wait for her. On one day he would think that good faith and proper consideration for Nora herself required him to keep silent; on the next he would tell himself that such maudlin chivalry as he was proposing to himself was sure to go to the wall and be neither rewarded nor recognised. So at last he sat down and wrote the following letter:

Lincoln's Inn Fields,
January, 186—.

DEAREST NORA,

Ever since I last saw you at St Diddulph's, I have been trying to teach myself what I ought to do in reference to you. Sometimes I think that because I am poor I ought to hold my tongue. At others I feel sure that I ought to speak out loud, because I love you so dearly. You may presume that just at this moment the latter opinion is in the ascendant.

As I do write I mean to be very bold—so bold that if I am wrong you will be thoroughly disgusted with me and will never willingly see me again. But I think it best to be true, and to say what I think. I do believe that you love me. According to all precedent I ought not to say so, but I do believe it. Ever since I was at St Diddulph's that belief has made me happy though there have been moments of doubt. If I thought that you did not love me, I would trouble you no further. A man may win his way to love when social circumstances are such as to throw him and the girl together; but such is not the case with us; and unless you love me now, you never will love me.' 'I do I do!' said Nora, pressing the letter to her bosom. 'If you do, I think that you owe it me to say so, and to let me have all the joy and all the feeling of responsibility which such am assurance will give me.' 'I will tell him so,' said Nora; 'I don't care what may come afterwards, but I will tell him the truth.' 'I know,' continued Hugh, 'that an engagement with me now would be hazardous, because what I earn is both scanty and precarious; but it seems to me that nothing could ever be done without some risk. There are risks of different kinds.' She wondered whether he was thinking when he wrote this of the rock on which her sister's barque had been split to pieces 'and we may hardly hope to avoid them all. For myself, I own that life would be tame to me, if there were no dangers to be overcome.

If you do love me, and will say so, I will not ask you to be my wife till I can give you a proper home; but the knowledge that I am the master of the treasure which I desire will give me a double energy, and will make me feel that when I have gained so much I cannot fail of adding to it all other smaller things that may be necessary.

Pray, pray send me an answer. I cannot reach you except by writing, as I was told by your aunt not to come to the house again.

Dearest Nora, pray believe
That I shall always be truly yours only,   HUGH STANBURY.

Write to him! Of course she would write to him. Of course she would confess to him the truth. 'He tells me that I owe it to him to say so, and I acknowledge the debt,' she said aloud to herself. 'And as for a proper home, he shall be the judge of that.' She resolved that she would not be a fine lady, not fastidious, not coy, not afraid to take her full share of the risk of which he spoke in such manly terms. 'It is quite true. As he has been able to make me love him, I have no right to stand aloof even if I wished it.' As she was walking up and down the room so resolving her sister came to her.

'Well, dear!' said Emily. 'May I ask what it is he says?'

Nora paused a moment, holding the letter tight in her hand, and then she held it out to her sister. 'There it is. You may read it.' Mrs Trevelyan took the letter and read it slowly, during which Nora stood looking out of the window. She would not watch her sister's face, as she did not wish to have to reply to any outward signs of disapproval. 'Give it me back,' she said, when she heard by the refolding of the paper that the perusal was finished.

'Of course I shall give it you back, dear.'

'Yes thanks. I did not mean to doubt you.'

'And what will you do, Nora?'

'Answer it of course.'

'I would think a little before I answered it,' said Mrs Trevelyan.

'I have thought a great deal, already.'

'And how will you answer it?'

Nora paused again before she replied. 'As nearly as I know how to do in such words as he would put into my mouth. I shall strive to write just what I think he would wish me to write.'

'Then you will engage yourself to him, Nora?'

'Certainly I shall. I am engaged to him already. I have been ever since he came here.'

'You told me that there was nothing of the kind.'

'I told you that I loved him better than anybody in the world, and that ought to have made you know what it must come to. When I am thinking of him every day, and every hour, how can I not be glad to have an engagement settled with him? I couldn't marry anybody else, and I don't want to remain as I am.' The tears came into the married sister's eyes, and rolled down her cheeks, as this was said to her. Would it not have been better for her had she remained as she was? 'Dear Emily,' said Nora, 'you have got Louey still.'

'Yes and they mean to take him from me. But I do not wish to speak of myself. Will you postpone your answer till mamma is here?'

'I cannot do that, Emily. What; receive such a letter as that, and send no reply to it!'

'I would write a line for you, and explain—'

'No, indeed, Emily. I choose to answer my own letters. I have shewn you that, because I trust you; but I have fully made up my mind as to what I shall write. It will have been written and sent before dinner.'

'I think you will be wrong, Nora.'

'Why wrong! When I came over here to stay with you, would mamma ever have thought of directing me not to accept any offer till her consent had been obtained all the way from the Mandarins? She would never have dreamed of such a thing.'

'Will you ask Aunt Mary?'

'Certainly not. What is Aunt Mary to me? We are here in her house for a time, under the press of circumstances; but I owe her no obedience. She told Mr Stanbury not to come here; and he has not come; and I shall not ask him to come. I would not willingly bring any one into Uncle Oliphant's house that he and she do not wish to see. But I will not admit that either of them have any authority over me.'

'Then who has, dearest?'

'Nobody except papa and mamma; and they have chosen to leave me to myself.'

Mrs Trevelyan found it impossible to shake her sister's firmness, and could herself do nothing, except tell Mrs Outhouse what was the state of affairs. When she said that she should do this, there almost came to be a flow of high words between the sisters; but at last Nora assented. 'As for knowing, I don't care if all the world knows it. I shall do nothing in a corner. I don't suppose Aunt Mary will endeavour to prevent my posting my letter.'

Emily at last went to seek Mrs Outhouse, and Nora at once sat down to her desk. Neither of the sisters felt at all sure that Mrs Outhouse would not attempt to stop the emission of the letter from her house; but, as it happened, she was out, and did not return till Nora had come back from her journey to the neighbouring post-office. She would trust her letter, when written, to no hands but her own; and as she herself dropped it into the safe custody of the Postmaster-General, it also shall be revealed to the public:

Parsonage,
St Diddulph's,
January, 186—.

Dear Hugh,

For I suppose I may as well write to you in that way now. I have been made so happy by your affectionate letter. Is not that a candid confession for a young lady? But you tell me that I owe you the truth, and so I tell you the truth. Nobody will ever be anything to me, except you; and you are everything. I do love you; and should it ever be possible, I will become your wife.

I have said so much, because I feel that I ought to obey the order you have given me; but pray do not try to see me or write to me till mamma has arrived. She and papa will be here in the spring, quite early in the spring, we hope; and then you may come to us. What they may say, of course, I cannot tell; but I shall be true to you.

Your own, with truest affection,   NORA.

Of course, you knew that I loved you, and I don't think that you are a conjuror at all.

As soon as ever the letter was written, she put on her bonnet, and went forth with it herself to the post-office. Mrs Trevelyan stopped her on the stairs, and endeavoured to detain her, but Nora would not be detained. 'I must judge for myself about this,' she said. 'If mamma were here, it would be different, but, as she is not here, I must judge for myself.'

What Mrs Outhouse might have done had she been at home at the time, it would be useless to surmise. She was told what had happened when it occurred, and questioned Nora on the subject. 'I thought I understood from you,' she said, with something of severity in her countenance, 'that there was to be nothing between you and Mr Stanbury at any rate, till my brother came home?'

'I never pledged myself to anything of the kind, Aunt Mary,' Nora said. 'I think he promised that he would not come here, and I don't suppose that he means to come. If he should do so, I shall not see him.'

With this Mrs Outhouse was obliged to be content. The letter was gone, and could not be stopped. Nor, indeed, had any authority been delegated to her by which she would have been justified in stopping it. She could only join her husband in wishing that they both might be relieved, as soon as possible, from the terrible burden which had been thrown upon them. 'I call it very hard,' said Mr Outhouse 'very hard, indeed. If we were to desire them to leave the house, everybody would cry out upon us for our cruelty; and yet, while they remain here, they will submit themselves to no authority. As far as I can see, they may, both of them, do just what they please, and we can't stop it.'

CHAPTER LIV. MR GIBSON'S THREAT

Miss Stanbury for a long time persisted in being neither better nor worse. Sir Peter would not declare her state to be precarious, nor would he say that she was out of danger; and Mr Martin had been so utterly prostrated by the nearly-fatal effects of his own mistake that he was quite unable to rally himself and talk on the subject with any spirit or confidence. When interrogated he would simply reply that Sir Peter said this and Sir Peter said that, and thus add to, rather than diminish, the doubt, and excitement, and varied opinion which prevailed through the city. On one morning it was absolutely asserted within the limits of the Close that Miss Stanbury was dying, and it was believed for half a day at the bank that she was then lying *in articulo mortis*. There had got about, too, a report that a portion of the property had only been left to Miss Stanbury for her life, that the Burgesses would be able to reclaim the houses in the city, and that a will had been made altogether in favour of Dorothy, cutting out even Brooke from any share in the inheritance; and thus Exeter had a good deal to say respecting the affairs and state of health of our old friend. Miss Stanbury's illness, however, was true enough. She was much too ill to hear anything of what was going on, too ill to allow Martha to talk to her at all about the outside public. When the invalid herself would ask questions about the affairs of the world, Martha would be very discreet and turn away from the subject. Miss Stanbury, for instance, ill as she was, exhibited a most mundane interest, not exactly in Camilla French's marriage, but in the delay which that marriage seemed destined to encounter. 'I dare say he'll slip out of it yet,' said the sick lady to her confidential servant. Then Martha had thought it right to change the subject, feeling it to be wrong that an old lady on her death-bed should be taking joy in the disappointment of her young neighbour. Martha changed the subject, first to jelly, and then to the psalms of the day. Miss Stanbury was too weak to resist; but the last verse of the last psalm of the evening had hardly been finished before she remarked that she would never believe it till she saw it. 'It's all in the hands of Him as is on high, mum,' said Martha, turning her eyes up to the ceiling, and closing the book at the same time, with a look strongly indicative of displeasure.

Miss Stanbury understood it all as well as though she were in perfect health. She knew her own failings, was conscious of her worldly tendencies, and perceived that her old servant was thinking of it. And then sundry odd thoughts, half-digested thoughts, ideas too difficult for her present strength, crossed her brain. Had it been wicked of her when she was well to hope that a scheming woman should not succeed in betraying a man by her schemes into an ill-assorted marriage; and if not wicked then, was it wicked now because she was ill? And from that thought her mind travelled on to the ordinary practices of death-bed piety. Could an assumed devotion be of use to her now, such a devotion as Martha was enjoining upon her from hour to hour, in pure and affectionate solicitude for her soul? She had spoken one evening of a game of cards, saying that a game of cribbage would have consoled her. Then Martha, with a shudder, had suggested a hymn, and had had recourse at once to a sleeping draught. Miss Stanbury had submitted, but had understood it all. If cards were wicked, she had indeed been a terrible sinner. What hope could there be now, on her death-bed, for one so sinful? And she could not repent of her cards, and would not try to repent of them, not seeing the evil of them; and if they were innocent, why should she not have the consolation now when she so much wanted it? Yet she knew that the whole household, even Dorothy, would be in arms against her, were she to suggest such a thing. She took the hymn and the sleeping draught, telling herself that it would be best for her to banish such ideas from her mind. Pastors and masters had laid down for her a mode of living, which she had followed, but indifferently perhaps, but still with an intention of obedience. They had also laid down a mode of dying, and it would be well that she should follow that as closely as possible. She would say nothing more about cards. She would think nothing more of Camilla French. But, as she so resolved, with intellect half asleep, with her mind wandering between fact and dream, she was unconsciously comfortable with an assurance that if Mr Gibson did marry Camilla French, Camilla French would lead him the very devil of a life.

During three days Dorothy went about the house as quiet as a mouse, sitting nightly at her aunt's bedside, and tending the sick woman with the closest care. She, too, had been now and again somewhat startled by the seeming worldliness of her aunt in her illness. Her aunt talked to her about rents, and gave her messages for Brooke Burgess on subjects which seemed to Dorothy to be profane when spoken of on what might perhaps be a death-bed. And this struck her the more strongly, because she had a matter of her own on which she would have much wished to ascertain her aunt's opinion, if she had not thought that it would have been exceedingly wrong of her to trouble her aunt's mind at such a time by any such matter. Hitherto she had said not a word of Brooke's proposal to any living being. At present it was a secret with herself, but a secret so big that it almost caused her bosom to burst with the load that it bore. She could not, she thought, write to Priscilla till she had told her aunt. If she were to write a word on the subject to any one, she could not fail to make manifest the extreme longing of her own heart. She could not have written Brooke's name on paper, in reference to his words to herself without covering it with epithets of love. But all that must be known to no one if her love was to be of no avail to her. And she had an idea that her aunt would not wish Brooke to marry her, would think that Brooke should do better; and she was quite clear that in such a matter as this her aunt's wishes must be law. Had not her aunt the power of disinheriting Brooke altogether? And what then if her aunt should die, should die now, leaving Brooke at liberty to do as he pleased? There was something so distasteful to her in this view of the matter that she would not look at it. She would not allow herself to think of any success which might possibly accrue to herself by reason of her aunt's death. Intense as was the longing in her heart for permission from those in authority over her to give herself to Brooke Burgess, perfect as was the earthly Paradise which appeared to be open to her when she thought of the good thing which had befallen her in that matter, she conceived that she would be guilty of the grossest ingratitude were she in any degree to curtail even her own estimate of her aunt's prohibitory powers because of her aunt's illness. The remembrance of the words which Brooke had spoken to her was with her quite perfect. She was entirely conscious of the joy which would he hers, if she might accept those words as properly sanctioned; but she was a creature in her aunt's hands according to her own ideas of her own duties; and while her aunt was ill she could not even learn what might be the behests which she would be called on to obey.

She was sitting one evening alone, thinking of all this, having left Martha with her aunt, and was trying to reconcile the circumstances of her life as it now existed with the circumstances as they had been with her in the old days at Nuncombe Putney, wondering at herself in that she should have a lover, and trying to convince herself that for her this little episode of romance could mean nothing serious, when Martha crept down into the room to her. Of late days—the alteration might perhaps be dated from the rejection of Mr Gibson—Martha, who had always been very kind, had become more respectful in her manner to Dorothy than had heretofore been usual with her. Dorothy was quite aware of it, and was not unconscious of a certain rise in the world which was thereby indicated. 'If you please, miss,' said Martha, 'who do you think is here?'

'But there is nobody with my aunt?' said Dorothy.

'She is sleeping like a babby, and I came down just for a moment. Mr Gibson is here, miss in the house! He asked for your aunt, and when, of course, he could not see her, he asked for you.' Dorothy for a few minutes was utterly disconcerted, but at last she consented to see Mr Gibson. 'I think it is best,' said Martha, 'because it is bad to be fighting, and missus so ill. "Blessed are the peace-makers," miss, "for they shall be called the children of God."' Convinced by this argument, or by the working of her own mind, Dorothy directed that Mr Gibson might be shewn into the room. When he came, she found herself unable to address him. She remembered the last time in which she had seen him, and was lost in wonder that he should be there. But she shook hands with him, and went through some form of greeting in which no word was uttered.

'I hope you will not think that I have done wrong,' said he, 'in calling to ask after my old friend's state of health?'

'Oh dear, no,' said Dorothy, quite bewildered.

'I have known her for so very long, Miss Dorothy, that now in the hour of her distress, and perhaps mortal malady, I cannot stop to remember the few harsh words that she spoke to me lately.'

'She never means to be harsh, Mr Gibson.'

'Ah; well; no perhaps not. At any rate I have learned to forgive and forget. I am afraid your aunt is very ill, Miss Dorothy.'

'She is ill, certainly, Mr Gibson.'

'Dear, dear! We are all as the grass of the field, Miss Dorothy, here to-day and gone to-morrow, as sparks fly upwards. Just fit to be cut down and cast into the oven. Mr Jennings has been with her, I believe?' Mr Jennings was the other minor canon.

'He comes three times a week, Mr Gibson.'

'He is an excellent young man, a very good young man. It has been a great comfort to me to have Jennings with me. But he's very young, Miss Dorothy; isn't he?' Dorothy muttered something, purporting to declare, that she was not acquainted with the exact circumstances of Mr Jennings' age. 'I should be so glad to come if my old friend would allow me,' said Mr Gibson, almost with a sigh. Dorothy was clearly of opinion that any change at the present would be bad for her aunt, but she did not know how to express her opinion; so she stood silent and looked at him. 'There needn't be a word spoken, you know, about the ladies at Heavitree,' said Mr Gibson.

'Oh dear, no,' said Dorothy. And yet she knew well that there would be such words spoken if Mr Gibson were to make his way into her aunt's room. Her aunt was constantly alluding to the ladies at Heavitree, in spite of all the efforts of her old servant to restrain her.

'There was some little misunderstanding,' said Mr Gibson; 'but all that should be over now. We both intended for the best, Miss Dorothy; and I'm sure nobody here can say that I wasn't sincere.' But Dorothy, though she could not bring herself to answer Mr Gibson plainly, could not be induced to assent to his proposition. She muttered something about her aunt's weakness, and the great attention which Mr Jennings shewed. Her aunt had become very fond of Mr Jennings, and she did at last express her opinion, with some clearness, that her aunt should not be disturbed by any changes at present. 'After that I should not think of pressing it, Miss Dorothy,' said Mr Gibson; 'but, still, I do hope that I may have the privilege of seeing her yet once again in the flesh. And touching my approaching marriage, Miss Dorothy—' He paused, and Dorothy felt that she was blushing up to the roots of her hair. 'Touching my marriage,' continued Mr Gibson, 'which however will not be solemnized till the end of March;'—it was manifest that he regarded this as a point that would in that household be regarded as an argument in his favour—'I do hope that you will look upon it in the most favourable light and your excellent aunt also, if she be spared to us.'

'I am sure we hope that you will be happy, Mr Gibson.'

'What was I to do, Miss Dorothy? I know that I have been very much blamed but so unfairly! I have never meant to be untrue to a mouse, Miss Dorothy.' Dorothy did not at all understand whether she were the mouse, or Camilla French, or Arabella. 'And it is so hard to find that one is ill-spoken of because things have gone a little amiss.' It was quite impossible that Dorothy should make any answer to this, and at last Mr Gibson left her, assuring her with his last word that nothing would give him so much pleasure as to be called upon once more to see his old friend in her last moments.

Though Miss Stanbury had been described as sleeping 'like a babby,' she had heard the footsteps of a strange man in the house, and had made Martha tell her whose footsteps they were. As soon as Dorothy went to her, she darted upon the subject with all her old keenness.

'What did he want here, Dolly?'

'He said he would like to see you, aunt when you are a little better, you know. He spoke a good deal of his old friendship and respect.'

'He should have thought of that before. How am I to see people now?'

'But when you are better, aunt ?'

'How do I know that I shall ever be better? He isn't off with those people at Heavitree is he?'

'I hope not, aunt.'

'Psha! A poor, weak, insufficient creature, that's what he is. Mr Jennings is worth twenty of him.' Dorothy, though she put the question again in its most alluring form of Christian charity and forgiveness, could not induce her aunt to say that she would see Mr Gibson. 'How can I see him, when you know that Sir Peter has forbidden me to see anybody, except Mrs Clifford and Mr Jennings?'

Two days afterwards there was an uncomfortable little scene at Heavitree. It must, no doubt, have been the case, that the same train of circumstances which had produced Mr Gibson's visit to the Close, produced also the scene in question. It was suggested by some who were attending closely to the matter that Mr Gibson had already come to repent his engagement with Camilla French; and, indeed, there were those who pretended to believe that he was induced, by the prospect of Miss Stanbury's demise, to transfer his allegiance yet again, and to bestow his hand upon Dorothy at last. There were many in the city who could never be persuaded that Dorothy had refused him, these being, for the most part, ladies in whose estimation the value of a husband was counted so great, and a beneficed clergyman so valuable among suitors, that it was to their thinking impossible that Dorothy Stanbury should in her sound senses have rejected such an offer. 'I don't believe a bit of it,' said Mrs Crumbie to Mrs Apjohn; 'is it likely?' The ears of all the French family were keenly alive to rumours, and to rumours of rumours. Reports of these opinions respecting Mr Gibson reached Heavitree, and had their effect. As long as Mr Gibson was behaving well as a suitor, they were inoperative there. What did it matter to them how the prize might have been struggled for, might still be struggled for elsewhere, while they enjoyed the consciousness of possession? But when the consciousness of possession became marred by a cankerous doubt, such rumours were very important. Camilla heard of the visit in the Close, and swore that she would have justice done her. She gave her mother to understand that, if any trick were played upon her, the diocese should be made to ring of it, in a fashion that would astonish them all, from the bishop downwards. Whereupon Mrs French, putting much faith in her daughter's threats, sent for Mr Gibson.

'The truth is, Mr Gibson,' said Mrs French, when the civilities of their first greeting had been completed, 'my poor child is pining.'

'Pining, Mrs French!'

'Yes pining, Mr Gibson. I am afraid that you little understand how sensitive is that young heart. Of course, she is your own now. To her thinking, it would be treason to you for her to indulge in conversation with any other gentleman; but, then, she expects that you should spend your evenings with her of course!'

'But, Mrs French, think of my engagements, as a clergyman.'

'We know all about that, Mr Gibson. We know what a clergyman's calls are. It isn't like a doctor's, Mr Gibson.'

'It's very often worse, Mrs French.'

'Why should you go calling in the Close, Mr Gibson?' Here was the gist of the accusation.

'Wouldn't you have me make my peace with a poor dying sister?' pleaded Mr Gibson.

'After what has occurred,' said Mrs French, shaking her head at him, 'and while things are just as they are now, it would be more like an honest man of you to stay away. And, of course, Camilla feels it. She feels it very much and she won't put up with it neither.'

'I think this is the cruellest, cruellest thing I ever heard,' said Mr Gibson.

'It is you that are cruel, sir.'

Then the wretched man turned at bay. 'I tell you what it is, Mrs French if I am treated in this way, I won't stand it. I won't, indeed. I'll go away. I'm not going to be suspected, nor yet blown up. I think I've behaved handsomely, at any rate to Camilla.'

'Quite so, Mr Gibson, if you would come and see her on evenings,' said Mrs French, who was falling back into her usual state of timidity.

'But, if I'm to be treated in this way, I will go away. I've thoughts of it as it is. I've been already invited to go to Natal, and if I hear anything more of these accusations, I shall certainly make up my mind to go.' Then he left the house, before Camilla could be down upon him from her perch on the landing-place.

CHAPTER LV. THE REPUBLICAN BROWNING

Mr Glascock had returned to Naples after his sufferings in the dining-room of the American Minister, and by the middle of February was back again in Florence. His father was still alive, and it was said that the old lord would now probably live through the winter. And it was understood that Mr Glascock would remain in Italy. He had declared that he would pass his time between Naples, Rome, and Florence; but it seemed to his friends that Florence was, of the three, the most to his taste. He liked his room, he said; at the York Hotel, and he liked being in the capital. That was his own statement. His friends said that he liked being with Carry Spalding, the daughter of the American Minister; but none of them, then in Italy, were sufficiently intimate with him to express that opinion to himself.

It had been expressed more than once to Carry Spalding. The world in general says such things to ladies more openly than it does to men, and the probability of a girl's success in matrimony is canvassed in her hearing by those who are nearest to her with a freedom which can seldom be used in regard to a man. A man's most intimate friend hardly speaks to him of the prospect of his marriage till he himself has told that the engagement exists. The lips of no living person had suggested to Mr Glascock that the American girl was to become his wife; but a great deal had been said to Carry Spalding about the conquest she had made. Her uncle, her aunt, her sister, and her great friend Miss Petrie, the poetess—the Republican Browning as she was called—had all spoken to her about it frequently. Olivia had declared her conviction that the thing was to be. Miss Petrie had, with considerable eloquence, explained to her friend that that English title, which was but the clatter of a sounding brass, should be regarded as a drawback rather than as an advantage. Mrs Spalding, who was no poetess, would undoubtedly have welcomed Mr Glascock as her niece's husband with all an aunt's energy. When told by Miss Petrie that old Lord Peterborough was a tinkling cymbal she snapped angrily at her gifted countrywoman. But she was too honest a woman, and too conscious also of her niece's strength, to say a word to urge her on. Mr Spalding as an American minister, with full powers at the court of a European sovereign, felt that he had full as much to give as to receive; but he was well inclined to do both. He would have been much pleased to talk about his nephew Lord Peterborough, and he loved his niece dearly. But by the middle of February he was beginning to think that the matter had been long enough in training. If the Honourable Glascock meant anything, why did he not speak out his mind plainly? The American Minister in such matters was accustomed to fewer ambages than were common in the circles among which Mr Glascock had lived.

In the meantime Caroline Spalding was suffering. She had allowed herself to think that Mr Glascock intended to propose to her, and had acknowledged to herself that were he to do so she would certainly accept him. All that she had seen of him, since the day on which he had been courteous to her about the seat in the diligence, had been pleasant to her. She had felt the charm of his manner, his education, and his gentleness; and had told herself that with all her love for her own country, she would willingly become an Englishwoman for the sake of being that man's wife. But nevertheless the warnings of her great friend, the poetess, had not been thrown away upon her. She would put away from herself as far as she could any desire to become Lady Peterborough. There should be no bias in the man's favour on that score. The tinkling cymbal and the sounding brass should be nothing to her. But yet—yet what a chance was there here for her? 'They are dishonest, and rotten at the core,' said Miss Petrie, trying to make her friend understand that a free American should under no circumstances place trust in an English aristocrat. 'Their country, Carry, is a game played out, while we are still breasting the hill with our young lungs full of air.' Carry Spalding was proud of her intimacy with the Republican Browning; but nevertheless she liked Mr Glascock; and when Mr Glascock had been ten days in Florence, on his third visit to the city, and had been four or five times at the embassy without expressing his intentions in the proper form, Carry Spalding began to think that she had better save herself from a heartbreak while salvation might be within her reach. She perceived that her uncle was gloomy and almost angry when he spoke of Mr Glascock, and that her aunt was fretful with disappointment. The Republican Browning had uttered almost a note of triumph; and had it not been that Olivia persisted, Carry Spalding would have consented to go away with Miss Petrie to Rome. 'The old stones are rotten too,' said the poetess; 'but their dust tells no lies.' That well known piece of hers 'Ancient Marbles, while ye crumble,' was written at this time, and contained an occult reference to Mr Glascock and her friend.

But Livy Spalding clung to the alliance. She probably knew her sister's heart better than did the others; and perhaps also had a clearer insight into Mr Glascock's character. She was at any rate clearly of opinion that there should be no running away. 'Either you do like him, or you don't. If you do, what are you to get by going to Rome?' said Livy.

'I shall get quit of doubt and trouble.'

'I call that cowardice. I would never run away from a man, Carry. Aunt Sophie forgets that they don't manage these things in England just as we do.'

'I don't know why there should be a difference.'

'Nor do I, only that there is. You haven't read so many of their novels as I have.'

'Who would ever think of learning to live out of an English novel?' said Carry.

'I am not saying that. You may teach him to live how you like afterwards. But if you have anything to do with people it must be well to know what their manners are. I think the richer sort of people in England slide into these things more gradually than we do. You stand your ground, Carry, and hold your own, and take the goods the gods provide you.' Though Caroline Spalding opposed her sister's arguments, and was particularly hard upon that allusion to 'the richer sort of people,' which, as she knew, Miss Petrie would have regarded as evidence of reverence for sounding brasses and tinkling cymbals, nevertheless she loved Livy dearly for what she said, and kissed the sweet counsellor, and resolved that she would for the present decline the invitation of the poetess. Then was Miss Petrie somewhat indignant with her friend, and threw out her scorn in those lines which have been mentioned.

But the American Minister hardly knew how to behave himself when he met Mr Glascock, or even when he was called upon to speak of him. Florence no doubt is a large city, and is now the capital of a great kingdom; but still people meet in Florence much more frequently than they do in Paris or in London. It may almost be said that they whose habit it is to go into society, and whose circumstances bring them into the same circles, will see each other every day. Now the American Minister delighted to see and to be seen in all places frequented by persons of a certain rank and position in Florence. Having considered the matter much, he had convinced himself that he could thus best do his duty as minister from the great Republic of Free States to the newest and as he called it 'the free-est of the European kingdoms.' The minister from France was a marquis; he from England was an earl; from Spain had come a count and so on. In the domestic privacy of his embassy Mr Spalding would be severe enough upon the sounding brasses and the tinkling cymbals, and was quite content himself to be the Honourable Jonas G. Spalding—Honourable because selected by his country for a post of honour; but he liked to be heard among the cymbals and seen among the brasses, and to feel that his position was as high as theirs. Mr Glascock also was frequently in the same circles, and thus it came to pass that the two gentlemen saw each other almost daily. That Mr Spalding knew well how to bear himself in his high place no one could doubt; but he did not quite know how to carry himself before Mr Glascock. At home at Boston he would have been more completely master of the situation.

He thought too that he began to perceive that Mr Glascock avoided him, though he would hear on his return home that that gentleman had been at the embassy, or had been walking in the Cascine with his nieces. That their young ladies should walk in public places with unmarried gentlemen is nothing to American fathers and guardians. American young ladies are accustomed to choose their own companions. But the minister was tormented by his doubts as to the ways of Englishmen, and as to the phase in which English habits might most properly exhibit themselves in Italy. He knew that people were talking about Mr Glascock and his niece. Why then did Mr Glascock avoid him? It was perhaps natural that Mr Spalding should have omitted to observe that Mr Glascock was not delighted by those lectures on the American constitution which formed so large a part of his ordinary conversation with Englishmen.

It happened one afternoon that they were thrown together so closely for nearly an hour that neither could avoid the other. They were both at the old palace in which the Italian parliament is held, and were kept waiting during some long delay in the ceremonies of the place. They were seated next to each other, and during such delay there was nothing for them but to talk. On the other side of each of them was a stranger, and not to talk in such circumstances would be to quarrel. Mr Glascock began by asking after the ladies.

'They are quite well, sir, thank you,' said the minister. 'I hope that Lord Peterborough was pretty well when last you heard from Naples, Mr Glascock.' Mr Glascock explained that his father's condition was not much altered, and then there was silence for a moment.

'Your nieces will remain with you through the spring I suppose?' said Mr Glascock.

'Such is their intention, sir.'

'They seem to like Florence, I think.'

'Yes yes; I think they do like Florence. They see this capital, sir, perhaps under more favourable circumstances than are accorded to most of my countrywomen. Our republican simplicity, Mr Glascock, has this drawback, that away from home it subjects us somewhat to the cold shade of unobserved obscurity. That it possesses merits which much more than compensate for this trifling evil I should be the last man in Europe to deny.' It is to be observed that American citizens are always prone to talk of Europe. It affords the best counterpoise they know to that other term, America, and America and the United States are of course the same. To speak of France or of England as weighing equally against their own country seems to an American to be an absurdity and almost an insult to himself. With Europe he can compare himself, but even this is done generally in the style of the Republican Browning when she addressed the Ancient Marbles.

'Undoubtedly,' said Mr Glascock, 'the family of a minister abroad has great advantages in seeing the country to which he is accredited.'

'That is my meaning, sir. But, as I was remarking, we carry with us as a people no external symbols of our standing at home. The wives and daughters, sir, of the most honoured of our citizens have no nomenclature different than that which belongs to the least noted among us. It is perhaps a consequence of this that Europeans who are accustomed in their social intercourse to the assistance of titles, will not always trouble themselves to inquire who and what are the American citizens who may sit opposite to them at table. I have known, Mr Glascock, the wife and daughter of a gentleman who has been thrice sent as senator from his native State to Washington, to remain as disregarded in the intercourse of a European city, as though they had formed part of the family of some grocer from your Russell Square!'

'Let the Miss Spaldings go where they will,' said Mr Glascock, 'they will not fare in that way.'

'The Miss Spaldings, sir, are very much obliged to you,' said the minister with a bow.

'I regard it as one of the luckiest chances of my life that I was thrown in with them at St Michael as I was,' said Mr Glascock with something like warmth.

'I am sure, sir, they will never forget the courtesy displayed by you on that occasion,' said the minister bowing again.

'That was a matter of course. I and my friend would have done the same for the grocer's wife and daughter of whom you spoke. Little services such as that do not come from appreciation of merit, but are simply the payment of the debt due by all men to all women.'

'Such is certainly the rule of living in our country, sir,' said Mr Spalding.

'The chances are,' continued the Englishman, 'that no further observation follows the payment of such a debt. It has been a thing of course.'

'We delight to think it so, Mr Glascock, in our own cities.'

'But in this instance it has given rise to one of the pleasantest, and as I hope most enduring friendships that I have ever formed,' said Mr Glascock with enthusiasm. What could the American Minister do but bow again three times? And what other meaning could he attach to such words than that which so many of his friends had been attributing to Mr Glascock for some weeks past? It had occurred to Mr Spalding, even since he had been sitting in his present close proximity to Mr Glascock, that it might possibly be his duty as an uncle having to deal with an Englishman, to ask that gentleman what were his intentions. He would do his duty let it be what it might; but the asking of such a question would be very disagreeable to him. For the present he satisfied himself with inviting his neighbour to come and drink tea with Mrs Spalding on the next evening but one. 'The girls will be delighted, I am sure,' said he, thinking himself to be justified in this friendly familiarity by Mr Glascock's enthusiasm. For Mr Spalding was clearly of opinion that, let the value of republican simplicity be what it might, an alliance with the crumbling marbles of Europe would in his niece's circumstances be not inexpedient. Mr Glascock accepted the invitation with alacrity, and the minister when he was closeted with his wife that evening declared his opinion that after all the Britisher meant fighting. The aunt told the girls that Mr Glascock was coming, and in order that it might not seem that a net was being specially spread for him, others were invited to join the party. Miss Petrie consented to be there, and the Italian, Count Buonarosci, to whose presence, though she could not speak to him, Mrs Spalding was becoming accustomed. It was painful to her to feel that she could not communicate with those around her, and for that reason she would have avoided Italians. But she had an idea that she could not thoroughly realise the advantages of foreign travel unless she lived with foreigners; and, therefore, she was glad to become intimate at any rate with the outside of Count Buonarosci.

'I think your uncle is wrong, dear,' said Miss Petrie early in the day to her friend.

'But why? He has done nothing more than what is just civil.'

'If Mr Glascock kept a store in Broadway he would not have thought it necessary to shew the same civility.'

'Yes if we all liked the Mr Glascock who kept the store.'

'Caroline,' said the poetess with severe eloquence, 'can you put your hand upon your heart and say that this inherited title, this tinkling cymbal as I call it, has no attraction for you or yours? Is it the unadorned simple man that you welcome to your bosom, or a thing of stars and garters, a patch of parchment, the minion of a throne, the lordling of twenty descents, in which each has been weaker than that before it, the hero of a scutcheon, whose glory is in his quarterings, and whose worldly wealth comes from the sweat of serfs whom the euphonism of an effete country has learned to decorate with the name of tenants?'

But Caroline Spalding had a spirit of her own, and had already made up her mind that she would not be talked down by Miss Petrie. 'Uncle Jonas,' said she, 'asks him because we like him; and would do so too if he kept the store in Broadway. But if he did keep the store perhaps we should not like him.'

'I trow not,' said Miss Petrie.

Livy was much more comfortable in her tactics, and without consulting anybody sent for a hairdresser. 'It's all very well for Wallachia,' said Livy Miss Petrie's name was Wallachia 'but I know a nice sort of man when I see him, and the ways of the world are not to be altered because Wally writes poetry.'

When Mr Glascock was announced, Mrs Spalding's handsome rooms were almost filled, as rooms in Florence are filled, obstruction in every avenue, a crowd in every corner, and a block at every doorway, not being among the customs of the place. Mr Spalding immediately caught him, intercepting him between the passages and the ladies, and engaged him at once in conversation.

'Your John S. Mill is a great man,' said the minister.

'They tell me so,' said Mr Glascock. 'I don't read what he writes myself.'

This acknowledgment seemed to the minister to be almost disgraceful, and yet he himself had never read a word of Mr Mill's writings. 'He is a far-seeing man,' continued the minister. 'He is one of the few Europeans who can look forward, and see how the rivers of civilization are running on. He has understood that women must at last be put upon an equality with men.'

'Can he manage that men shall have half the babies?' said Mr Glascock, thinking to escape by an attempt at playfulness.

But the minister was down upon him at once, had him by the lappet of his coat, though he knew how important it was for his dear niece that he should allow Mr Glascock to amuse himself this evening after another fashion. 'I have an answer ready, sir, for that difficulty,' he said.'step aside with me for a moment. The question is important, and I should be glad if you would communicate my ideas to your great philosopher. Nature, sir, has laid down certain laws, which are immutable; and, against them—'

But Mr Glascock had not come to Florence for this. There were circumstances in his present position which made him feel that he would be gratified in escaping, even at the cost of some seeming incivility. 'I must go in to the ladies at once,' he said, 'or I shall never get a word with them.' There came across the minister's brow a momentary frown of displeasure, as though he felt that he were being robbed of that which was justly his own. For an instant his grasp fixed itself more tightly to the coat. It was quite within the scope of his courage to hold a struggling listener by physical strength but he remembered that there was a purpose, and he relaxed his hold.

'I will take another opportunity,' said the minister. 'As you have raised that somewhat trite objection of the bearing of children, which we in our country, sir, have altogether got over, I must put you in possession of my views on that subject; but I will find another occasion.' Then Mr Glascock began to reflect whether an

American lady, married in England, would probably want to see much of her uncle in her adopted country.

Mrs Spalding was all smiles when her guest reached her. 'We did not mean to have such a crowd of people,' she said, whispering; 'but you know how one thing leads to another, and people here really like short invitations.' Then the minister's wife bowed very low to an Italian lady, and for the moment wished herself in Beacon Street. It was a great trouble to her that she could not pluck up courage to speak a word in Italian. 'I know more about it than some that are glib enough,' she would say to her niece Livy, 'but these Tuscans are so particular with their Bocca Tostana.'

It was almost spiteful on the part of Miss Petrie the manner in which, on this evening, she remained close to her friend Caroline Spalding. It is hardly possible to believe that it came altogether from high principle, from a determination to save her friend from an impending danger. One's friend has no right to decide for one what is, and what is not dangerous. Mr Glascock after awhile found himself seated on a fixed couch, that ran along the wall, between Carry Spalding and Miss Petrie; but Miss Petrie was almost as bad to him as had been the minister himself. 'I am afraid,' she said, looking up into his face with some severity, and rushing upon her subject with audacity, 'that the works of your Browning have not been received in your country with that veneration to which they are entitled.'

'Do you mean Mr or Mrs Browning?' asked Mr Glascock perhaps with some mistaken idea that the lady was out of her depth, and did not know the difference.

'Either, both; for they are one, the same, and indivisible. The spirit and germ of each is so reflected in the outcome of the other, that one sees only the result of so perfect a combination, and one is tempted to acknowledge that here and there a marriage may have been arranged in Heaven. I don't think that in your country you have perceived this, Mr Glascock.'

'I am not quite sure that we have,' said Mr Glascock. 'Yours is not altogether an inglorious mission,' continued Miss Petrie.

'I've got no mission,' said Mr Glascock 'either from the Foreign Office, or from my own inner convictions.'

Miss Petrie laughed with a scornful laugh. 'I spoke, sir, of the mission of that small speck on the earth's broad surface, of which you think so much, and which we call Great Britain.'

'I do think a good deal of it,' said Mr Glascock.

'It has been more thought of than any other speck of the same size,' said Carry Spalding.

'True,' said Miss Petrie, sharply 'because of its iron and coal. But the mission I spoke of was this.' And she put forth her hand with an artistic motion as she spoke. 'It utters prophecies, though it cannot read them. It sends forth truth, though it cannot understand it. Though its own ears are deaf as adder's, it is the nursery of poets, who sing not for their own countrymen, but for the higher sensibilities and newer intelligences of lands in which philanthropy has made education as common as the air that is breathed.'

'Wally,' said Olivia, coming up to the poetess, in anger that was almost apparent, 'I want to take you, and introduce you to the Marchesa Pulti.'

But Miss Petrie no doubt knew that the eldest son of an English lord was at least as good as an Italian marchesa. 'Let her come here,' said the poetess, with her grandest smile.

CHAPTER LVI. WITHERED GRASS

When Caroline Spalding perceived how direct an attempt had been made by her sister to take the poetess away, in order that she might thus be left alone with Mr Glascock, her spirit revolted against the manoeuvre, and she took herself away amidst the crowd. If Mr Glascock should wish to find her again he could do so. And there came across her mind something of a half-formed idea that, perhaps after all her friend Wallachia was right. Were this man ready to take her and she ready to be taken, would such an arrangement be a happy one for both of them? His high-born, wealthy friends might very probably despise her, and it was quite possible that she also might despise them. To be Lady Peterborough, and have the spending of a large fortune, would not suffice for her happiness. She was sure of that. It would be a leap in the dark' and all such leaps must needs be dangerous, and therefore should be avoided. But she did like the man. Her friend was untrue to her and cruel in those allusions to tinkling cymbals. It might be well for her to get over her liking, and to think no more of one who was to her a foreigner and a stranger, of whose ways of living in his own home she knew so little, whose people might be antipathetic to her, enemies instead of friends, among whom her life would be one long misery; but it was not on that ground that Miss Petrie had recommended her to start for Rome as soon as Mr Glascock had reached Florence. 'There is no reason,' she said to herself, 'why I should not marry a man if I like him, even though he be a lord. And of him I should not be the least afraid. It's the women that I fear.' And then she called to mind all that she had ever heard of English countesses and duchesses. She thought that she knew that they were generally cold and proud, and very little given to receive outsiders graciously within their ranks. Mr Glascock had an aunt who was a Duchess, and a sister who would be a Countess. Caroline Spalding felt how her back would rise against these new relations, if it should come to pass that they should look unkindly upon her when she was taken to her own home; how she would fight with them, giving them scorn for scorn; how unutterably miserable she would be; how she would long to be back among her own equals, in spite even of her love for her husband. 'How grand a thing it is,' she said, 'to be equal with those whom you love!' And yet she was to some extent allured by the social position of the man. She could perceive that he had a charm of manner which her countrymen lacked. He had read, perhaps, less than her uncle knew, perhaps, less than most of those men with whom she had been wont to associate in her own city life at home, was not braver, or more virtuous, or more self-denying than they; but there was a softness and an ease in his manner which was palatable to her, and an absence of that too visible effort of the intellect which is so apt to mark and mar the conversation of Americans. She almost wished that she had been English, in order that the man's home and friends might have suited her. She was thinking of all this as she stood pretending to talk to an American lady, who was very eloquent on the delights of Florence.

In the meantime Olivia and Mr Glascock had moved away together, and Miss Petrie was left alone. This was no injury to Miss Petrie, as her mind at once set itself to work on a sonnet touching the frivolity of modern social gatherings; and when she complained afterwards to Caroline that it was the curse of their mode of life that no moment could be allowed for thought, in which she referred specially to a few words that Mr Gore had addressed to her at this moment of her meditations, she was not wilfully a hypocrite. She was painfully turning her second set of rhymes, and really believed that she had been subjected to a hardship. In the meantime Olivia and Mr Glascock were discussing her at a distance.

'You were being put through your facings, Mr Glascock,' Olivia had said.

'Well; yes; and your dear friend, Miss Petrie, is rather a stern examiner.'

'She is Carry's ally, not mine,' said Olivia. Then she remembered that by saying this she might be doing her sister an injury. Mr Glascock might object to such a bosom friend for his wife. 'That is to say, of course we are all intimate with her? but just at this moment Carry is most in favour.'

'She is very clever, I am quite sure,' said he.

'Oh yes she's a genius. You must not doubt that on the peril of making every American in Italy your enemy.'

'She is a poet is she not?'

'Mr Glascock!'

'Have I said anything wrong?' he asked.

'Do you mean to look me in the face and tell me that you are not acquainted with her works, that you don't know pages of them by heart, that you don't sleep with them under your pillow, don't travel about with them in your dressing-bag? I'm afraid we have mistaken you, Mr Glascock.'

'Is it so great a sin?'

'If you'll own up honestly, I'll tell you something in a whisper. You have not read a word of her poems?'

'Not a word.'

'Neither have I. Isn't it horrible? But, perhaps, if I heard Tennyson talking every day, I shouldn't read Tennyson. Familiarity does breed contempt, doesn't it? And then poor dear Wallachia is such a bore. I sometimes wonder, when English people are listening to her, whether they think that American girls generally talk like that.'

'Not all, perhaps, with that perfected eloquence.'

'I dare say you do,' continued Olivia, craftily. 'That is just the way in which people form their opinions about foreigners. Some specially self-asserting American speaks his mind louder than other people, and then you say that all Americans are self-asserting.'

'But you are a little that way given, Miss Spalding.'

'Because we are always called upon to answer accusations against us, expressed or unexpressed. We don't think ourselves a bit better than you; or, if the truth were known, half as good. We are always struggling to be as polished and easy as the French, or as sensible and dignified as the English; but when our defects are thrown in our teeth—'

'Who throws them in your teeth, Miss Spalding?'

'You look it, all of you, if you do not speak it out. You do assume a superiority, Mr Glascock; and that we cannot endure.'

'I do not feel that I assume anything,' said Mr Glascock, meekly.

'If three gentlemen be together, an Englishman, a Frenchman, and an American, is not the American obliged to be on his mettle to prove that he is somebody among the three? I admit that he is always claiming to be the first; but he does so only that he may not be too evidently the last. If you knew us, Mr Glascock, you would find us to be very mild, and humble, and nice, and good, and clever, and kind, and charitable, and beautiful—in short, the finest people that have as yet been created on the broad face of God's smiling earth.' These last words she pronounced with a nasal twang, and in a tone of voice which almost seemed to him to be a direct mimicry of the American Minister. The upshot of the conversation, however, was that the disgust against Americans which, to a certain degree, had been excited in Mr Glascock's mind by the united efforts of Mr Spalding and the poetess, had been almost entirely dispelled. From all of which the reader ought to understand that Miss Olivia Spalding was a very clever young woman.

But nevertheless Mr Glascock had not quite made up his mind to ask the elder sister to be his wife. He was one of those men to whom love-making does not come very easy, although he was never so much at his ease as when he was in company with ladies. He was sorely in want of a wife, but he was aware that at different periods during the last fifteen years he had been angled for as a fish. Mothers in England had tried to catch him, and of such mothers he had come to have the strongest possible detestation. He had seen the hooks or perhaps had fancied that he saw them when they were not there. Lady Janes and Lady Sarahs had been hard upon him, till he learned to buckle himself into triple armour when he went amongst them, and yet he wanted a wife; no man more sorely wanted one. The reader will perhaps remember how he went down to Nuncombe Putney in quest of a wife, but all in vain. The lady in that case had been so explicit with him that he could not hope for a more favourable answer; and, indeed, he would not have cared to marry a girl who had told him that she preferred another man to himself, even if it had been possible for him to do so. Now he had met a lady very different from those with whom he had hitherto associated but not the less manifestly a lady. Caroline Spalding was bright, pleasant, attractive, very easy to talk to, and yet quite able to hold her own. But the American Minister was a bore; and Miss Petrie was unbearable. He had often told himself that in this matter of marrying a wife he would please himself altogether, that he would allow himself to be tied down by no consideration of family pride, that he would consult nothing but his own heart and feelings.

As for rank, he could give that to his wife. As for money, he had plenty of that also. He wanted a woman that was not *blasée* with the world, that was not a fool, and who would respect him. The more he thought of it, the more sure he was that he had seen none who pleased him so well as Caroline Spalding; and yet he was a little afraid of taking a step that would be irrevocable. Perhaps the American Minister might express a wish to end his days at Monkhams, and might think it desirable to have Miss Petrie always with him as a private secretary in poetry!

'Between you and us, Mr Glascock, the spark of sympathy does not pass with a strong flash,' said a voice in his ear. As he turned round rapidly to face his foe, he was quite sure, for the moment, that under no possible circumstances would he ever take an American woman to his bosom as his wife.

'No,' said he; 'no, no. I rather think that I agree with you.'

'The antipathy is one,' continued Miss Petrie, 'which has been common on the face of the earth since the clown first trod upon the courtier's heels. It is the instinct of fallen man to hate equality, to desire ascendancy, to crush, to oppress, to tyrannise, to enslave. Then, when the slave is at last free, and in his freedom demands equality, man is not great enough to take his enfranchised brother to his bosom.'

'You mean negroes,' said Mr Glascock, looking round and planning for himself a mode of escape.

'Not negroes only, not the enslaved blacks, who are now enslaved no more, but the rising nations of white men wherever they are to be seen. You English have no sympathy with a people who claim to be at least your equals. The clown has trod upon the courtier's heels till the clown is clown no longer, and the courtier has hardly a court in which he may dangle his sword-knot.'

'If so the clown might as well spare the courtier,' not meaning the rebuke which his words implied.

'Ah h but the clown will not spare the courtier, Mr Glascock. I understand the gibe, and I tell you that the courtier shall be spared no longer because he is useless. He shall be cut down together with the withered grasses and thrown into the oven, and there shall be an end of him.' Then she turned round to appeal to an American gentleman who had joined them, and Mr Glascock made his escape. 'I hold it to be the holiest duty which I owe to my country never to spare one of them when I meet him.'

'They are all very well in their way,' said the American gentleman.

'Down with them, down with them!' exclaimed the poetess, with a beautiful enthusiasm. In the meantime Mr Glascock had made up his mind that he could not dare to ask Caroline Spalding to be his wife. There were certain forms of the American female so dreadful that no wise man would wilfully come in contact with them. Miss Petrie's ferocity was distressing to him, but her eloquence and enthusiasm were worse even than her ferocity. The personal incivility of which she had been guilty in calling him a withered grass was distasteful to him, as being opposed to his ideas of the customs of society; but what would be his fate if his wife's chosen friend should be for ever dinning her denunciation of withered grasses into his ear?

He was still thinking of all this when he was accosted by Mrs Spalding. 'Are you going to dear Lady Banbury's to-morrow?' she asked. Lady Banbury was the wife of the English Minister.

'I suppose I shall be there in the course of the evening.'

'How very nice she is; is she not? I do like Lady Banbury—so soft, and gentle, and kind.'

'One of the pleasantest old ladies I know,' said Mr Glascock.

'It does not strike you so much as it does me,' said Mrs Spalding, with one of her sweetest smiles. 'The truth is, we all value what we have not got. There are no Lady Banburys in our country, and therefore we think the more of them when we meet them here. She is talking of going to Rome for the Carnival, and has asked

Caroline to go with her. I am so pleased to find that my dear girl is such a favourite.'

Mr Glascock immediately told himself that he saw the hook. If he were to be fished for by this American aunt as he had been fished for by English mothers, all his pleasure in the society of Caroline Spalding would be at once over. It would be too much, indeed, if in this American household he were to find the old vices of an aristocracy superadded to young republican sins! Nevertheless Lady Banbury was, as he knew well, a person whose opinion about young people was supposed to be very good. She noticed those only who were worthy of notice; and to have been taken by the hand by Lady Banbury was acknowledged to be a passport into good society. If Caroline Spalding was in truth going to Rome with Lady Banbury, that fact was in itself a great confirmation of Mr Glascock's good opinion of her. Mrs Spalding had perhaps understood this; but had not understood that having just hinted that it was so, she should have abstained from saying a word more about her dear girl. Clever and well-practised must, indeed, be the hand of the fisherwoman in matrimonial waters who is able to throw her fly without showing any glimpse of the hook to the fish for whom she angles. Poor Mrs Spalding, though with kindly instincts towards her niece she did on this occasion make some slight attempt at angling, was innocent of any concerted plan. It seemed to her to be so natural to say a good word in praise of her niece to the man whom she believed to be in love with her niece.

Caroline and Mr Glascock did not meet each other again till late in the evening, and just as he was about to take his leave. As they came together each of them involuntarily looked round to see whether Miss Petrie was near. Had she been there nothing would have been said beyond the shortest farewell greeting. But Miss Petrie was afar off, electrifying some Italian by the vehemence of her sentiments, and the audacious volubility of a language in which all arbitrary restrictions were ignored. 'Are you going?' she asked.

'Well I believe I am. Since I saw you last I've encountered Miss Petrie again, and I'm rather depressed.'

'Ah you don't know her. If you did you wouldn't laugh at her.'

'Laugh at her! Indeed I do not do that; but when I'm told that I'm to be thrown into the oven and burned because I'm such a worn-out old institution—'

'You don't mean to say that you mind that!'

'Not much, when it comes up in the ordinary course of conversation; but it palls upon one when it is asserted for the fourth or fifth time in an evening.'

'Alas, alas!' exclaimed Miss. Spalding, with mock energy.

'And why, alas?'

'Because it is so impossible to make the oil and vinegar of the old world and of the new mix together and suit each other.'

'You think it is impossible, Miss Spalding?'

'I fear so. We are so terribly tender, and you are always pinching us on our most tender spot. And we never meet you without treading on your gouty toes.'

'I don't think my toes are gouty,' said he.

'I apologise to your own, individually, Mr Glascock; but I must assert that nationally you are subject to the gout.'

'That is, when I'm told over and over again that I'm to be cut down and thrown into the oven—'

'Never mind the oven now, Mr Glascock. If my friend has been over-zealous I will beg pardon for her. But it does seem to me, indeed it does, with all the reverence and partiality I have for everything European,' the word European was an offence to him, and he shewed that it was so by his countenance 'that the idiosyncrasies of you and of us are so radically different, that we cannot be made to amalgamate and sympathise with each other thoroughly.'

He paused for some seconds before he answered her, but it was so evident by his manner that he was going to speak, that she could neither leave him nor interrupt him. 'I had thought that it might have been otherwise,' he said at last, and the tone of his voice was so changed as to make her know that he was in earnest.

But she did not change her voice by a single note. 'I'm afraid it cannot be so,' she said, speaking after her old fashion half in earnest, half in banter. 'We may make up our minds to be very civil to each other when we meet. The threats of the oven may no doubt be dropped on our side, and you may abstain from expressing in words your sense of our inferiority.'

'I never expressed anything of the kind,' he said, quite in anger.

'I am taking you simply as the sample Englishman, not as Mr Glascock, who helped me and my sister over the mountains. Such of us as have to meet in society may agree to be very courteous; but courtesy and cordiality are not only not the same, but they are incompatible.'

'Why so?'

'Courtesy is an effort, and cordiality is free. I must be allowed to contradict the friend that I love; but I assent too often falsely to what is said to me by a passing acquaintance. In spite of what the Scripture says, I think it is one of the greatest privileges of a brother that he may call his brother a fool.'

'Shall you desire to call your husband a fool?'

'My husband!'

'He will, I suppose, be at least as dear to you as a brother?'

'I never had a brother.'

'Your sister, then! It is the same, I suppose?'

'If I were to have a husband, I hope he would be the dearest to me of all. Unless he were so, he certainly would not be my husband. But between a man and his wife there does not spring up that playful, violent intimacy admitting of all liberties, which comes from early nursery associations; and, then, there is the difference of sex.'

'I should not like my wife to call me a fool,' he said.

'I hope she may never have occasion to do so, Mr Glascock. Marry an English wife in your own class as, of course, you will and then you will be safe.'

'But I have set my heart fast on marrying an American wife,' he said.

'Then I can't tell what may befall you. It's like enough, if you do that, that you may be called by some name you will think hard to bear. But you'll think better of it. Like should pair with like, Mr Glascock. If you were to marry one of our young women, you would lose in dignity as much as she would lose in comfort.' Then they parted, and she went off to say farewell to other guests. The manner in which she had answered what he had said to her had certainly been of a nature to stop any further speech of the same kind. Had she been gentle with him, then he would certainly have told her that she was the American woman whom he desired to take with him to his home in England.

CHAPTER LVII. DOROTHY'S FATE

Towards the end of February Sir Peter Mancrudy declared Miss Stanbury to be out of danger, and Mr Martin began to be sprightly on the subject, taking to himself no inconsiderable share of the praise accruing to the medical faculty in Exeter generally for the saving of a life so valuable to the city. 'Yes, Mr Burgess,' Sir Peter said to old Barty of the bank, 'our friend will get over it this time, and without any serious damage to her constitution, if she will only take care of herself.' Barty made some inaudible grunt, intended to indicate his own indifference on the subject, and expressed his opinion to the chief clerk that old Jemima Wideawake as he was pleased to call her was one of those tough customers who would never die. 'It would be nothing to us, Mr Barty, one way or the other,' said the clerk; to which Barty Burgess assented with another grunt.

Camilla French declared that she was delighted to hear the news. At this time there had been some sort of a reconciliation between her and her lover. Mrs French had extracted from him a promise that he would not go to Natal; and Camilla had commenced the preparations for her wedding. His visits to Heavitree were as few and far between as he could make them with any regard to decency; but the 31st of March was coming on quickly, and as he was to be made a possession of them for ever, it was considered to be safe and well to allow him some liberty in his present condition. 'My dear, if they are driven, there is no knowing what they won't do,' Mrs French said to her daughter. Camilla had submitted with compressed lips and a slight nod of her head. She had worked very hard, but her day of reward was coming. It was impossible not to perceive both for her and her mother that the scantiness of Mr Gibson's attention to his future bride was cause of some weak triumph to Arabella. She said that it was very odd that he did not come and once added with a little sigh that he used to come in former days, alluding to those happy days in which another love was paramount. Camilla could not endure this with an equal mind. 'Bella, dear,' she said, 'we know what all that means. He has made his choice, and if I am satisfied with what he does now, surely you need not grumble.' Miss Stanbury's illness had undoubtedly been a great source of contentment to the family at Heavitree, as they had all been able to argue that her impending demise was the natural consequence of her great sin in the matter of Dorothy's proposed marriage. When, however, they heard from Mr Martin that she would certainly recover, that Sir Peter's edict to that effect had gone forth, they were willing to acknowledge that Providence, having so far punished the sinner, was right in staying its hand and abstaining from the final blow. 'I'm sure we are delighted,' said Mrs French, 'for though she has said cruel things of us and so untrue, too, yet of course it is our duty to forgive her. And we do forgive her.'

Dorothy had written three or four notes to Brooke since his departure, which contained simple bulletins of her aunt's health. She always began her letters with 'My dear Mr Burgess,' and ended them with 'yours truly.' She never made any allusion to Brooke's declaration of love, or gave the slightest sign in her letters to shew that she even remembered it. At last she wrote to say that her aunt was convalescent; and, in making this announcement, she allowed herself some enthusiasm of expression. She was so happy, and was so sure that Mr Burgess would be equally so! And her aunt had asked after her 'dear Brooke,' expressing her great satisfaction with him, in that he had come down to see her when she had been almost too ill to see anyone. In answer to this there came to her a real love-letter from Brooke Burgess. It was the first occasion on which he had written to her. The little bulletins had demanded no replies, and had received none. Perhaps there had been a shade of disappointment on Dorothy's side, in that she had written thrice, and had been made rich with no word in return. But, although her heart had palpitated on hearing the postman's knock, and had palpitated in vain, she had told herself that it was all as it should be. She wrote to him, because she possessed information which it was necessary that she should communicate. He did not write to her, because there was nothing for him to tell. Then had come the love-letter, and in the love-letter there was an imperative demand for a reply.

What was she to do? To have recourse to Priscilla for advice was her first idea; but she herself believed that she owed a debt of gratitude to her aunt, which Priscilla would not take into account—the existence of which Priscilla would by no means admit. She knew Priscilla's mind in this matter, and was sure that Priscilla's advice, whatever it might be, would be given without any regard to her aunt's views. And then Dorothy was altogether ignorant of her aunt's views. Her aunt had been very anxious that she should marry Mr Gibson, but had clearly never admitted into her mind the idea that she might possibly marry Brooke Burgess; and it seemed to her that she herself would be dishonest, both to her aunt and to her lover, if she were to bind this man to herself without her aunt's knowledge. He was to be her aunt's heir, and she was maintained by her aunt's liberality! Thinking of all this, she at last resolved that she would take the bull by the horns, and tell her aunt. She felt that the task would be one almost beyond her strength. Thrice she went into her aunt's room, intending to make a clean breast; Thrice her courage failed her, and she left the room with her tale untold, excusing herself on various pretexts. Her aunt had seemed to be not quite so well, or had declared herself to be tired, or had been a little cross or else Martha had come in at the nick of time. But there was Brooke Burgess's letter unanswered, a letter that was read night and morning, and which was never for an instant out of her mind. He had demanded a reply, and he had a right at least to that. The letter had been with her for four entire days before she had ventured to speak to her aunt on the subject.

On the first of March Miss Stanbury came out of her bed-room for the first time. Dorothy, on the previous day, had decided on postponing her communication for this occasion; but, when she found herself sitting in the little sitting-room up stairs close at her aunt's elbow, and perceived the signs of weakness which the new move had made conspicuous, and heard the invalid declare that the little journey had been almost too much for her, her heart misgave her. She ought to have told her tale while her aunt was still in bed. But presently there came a question, which put her into such a flutter that she was for the time devoid of all resolution. 'Has Brooke written?' said Miss Stanbury.

'Yes aunt; he has written.'

'And what did he say?' Dorothy was struck quite dumb. 'Is there anything wrong?' And now, as Miss Stanbury asked the question, she seemed herself to have forgotten that she had two minutes before declared herself to be almost too feeble to speak. 'I'm sure there is something wrong. What is it? I will know'

'There is nothing wrong, Aunt Stanbury'

'Where is the letter? Let me see it.'

'I mean there is nothing wrong about him.'

'What is it, then?'

'He is quite well, Aunt Stanbury.'

'Shew me the letter. I will see the letter. I know that there is something the matter. Do you mean to say you won't shew me Brooke's letter?'

There was a moment's pause before Dorothy answered. 'I will shew you his letter though I am sure he didn't mean that I should shew it to anyone.'

'He hasn't written evil of me?'

'No; no; no. He would sooner cut his hand off than say a word bad of you. He never says or writes anything bad of anybody. But Oh, aunt; I'll tell you everything. I should have told you before, only that you were ill.'

Then Miss Stanbury was frightened. 'What is it?' she said hoarsely, clasping the arms of the great chair, each with a thin, shrivelled hand.

'Aunt Stanbury, Brooke—Brooke wants me to be his wife!'

'What!'

'You cannot be more surprised than I have been, Aunt Stanbury; and there has been no fault of mine.'

'I don't believe it,' said the old woman.

'Now you may read the letter,' said Dorothy, standing up. She was quite prepared to be obedient, but she felt that her aunt's manner of receiving the information was almost an insult.

'He must be a fool,' said Miss Stanbury.

This was hard to hear, and the colour went and came rapidly across Dorothy's cheeks as she gave herself a few moments to prepare an answer. She already perceived that her aunt would be altogether adverse to the marriage, and that therefore the marriage could never take place. She had never for a moment allowed herself to think otherwise, but, nevertheless, the blow was heavy on her. We all know how constantly hope and expectation will rise high within our own bosoms in opposition to our own judgment, how we become sanguine in regard to events which we almost know can never come to pass. So it had been with Dorothy. Her heart had been almost in a flutter of happiness since she had had Brooke's letter in her possession, and yet she never ceased to declare to herself her own conviction that that letter could lead to no good result. In regard to her own wishes on the subject she had never asked herself a single question. As it had been quite beyond her power to bring herself to endure the idea of marrying Mr Gibson, so it had been quite impossible to her not to long to be Brooke's wife from the moment in which a suggestion to that effect had fallen from his lips. This was a state of things so certain, so much a matter of course, that, though she had not spoken a word to him in which she owned her love, she had never for a moment doubted that he knew the truth and that everybody else concerned would know it too. But she did not suppose that her wishes would go for anything with her aunt. Brooke Burgess was to become a rich man as her aunt's heir, and her aunt would of course have her own ideas about Brooke's advancement in life. She was quite prepared to submit without quarrelling when her aunt should tell her that the idea must not be entertained. But the order might be given, the prohibition might be pronounced, without an insult to her own feelings as a woman. 'He must he a fool,' Miss Stanbury had said, and Dorothy took time to collect her thoughts before she would reply. In the meantime her aunt finished the reading of the letter.

'He may be foolish in this,' Dorothy said; 'but I don't think you should call him a fool.'

'I shall call him what I please. I suppose this was going on at the time when you refused Mr Gibson.'

'Nothing was going on. Nothing has gone on at all,' said Dorothy, with as much indignation as she was able to assume.

'How can you tell me that? That is an untruth.'

'It is not an untruth,' said Dorothy, almost sobbing, but driven at the same time to much anger.

'Do you mean to say that this is the first you ever heard of it?' And she held out the letter, shaking it in her thin hand.

'I have never said so, Aunt Stanbury.'

'Yes, you did.'

'I said that nothing was going on, when Mr Gibson was—. If you choose to suspect me, Aunt Stanbury, I'll go away. I won't stay here if you suspect me. When Brooke spoke to me, I told him you wouldn't like it.'

'Of course I don't like it.' But she gave no reason why she did not like it.

'And there was nothing more till this letter came. I couldn't help his writing to me. It wasn't my fault.'

'Psha!'

'If you are angry, I am very sorry. But you haven't a right to be angry.'

'Go on, Dorothy; go on. I'm so weak that I can hardly stir myself; it's the first moment that I've been out of my bed for weeks and of course you can say what you please. I know what it will be. I shall have to take to my bed again, and then in a very little time you can both make fools of yourselves just as you like.'

This was an argument against which Dorothy of course found it to be quite impossible to make continued combat. She could only shuffle her letter back into her pocket, and be, if possible, more assiduous than ever in her attentions to the invalid. She knew that she had been treated most unjustly, and there would be a question to be answered as soon as her aunt should be well as to the possibility of her remaining in the Close subject to such injustice; but let her aunt say what she might, or do what she might, Dorothy could not leave her for the present. Miss Stanbury sat for a considerable time quite motionless, with her eyes closed, and did not stir or make signs of life till Dorothy touched her arm, asking her whether she would not take some broth which had been prepared for her. 'Where's Martha? Why does not Martha come?' said Miss Stanbury. This was a hard blow, and from that moment Dorothy believed that it would be expedient that she should return to Nuncombe Putney. The broth, however, was taken, while Dorothy sat by in silence. Only one word further was said that evening by Miss Stanbury about

Brooke and his love-affair. 'There must be nothing more about this, Dorothy; remember that; nothing at all. I won't have it.' Dorothy made no reply. Brooke's letter was in her pocket, and it should be answered that night. On the following day she would let her aunt know what she had said to Brooke. Her aunt should not see the letter, but should be made acquainted with its purport in reference to Brooke's proposal of marriage.

'I won't have it!' That had been her aunt's command. What right had her aunt to give any command upon the matter? Then crossed Dorothy's mind, as she thought of this, a glimmering of an idea that no one can be entitled to issue commands who cannot enforce obedience. If Brooke and she chose to become man and wife by mutual consent, how could her aunt prohibit the marriage? Then there followed another idea, that commands are enforced by the threatening and, if necessary, by the enforcement of penalties. Her aunt had within her hand no penalty of which Dorothy was afraid on her own behalf; but she had the power of inflicting a terrible punishment on Brooke Burgess. Now Dorothy conceived that she herself would be the meanest creature alive if she were actuated by fears as to money in her acceptance or rejection of a man whom she loved as she did Brooke Burgess. Brooke had an income of his own which seemed to her to be ample for all purposes. But that which would have been sordid in her, did not seem to her to have any stain of sordidness for him. He was a man, and was bound to be rich if he could. And, moreover, what had she to offer in herself, such a poor thing as was she, to make compensation to him for the loss of fortune? Her aunt could inflict this penalty, and therefore the power was hers, and the power must be obeyed. She would write to Brooke in a manner that should convey to him her firm decision.

But not the less on that account would she let her aunt know that she thought herself to have been ill-used. It was an insult to her, a most ill-natured insult that telling her that Brooke had been a fool for loving her. And then that accusation against her of having been false, of having given one reason for refusing Mr Gibson, while there was another reason in her heart, of having been cunning and then untrue, was not to be endured. What would her aunt think of her if she were to bear such allegations without indignant protest? She would write her letter, and speak her mind to her aunt as soon as her aunt should be well enough to hear it.

As she had resolved, she wrote her letter that night before she went to bed. She wrote it with floods of tears, and a bitterness of heart which almost conquered her. She too had heard of love, and had been taught to feel that the success or failure of a woman's life depended upon that whether she did, or whether she did not, by such gifts as God might have given to her, attract to herself some man strong enough, and good enough, and loving enough to make straight for her her paths, to bear for her her burdens, to be the father of her children, the staff on which she might lean, and the wall against which she might grow, feeling the sunshine, and sheltered from the wind. She had ever estimated her own value so lowly as to have told herself often that such success could never come in her way. From her earliest years she had regarded herself as outside the pale within which such joys are to be found. She had so strictly taught herself to look forward to a blank existence, that she had learned to do so without active misery. But not the less did she know where happiness lay; and when the good thing came almost within her reach, when it seemed that God had given her gifts which might have sufficed, when a man had sought her hand whose nature was such that she could have leaned on him with a true worship, could have grown against him as against a wall with perfect confidence, could have lain with her head upon his bosom, and have felt that of all spots that in the world was the most fitting for her when this was all but grasped, and must yet be abandoned, there came upon her spirit an agony so bitter that she had not before known how great might be the depth of human disappointment. But the letter was at last written, and when finished was as follows:

The Close,
Exeter,
March 1, 186—.

DEAR BROOKE.

There had been many doubts about this; but at last they were conquered, and the name was written.

I have shewn your letter to my aunt, as I am sure you will think was best. I should have answered it before, only that I thought that she was not quite well enough to talk about it. She says, as I was sure she would, that what you propose is quite out of the question. I am aware that I am bound to obey her; and as I think that you also ought to do so, I shall think no more of what you have said to me and have written. It is quite impossible now, even if it might have been possible under other circumstances. I shall always remember your great kindness to me. Perhaps I ought to say that I am very grateful for the compliment you have paid me. I shall think of you always till I die.

Believe me to be,

Your very sincere friend,   DOROTHY STANBURY.

The next day Miss Stanbury again came out of her room, and on the third day she was manifestly becoming stronger. Dorothy had as yet not spoken of her letter, but was prepared to do so as soon as she thought that a fitting opportunity had come. She had a word or two to say for herself; but she must not again subject herself to being told that she was taking her will of her aunt because her aunt was too ill to defend herself. But on the third day Miss Stanbury herself asked the question. 'Have you written anything to Brooke?' she asked.

'I have answered his letter, Aunt Stanbury.'

'And what have you said to him?'

'I have told him that you disapproved of it, and that nothing more must be said about it.'

'Yes of course you made me out to be an ogre.'

'I don't know what you mean by that, aunt. I am sure that I told him the truth.'

'May I see the letter?'

'It has gone.'

'But you have kept a copy,' said Miss Stanbury.

'Yes; I have got a copy,' replied Dorothy; 'but I would rather not shew it. I told him just what I tell you.'

'Dorothy, it is not at all becoming that you should have a correspondence with any young man of such a nature that you should be ashamed to shew it to your aunt.'

'I am not ashamed of anything,' said Dorothy sturdily.

'I don't know what young women in these days have come to,' continued Miss Stanbury. 'There is no respect, no subjection, no obedience, and too often no modesty.'

'Does that mean me, Aunt Stanbury?' asked Dorothy.

'To tell you the truth, Dorothy, I don't think you ought to have been receiving love-letters from Brooke Burgess when I was lying ill in bed. I didn't expect it of you. I tell you fairly that I didn't expect it of you.'

Then Dorothy spoke out her mind. 'As you think that, Aunt Stanbury, I had better go away. And if you please I will when you are well enough to spare me.'

'Pray don't think of me at all,' said her aunt.

'And as for love-letters, Mr Burgess has written to me once. I don't think that there can be anything immodest in opening a letter when it comes by the post. And as soon as I had it I determined to shew it to you. As for what happened before, when Mr Burgess spoke to me, which was long, long after all that about Mr Gibson was over, I told him that it couldn't be so; and I thought there would be no more about it. You were so ill that I could not tell you. Now you know it all.'

'I have not seen your letter to him.'

'I shall never shew it to anybody. But you have said things, Aunt Stanbury, that are very cruel.'

'Of course! Everything I say is wrong.'

'You have told me that I was telling untruths, and you have called me immodest. That is a terrible word.'

'You shouldn't deserve it then.'

'I never have deserved it, and I won't bear it. No; I won't. If Hugh heard me called that word, I believe he'd tear the house down.'

'Hugh, indeed! He's to be brought in between us is he?'

'He's my brother, and of course I'm obliged to think of him. And if you please, I'll go home as soon as you are well enough to spare me.'

Quickly after this there were many letters coming and going between the house in the Close and the ladies at Nuncombe Putney, and Hugh Stanbury, and Brooke Burgess. The correspondent of Brooke Burgess was of course Miss Stanbury herself. The letters to Hugh and to Nuncombe Putney were written by Dorothy. Of the former we need be told nothing at the present moment; but the upshot of all poor Dolly's letters was, that on the tenth of March she was to return home to Nuncombe Putney, share once more her sister's bed and mother's poverty, and abandon the comforts of the Close. Before this became a definite arrangement Miss Stanbury had given way in a certain small degree. She had acknowledged that Dorothy had intended no harm. But this was not enough for Dorothy, who was conscious of no harm either done or intended. She did not specify her terms, or require specifically that her aunt should make apology for that word, immodest, or at least withdraw it; but she resolved that she would go unless it was most absolutely declared to have been applied to her without the slightest reason. She felt, moreover, that her aunt's house ought to be open to Brooke Burgess, and that it could not be open to them both. And so she went having resided under her aunt's roof between nine and ten months.

'Good-bye, Aunt Stanbury,' said Dorothy, kissing her aunt, with a tear in her eye and a sob in her throat.

'Good-bye, my dear, good-bye.' And Miss Stanbury, as she pressed her niece's hand, left in it a bank-note.

'I'm much obliged, aunt; I am indeed; but I'd rather not.' And the bank-note was left on the parlour table.

CHAPTER LVIII. DOROTHY AT HOME

Dorothy was received at home with so much affection and such expressions of esteem as to afford her much consolation in her misery. Both her mother and her sister approved of her conduct. Mrs Stanbury's approval was indeed accompanied by many expressions of regret as to the good things lost. She was fully alive to the fact that life in the Close at Exeter was better for her daughter than life in their little cottage at Nuncombe Putney. The outward appearance which Dorothy bore on her return home was proof of this. Her clothes, the set of her hair, her very gestures and motions had framed themselves on town ideas. The faded, wildered, washed-out look, the uncertain, purposeless bearing which had come from her secluded life and subjection to her sister had vanished from her. She had lived among people, and had learned something of their gait and carriage. Money we know will do almost everything, and no doubt money had had much to do with this. It is very pretty to talk of the alluring simplicity of a clean calico gown; but poverty will shew itself to be meagre, dowdy, and draggled in a woman's dress, let the woman be ever so simple, ever so neat, ever so independent, and ever so high-hearted. Mrs Stanbury was quite alive to all that her younger daughter was losing. Had she not received two offers of marriage while she was at Exeter? There was no possibility that offers of marriage should be made in the cottage at Nuncombe Putney. A man within the walls of the cottage would have been considered as much out of place as a wild bull. It had been matter of deep regret to Mrs Stanbury that her daughter should not have found herself able to marry Mr Gibson. She knew that there was no matter for reproach in this, but it was a misfortune, a great misfortune. And in the mother's breast there had been a sad, unrepressed feeling of regret that young people should so often lose their chances in the world through over-fancifulness, and ignorance as to their own good. Now when she heard the story of Brooke Burgess, she could not but think that had Dorothy remained at Exeter, enduring patiently such hard words as her aunt might speak, the love affair might have been brought at some future time to a happy conclusion. She did not say all this; but there came on her a silent melancholy, made expressive by constant little shakings of the head and a continued reproachful sadness of demeanour, which was quite as intelligible to Priscilla as would have been any spoken words. But Priscilla's approval of her sister's conduct was clear, outspoken, and satisfactory. She had been quite sure that her sister had been right about Mr Gibson; and was equally sure that she was now right about Brooke Burgess.

Priscilla had in her mind an idea that if B. B., as they called him, was half as good as her sister represented him to be—for indeed Dorothy endowed him with every virtue consistent with humanity—he would not be deterred from his pursuit either by Dolly's letter or by Aunt Stanbury's commands. But of this she thought it wise to say nothing. She paid Dolly the warm and hitherto unaccustomed compliment of equality, assuming to regard her sister's judgment and persistent independence to be equally strong with her own; and, as she knew well, she could not have gone further than this. 'I never shall agree with you about Aunt Stanbury,' she said. 'To me she seems to be so imperious, so exacting, and also so unjust, as to be unbearable.'

'But she is affectionate,' said Dolly.

'So is the dog that bites you, and, for aught I know, the horse that kicks you. But it is ill living with biting dogs and kicking horses. But all that matters little as you are still your own mistress. How strange these nine months have been, with you in Exeter, while we have been at the Clock House. And here we are, together again in the old way, just as though nothing had happened.' But Dorothy knew well that a great deal had happened, and that her life could never be as it had been heretofore. The very tone in which her sister spoke to her was proof of this. She had an infinitely greater possession in herself than had belonged to her before her residence at Exeter; but that possession was so heavily mortgaged and so burthened as to make her believe that the change was to be regretted.

At the end of the first week there came a letter from Aunt Stanbury to Dorothy. It began by saying that Dolly had left behind her certain small properties which had now been made up in a parcel and sent by the railway, carriage paid. 'But they weren't mine at all,' said Dolly, alluding to certain books in which she had taken delight.' She means to give them to you,' said Priscilla, 'and I think you must take them.' 'And the shawl is no more mine than it is yours, though I wore it two or three times in the winter.' Priscilla was of opinion that the shawl must be taken also. Then the letter spoke of the writer's health, and at last fell into such a strain of confidential gossip that Mrs Stanbury, when she read it, could not understand that there had been a quarrel. 'Martha says that she saw Camilla French in the street to-day, such a guy in her new finery as never was seen before except on May-day.' Then in the postscript Dorothy was enjoined to answer this letter quickly. 'None of your short scraps, my dear,' said Aunt Stanbury.

'She must mean you to go back to her,' said Mrs Stanbury.

'No doubt she does,' said Priscilla; 'but Dolly need not go because my aunt means it. We are not her creatures.'

But Dorothy answered her aunt's letter in the spirit in which it had been written. She asked after her aunt's health, thanked her aunt for the gift of the books in each of which her name had been clearly written, protested about the shawl, sent her love to Martha and her kind regards to Jane, and expressed a hope that C. F. enjoyed her new clothes. She described the cottage, and was funny about the cabbage stumps in the garden, and at last succeeded in concocting a long epistle. 'I suppose there will he a regular correspondence,' said Priscilla.

Two days afterwards, however, the correspondence took altogether another form. The cottage in which they now lived was supposed to be beyond the beat of the wooden-legged postman, and therefore it was necessary that they should call at the post-office for their letters. On the morning in question Priscilla obtained a thick letter from Exeter for her mother, and knew that it had come from her aunt. Her aunt could hardly have found it necessary to correspond with Dorothy's mother so soon after that letter to Dorothy had been written had there not arisen some very peculiar cause. Priscilla, after much meditation, thought it better that the letter should be opened in Dorothy's absence, and in Dorothy's absence the following letter was read both by Priscilla and her mother.

The Close,
March 19, 186—.

Dear Sister Stanbury,

After much consideration, I think it best to send under cover to you the enclosed letter from Mr Brooke Burgess, intended for your daughter Dorothy. You will see that I have opened it and read it as I was clearly entitled to do, the letter having been addressed to my niece while she was supposed to be under my care. I do not like to destroy the letter, though, perhaps, that would be best; but I would advise you to do so, if it be possible, without shewing it to Dorothy. I have told Mr Brooke Burgess what I have done.

I have also told him that I cannot sanction a marriage between him and your daughter. There are many reasons of old date, not to speak of present reasons, also, which would make such a marriage highly inexpedient. Mr Brooke Burgess is, of course, his own master, but your daughter understands completely how the matter stands.

Yours truly,

Jemima Stanbury.

'What a wicked old woman!' said Priscilla. Then there arose a question whether they should read Brooke's letter, or whether they should give it unread to Dorothy. Priscilla denounced her aunt in the strongest language she could use for having broken the seal. "Clearly entitled," because Dorothy had been living with her!' exclaimed Priscilla. 'She can have no proper conception of honour or of honesty.

She had no more right to open Dorothy's letter than she had to take her money.' Mrs Stanbury was very, anxious to read Brooke's letter, alleging that they would then be able to judge whether it should be handed over to Dorothy. But Priscilla's sense of right would not admit of this. Dorothy must receive the letter from her lover with no further stain from unauthorised eyes than that to which it had been already subjected. She was called in, therefore, from the kitchen, and the whole packet was given to her. 'Your aunt has read the enclosure, Dolly; but we have not opened it.'

Dorothy took the packet without a word and sat herself down. She first read her aunt's letter very slowly. 'I understand perfectly,' she said, folding it up, almost listlessly, while Brooke's letter lay still unopened on her lap. Then she took it up, and held it awhile in both hands, while her mother and Priscilla watched her. 'Priscilla,' she said, 'do you read it first.'

Priscilla was immediately at her side, kissing her. 'No, my darling; no,' she said; 'it is for you to read it.' Then Dorothy took the precious contents from the envelope, and opened the folds of the paper. When she had read a dozen words, her eyes were so suffused with tears, that she could hardly make herself mistress of the contents of the letter; but she knew that it contained renewed assurances of her lover's love, and assurance on his part that he would take no refusal from her based on any other ground than that of her own indifference to him. He had written to Miss Stanbury to the same effect; but he had not thought it necessary to explain this to Dorothy; nor did Miss Stanbury in her letter tell them that she had received any communication from him.'shall I read it now?' said Priscilla, as soon as Dorothy again allowed the letter to fall into her lap.

Both Priscilla and Mrs Stanbury read it, and for awhile they sat with the two letters among them without much speech about them. Mrs Stanbury was endeavouring to make herself believe that her sister-in-law's opposition might be overcome, and that then Dorothy might be married. Priscilla was inquiring of herself whether it would be well that Dorothy should defy her aunt so much, at any rate, and marry the man, even to his deprivation of the old woman's fortune. Priscilla had her doubts about this, being very strong in her ideas of self-denial. That her sister should put up with the bitterest disappointment rather than injure the man she loved was right but then it would also be so extremely right to defy Aunt Stanbury to her teeth! But Dorothy, in whose character was mixed with her mother's softness much of the old Stanbury strength, had no doubt in her mind. It was very sweet to be so loved. What gratitude did she not owe to a man who was so true to her! What was she that she should stand in his way? To lay herself down that she might be crushed in his path was no more than she owed to him. Mrs Stanbury was the first to speak.

'I suppose he is a very good young man,' she said.

'I am sure he is a noble, true-hearted man,' said Priscilla.

'And why shouldn't he marry whom he pleases, as long as she is respectable?' said Mrs Stanbury.

'In some people's eyes poverty is more disreputable than vice,' said Priscilla.

'Your aunt has been so fond of Dorothy,' pleaded Mrs Stanbury.

'Just as she is of her servants,' said Priscilla.

But Dorothy said nothing. Her heart was too full to enable her to defend her aunt; nor at the present moment was she strong enough to make her mother understand that no hope was to be entertained. In the course of the day she walked out with her sister on the road towards Ridleigh, and there, standing among the rocks and ferns, looking down upon the river, with the buzz of the little mill within her ears, she explained the feelings of her heart and her many thoughts with a flow of words stronger, as Priscilla thought, than she had ever used before.

'It is not what he would suffer now, Pris, or what he would feel, but what he would feel ten, twenty years hence, when he would know that his children would have been all provided for, had, he not lost his fortune by marrying me.'

'He must be the only judge whether he prefers you to the old woman's money,' said Priscilla.

'No, dear; not the only judge. And it isn't that, Pris, not which he likes best now, but which it is best for him that he should have. What could I do for him?'

'You can love him.'

'Yes I can do that.' And Dorothy paused a moment, to think how exceedingly well she could do that one thing. 'But what is that? As you said the other day, a dog can do that. I am not clever. I can't play, or talk French, or do things that men like their wives to do. And I have lived here all my life; and what am I, that for me he should lose a great fortune?'

'That is his look out.'

'No, dearest, it is mine, and I will look out. I shall be able, at any rate, to remember always that I have loved him, and have not injured him. He may be angry with me now,' and there was a feeling of pride at her heart, as she thought that he would be angry with her, because she did not go to him 'but he will know at last that I have been as good to him as I knew how to be.'

Then Priscilla wound her arms round Dorothy, and kissed her. 'My sister,' she said; 'my own sister!' They walked on further, discussing the matter in all its bearings, talking of the act of self-denial which Dorothy was called on to perform, as though it were some abstract thing, the performance of which was, or perhaps was not, imperatively demanded by the laws which should govern humanity; but with no idea on the mind of either of them that there was any longer a doubt as to this special matter in hand. They were away from home over three hours; and, when they returned, Dorothy at once wrote her two letters. They were very simple, and very short. She told Brooke, whom she now addressed as 'Dear Mr Burgess,' that it could not be as he would have it; and she told her aunt with some terse independence of expression, which Miss Stanbury quite understood, that she had considered the matter, and had thought it right to refuse Mr Burgess's offer.

'Don't you think she is very much changed?' said Mrs Stanbury to her eldest daughter.

'Not changed in the least, mother; but the sun has opened the bud, and now we see the fruit.'

CHAPTER LIX. MR BOZZLE AT HOME

It had now come to pass that Trevelyan had not a friend in the world to whom he could apply in the matter of his wife and family. In the last communication which he had received from Lady Milborough she had scolded him, in terms that were for her severe, because he had not returned to his wife and taken her off with him to Naples. Mr Bideawhile had found himself obliged to decline to move in the matter at all. With Hugh Stanbury, Trevelyan had had a direct quarrel. Mr and Mrs Outhouse he regarded as bitter enemies, who had taken the part of his wife without any regard to the decencies of life. And now it had come to pass that his sole remaining ally, Mr Samuel Bozzle, the ex-policeman, was becoming weary of his service. Trevelyan remained in the north of Italy up to the middle of March, spending a fortune in sending telegrams to Bozzle, instigating Bozzle by all the means in his power to obtain possession of the child, desiring him at one time to pounce down upon the parsonage of St. Diddulph's with a battalion of policemen armed to the teeth with the law's authority, and at another time suggesting to him to find his way by stratagem into Mr Outhouse's castle and carry off the child in his arms. At last he sent word to say that he himself would be in England before the end of March, and would see that the majesty of the law should be vindicated in his favour.

Bozzle had in truth made but one personal application for the child at St. Diddulph's. In making this he had expected no success, though, from the energetic nature of his disposition, he had made the attempt with some zeal. But he had never applied again at the parsonage, disregarding the letters, the telegrams, and even the promises which had come to him from his employer with such frequency. The truth was that Mrs Bozzle was opposed to the proposed separation of the mother and the child, and that Bozzle was a man who listened to the words of his wife. Mrs Bozzle was quite prepared to admit that Madame T. as Mrs Trevelyan had come to be called at No. 55, Stony Walk, was no better than she should be. Mrs Bozzle was disposed to think that ladies of quality, among whom Madame T. was entitled in her estimation to take rank, were seldom better than they ought to be, and she was quite willing that her husband should earn his bread by watching the lady or the lady's lover. She had participated in Bozzle's triumph when he had discovered that the Colonel had gone to Devonshire, and again when he had learned that the Lothario had been at St. Diddulph's. And had the case been brought before the judge ordinary by means of her husband's exertions, she would have taken pleasure in reading every word of the evidence, even though her husband should have been ever so roughly handled by the lawyers. But now, when a demand was made upon Bozzle to violate the sanctity of the clergyman's house, and withdraw the child by force or stratagem, she began to perceive that the palmy days of the Trevelyan affair were over for them, and that it would be wise on her husband's part gradually to back out of the gentleman's employment. 'Just put it on the fire-back, Bozzle,' she said one morning, as her husband stood before her reading for the second time a somewhat lengthy epistle which had reached him from Italy, while he held the baby over his shoulder with his left arm. He had just washed himself at the sink, and though his face was clean, his hair was rough, and his shirt sleeves were tucked up.

'That's all very well, Maryanne; but when a party has took a gent's money, a party is bound to go through with the job.'

'Gammon, Bozzle.'

'It's all very well to say gammon; but his money has been took and there's more to come.'

'And ain't you worked for the money down to Hexeter one time, across the water pretty well day and night watching that ere clergyman's 'ouse like a cat? What more'd he have? As to the child, I won't hear of it, B. The child shan't come here. We'd all be shewed up in the papers as that black, that they'd hoot us along the streets. It ain't the regular line of business, Bozzle; and there ain't no good to be got, never, by going off the regular line.' Whereupon Bozzle scratched his head and again read the letter. A distinct promise of a hundred pounds was made to him, if he would have the child ready to hand over to Trevelyan on Trevelyan's arrival in England.

'It ain't to be done, you know,' said Bozzle.

'Of course it ain't,' said Mrs Bozzle.

'It ain't to be done, anyways, not in my way of business. Why didn't he go to Skint, as I told him, when his own lawyer was too dainty for the job? The paternal parent has a right to his hinfants, no doubt.' That was Bozzle's law.

'I don't believe it, B.'

'But he have, I tell you.'

'He can't suckle 'em can he? I don't believe a bit of his rights.'

'When a married woman has followers, and the husband don't go the wrong side of the post too, or it ain't proved again him that he do, they'll never let her have nothing to do with the children. It's been before the court a hundred times. He'll get the child fast enough if he'll go before the court.'

'Anyways it ain't your business, Bozzle, and don't you meddle nor make. The money's good money as long as it's honest earned; but when you come to rampaging and breaking into a gent's house, then I say money may be had a deal too hard.' In this special letter, which had now come to hand, Bozzle was not instructed to 'rampage.' He was simply desired to make a further official requisition for the boy at the parsonage, and to explain to Mr Outhouse, Mrs Outhouse, and Mrs Trevelyan, or to as many of them as he could contrive to see, that Mr Trevelyan was immediately about to return to London, and that he would put the law into execution if his son were not given up to him at once. 'I'll tell you what it is, B.,' exclaimed Mrs Bozzle, 'it's my belief as he ain't quite right up here;' and Mrs Bozzle touched her forehead.

'It's love for her as has done it then,' said Bozzle, shaking his head.

'I'm not a taking of her part, B. A woman as has a husband as finds her with her wittels regular, and with what's decent and comfortable beside, ought to be contented. I've never said no other than that. I ain't no patience with your saucy madames as can't remember as they're eating an honest man's bread. Drat 'em all; what is it they wants? They don't know what they wants. It's just hidleness cause there ain't a ha'porth for 'em to do. It's that as makes 'em, I won't say what. But as for this here child, B....' At that moment there came a knock at the door. Mrs Bozzle going into the passage, opened it herself, and saw a strange gentleman. Bozzle, who had stood at the inner door, saw that the gentleman was Mr Trevelyan.

The letter, which was still in the ex-policeman's hand, had reached Stony Walk on the previous day; but the master of the house had been absent, finding out facts, following up his profession, and earning an honest penny. Trevelyan had followed his letter quicker than he had intended when it was written, and was now with his prime minister, before his prime minister had been able to take any action on the last instruction received. 'Does one Mr Samuel Bozzle live here?' asked Trevelyan. Then Bozzle came forward and introduced his wife. There was no one else present except the baby, and Bozzle intimated that let matters be as delicate as they might, they could be discussed with perfect security in his wife's presence. But Trevelyan was of a different opinion, and he was disgusted and revolted most unreasonably by the appearance of his minister's domestic arrangements. Bozzle had always waited upon him with a decent coat, and a well-brushed hat, and clean shoes. It is very much easier for such men as Mr Bozzle to carry decency of appearance about with them than to keep it at home. Trevelyan had never believed his ally to be more than an ordinary ex-policeman, but he had not considered how unattractive might be the interior of a private detective's private residence. Mrs Bozzle had set a chair for him, but he had declined to sit down. The room was dirty, and very close as though no breath of air was ever allowed to find entrance there. 'Perhaps you could put on your coat, and walk out with me for a few minutes,' said Trevelyan. Mrs Bozzle, who well understood that business was business, and that wives were not business, felt no anger at this, and handed her husband his best coat. The well-brushed hat was fetched from a cupboard, and it was astonishing to see how easily and how quickly the outer respectability of Bozzle was restored.

'Well?' said Trevelyan, as soon as they were together in the middle of Stony Walk.

'There hasn't been nothing to be done, sir,' said Bozzle.

'Why not?' Trevelyan could perceive at once that the authority which he had once respected had gone from the man. Bozzle away from his own home, out on business, with his coat buttoned over his breast, and his best hat in his hand, was aware that he commanded respect and he could carry himself accordingly. He knew himself to be somebody, and could be easy, self-confident, confidential, severe, authoritative, or even arrogant, as the circumstances of the moment might demand. But he had been found with his coat off, and a baby in his arms, and he could not recover himself. 'I do not suppose that anybody will question my right to have the care of my own child,' said Trevelyan.

'If you would have gone to Mr Skint, sir ,' suggested Bozzle. 'There ain't no smarter gent in all the profession, sir, than Mr Skint.'

Mr Trevelyan made no reply to this, but walked on in silence, with his minister at his elbow. He was very wretched, understanding well the degradation to which he was subjecting himself in discussing his wife's conduct with this man; but with whom else could he discuss it? The man seemed to be meaner now than he had been before he had been seen in his own home. And Trevelyan was conscious too that he himself was not in outward appearance as he used to be, that he was ill-dressed, and haggard, and worn, and visibly a wretched being. How can any man care to dress himself with attention who is always alone, and always miserable when alone? During the months which had passed over him since he had sent his wife away from him, his very nature had been altered, and he himself was aware of the change. As he went about, his eyes were ever cast downwards, and he walked with a quick shuffling gait, and he suspected others, feeling that he himself was suspected. And all work had ceased with him. Since she had left him he had not read a single book that was worth the reading. And he knew it all. He was conscious that he was becoming disgraced and degraded. He would sooner have shot himself than have walked into his club, or even have allowed himself to be seen by daylight in Pall Mall, or Piccadilly. He had taken in his misery to drinking little drops of brandy in the morning, although he knew well that there was no shorter road to the devil than that opened by such a habit. He looked up for a moment at Bozzle, and then asked him a question. 'Where is he now?'

'You mean the Colonel, sir. He up in town, sir, a minding of his parliamentary duties. He have been up all this month, sir.'

'They haven't met?'

Bozzle paused a moment before he replied, and then smiled as he spoke. 'It is so hard, to say, sir. Ladies is so cute and cunning. I've watched as sharp as watching can go, pretty near. I've put a youngster on at each bend, and both of 'em'd hear a mouse stirring in his sleep. I ain't got no evidence, Mr Trevelyan. But if you ask me my opinion, why in course they've been together somewhere. It stands to reason, Mr Trevelyan; don't it?' And Bozzle as he said this smiled almost aloud.

'D—n and b—t it all for ever!' said Trevelyan, gnashing his teeth, and moving away into Union Street as fast as he could walk. And he did go away, leaving Bozzle standing in the middle of Stony Walk.

'He's disturbed in his mind quite 'orrid,' Bozzle said when he got back to his wife. 'He cursed and swore as made even me feel bad.'

'B.,' said is wife, 'do you listen to me. Get in what's a howing and don't you have any more to do with it.'

CHAPTER LX. ANOTHER STRUGGLE

Sir Marmaduke and Lady Rowley were to reach England about the end of March or the beginning of April, and both Mrs Trevelyan and Nora Rowley were almost sick for their arrival. Both their uncle and aunt had done very much for them, had been true to them in their need, and had submitted to endless discomforts in order that their nieces might have respectable shelter in their great need; but nevertheless their conduct had not been of a kind to produce either love or friendship. Each of the sisters felt that she had been much better off at Nuncombe Putney; and that either the weakness of Mrs Stanbury, or the hardness of Priscilla, was preferable to the repulsive forbearance of their clerical host. He did not scold them. He never threw it in Mrs Trevelyan's teeth that she had been separated from her husband by her own fault; he did not tell them of his own discomfort. But he showed it in every gesture, and spoke of it in every tone of his voice, so that Mrs Trevelyan could not refrain from apologising for the misfortune of her presence.

'My dear,' he said, 'things can't be pleasant and unpleasant at the same time. You were quite right to come here. I am glad for all our sakes that Sir Marmaduke will be with us so soon.'

She had almost given up in her mind the hope that she had long cherished, that she might some day be able to live again with her husband. Every step which he now took in reference to her seemed to be prompted by so bitter an hostility, that she could not but believe that she was hateful to him. How was it possible that a husband and his wife should again come together, when there had been between them such an emissary as a detective policeman? Mrs Trevelyan had gradually come to learn that Bozzle had been at Nuncombe Putney, watching her, and to be aware that she was still under the surveillance of his eye. For some months past now she had neither seen Colonel Osborne, nor heard from him. He had certainly by his folly done much to produce the ruin which had fallen upon her; but it never occurred to her to blame him. Indeed she did not know that he was liable to blame. Mr Outhouse always spoke of him with indignant scorn, and Nora had learned to think that much of their misery was due to his imprudence. But Mrs Trevelyan would not see this, and, not seeing it, was more widely separated from her husband than she would have been had she acknowledged that any excuse for his misconduct had been afforded by the vanity and folly of the other man.

Lady Rowley had written to have a furnished house taken for them from the first of April, and a house had been secured in Manchester Street. The situation in question is not one which is of itself very charming, nor is it supposed to be in a high degree fashionable; but Nora looked forward to her escape from St. Diddulph's to Manchester Street as though Paradise were to be re-opened to her as soon as she should be there with her father and mother. She was quite clear now as to her course about Hugh Stanbury. She did not doubt that that she could so argue the matter as to get the consent of her father and mother. She felt herself to be altogether altered in her views of life, since experience had come upon her, first at Nuncombe Putney, and after that, much more heavily and seriously, at St. Diddulph's. She looked back as though to a childish dream to the ideas which had prevailed with her when she had told herself, as she used to do so frequently, that she was unfit to be a poor man's wife. Why should she be more unfit for such a position than another? Of course there were many thoughts in her mind, much of memory if nothing of regret, in regard to Mr Glascock and the splendour that had been offered to her. She had had her chance of being a rich man's wife, and had rejected it—had rejected it twice, with her eyes open. Readers will say that if she loved Hugh Stanbury with all her heart, there could be nothing of regret in her reflections. But we are perhaps accustomed in judging for ourselves and of others to draw the lines too sharply, and to say that on this side lie vice, folly, heartlessness, and greed and on the other honour, love, truth, and wisdom, the good and the bad each in its own domain. But the good and the bad mix themselves so thoroughly in our thoughts, even in our aspirations, that we must look for excellence rather in overcoming evil than in freeing ourselves from its influence. There had been many moments of regret with Nora but none of remorse. At the very moment in which she had sent Mr Glascock away from her, and had felt that he had now been sent away for always, she had been full of regret. Since that there had been many hours in which she had thought of her own self-lesson, of that teaching by which she had striven to convince herself that she could never fitly become a poor man's wife. But the upshot of it all was a healthy pride in what she had done, and a strong resolution that she would make shirts and hem towels for her husband if he required it. It had been given her to choose, and she had chosen. She had found herself unable to tell a man that she loved him when she did not love him and equally unable to conceal the love which she did feel. 'If he wheeled a barrow of turnips about the street, I'd marry him tomorrow,' she said to her sister one afternoon as they were sitting together in the room which ought to have been her uncle's study.

'If he wheeled a big barrow, you'd have to wheel a little one,' said her sister.

'Then I'd do it. I shouldn't mind. There has been this advantage in St. Diddulph's, that nothing can be *triste*, nothing dull, nothing ugly after it.'

'It may be so with you, Nora, that is in imagination.'

'What I mean is that living here has taught me much that I never could have learned in Curzon Street. I used to think myself such a fine young woman but, upon my word, I think myself a finer one now.'

'I don't quite know what you mean.'

'I don't quite know myself; but I nearly know. I do know this, that I've made up my own mind about what I mean to do.'

'You'll change it, dear, when mamma is here, and things are comfortable again. It's my belief that Mr Glascock would come to you again tomorrow if you would let him.' Mrs Trevelyan was, naturally, in complete ignorance of the experience of transatlantic excellence which Mr Glascock had encountered in Italy.

'But I certainly should not let him. How would it be possible after what I wrote to Hugh?'

'All that might pass away,' said Mrs Trevelyan slowly, after a long pause.

'All what might pass away? Have I not given him a distinct promise? Have I not told him that I loved him, and sworn that I would be true to him? Can that be made to pass away, even if one wished it?'

'Of course it can. Nothing need be fixed for you till you have stood at the altar with a man and been made his wife. You may choose still. I can never choose again.'

'I never will, at any rate,' said Nora.

Then there was another pause. 'It seems strange to me, Nora,' said the elder sister, 'that after what you have seen you should be so keen to be married to any one.'

'What is a girl to do?'

'Better drown herself than do as I have done. Only think what there is before me. What I have gone through is nothing to it. Of course I must go back to the Islands. Where else am I to live? Who else will take me?'

'Come to us,' said Nora.

'Us, Nora! Who are the us? But in no way would that be possible. Papa will be here, perhaps, for six months.' Nora thought it quite possible that she might have a home of her own before six months were passed, even though she might be wheeling the smaller barrow, but she would not say so. 'And by that time everything must be decided.'

'I suppose it must.'

'Of course papa and mamma must go back,' said Mrs Trevelyan.

'Papa might take a pension. He's entitled to a pension now.'

'He'll never do that as long as he can have employment. They'll go back, and I must go with them. Who else would take me in?'

'I know who would take you in, Emily.'

'My darling, that is romance. As for myself, I should not care where I went. If it were even to remain here, I could bear it.'

'I could not,' said Nora, decisively.

'It is so different with you, dear. I don't suppose it is possible I should take my boy with me to the Islands; and how am I to go anywhere without him?' Then she broke down, and fell into a paroxysm of sobs, and was in very truth a broken-hearted woman.

Nora was silent for some minutes, but at last she spoke. 'Why do you not go back to him, Emily?'

'How am I to go back to him? What am I to do to make him take me back?' At this very moment Trevelyan was in the house, but they did not know it.

'Write to him,' said Nora.

'What am I to say? In very truth I do believe that he is mad. If I write to him, should I defend myself or accuse myself? A dozen times I have striven to write such a letter, not that I might send it, but that I might find what I could say should I ever wish to send it. And it is impossible. I can only tell him how unjust he has been, how cruel, how mad, how wicked!'

'Could you not say to him simply this? "Let us be together, wherever it may be; and let bygones be bygones."'

'While he is watching me with a policeman? While he is still thinking that I entertain a lover? While he believes that I am the base thing that he has dared to think me?'

'He has never believed it.'

'Then how can he be such a villain as to treat me like this? I could not go to him, Nora not unless I went to him as one who was known to be mad, over whom in his wretched condition it would be my duty to keep watch. In no other way could I overcome my abhorrence of the outrages to which he has subjected me.'

'But for the child's sake, Emily.'

'Ah, yes! If it were simply to grovel in the dust before him it should be done. If humiliation would suffice, or any self-abasement that were possible to me! But I should be false if I said that I look forward to any such possibility. How can he wish to have me back again after what he has said and done? I am his wife, and he has disgraced me before all men by his own words. And what have I done, that I should not have done; what left undone on his behalf that I should have done? It is hard that the foolish workings of a weak man's mind should be able so completely to ruin the prospects of a woman's life!'

Nora was beginning to answer this by attempting to shew that the husband's madness was, perhaps, only temporary, when there came a knock at the door, and Mrs Outhouse was at once in the room. It will be well that the reader should know what had taken place at the parsonage while the two sisters had been together upstairs, so that the nature of Mrs Outhouse's mission to them may explain itself. Mr Outhouse had been in his closet downstairs, when the maid-servant brought word to him that Mr Trevelyan was in the parlour, and was desirous of seeing him.

'Mr Trevelyan!' said the unfortunate clergyman, holding up both his hands. The servant understood the tragic importance of the occasion quite as well as did her master, and simply shook her head. 'Has your mistress seen him?' said the master. The girl again shook her head. 'Ask your mistress to come to me,' said the clergyman. Then the girl disappeared; and in a few minutes Mrs Outhouse, equally imbued with the tragic elements of the day, was with her husband.

Mr Outhouse began by declaring that no consideration should induce him to see Trevelyan, and commissioned his wife to go to the man and tell him that he must leave the house. When the unfortunate woman expressed an opinion that Trevelyan had some legal rights upon which he might probably insist, Mr Outhouse asserted roundly that he could have no legal right to remain in that parsonage against the will of the rector. 'If he wants to claim his wife and child, he must do it by law not by force; and thank God, Sir Marmaduke will be here before he can do that.' 'But I can't make him go,' said Mrs Outhouse. 'Tell him that you'll send for a policeman,' said the clergyman.

It had come to pass that there had been messages backwards and forwards between the visitor and the master of the house, all carried by that unfortunate lady.

Trevelyan did not demand that his wife and child should be given up to him, did not even, on this occasion, demand that his boy should be surrendered to him now, at once. He did say, very repeatedly, that of course he must have his boy, but seemed to imply that, under certain circumstances, he would be willing to take his wife to live with him again. This appeared to Mrs Outhouse to be so manifestly the one thing that was desirable, to be the only solution of the difficulty that could be admitted as a solution at all, that she went to work on that hint, and ventured to entertain a hope that a reconciliation might be effected. She implored her husband to lend a hand to the work, by which she intended to imply that he should not only see Trevelyan, but consent to meet the sinner on friendly terms. But Mr Outhouse was on the occasion ever more than customarily obstinate. His wife might do what she liked. He would neither meddle nor make. He would not willingly see Mr Trevelyan in his own house unless, indeed, Mr Trevelyan should attempt to force his way up into the nursery. Then he said that which left no doubt on his wife's mind that, should any violence be attempted, her husband would manfully join the *mêlée*.

But it soon became evident that no such attempt was to be made on that day. Trevelyan was lachrymose, heartbroken, and a sight pitiable to behold. When Mrs Outhouse loudly asserted that his wife had not sinned against him in the least; 'not in a tittle, Mr Trevelyan,' she repeated over and over again he began to assert himself, declaring that she had seen the man in Devonshire, and corresponded with him since she had been at St. Diddulph's; and when the lady had declared that the latter assertion was untrue, he had shaken his head, and had told her that perhaps she did not know all. But the misery of the man had its effect upon her, and at last she proposed to be the bearer of a message to his wife. He had demanded to see his child, offering his promise that he would not attempt to take the boy by force on this occasion saying, also, that his claim by law was so good, that no force could be necessary. It was proposed by Mrs Outhouse that he should first see the mother, and to this he at last assented. How blessed a thing would it be if these two persons could be induced to forget the troubles of the last twelve months, and once more to love and trust each other! 'But, sir,' said Mrs Outhouse, putting her hand upon his arm 'you must not upbraid her, for she will not bear it. 'She knows nothing of what is due to a husband,' said Trevelyan, gloomily. The task was not hopeful; but, nevertheless, the poor woman resolved to do her best.

And now Mrs Outhouse was in her niece's room, asking her to go down and see her husband. Little Louis had at the time been with the nurse, and the very moment that the mother heard that the child's father was in the house, she jumped up and rushed away to get possession of her treasure. 'Has he come for baby?' Nora asked in dismay. Then Mrs Outhouse, anxious to obtain a convert to her present views, boldly declared that Mr Trevelyan had no such intention. Mrs Trevelyan came back at once with the boy, and then listened to all her aunt's arguments. 'But I will not take baby with me,' she said. At last it was decided that she should go down alone, and that the child should afterwards be taken to his father in the drawing-room; Mrs Outhouse pledging herself that the whole household should combine in her defence if Mr Trevelyan should attempt to take the child out of that room. 'But what am I to say to him?' she asked.

'Say as little as possible,' said Mrs Outhouse 'except to make him understand that he has been in error in imputing fault to you.'

'He will never understand that,' said Mrs Trevelyan.

A considerable time elapsed after that before she could bring herself to descend the stairs. Now that her husband was so near her, and that her aunt had assured her that she might reinstate herself in her position, if she could only abstain from saying hard words to him, she wished that he was away from her again, in Italy. She knew that she could not refrain from hard words.

How was it possible that she should vindicate her own honour, without asserting with all her strength that she had been ill-used; and, to speak truth on the matter, her love for the man, which had once been true and eager, had been quelled by the treatment she had received. She had clung to her love in some shape, in spite of the accusations made against her, till she had heard that the policeman had been set upon her heels. Could it be possible that any woman should love a man, or at least that any wife should love a husband, after such usage as that? At last she crept gently down the stairs, and stood at the parlour-door. She listened, and could hear his steps, as he paced backwards and forwards through the room. She looked back, and could see the face of the servant peering round from the kitchen-stairs. She could not endure to be watched in her misery, and, thus driven, she opened the parlour-door.' 'Louis,' she said, walking into the room, 'Aunt Mary has desired me to come to you.'

'Emily!' he exclaimed, and ran to her and embraced her. She did not seek to stop him, but she did not return the kiss which he gave her. Then he held her by her hands, and looked into her face, and she could see how strangely he was altered. She thought that she would hardly have known him, had she not been sure that it was he. She herself was also changed. Who can bear sorrow without such change, till age has fixed the lines of the face, or till care has made them hard and unmalleable? But the effect on her was as nothing to that which grief, remorse, and desolation had made on him. He had had no child with him, no sister, no friend. Bozzle had been his only refuge, a refuge not adapted to make life easier to such a man as Trevelyan; and he, in spite of the accusations made by himself against his wife, within his own breast hourly since he had left her had found it to be very difficult to satisfy his own conscience. He told himself from hour to hour that he knew that he was right, but in very truth he was ever doubting his own conduct.

'You have been ill, Louis,' she said, looking at him.

'Ill at ease, Emily, very ill at ease! A sore heart will make the face thin, as well as fever or ague. Since we parted I have not had much to comfort me.'

'Nor have I, nor any of us,' said she. 'How was comfort to come from such a parting?'

Then they both stood silent together. He was still holding her by the hand, but she was careful not to return his pressure. She would not take her hand away from him; but she would show him no sign of softness till he should have absolutely acquitted her of the accusation he had made against her. 'We are man and wife,' he said after awhile. 'In spite of all that has come and gone, I am yours, and you are mine.'

'You should have remembered that always, Louis.'

'I have never forgotten it, never. In no thought have I been untrue to you. My heart has never changed since first I gave it you.' There came a bitter frown upon her face, of which she was so conscious herself, that she turned her face away from him. She still remembered her lesson, that she was not to anger him, and, therefore, she refrained from answering him at all.

But the answer was there, hot within her bosom. Had he loved her and yet suspected that she was false to him and to her vows, simply because she had been on terms of intimacy with an old friend? Had he loved her, and yet turned her from his house? Had he loved her and set a policeman to watch her? Had he loved her, and yet spoken evil of her to all their friends? Had he loved her, and yet striven to rob her of her child? 'Will you come to me?' he said.

'I suppose it will be better so,' she answered slowly.

'Then you will promise me—' He paused, and attempted to turn her towards him, so that he might look her in the face.

'Promise what?' she said, quickly glancing round at him, and drawing her hand away from him as she did so.

'That all intercourse with Colonel Osborne shall be at an end.'

'I will make no promise. You come to me to add one insult to another. Had you been a man, you would not have named him to me after what you have done to me.'

'That is absurd. I have a right to demand from you such a pledge. I am willing to believe that you have not—'

'Have not what?'

'That you have not utterly disgraced me.'

'God in heaven, that I should hear this!' she exclaimed. 'Louis Trevelyan, I have not disgraced you at all in thought, in word, in deed, in look, or in gesture. It is you that have disgraced yourself, and ruined me, and degraded even your own child.'

'Is this the way in which you welcome me?'

'Certainly it is in this way and in no other if you speak to me of what is past, without acknowledging your error.' Her brow became blacker and blacker as she continued to speak to him. 'It would be best that nothing should be said, not a word. That it all should be regarded as an ugly dream. But, when you come to me and at once go back to it all, and ask me for a promise'

'Am I to understand then that all idea of submission to your husband is to be at an end?'

'I will submit to no imputation on my honour even from you. One would have thought that it would have been for you to preserve it untarnished.'

'And you will give me no assurance as to your future life?'

'None, certainly none. If you want promises from me, there can be no hope for the future. What am I to promise? That I will not have a lover? What respect can I enjoy as your wife if such a promise be needed? If you should choose to fancy that it had been broken you would set your policeman to watch me again! Louis, we can never live together again, ever, with comfort, unless you acknowledge in your own heart that you have used me shamefully.'

'Were you right to see him in Devonshire?'

'Of course I was right. Why should I not see him or any one?'

'And you will see him again?'

'When papa comes, of course I shall see him.'

'Then it is hopeless,' said he, turning away from her.

'If that man is to be a source of disquiet to you, it is hopeless,' she answered. 'If you cannot so school yourself that he shall be the same to you as other men, it is quite hopeless. You must still be mad as you have been mad hitherto.'

He walked about the room restlessly for a time, while she stood with assumed composure near the window.'send me my child,' he said at last.

'He shall come to you, Louis for a little; but he is not to be taken out from hence. Is that a promise?'

'You are to exact promises from me, where my own rights are concerned, while you refuse to give me any, though I am entitled to demand them! I order you to send the boy to me. Is he not my own?'

'Is he not mine too? And is he not all that you have left to me?'

He paused again, and then gave the promise. 'Let him be brought to me. He shall not be removed now. I intend to have him. I tell you so fairly. He shall be taken from you unless you come back to me with such assurances as to your future conduct as I have a right to demand. There is much that the law cannot give me. It cannot procure wife-like submission, love, gratitude, or even decent matronly conduct. But that which it can give me, I will have.'

She walked off to the door, and then as she was quitting the room she spoke to him once again. 'Alas, Louis,' she said, 'neither can the law, nor medicine, nor religion, restore to you that fine intellect which foolish suspicions have destroyed.' Then she left him and returned to the room in which her aunt, and Nora, and the child were all clustered together, waiting to learn the effects of the interview. The two women asked their questions with their eyes, rather than with spoken words. 'It is all over,' said Mrs Trevelyan. 'There is nothing left for me but to go back to papa. I only hear the same accusations, repeated again and again, and make myself subject to the old insults.' Then Mrs Outhouse knew that she could interfere no further, and that in truth nothing could be done till the return of Sir Marmaduke should relieve her and her husband from all further active concern in the matter.

But Trevelyan was still down-stairs waiting for the child. At last it was arranged that Nora should take the boy into the drawing-room, and that Mrs Outhouse should fetch the father up from the parlour to the room above it. Angry as was Mrs Trevelyan with her husband, not the less was she anxious to make the boy good-looking and seemly in his father's eyes. She washed the child's face, put on him a clean frill and a pretty ribbon; and, as she did so, she bade him kiss his papa, and speak nicely to him, and love him. 'Poor papa is unhappy,' she said, 'and Louey must be very good to him.' The boy, child though he was, understood much more of what was passing around him than his mother knew. How was he to love papa when mamma did not do so? In some shape that idea had framed itself in his mind; and, as he was taken down, he knew it was impossible that he should speak nicely to his papa. Nora did as she was bidden, and went down to the first-floor. Mrs Outhouse, promising that even if she were put out of the room by Mr Trevelyan she would not stir from the landing outside the door, descended to the parlour and quickly returned with the unfortunate father. Mr Outhouse, in the meantime, was still sitting in his closet, tormented with curiosity, but yet determined not to be seen till the intruder should have left his house.

'I hope you are well, Nora,' he said, as he entered the room with Mrs Outhouse.

'Quite well, thank you, Louis.'

'I am sorry that our troubles should have deprived you of the home you had been taught to expect.' To this Nora made no reply, but escaped, and went up to her sister. 'My poor little boy,' said Trevelyan, taking the child and placing it on his knee. 'I suppose you have forgotten your unfortunate father.' The child, of course, said nothing, but just allowed himself to be kissed.

'He is looking very well,' said Mrs Outhouse.

'Is he? I dare say he is well. Louey, my boy, are you happy?' The question was asked in a voice that was dismal beyond compare, and it also remained unanswered. He had been desired to speak nicely to his papa; but how was it possible that a child should speak nicely under such a load of melancholy? 'He will not speak to me,' said Trevelyan. 'I suppose it is what I might have expected.' Then the child was put off his knee on to the floor, and began to whimper. 'A few months since he would sit there for hours, with his head upon my breast,' said Trevelyan.

'A few months is a long time in the life of such an infant,' said Mrs Outhouse.

'He may go away,' said Trevelyan. Then the child was led out of the room, and sent up to his mother.

'Emily has done all she can to make the child love your memory,' said Mrs Outhouse.

'To love my memory! What, as though I were dead. I will teach him to love me as I am, Mrs Outhouse. I do not think that it is too late. Will you tell your husband from me, with my compliments, that I shall cause him to be served with a legal demand for the restitution of my child?'

'But Sir Marmaduke will be here in a few days.'

'I know nothing of that. Sir Marmaduke is nothing to me now. My child is my own and so is my wife. Sir Marmaduke has no authority over either one or the other. I find my child here, and it is here that I must look for him. I am sorry that you should be troubled, but the fault does not rest with me. Mr Outhouse has refused to give me up my own child, and I am driven to take such steps for his recovery as the law has put within my reach.'

'Why did you turn your wife out of doors, Mr Trevelyan?' asked Mrs Outhouse boldly.

'I did not turn her out of doors. I provided a fitting shelter for her. I gave her everything that she could want. You know what happened. That man went down and was received there. I defy you, Mrs Outhouse, to say that it was my fault.'

Mrs Outhouse did attempt to show him that it was his fault; but while she was doing so he left the house. 'I don't think she could go back to him,' said Mrs Outhouse to her husband. 'He is quite insane upon this matter.'

'I shall be insane, I know,' said Mr Outhouse, 'if Sir Marmaduke does not come home very quickly.' Nevertheless he quite ignored any legal power that might be brought to bear against him as to the restitution of the child to its father.

CHAPTER LXI. PARKER'S HOTEL, MOWBRAY STREET

Within a week of the occurrence which is related in the last chapter, there came a telegram from Southampton to the parsonage at St. Diddulph's, saying that Sir Marmaduke and Lady Rowley had reached England. On the evening of that day they were to lodge at a small family hotel in Baker Street, and both Mrs Trevelyan and Nora were to be with them. The leave-taking at the parsonage was painful, as on both sides there existed a feeling that affection and sympathy were wanting. The uncle and aunt had done their duty, and both Mrs Trevelyan and Nora felt that they ought to have been demonstrative and cordial in their gratitude, but they found it impossible to become so. And the rector could not pretend but that he was glad to be rid of his guests. There were, too, some last words about money to be spoken, which were grievous thorns in the poor man's flesh. Two bank notes, however, were put upon his table, and he knew that unless he took them he could not pay for the provisions which his unwelcome visitors had consumed. Surely there never was a man so cruelly ill-used as had been Mr Outhouse in all this matter. 'Another such winter as that would put me in my grave,' he said, when his wife tried to comfort him after they were gone. 'I know that they have both been very good to us,' said Mrs Trevelyan, as she and her sister, together with the child and the nurse, hurried away toward Baker Street in a cab, 'but I have never for a moment felt that they were glad to have us.' 'But how could they have been glad to have us,' she added afterwards, 'when we brought such trouble with us?' But they to whom they were going now would receive her with joy, would make her welcome with all her load of sorrows, would give to her a sympathy which it was impossible that she should receive from others. Though she might not be happy now, for in truth how could she be ever really happy again, there would be a joy to her in placing her child in her mother's arms, and in receiving her father's warm caresses. That her father would be very vehement in his anger against her husband she knew well, for Sir Marmaduke was a vehement man. But there would be some support for her in the very violence of his wrath, and at this moment it was such support that she most needed. As they journeyed together in the cab, the married sister seemed to be in the higher spirits of the two. She was sure, at any rate, that those to whom she was going would place themselves on her side. Nora had her own story to tell about Hugh Stanbury, and was by no means so sure that her tale would be received with cordial agreement. 'Let me tell them myself,' she whispered to her sister. 'Not tonight, because they will have so much to say to you; but I shall tell mamma to-morrow.'

The train by which the Rowleys were to reach London was due at the station at 7.30 p.m., and the two sisters timed their despatch from St. Diddulph's so as to enable them to reach the hotel at eight. 'We shall be there now before mamma,' said Nora, 'because they will have so much luggage, and so many things, and the trains are always late.' When they started from the door of the parsonage, Mr Outhouse gave the direction to the cabman, 'Gregg's Hotel, Baker Street.' Then at once he began to console himself in that they were gone.

It was a long drive from St. Diddulph's in the east, to Marylebone in the west, of London. None of the party in the cab knew anything of the region through which they passed. The cabman took the line by the back of the Bank, and Finsbury Square and the City Road, thinking it best, probably, to avoid the crush at Holborn Hill, though at the expense of something of a circuit. But of this Mrs Trevelyan and Nora knew nothing. Had their way taken them along Piccadilly, or through Mayfair, or across Grosvenor Square, they would have known where they were; but at present they were not thinking of those once much-loved localities. The cab passed the Angel, and up and down the hill at Pentonville, and by the King's Cross stations, and through Euston Square and then it turned up Gower Street. Surely the man should have gone on along the New Road, now that he had come so far out of his way. But of this the two ladies knew nothing nor did the nurse. It was a dark, windy night, but the lamps in the streets had given them light, so that they had not noticed the night. Nor did they notice it now as the streets became narrower and darker. They were hardly thinking that their journey was yet at an end, and the mother was in the act of covering her boy's face as he lay asleep on the nurse's lap, when the cab was stopped. Nora looking out through the window, saw the word 'Hotel' over a doorway, and was satisfied. 'shall I take the child, ma'am?' said a man in black, and the child was handed out. Nora was the first to follow, and she then perceived that the door of the hotel was not open. Mrs Trevelyan followed; and then they looked round them and the child was gone. They heard the rattle of another cab as it was carried away at a gallop round a distant corner and then some inkling of what had happened came upon them. The father had succeeded in getting possession of his child.

It was a narrow, dark street, very quiet, having about it a certain air of poor respectability an obscure, noiseless street, without even a sign of life. Some unfortunate one had endeavoured here to keep an hotel, but there was no hotel kept there now. There had been much craft in selecting the place in which the child had been taken from them. As they looked around them, perceiving the terrible misfortune which had befallen them, there was not a human being near them save the cabman, who was occupied in unchaining, or pretending to unchain the heavy mass of luggage on the roof. The windows of the house before which they were stopping, were closed, and Nora perceived at once that the hotel was not inhabited. The cabman must have perceived it also. As for the man who had taken the child, the nurse could only say that he was dressed in black, like a waiter, that he had a napkin under his arm, and no hat on his head. He had taken the boy tenderly in his arms and then she had seen nothing further. The first thing that Nora had seen, as she stood on the pavement, was the other cab moving off rapidly.

Mrs Trevelyan had staggered against the railings, and was soon screaming in her wretchedness. Before long there was a small crowd around them, comprising three or four women, a few boys, an old man or two and a policeman. To the policeman Nora had soon told the whole story, and the cabman was of course attacked. But the cabman played his part very well. He declared that he had done just what he had been told to do. Nora was indeed sure that she had heard her uncle desire him to drive to Gregg's Hotel in Baker Street. The cabman in answer to this, declared that he had not clearly heard the old gentleman's directions; but that a man whom he had conceived to be a servant, had very plainly told him to drive to Parker's Hotel, Mowbray Street, Gower Street. 'I comed ever so far out of my way,' said the cabman, 'to avoid the rumpus with the homnibuses at the hill cause the ladies things is so heavy we'd never got up if the 'otherwise had once jibbed.' All which, though it had nothing to do with the matter, seemed to impress the policeman with the idea that the cabman, if not a true man, was going to be too clever for them on this occasion. And the crafty cabman went on to declare that his horse was so tired with the road that he could not go on to Baker Street. They must get another cab. Take his number! Of course they could take his number. There was his number. His fare was four and six, that is, if the ladies wouldn't pay him anything extra for the terrible load; and he meant to have it. It would be sixpence more if they kept him there many minutes longer. The number was taken, and another cab was got, and the luggage was transferred, and the money was paid, while the unhappy mother was still screaming in hysterics against the railings. What had been done was soon clear enough to all those around her. Nora had told the policeman, and had told one of the women, thinking to obtain their sympathy and assistance. 'It's the kid's dada as has taken it,' said one man, 'and there ain't nothing to be done.' There was nothing to be done, nothing, at any rate, then and there.

Nora had been very eager that the cabman should be arrested; but the policeman assured her that such an arrest was out of the question, and would have been useless had it been possible. The man would be forthcoming if his presence should be again desired, but he had probably, so said the policeman, really been desired to drive to Mowbray Street. 'They knows where to find me if they wants me, only I must be paid my time,' said the cabman confidently. And the policeman was of opinion that as the boy had been kidnapped on behalf of the father, no legal steps could be taken either for the recovery of the child or for the punishment of the perpetrators of the act. He got up, however, on the box of the cab, and accompanied the party to the hotel in Baker Street. They reached it almost exactly at the same time with Sir Marmaduke and Lady Rowley, and the reader must imagine the confusion, the anguish, and the disappointment of that meeting. Mrs Trevelyan was hardly in possession of her senses when she reached her mother, and could not be induced to be tranquil even when she was assured by her father that her son would suffer no immediate evil by being transferred to his father's hands. She in her frenzy declared that she would never see her little one again, and seemed to think that the father might not improbably destroy the child. 'He is mad, papa, and does not know what he does. Do you mean to say that a madman may do as he pleases? that he may rob my child from me in the streets? that he may take him out of my very arms in that way?' And she was almost angry with her father because no attempt was made that night to recover the boy.

Sir Marmaduke, who was not himself a good lawyer, had been closeted with the policeman for a quarter of an hour, and had learned the policeman's views. Of course, the father of the child was the person who had done the deed. Whether the cabman had been in the plot or not, was not matter of much consequence. There could be no doubt that some one had told the man to go to Parker's Hotel, as the cab was starting; and it would probably be impossible to punish him in the teeth of such instructions. Sir Marmaduke, however, could doubtless have the cabman summoned. And as for the absolute abduction of the child, the policeman was of opinion that a father could not be punished for obtaining possession of his son by such a stratagem, unless the custody of the child had been made over to the mother by some court of law. The policeman, indeed, seemed to think that nothing could be done, and Sir Marmaduke was inclined to agree with him. When this was explained to Mrs Trevelyan by her mother, she again became hysterical in her agony, and could hardly be restrained from going forth herself to look for her lost treasure.

It need hardly be further explained that Trevelyan had planned the stratagem in concert with Mr Bozzle. Bozzle, though strongly cautioned by his wife to keep himself out of danger in the matter, was sorely tempted by his employer's offer of a hundred pounds. He positively refused to be a party to any attempt at violence at St. Diddulph's; but when he learned, as he did learn, that Mrs Trevelyan, with her sister and baby, were to be transferred from St. Diddulph's in a cab to Baker Street, and that the journey was luckily to be made during the shades of evening, his active mind went to work, and he arranged the plan. There were many difficulties, and even some pecuniary difficulty. He bargained that he should have his hundred pounds clear of all deduction for expenses, and then the attendant expenses were not insignificant. It was necessary that there should be four men in the service, all good and true; and men require to be well paid for such goodness and truth. There was the man, himself an ex-policeman, who gave the instructions to the first cabman, as he was starting. The cabman would not undertake the job at all unless he were so instructed on the spot, asserting that in this way he would be able to prove that the orders he obeyed came from the lady's husband. And there was the crafty pseudo-waiter, with the napkin and no hat, who had carried the boy to the cab in which his father was sitting. And there were the two cabmen. Bozzle planned it all, and with some difficulty arranged the preliminaries. How successful was the scheme, we have seen; and Bozzle, for a month, was able to assume a superiority over his wife, which that honest woman found to be very disagreeable.

'There ain't no fraudulent abduction in it at all,' Bozzle exclaimed, 'because a wife ain't got no rights again her husband, not in such a matter as that.' Mrs Bozzle replied that if her husband were to take her child away from her without her leave, she'd let him know something about it. But as the husband had in his possession the note for a hundred pounds, realized, Mrs Bozzle had not much to say in support of her view of the case.

On the morning after the occurrence, while Sir Marmaduke was waiting with his solicitor upon a magistrate to find whether anything could be done, the following letter was brought to Mrs Trevelyan at Gregg's Hotel:

Our child is safe with me, and will remain so. If you care to obtain legal advice you will find that I as his father have a right to keep him under my protection. I shall do so; but will allow you to see him as soon as I shall have received a full guarantee that you have no idea of withdrawing him from my charge.

A home for yourself with me is still open to you on condition that you will give me the promise that I have demanded from you; and as long as I shall not hear that you again see or communicate with the person to whose acquaintance I object. While, you remain away from me I will cause you to be paid £50 a month, as I do not wish that you should be a burden on others. But this payment will depend also on your not seeing or holding any communication with the person to whom I have alluded.

Your affectionate and offended husband,   LOUIS TREVELYAN.

A letter addressed to The Acrobats' Club will reach me.

Sir Rowley came home dispirited and unhappy, and could not give much comfort to his daughter. The magistrate had told him that though the cabman might probably be punished for taking the ladies otherwise than as directed, if the direction to Baker Street could be proved, nothing could be done to punish the father. The magistrate explained that under a certain Act of Parliament the mother might apply to the Court of Chancery for the custody of any children under seven years of age, and that the court would probably grant such custody unless it were shewn that the wife had left her husband without sufficient cause. The magistrate could not undertake to say whether or no sufficient cause had here been given or whether the husband was in fault or the wife. It was, however, clear that nothing could be done without application to the Court of Chancery. It appeared, so said the magistrate, that the husband had offered a home to his wife, and that in offering it he had attempted to impose no conditions which could be shewn to be cruel before a judge. The magistrate thought that Mr Trevelyan had done nothing illegal in taking the child from the cab. Sir Marmaduke, on hearing this, was of opinion that nothing could be gained by legal interference. His private desire was to get hold of Trevelyan and pull him limb from limb. Lady Rowley thought that her daughter had better go back to her husband, let the future consequences be what they might. And the poor desolate mother herself had almost brought herself to offer to do so, having in her brain some idea that she would after a while be able to escape with her boy. As for love for her husband, certainly there was none now left in her bosom. Nor could she teach herself to think it possible that she should ever live with him again on friendly terms. But she would submit to anything with the object of getting back her boy. Three or four letters were written to Mr Trevelyan in as many days from his wife, from Lady Rowley, and from Nora; in which various overtures were made. Trevelyan wrote once again to his wife. She knew, he said, already the terms on which she might come back. These terms were still open to her. As for the boy, he certainly should not leave his father. A meeting might be planned on condition that he, Trevelyan, were provided with a written assurance from his wife that she would not endeavour to remove the boy, and that he himself should be present at the meeting.

Thus the first week was passed after Sir Marmaduke's return, and a most wretched time it was for all the party at Gregg's Hotel.

CHAPTER LXII. LADY ROWLEY MAKES AN ATTEMPT

Nothing could be more uncomfortable than the state of Sir Marmaduke Rowley's family for the first ten days after the arrival in London of the Governor of the Mandarin Islands. Lady Rowley had brought with her two of her girls, the third and fourth, and, as we know, had been joined by the two eldest, so that there was a large family of ladies gathered together. A house had been taken in Manchester Street, to which they had intended to transfer themselves after a single night passed at Gregg's Hotel. But the trouble and sorrow inflicted upon them by the abduction of Mrs Trevelyan's child, and the consequent labours thrust upon Sir Marmaduke's shoulders had been so heavy, that they had slept six nights at the hotel, before they were able to move themselves into the house prepared for them. By that time all idea had been abandoned of recovering the child by any legal means to be taken as a consequence of the illegality of the abduction. The boy was with his father, and the lawyers seemed to think that the father's rights were paramount as he had offered a home to his wife without any conditions which a court of law would adjudge to be cruel. If she could shew that he had driven her to live apart from him by his own bad conduct, then probably the custody of her boy might be awarded to her, until the child should be seven years old. But when the circumstances of the case were explained to Sir Marmaduke's lawyer by Lady Rowley, that gentleman shook his head. Mrs Trevelyan had, he said, no case with which she could go into court. Then by degrees there were words whispered as to the husband's madness. The lawyer said that that was a matter for the doctors. If a certain amount of medical evidence could be obtained to show that the husband was in truth mad, the wife could, no doubt, obtain the custody of the child. When this was reported to Mrs Trevelyan, she declared that conduct such as her husband's must suffice to prove any man to be mad; but at this Sir Marmaduke shook his head, and Lady Rowley sat, sadly silent, with her daughter's hand within her own. They would not dare to tell her that she could regain her child by that plea.

During those ten days they did not learn whither the boy had been carried, nor did they know even where the father might be found. Sir Marmaduke followed up the address as given in the letter, and learned from the porter at 'The Acrobats' that the gentleman's letters were sent to No. 65, Stony Walk, Union Street, Borough. To this uncomfortable locality Sir Marmaduke travelled more than once. Thrice he went thither, intent on finding his son-in-law's residence. On the two first occasions he saw no one but Mrs Bozzle; and the discretion of that lady in declining to give any information was most admirable. 'Trewillian!' Yes, she had heard the name certainly. It might be that her husband had business engagements with a gent of that name. She would not say even that for certain, as it was not her custom ever to make any inquiries as to her husband's business engagements. Her husband's business engagements were, she said, much too important for the 'likes of she' to know anything about them. When was Bozzle likely to be at home? Bozzle was never likely to be at home. According to her showing, Bozzle was of all husbands the most erratic. He might perhaps come in for an hour or two in the middle of the day on a Wednesday, or perhaps would take a cup of tea at home on Friday evening. But anything so fitful and uncertain as were Bozzle's appearances in the bosom of his family was not to be conceived in the mind of woman. Sir Marmaduke then called in the middle of the day on Wednesday, but Bozzle was reported to be away in the provinces. His wife had no idea in which of the provinces he was at that moment engaged. The persevering governor from the islands called again on the Friday evening, and then, by chance, Bozzle was found at home. But Sir Marmaduke succeeded in gaining very little information even from Bozzle. The man acknowledged that he was employed by Mr Trevelyan. Any letter or parcel left with him for Mr Trevelyan should be duly sent to that gentleman. If Sir Marmaduke wanted Mr Trevelyan's address, he could write to Mr Trevelyan and ask for it. If Mr Trevelyan declined to give it, was it likely that he, Bozzle, should betray it? Sir Marmaduke explained who he was at some length. Bozzle with a smile assured the governor that he knew very well who he was. He let drop a few words to show that he was intimately acquainted with the whole course of Sir Marmaduke's family affairs. He knew all about the Mandarins, and Colonel Osborne, and Gregg's Hotel—not that he said anything about Parker's Hotel—and the Colonial Office. He spoke of Miss Nora, and even knew the names of the other two young ladies, Miss Sophia and Miss Lucy. It was a weakness with Bozzle, that of displaying his information. He would have much liked to be able to startle Sir Marmaduke by describing the Government House in the island, or by telling him something of his old carriage-horses. But of such information as Sir Marmaduke desired, Sir Marmaduke got none.

And there were other troubles which fell very heavily upon the poor governor, who had come home as it were for a holiday, and who was a man hating work naturally, and who, from the circumstances of his life, had never been called on to do much work. A man may govern the Mandarins and yet live in comparative idleness. To do such governing work well a man should have a good presence, a flow of words which should mean nothing, an excellent temper, and a love of hospitality. With these attributes Sir Rowley was endowed; for, though his disposition was by nature hot, for governing purposes it had been brought by practice under good control. He had now been summoned home through the machinations of his dangerous old friend Colonel Osborne, in order that he might give the results of his experience in governing before a committee of the House of Commons. In coming to England on this business he had thought much more of his holiday, of his wife and children, of his daughters at home, of his allowance per day while he was to be away from his government, and of his salary to be paid to him entire during his absence, instead of being halved as it would be if he were away on leave; he had thought much more in coming home on these easy and pleasant matters, than he did on the work that was to be required from him when he arrived. And then it came to pass that he felt himself almost injured, when the Colonial Office demanded his presence from day to day, and when clerks bothered him with questions as to which they expected ready replies, but in replying to which Sir Marmaduke was by no means ready. The working men at the Colonial Office had not quite thought that Sir Marmaduke was the most fitting man for the job in hand. There was a certain Mr Thomas Smith at another set of islands in quite another part of the world, who was supposed by these working men at home to be a very paragon of a governor. If he had been had home, so said the working men, no Committee of the House would have been able to make anything of him. They might have asked him questions week after week, and he would have answered them all fluently and would have committed nobody. He knew all the ins and outs of governing, did Mr Thomas Smith, and was a match for the sharpest Committee that ever sat at Westminster. Poor Sir Marmaduke was a man of a very different sort; all of which was known by the working men; but the Parliamentary interest had been too strong, and here was Sir Marmaduke at home. But the working men were not disposed to make matters so pleasant for Sir Marmaduke as Sir Marmaduke had expected. The Committee would not examine Sir Marmaduke till after Easter, in the middle of April; but it was expected of him that, he should read blue-books without number, and he was so catechised by the working men that he almost began to wish himself back at the Mandarins. In this way the new establishment in Manchester Street was not at first in a happy or even in a contented condition.

At last, after about ten days, Lady Rowley did succeed in obtaining an interview with Trevelyan. A meeting was arranged through Bozzle, and took place in a very dark and gloomy room at an inn in the City. Why Bozzle should have selected the Bremen Coffee House, in Poulter's Alley, for this meeting no fit reason can surely be given, unless it was that he conceived himself bound to select the most dreary locality within his knowledge on so melancholy an occasion. Poulter's Alley is a narrow dark passage somewhere behind the Mansion House; and the Bremen Coffee House—why so called no one can now tell—is one of those strange houses of public resort in the City at which the guests seem never to eat, never to drink, never to sleep, but to come in and out after a mysterious and almost ghostly fashion, seeing their friends or perhaps their enemies, in nooks and corners, and carrying on their conferences in low melancholy whispers. There is an aged waiter at the Bremen Coffee House; and there is certainly one private sitting-room upstairs. It was a dingy, ill-furnished room, with an old large mahogany table, an old horse-hair sofa, six horse-hair chairs, two old round mirrors, and an old mahogany press in a corner. It was a chamber so sad in its appearance that no wholesome useful work could have been done within it; nor could men have eaten there with any appetite, or have drained the flowing bowl with any touch of joviality. It was generally used for such purposes as that to which it was now appropriated, and no doubt had been taken by Bozzle on more than one previous occasion. Here Lady Rowley arrived precisely at the hour fixed, and was told that the gentleman was waiting up stairs for her.

There had, of course, been many family consultations as to the manner in which this meeting should be arranged. Should Sir Marmaduke accompany his wife or, perhaps, should Sir Marmaduke go alone? Lady Rowley had been very much in favour of meeting Mr Trevelyan without any one to assist her in the conference. As for Sir Marmaduke, no meeting could be concluded between him and his son-in-law without a personal, and probably a violent quarrel. Of that Lady Rowley had been quite sure. Sir Marmaduke, since he had been home, had, in the midst of his various troubles, been driven into so vehement a state of indignation against his son-in-law as to be unable to speak of the wretched man without strongest terms of opprobrium. Nothing was too bad to be said by him of one who had ill-treated his dearest daughter. It must be admitted that Sir Marmaduke had heard only one side of the question. He had questioned his daughter, and had constantly seen his old friend Osborne. The colonel's journey down to Devonshire had been made to appear the most natural proceeding in the world. The correspondence of which Trevelyan thought so much had been shown to consist of such notes as might pass between any old gentleman and any young woman. The promise which Trevelyan had endeavoured to exact, and which Mrs Trevelyan had declined to give, appeared to the angry father to be a monstrous insult. He knew that the colonel was an older man than himself, and his Emily was still to him only a young girl. It was incredible to him that anybody should have regarded his old comrade as his daughter's lover. He did not believe that anybody had, in truth, so regarded the man. The tale had been a monstrous invention on the part of the husband, got up because he had become tired of his young wife. According to Sir Marmaduke's way of thinking, Trevelyan should either be thrashed within an inch of his life, or else locked up in a mad-house. Colonel Osborne shook his head, and expressed a conviction that the poor man was mad.

But Lady Rowley was more hopeful. Though she was as confident about her daughter as was the father, she was less confident about the old friend. She, probably, was alive to the fact that a man of fifty might put on the airs and assume the character of a young lover; and acting on that suspicion, entertaining also some hope that bad as matters now were they might be mended, she had taken care that

Colonel Osborne and Mrs Trevelyan should not be brought together. Sir Marmaduke had fumed, but Lady Rowley had been firm. 'If you think so, mamma,' Mrs Trevelyan had said, with something of scorn in her tone 'of course let it be so.' Lady Rowley had said that it would be better so; and the two had not seen each other since the memorable visit to Nuncombe Putney. And now Lady Rowley was about to meet her son-in law with some slight hope that she might arrange affairs. She was quite aware that present indignation, though certainly a gratification, might be indulged in at much too great a cost. It would be better for all reasons that Emily should go back to her husband and her home, and that Trevelyan should be forgiven for his iniquities.

Bozzle was at the tavern during the interview, but he was not seen by Lady Rowley. He remained seated downstairs, in one of the dingy corners, ready to give assistance to his patron should assistance be needed. When Lady Rowley was shown into the gloomy sitting-room by the old waiter, she found Trevelyan alone, standing in the middle of the room, and waiting for her. 'This is a sad occasion,' he said, as he advanced to give her his hand.

'A very sad occasion, Louis.'

'I do not know what you may have heard of what has occurred, Lady Rowley. It is natural, however, to suppose that you must have heard me spoken of with censure.'

'I think my child has been ill used, Louis,' she replied.

'Of course you do. I could not expect that it should be otherwise. When it was arranged that I should meet you here, I was quite aware that you would have taken the side against me before you had heard my story. It is I that have been ill used—cruelly misused; but I do not expect that you should believe me. I do not wish you to do. I would not for worlds separate the mother from her daughter.'

'But why have you separated your own wife from her child?'

'Because it was my duty. What! Is a father not to have the charge of his own son. I have done nothing, Lady Rowley, to justify a separation which is contrary to the laws of nature.'

'Where is the boy, Louis?'

'Ah that is just what I am not prepared to tell any one who has taken my wife's side till I know that my wife has consented to pay to me that obedience which I, as her husband, have a right to demand. If Emily will do as I request of her, as I command her,' as Trevelyan said this, he spoke in a tone which was intended to give the highest possible idea of his own authority and dignity, 'then she may see her child without delay.'

'What is it you request of my daughter?'

'Obedience, simply that. Submission to my will, which is surely a wife's duty. Let her beg my pardon for what has occurred.'

'She cannot do that, Louis.'

'And solemnly promise me,' continued Trevelyan, not deigning to notice Lady Rowley's interruption, 'that she will hold no further intercourse with that snake in the grass who wormed his way into my house; let her be humble, and penitent, and affectionate, and then she shall be restored to her husband and to her child.' He said this walking up and down the room, and waving his hand, as though he were making a speech that was intended to be eloquent, as though he had conceived that he was to overcome his mother-in-law by the weight of his words and the magnificence of his demeanour. And yet his demeanour was ridiculous, and his words would have had no weight had they not tended to show Lady Rowley how little prospect there was that she should be able to heal this breach. He himself, too, was so altered in appearance since she had last seen him, bright with the hopes of his young married happiness, that she would hardly have recognised him had she met him in the street. He was thin, and pale, and haggard, and mean. And as he stalked up and down the room, it seemed to her that the very character of the man was changed. She had not previously known him to be pompous, unreasonable, and absurd. She did not answer him at once, as she perceived that he had not finished his address and, after a moment's pause, he continued. 'Lady Rowley, there is nothing I would not have done for your daughter, for my wife. All that I had was hers. I did not dictate to her any mode of life; I required from her no sacrifices; I subjected her to no caprices; but I was determined to be master in my own house.'

'I do not think, Louis, that she has ever denied your right to be master.'

'To be master in my own house, and to be paramount in my influence over her. So much I had a right to demand.'

'Who has denied your right?'

'She has submitted herself to the counsels and to the influences of a man who has endeavoured to undermine me in her affection. In saying that I make my accusation as light against her as is possible. I might make it much heavier, and yet not sin against the truth.'

'This is an illusion, Louis.'

'Ah well. No doubt it becomes you to defend your child. Was it an illusion when he went to Devonshire? Was it an illusion when he corresponded with her contrary to my express orders both before and after that unhallowed journey? Lady Rowley, there must be no more such illusions. If my wife means to come back to me, and to have her child in her own hands, she must be penitent as regards the past, and obedient as regards the future.'

There was a wicked bitterness in that word penitent which almost maddened Lady Rowley. She had come to this meeting believing that Trevelyan would be rejoiced to take back his wife, if details could be arranged for his doing so which should not subject him to the necessity of crying, *peccavi*; but she found him speaking of his wife as though he would be doing her the greatest possible favour in allowing her to come back to him dressed in sackcloth, and with ashes on her head. She could understand from what she had heard that his tone and manner were much changed since he obtained possession of the child, and that he now conceived that he had his wife within his power. That he should become a tyrant because he had the power to tyrannise was not in accordance with her former conception of the man's character, but then he was so changed, that she felt that she knew nothing of the man who now stood before her. 'I cannot acknowledge that my daughter has done anything that requires penitence,' said Lady Rowley.

'I dare say not, but my view is different.'

'She cannot admit herself to be wrong when she knows herself to be right. You would not have her confess to a fault, the very idea of which has always been abhorrent to her?'

'She must be crushed in spirit, Lady Rowley, before she can again become a pure and happy woman.'

'This is more than I can bear,' said Lady Rowley, now, at last, worked up to a fever of indignation. 'My daughter, sir, is as pure a woman as you have ever known, or are likely to know. You, who should have protected her against the world, will some day take blame to yourself as you remember that you have so cruelly maligned her.' Then she walked away to the door, and would not listen to the words which he was hurling after her. She went down the stairs, and out of the house, and at the end of Poulter's Alley found the cab which was waiting for her.

Trevelyan, as soon as he was alone, rang the bell, and sent for Bozzle. And while the waiter was coming to him, and until his myrmidon had appeared, he continued to stalk up and down the room, waving his hand in the air as though he were continuing his speech. 'Bozzle,' said he, as soon as the man had closed the door, 'I have changed my mind.'

'As how, Mr Trewillian?'

'I shall make no further attempt. I have done all that man can do, and have done it in vain. Her father and mother uphold her in her conduct, and she is lost to me for ever.'

'But the boy, Mr T.?'

'I have my child. Yes I have my child. Poor infant. Bozzle, I look to you to see that none of them learn our retreat.'

'As for that, Mr Trewillian, why, facts is to be come at by one party pretty well as much as by another. Now, suppose the things was changed, wicey warsey, and as I was hacting for the Colonel's party.'

'D— the Colonel!' exclaimed Trevelyan.

'Just so, Mr Trewillian; but if I was hacting for the other party, and they said to me, "Bozzle where's the boy?" why, in three days I'd be down on the facts. Facts is open, Mr Trewillian, if you knows where to look for them.'

'I shall take him abroad at once.'

'Think twice of it, Mr T. The boy is so young, you see, and a mother's 'art is softer and lovinger than anything. I'd think twice of it, Mr T., before I kept 'em apart.' This was a line of thought which Mr Bozzle's conscience had not forced him to entertain to the prejudice of his professional arrangements; but now, as he conversed with his employer, and became by degrees aware of the failure of Trevelyan's mind, some shade of remorse came upon him, and made him say a word on behalf of the 'other party.'

'Am I not always thinking of it? What else have they left me to think of? That will do for to-day. You had better come down to me to-morrow afternoon.' Bozzle promised obedience to these instructions, and as soon as his patron had started he paid the bill, and took himself home.

Lady Rowley, as she travelled back to her house in Manchester Street, almost made up her mind that the separation between her daughter and her son-in-law had better be continued. It was a very sad conclusion to which to come, but she could not believe that any high-spirited woman could long continue to submit herself to the caprices of a man so unreasonable and dictatorial as he to whom she had just been listening. Were it not for the boy, there would, she felt, be no doubt upon the matter. And now, as matters stood, she thought that it should be their great object to regain possession of the child. Then she endeavoured to calculate what would be the result to her daughter, if in very truth it should be found that the wretched man was mad. To hope for such a result seemed to her to be very wicked and yet she hardly knew how not to hope for it.

'Well, mamma,' said Emily Trevelyan, with a faint attempt at a smile, 'you saw him?'

'Yes, dearest, I saw him. I can only say that he is a most unreasonable man.'

'And he would tell you nothing of Louey?'

'No dear not a word.'

CHAPTER LXIII. SIR MARMADUKE AT HOME

Nora Rowley had told her lover that there was to be no further communication between them till her father and mother should be in England; but in telling him so, had so frankly confessed her own affection for him and had so sturdily promised to be true to him, that no lover could have been reasonably aggrieved by such an interdiction. Nora was quite conscious of this, and was aware that Hugh Stanbury had received such encouragement as ought, at any rate to, bring him to the new Rowley establishment, as soon as he should learn where it had fixed itself. But when at the end of ten days he had not shown himself, she began to feel doubts. Could it be that he had changed his mind, that he was unwilling to encounter refusal from her father, or that he had found, on looking into his own affairs more closely, that it would be absurd for him to propose to take a wife to himself while his means were so poor and so precarious? Sir Marmaduke during this time had been so unhappy, so fretful, so indignant, and so much worried, that Nora herself had become almost afraid of him; and, without much reasoning on the matter, had taught herself to believe that Hugh might be actuated by similar fears. She had intended to tell her mother of what had occurred between her and Stanbury the first moment that she and Lady Rowley were together; but then there had fallen upon them that terrible incident of the loss of the child, and the whole family had become at once so wrapped up in the agony of the bereaved mother, and so full of rage against the unreasonable father, that there seemed to Nora to be no possible opportunity for the telling of her own love-story. Emily herself appeared to have forgotten it in the midst of her own misery, and had not mentioned Hugh Stanbury's name since they had been in Manchester Street. We have all felt how on occasions our own hopes and fears, nay, almost our own individuality, become absorbed in and obliterated by the more pressing cares and louder voices of those around us. Nora hardly dared to allude to herself while her sister's grief was still so prominent, and while her father was daily complaining of his own personal annoyances at the Colonial Office. It seemed to her that at such a moment she could not introduce a new matter for dispute, and perhaps a new subject of dismay.

Nevertheless, as the days passed by, and as she saw nothing of Hugh Stanbury, her heart became sore and her spirit vexed. It seemed to her that if she were now deserted by him, all the world would be over for her. The Glascock episode in her life had passed by, that episode which might have been her history, which might have been a history so prosperous, so magnificent, and probably so happy. As she thought of herself and of circumstances as they had happened to her, of the resolutions which she had made as to her own career when she first came to London, and of the way in which she had thrown all those resolutions away in spite of the wonderful success which had come in her path, she could not refrain from thinking that she had brought herself to shipwreck by her own indecision. It must not be imagined that she regretted what she had done. She knew very well that to have acted otherwise than she did when Mr Glascock came to her at Nuncombe Putney would have proved her to be heartless, selfish, and unwomanly. Long before that time she had determined that it was her duty to marry a rich man and, if possible, a man in high position. Such a one had come to her, one endowed with all the good things of the world beyond her most sanguine expectation, and she had rejected him! She knew that she had been right because she had allowed herself to love the other man. She did not repent what she had done, the circumstances being as they were, but she almost regretted that she had been so soft in heart, so susceptible of the weakness of love, so little able to do as she pleased with herself. Of what use to her was it that she loved this man with all her strength of affection when he never came to her, although the time at which he had been told that he might come was now ten days past?

She was sitting one afternoon in the drawing-room listlessly reading, or pretending to read, a novel, when, on a sudden, Hugh Stanbury was announced. The circumstances of the moment were most unfortunate for such a visit. Sir Marmaduke, who had been down at Whitehall in the morning, and from thence had made a journey to St. Diddulph's-in-the-East and back, was exceedingly cross and out of temper. They had told him at his office that they feared he would not suffice to carry through the purpose for which he had been brought home. And his brother-in-law, the parson, had expressed to him an opinion that he was in great part responsible for the misfortune of his daughter, by the encouragement which he had given to such a man as Colonel Osborne. Sir Marmaduke had in consequence quarrelled both with the chief clerk and with Mr Outhouse, and had come home surly and discontented. Lady Rowley and her eldest daughter were away, closeted at the moment with Lady Milborough, with whom they were endeavouring to arrange some plan by which the boy might at any rate be given back. Poor Emily Trevelyan was humble enough now to Lady Milborough, was prepared to be humble to any one, and in any circumstances, so that she should not be required to acknowledge that she had entertained Colonel Osborne as her lover. The two younger girls, Sophy and Lucy, were in the room when Stanbury was announced, as was also Sir Marmaduke, who at that very moment was uttering angry growls at the obstinacy and want of reason with which he had been treated by Mr Outhouse. Now Sir Marmaduke had not so much as heard the name of Hugh Stanbury as yet; and Nora, though her listlessness was all at an end, at once felt how impossible it would be to explain any of the circumstances of her case in such an interview as this. While, however, Hugh's dear steps were heard upon the stairs, her feminine mind at once went to work to ascertain in what best mode, with what most attractive reason for his presence, she might introduce the young man to her father. Had not the girls been then present, she thought that it might have been expedient to leave Hugh to tell his own story to Sir Marmaduke. But she had no opportunity of sending her sisters away; and, unless chance should remove them, this could not be done.

'He is son of the lady we were with at Nuncombe Putney,' she whispered to her father as she got up to move across the room to welcome her lover. Now Sir Marmaduke had expressed great disapproval of that retreat to Dartmoor, and had only understood respecting it that it had been arranged between Trevelyan and the family in whose custody his two daughters had been sent away into banishment. He was not therefore specially disposed to welcome Hugh Stanbury in consequence of this mode of introduction.

Hugh, who had asked for Lady Rowley and Mrs Trevelyan and had learned that they were out before he had mentioned Miss Rowley's name, was almost prepared to take his sweetheart into his arms. In that half-minute he had taught himself to expect that he would meet her alone, and had altogether forgotten Sir Marmaduke. Young men when they call at four o'clock in the day never expect to find papas at home. And of Sophia and Lucy he had either heard nothing or had forgotten what he had heard. He repressed himself however in time, and did not commit either Nora or himself by any very vehement demonstration of affection. But he did hold her hand longer than he should have done, and Sir Marmaduke saw that he did so.

'This is papa,' said Nora. 'Papa, this is our friend, Mr Hugh Stanbury.' The introduction was made in a manner almost absurdly formal, but poor Nora's difficulties lay heavy upon her. Sir Marmaduke muttered something but it was little more than a grunt. 'Mamma and Emily are out,' continued Nora. 'I dare say they will be in soon.' Sir Marmaduke looked round sharply at the man. Why was he to be encouraged to stay till Lady Rowley should return? Lady Rowley did not want to see him. It seemed to Sir Marmaduke, in the midst of his troubles, that this was no time to be making new acquaintances. 'These are my sisters, Mr Stanbury,' continued Nora. 'This is Sophia, and this is Lucy.' Sophia and Lucy would have been thoroughly willing to receive their sister's lover with genial kindness if they had been properly instructed, and if the time had been opportune; but, as it was, they had nothing to say. They, also, could only mutter some little sound intended to be more courteous than their father's grunt. Poor Nora!

'I hope you are comfortable here,' said Hugh.

'The house is all very well,' said Nora, 'but we don't like the neighbourhood.'

Hugh also felt that conversation was difficult. He had soon come to perceive before he had been in the room half a minute that the atmosphere was not favourable to his mission. There was to be no embracing or permission for embracing on the present occasion. Had he been left alone with Sir Marmaduke he would probably have told his business plainly, let Sir Marmaduke's manner to him have been what it might; but it was impossible for him to do this with three young ladies in the room with him. Seeing that Nora was embarrassed by her difficulties, and that Nora's father was cross and silent, he endeavoured to talk to the other girls, and asked them concerning their journey and the ship in which they had come. But it was very up-hill work. Lucy and Sophy could talk as glibly as any young ladies home from any colony, and no higher degree of fluency can be expressed, but now they were cowed. Their elder sister was shamefully and most undeservedly disgraced, and this man had had something—they knew not what—to do with it. 'Is Priscilla quite well?' Nora asked at last.

'Quite well. I heard from her yesterday. You know they have left the Clock House.'

'I had not heard it.'

'Oh yes and they are living in a small cottage just outside the village. And what else do you think has happened?'

'Nothing bad, I hope, Mr Stanbury.'

'My sister Dorothy has left her aunt, and is living with them again at Nuncombe.'

'Has there been a quarrel, Mr Stanbury?'

'Well, yes after a fashion there has, I suppose. But it is a long story and would not interest Sir Marmaduke. The wonder is that Dorothy should have been able to stay so long with my aunt. I will tell it you all some day.' Sir Marmaduke could not understand why a long story about this man's aunt and sister should be told to his daughter. He forgot, as men always do in such circumstances forget that, while he was living in the Mandarins, his daughter, living in England, would of course pick up new interest and become intimate with new histories. But he did not forget that pressure of the hand which he had seen, and he determined that his daughter Nora could not have any worse lover than the friend of his elder daughter's husband.

Stanbury had just determined that he must go, that there was no possibility for him either to say or do anything to promote his cause at the present moment, when the circumstances were all changed by the return home of Lady Rowley and Mrs Trevelyan. Lady Rowley knew, and had for some days known, much more of Stanbury than had come to the ears of Sir Marmaduke. She understood in the first place that the Stanburys had been very good to her daughter, and she was aware that Hugh Stanbury had thoroughly taken her daughter's part against his old friend

Trevelyan. She would therefore have been prepared to receive him kindly had he not on this very morning been the subject of special conversation between her and Emily. But, as it had happened, Mrs Trevelyan had this very day told Lady Rowley the whole story of Nora's love. The elder sister had not intended to be treacherous to the younger; but in the thorough confidence which mutual grief and close conference had created between the mother and daughter, everything had at last come out, and Lady Rowley had learned the story, not only of Hugh Stanbury's courtship, but of those rich offers which had been made by the heir to the barony of Peterborough.

It must be acknowledged that Lady Rowley was greatly grieved and thoroughly dismayed. It was not only that Mr Glascock was the eldest son of a peer, but that he was represented by the poor suffering wife of the ill-tempered man to be a man blessed with a disposition sweet as an angel's. 'And she would have liked him,' Emily had said, 'if it had not been for this unfortunate young man.' Lady Rowley was not worse than are other mothers, not more ambitious, or more heartless, or more worldly. She was a good mother, loving her children, and thoroughly anxious for their welfare. But she would have liked to be the mother-in-law of Lord Peterborough, and she would have liked, dearly, to see her second daughter removed from the danger of those rocks against which her eldest child had been shipwrecked. And when she asked after Hugh Stanbury, and his means of maintaining a wife, the statement which Mrs Trevelyan made was not comforting. 'He writes for a penny newspaper and, I believe, writes very well,' Mrs Trevelyan had said.

'For a penny newspaper! Is that respectable?'

'His aunt, Miss Stanbury, seemed to think not. But I suppose men of education do write for such things now. He says himself that it is very precarious as an employment.'

'It must be precarious, Emily. And has he got nothing?'

'Not a penny of his own,' said Mrs Trevelyan.

Then Lady Rowley had thought again of Mr Glascock, and of the family title, and of Markhams. And she thought of her present troubles, and of the Mandarins, and the state of Sir Marmaduke's balance at the bankers and of the other girls, and of all there was before her to do. Here had been a very Apollo among suitors kneeling at her child's feet, and the foolish girl had sent him away for the sake of a young man who wrote for a penny newspaper! Was it worth the while of any woman to bring up daughters with such results? Lady Rowley, therefore, when she was first introduced to Hugh Stanbury, was not prepared to receive him with open arms.

On this occasion the task of introducing him fell to Mrs Trevelyan, and was done with much graciousness. Emily knew that Hugh Stanbury was her friend, and would sympathise with her respecting her child. 'You have heard what has happened to me?' she said. Stanbury, however, had heard nothing of that kidnapping of the child. Though to the Rowleys it seemed that such a deed of iniquity, done in the middle of London, must have been known to all the world, he had not as yet been told of it, and now the story was given to him. Mrs Trevelyan herself told it, with many tears and an agony of fresh grief; but still she told it as to one whom she regarded as a sure friend, and from whom she knew that she would receive sympathy. Sir Marmaduke sat by the while, still gloomy and out of humour. Why was their family sorrow to be laid bare to this stranger?

'It is the cruellest thing I ever heard,' said Hugh.

'A dastardly deed,' said Lady Rowley.

'But we all feel that for the time he can hardly know what he does,' said Nora.

'And where is the child?' Stanbury asked.

'We have not the slightest idea,' said Lady Rowley. 'I have seen him, and he refuses to tell us. He did say that my daughter should see her boy; but he now accompanies his offer with such conditions that it is impossible to listen to him.'

'And where is he?'

'We do not know where he lives. We can reach him only through a certain man.'

'Ah, I know the man,' said Stanbury; 'one who was a policeman once. His name is Bozzle.'

'That is the man,' said Sir Marmaduke. 'I have seen him.'

'And of course he will tell us nothing but what he is told to tell us,' continued Lady Rowley. 'Can there be anything so horrible as this that a wife should be bound to communicate with her own husband respecting her own child through such a man as that?'

'One might possibly find out where he keeps the child,' said Hugh.

'If you could manage that, Mr Stanbury!' said Lady Rowley.

'I hardly see that it would do much good,' said Hugh. 'Indeed I do not know why he should keep the place a secret. I suppose he has a right to the boy until the mother shall have made good her claim before the court.' He promised, however, that he would do his best to ascertain where the child was kept, and where Trevelyan resided, and then having been nearly an hour at the house he was forced to get up and take his leave. He had said not a word to any one of the business that had brought him there. He had not even whispered an assurance of his affection to Nora. Till the two elder ladies had come in, and the subject of the taking of the boy had been mooted, he had sat there as a perfect stranger. He thought that it was manifest enough that Nora had told her secret to no one. It seemed to him that Mrs Trevelyan must have forgotten it—that Nora herself must have forgotten it, if such forgetting could be possible! He got up, however, and took his leave, and was comforted in some slight degree by seeing that there was a tear in Nora's eye.

'Who is he?' demanded Sir Marmaduke, as soon as the door was closed.

'He is a young man who was an intimate friend of Louis's,' answered Mrs Trevelyan; 'but he is so no longer, because he sees how infatuated Louis has been.'

'And why does he come here?'

'We know him very well,' continued Mrs Trevelyan. 'It was he that arranged our journey down to Devonshire. He was very kind about it, and so were his mother and sister. We have every reason to be grateful to Mr Stanbury.' This was all very well, but Nora nevertheless felt that the interview had been anything but successful.

'Has he any profession?' asked Sir Marmaduke.

'He writes for the press,' said Mrs Trevelyan.

'What do you mean—books?'

'No, for a newspaper.'

'For a penny newspaper,' said Nora boldly 'for the *Daily Record*.'

'Then I hope he won't come here any more,' said Sir Marmaduke. Nora paused a moment, striving to find words for some speech which might be true to her love and yet not unseemly; but finding no such words ready, she got up from her seat and walked out of the room. 'What is the meaning of it all?' asked Sir Marmaduke. There was a silence for a while, and then he repeated his question in another form. 'Is there any reason for his coming here—about Nora?'

'I think he is attached to Nora,' said Mrs Trevelyan. 'My dear,' said Lady Rowley, 'perhaps we had better not speak about it just now.'

'I suppose he has not a penny in the world,' said Sir Marmaduke.

'He has what he earns,' said Mrs Trevelyan.

'If Nora understands her duty she will never let me hear his name again,' said Sir Marmaduke. Then there was nothing more said, and as soon as they could escape, both Lady Rowley and Mrs Trevelyan left the room.

'I should have told you everything,' said Nora to her mother that night. 'I had no intention to keep anything a secret from you. But we have all been so unhappy about Louey, that we have had no heart to talk of anything else.'

'I understand all that, my darling.'

'And I had meant that you should tell papa, for I supposed that he would come. And I meant that he should go to papa himself. He intended that himself, only, to-day as things turned out.'

'Just so, dearest, but it does not seem that he has got any income. It would be very rash, wouldn't it?'

'People must be rash sometimes. Everybody can't have an income without earning it. I suppose people in professions do marry without having fortunes.'

'When they have settled professions, Nora.'

'And why is not his a settled profession? I believe he receives quite as much at seven and twenty as Uncle Oliphant does at sixty.'

'But your Uncle Oliphant's income is permanent.'

'Lawyers don't have permanent incomes, or doctors or merchants.'

'But those professions are regular and sure. They don't marry, without fortunes, till they have made their incomes sure.'

'Mr Stanbury's income is sure. I don't know why it shouldn't be sure. He goes on writing and writing every day, and it seems to me that of all professions in the world it is the finest. I'd much sooner write for a newspaper than be one of those old musty, fusty lawyers, who'll say anything that they're paid to say.'

'My dearest Nora, all that is nonsense. You know as well as I do that you should not marry a man when there is a doubt whether he can keep a house over your head that is his position.'

'It is good enough for me, mamma.'

'And what is his income from writing?'

'It is quite enough for me, mamma. The truth is I have promised, and I cannot go back from it. Dear, dear mamma, you won't quarrel with us, and oppose us, and make papa hard against us. You can do what you like with papa. I know that. Look at poor Emily. Plenty of money has not made her happy.'

'If Mr Glascock had only asked you a week sooner,' said Lady Rowley, with a handkerchief to her eyes.

'But you see, he didn't, mamma.'

'When I think of it I cannot but weep;' and the poor mother burst out into a full flood of tears 'such a man, so good, so gentle, and so truly devoted to you.'

'Mamma, what's the good of that now?'

'Going down all the way to Devonshire after you!'

'So did Hugh, mamma.'

'A position that any girl in England would have envied you. I cannot but feel it. And Emily says she is sure he would come back, if he got the very slightest encouragement.'

'That is quite impossible, mamma.'

'Why should it be impossible? Emily declares that she never saw a man so much in love in her life, and she says also that she believes he is abroad now simply because he is broken-hearted about it.'

'Mr Glascock, mamma, was very nice and good and all that; but indeed he is not the man to suffer from a broken heart. And Emily is quite mistaken. I told him the whole truth.'

'What truth?'

'That there was somebody else that I did love. Then he said that of course that put an end to it all, and he wished me good-bye ever so calmly.'

'How could you be so infatuated? Why should you have cut the ground away from your feet in that way?'

'Because I chose that there should be an end to it. Now there has been an end to it; and it is much better, mamma, that we should not think about Mr Glascock any more. He will never come again to me and if he did, I could only say the same thing.'

'You mustn't be surprised, Nora, if I'm unhappy; that is all. Of course I must feel it. Such a connection as it would have been for your sisters! Such a home for poor Emily in her trouble! And as for this other man—'

'Mamma, don't speak ill of him.'

'If I say anything of him, I must say the truth,' said Lady Rowley.

'Don't say anything against him, mamma, because he is to be my husband. Dear, dear mamma, you can't change me by anything you say. Perhaps I have been foolish; but it is settled now. Don't make me wretched by speaking against the man whom I mean to love all my life better than all the world.'

'Think of Louis Trevelyan.'

'I will think of no one but Hugh Stanbury. I tried not to love him, mamma. I tried to think that it was better to make believe that I loved Mr Glascock. But he got the better of me, and conquered me, and I will never rebel against him. You may help me, mamma but you can't change me.'

CHAPTER LXIV. SIR MARMADUKE AT HIS CLUB

Sir Marmaduke had come away from his brother-in-law the parson in much anger, for Mr Outhouse, with that mixture of obstinacy and honesty which formed his character, had spoken hard words of Colonel Osborne, and words which by implication had been hard also against Emily Trevelyan. He had been very staunch to his niece when attacked by his niece's husband; but when his sympathies and assistance were invoked by Sir Marmaduke it seemed as though he had transferred his allegiance to the other side. He pointed out to the unhappy father that Colonel Osborne had behaved with great cruelty in going to Devonshire, that the Stanburys had been untrue to their trust in allowing him to enter the house, and that Emily had been 'indiscreet' in receiving him. When a young woman is called indiscreet by her friends it may be assumed that her character is very seriously assailed. Sir Marmaduke had understood this, and on hearing the word had become wroth with his brother-in-law. There had been hot words between them, and Mr Outhouse would not yield an inch or retract a syllable. He conceived it to be his duty to advise the father to caution his daughter with severity, to quarrel absolutely with Colonel Osborne, and to let Trevelyan know that this had been done. As to the child, Mr Outhouse expressed a strong opinion that the father was legally entitled to the custody of his boy, and that nothing could be done to recover the child, except what might be done with the father's consent. In fact, Mr Outhouse made himself exceedingly disagreeable, and sent away Sir Marmaduke with a very heavy heart. Could it really be possible that his old friend Fred Osborne, who seven or eight-and-twenty years ago had been potent among young ladies, had really been making love to his old friend's married daughter? Sir Marmaduke looked into himself, and conceived it to be quite out of the question that he should make love to any one. A good dinner, good wine, a good cigar, an easy chair, and a rubber of whist—all these things, with no work to do, and men of his own standing around him—were the pleasures of life which Sir Marmaduke desired. Now Fred Osborne was an older man than he, and, though Fred Osborne did keep up a foolish system of padded clothes and dyed whiskers, still at fifty-two or fifty-three surely a man might be reckoned safe. And then, too, that ancient friendship! Sir Marmaduke, who had lived all his life in the comparative seclusion of a colony, thought perhaps more of that ancient friendship than did the Colonel, who had lived amidst the blaze of London life, and who had had many opportunities of changing his friends.

Some inkling of all this made its way into Sir Marmaduke's bosom, as he thought of it with bitterness; and he determined that he would have it out with his friend.

Hitherto he had enjoyed very few of those pleasant hours which he had anticipated on his journey homewards. He had had no heart to go to his club, and he had fancied that Colonel Osborne had been a little backward in looking him up, and providing him with amusement. He had suggested this to his wife, and she had told him that the Colonel had been right not to come to Manchester Street. 'I have told Emily,' said Lady Rowley, 'that she must not meet him, and she is quite of the same opinion.' Nevertheless, there had been remissness. Sir Marmaduke felt that it was so, in spite of his wife's excuses. In this way he was becoming sore with everybody, and very unhappy. It did not at all improve his temper when he was told that his second daughter had refused an offer from Lord Peterborough's eldest son. 'Then she may go into the workhouse for me,' the angry father had said, declaring at the same time that he would never give his consent to her marriage with the man who 'did dirty work' for the *Daily Record* as he, with his paternal wisdom, chose to express it. But this cruel phrase was not spoken in Nora's hearing, nor was it repeated to her. Lady Rowley knew her husband, and was aware that he would on occasions change his opinion.

It was not till two or three days after his visit to St. Diddulph's that he met Colonel Osborne. The Easter recess was then over, and Colonel Osborne had just returned to London. They met on the door-steps of 'The Acrobats,' and the Colonel immediately began with an apology. 'I have been so sorry to be away just when you are here—upon my word I have. But I was obliged to go down to the duchess's. I had promised early in the winter; and those people are so angry if you put them off. By George, it's almost as bad as putting off royalty.'

'D—n the duchess,' said Sir Marmaduke.

'With all my heart,' said the Colonel 'only I thought it as well that I should tell you the truth.'

'What I mean is, that the duchess and her people make no difference to me. I hope you had a pleasant time; that's all.'

'Well yes, we had. One must get away somewhere at Easter. There is no one left at the club, and there's no House, and no one asks one to dinner in town. In fact, if one didn't go away one wouldn't know what to do. There were ever so many people there that I liked to meet. Lady Glencora was there, and uncommon pleasant she made it. That woman has more to say for herself than any half-dozen men that I know. And Lord Cantrip, your chief, was there. He said a word or two to me about you.'

'What sort of word?'

'He says he wishes you would read up some blue books, or papers, or reports, or something of that kind, which he says that some of his fellows have sent you. It seems that there are some new rules, or orders, or fashions, which he wants you to have at your finger's ends. Nothing could be more civil than he was, but he just wished me to mention this, knowing that you and I are likely to see each other.'

'I wish I had never come over,' said Sir Marmaduke.

'Why so?'

'They didn't bother me with their new rules and fashions over there. When the papers came somebody read them, and that was enough. I could do what they wanted me to do there.'

'And so you will here after a bit.'

'I'm not so sure of that. Those young fellows seem to forget that an old dog can't learn new tricks. They've got a young brisk fellow there who seems to think that a man should be an encyclopaedia of knowledge because he has lived in a colony over twenty years.'

'That's the new under-secretary.'

'Never mind who it is. Osborne, just come up to the library, will you? I want to speak to you.'

Then Sir Marmaduke, with considerable solemnity, led the way up to the most deserted room in the club, and Colonel Osborne followed him, well knowing that something was to be said about Emily Trevelyan.

Sir Marmaduke seated himself on a sofa, and his friend sat close beside him. The room was quite deserted. It was four o'clock in the afternoon, and the club was full of men. There were men in the morning-room, and men in the drawing-room, and men in the card-room, and men in the billiard-room; but no better choice of a chamber for a conference intended to be silent and secret could have been made in all London than that which had induced Sir Marmaduke to take his friend into the library of 'The Acrobats.' And yet a great deal of money had been spent in providing this library for 'The Acrobats.' Sir Marmaduke sat for awhile silent, and had he sat silent for an hour, Colonel Osborne would not have interrupted him. Then, at last, he began, with a voice that was intended to be serious, but which struck upon the ear of his companion as being affected and unlike the owner of it. 'This is a very sad thing about my poor girl,' said Sir Marmaduke.

'Indeed it is. There is only one thing to be said about it, Rowley.'

'And what's that?'

'The man must be mad.'

'He is not so mad as to give us any relief by his madness, poor as such comfort would be. He has got Emily's child away from her, and I think it will about kill her. And what is to become of her? As to taking her back to the islands without her child, it is out of the question. I never knew anything so cruel in my life.'

'And so absurd, you know.'

'Ah that's just the question. If anybody had asked me, I should have said that you were the man of all men whom I could have best trusted.'

'Do you doubt it now?'

'I don't know what to think.'

'Do you mean to say that you suspect me and your daughter, too?'

'No, by heavens! Poor dear. If I suspected her, there would be an end of all things with me. I could never get over that. No I don't suspect her!' Sir Marmaduke had now dropped his affected tone, and was speaking with natural energy.

'But you do me?'

'No; if I did, I don't suppose I should be sitting with you here; but they tell me—'

'They tell you what?'

'They tell me that that you did not behave wisely about it. Why could you not let her alone when you found out how matters were going?'

'Who has been telling you this, Rowley?'

Sir Marmaduke considered for awhile, and then, remembering that Colonel Osborne could hardly quarrel with a clergyman, told him the truth. 'Outhouse says that you have done her an irretrievable injury by going down to Devonshire to her, and by writing to her.'

'Outhouse is an ass.'

'That is easily said, but why did you go?'

'And why should I not go? What the deuce! Because a man like that chooses to take vagaries into his head I am not to see my own godchild!' Sir Marmaduke tried to remember whether the Colonel was in fact the godfather of his eldest daughter, but he found that his mind was quite a blank about his children's godfathers and godmothers. 'And as for the letters, I wish you could see them. The only letters which had in them a word of importance were those about your coming home. I was anxious to get that arranged, not only for your sake, but because she was so eager about it.'

'God bless her, poor child,' said Sir Marmaduke, rubbing the tears away from his eyes with his red silk pocket-handkerchief.

'I will acknowledge that those letters—there may have been one or two— were the beginning of the trouble. It was these that made this man show himself to be a lunatic. I do admit that. I was bound not to talk about your coming, and I told her to keep the secret. He went spying about, and found her letters, I suppose, and then he took fire because there was to be a secret from him. Dirty, mean dog! And now I'm to be told by such a fellow as Outhouse that it's my fault, that I have caused all the trouble, because, when I happened to be in Devonshire, I went to see your daughter!' We must do the Colonel the justice of supposing that he had by this time quite taught himself to believe that the church porch at Cockchaffington had been the motive cause of his journey into Devonshire. 'Upon my word it is too hard,' continued he indignantly. 'As for Outhouse, only for the gown upon his back, I'd pull his nose. And I wish that you would tell him that I say so.'

'There is trouble enough without that,' said Sir Marmaduke.

'But it is hard. By G—, it is hard. There is this comfort: if it hadn't been me, it would have been some one else. Such a man as that couldn't have gone two or three years without being jealous of some one. And as for poor Emily, she is better off perhaps with an accusation so absurd as this, than she might have been had her name been joined with a younger man, or with one whom you would have less reason for trusting.'

There was so much that seemed to be sensible in this, and it was spoken with so well assumed a tone of injured innocence, that Sir Marmaduke felt that he had nothing more to say. He muttered something further about the cruelty of the case, and then slunk away out of the club, and made his way home to the dull gloomy house in Manchester Street. There was no comfort for him there but neither was there any comfort for him at the club. And why did that vexatious Secretary of State send him messages about blue books? As he went, he expressed sundry wishes that he was back at the Mandarins, and told himself that it would be well that he should remain there till he died.

CHAPTER LXV. MYSTERIOUS AGENCIES

When the thirty-first of March arrived, Exeter had not as yet been made gay with the marriage festivities of Mr Gibson and Camilla French. And this delay had not been the fault of Camilla. Camilla had been ready, and when, about the middle of the month, it was hinted to her that some postponement was necessary, she spoke her mind out plainly, and declared that she was not going to stand that kind of thing. The communication had not been made to her by Mr Gibson in person. For some days previously he had not been seen at Heavitree, and Camilla had from day to day become more black, gloomy, and harsh in her manners both to her mother and her sister. Little notes had come and little notes had gone, but no one in the house, except Camilla herself, knew what those notes contained. She would not condescend to complain to Arabella; nor did she say much in condemnation of her lover to Mrs French, till the blow came. With unremitting attention she pursued the great business of her wedding garments, and exacted from the unfortunate Arabella an amount of work equal to her own, of thankless work, as is the custom of embryo brides with their unmarried sisters. And she drew with great audacity on the somewhat slender means of the family for the amount of feminine gear necessary to enable her to go into Mr Gibson's house with something of the *éclat* of a well-provided bride. When Mrs French hesitated, and then expostulated, Camilla replied that she did not expect to be married above once, and that in no cheaper or more productive way than this could her mother allow her to consume her share of the family resources. 'What matter, mamma, if you do have to borrow a little money? Mr Burgess will let you have it when he knows why. And as I shan't be eating and drinking at home any more, nor yet getting my things here, I have a right to expect it.' And she ended by expressing an opinion, in Arabella's hearing, that any daughter of a house who proves herself to be capable of getting a husband for herself, is entitled to expect that those left at home shall pinch themselves for a time, in order that she may go forth to the world in a respectable way, and be a credit to the family.

Then came the blow. Mr Gibson had not been at the house for some days, but the notes had been going and coming. At last Mr Gibson came himself; but, as it happened, when he came Camilla was out shopping. In these days she often did go out shopping between eleven and one, carrying her sister with her. It must have been but a poor pleasure for Arabella, this witnessing the purchases made, seeing the pleasant draperies and handling the real linens and admiring the fine cambrics spread out before them on the shop counters by obsequious attendants. And the questions asked of her by her sister, whether this was good enough for so august an occasion, or that sufficiently handsome, must have been harassing. She could not have failed to remember that it ought all to have been done for her, that had she not been treated with monstrous injustice, with most unsisterly cruelty, all these good things would have been spread on her behoof. But she went on and endured it, and worked diligently with her needle, and folded and unfolded as she was desired, and became as it were quite a younger sister in the house, creeping out by herself now and again into the purlieus of the city, to find such consolation as she might receive from her solitary thoughts.

But Arabella and Camilla were both away when Mr Gibson called to tell Mrs French of his altered plans. And as he asked, not for his lady-love, but for Mrs French herself, it is probable that he watched his opportunity and that he knew to what cares his Camilla was then devoting herself. 'Perhaps it is quite as well that I should find you alone,' he said, after sundry preludes, to his future mother-in-law, 'because you can make Camilla understand this better than I can. I must put off the day for about three weeks.'

'Three weeks, Mr Gibson?'

'Or a month. Perhaps we had better say the 29th of April.' Mr Gibson had by this time thrown off every fear that he might have entertained of the mother, and could speak to her of such an unwarrantable change of plans with tolerable equanimity.

'But I don't know that that will suit Camilla at all.'

'She can name any other day she pleases, of course, that is in May.'

'But why is this to be?'

'There are things about money, Mrs French, which I cannot arrange sooner. And I find that unfortunately I must go up to London.' Though many other questions were asked, nothing further was got out of Mr Gibson on that occasion; and he left the house with a perfect understanding on his own part and on that of Mrs French that the marriage was postponed till some day still to be fixed, but which could not and should not be before the 29th of April. Mrs French asked him why he did not come up and see Camilla. He replied, false man that he was, that he had hoped to have seen her this morning, and that he would come again before the week was over.

Then it was that Camilla spoke her mind out plainly. 'I shall go to his house at once,' she said, 'and find out all about it. I don't understand it. I don't understand it at all; and I won't put up with it. He shall know who he has to deal with, if he plays tricks upon me. Mamma, I wonder you let him out of the house, till you had made him come back to his old day.'

'What could I do, my dear?'

'What could you do? Shake him out of it as I would have done. But he didn't dare to tell me because he is a coward.'

Camilla in all this showed her spirit; but she allowed her anger to hurry her away into an indiscretion. Arabella was present, and Camilla should have repressed her rage.

'I don't think he's at all a coward,' said Arabella.

'That's my business. I suppose I'm entitled to know what he is better than you.'

'All the same I don't think Mr Gibson is at all a coward,' said Arabella, again pleading the cause of the man who had misused her.

'Now, Arabella, I won't take any interference from you; mind that. I say it was cowardly, and he should have come to me. It's my concern, and I shall go to him. I'm not going to be stopped by any shilly-shally nonsense, when my future respectability, perhaps, is at stake. All Exeter knows that the marriage is to take place on the 31st of this month.'

On the next day Camilla absolutely did go to Mr Gibson's house at an early hour, at nine, when, as she thought, he would surely be at breakfast. But he had flown. He had left Exeter that morning by an early train, and his servant thought that he had gone to London. On the next morning Camilla got a note from him, written in London. It affected to be very cheery and affectionate, beginning 'DEAREST CAMMY,' and alluding to the postponement of his wedding as though it were a thing so fixed as to require no further question. Camilla answered this letter, still in much wrath, complaining, protesting, expostulating throwing in his teeth the fact that the day had been fixed by him, and not by her. And she added a postscript in the following momentous words 'If you have any respect for the name of your future wife, you will fall back upon your first arrangement.' To this she got simply a line of an answer, declaring that this falling back was impossible, and then nothing was heard of him for ten days.

He had gone from Tuesday to Saturday week, and the first that Camilla saw of him was his presence in the reading desk when he chaunted the cathedral service as priest-vicar on the Sunday.

At this time Arabella was very ill, and was confined to her bed. Mr Martin declared that her system had become low from over anxiety, that she was nervous, weak, and liable to hysterics, that her feelings were in fact too many for her, and that her efforts to overcome them, and to face the realities of the world, had exhausted her. This was, of course, not said openly, at the town-cross of Exeter; but such was the opinion which Mr Martin gave in confidence to the mother. 'Fiddle-de-dee!' said

Camilla, when she was told of feelings, susceptibilities, and hysterics. At the present moment she had a claim to the undivided interest of the family, and she believed that her sister's illness was feigned in order to defraud her of her rights. 'My dear, she is ill,' said Mrs French. 'Then let her have a dose of salts,' said the stern Camilla. This was on the Sunday afternoon. Camilla had endeavoured to see Mr Gibson as he came out of the cathedral, but had failed. Mr Gibson had been detained within the building no doubt by duties connected with the choral services. On that evening he got a note from Camilla, and quite early on the Monday morning he came up to Heavitree.

'You will find her in the drawing-room,' said Mrs French, as she opened the hall-door for him. There was a smile on her face as she spoke, but it was a forced smile. Mr Gibson did not smile at all.

'Is it all right with her?' he asked.

'Well you had better go to her. You see, Mr Gibson, young ladies, when they are going to be married, think that they ought to have their own way a little, just for the last time, you know.' He took no notice of the joke, but went with slow steps up to the drawing-room. It would be inquiring too curiously to ask whether Camilla, when she embraced him, discerned that he had fortified his courage that morning with a glass of curaçoa.

'What does all this mean, Thomas?' was the first question that Camilla asked when the embrace was over.

'All what mean, dear?'

'This untoward delay? Thomas, you have almost broken my heart. You have been away, and I have not heard from you.'

'I wrote twice, Camilla.'

'And what sort of letters? If there is anything the matter, Thomas, you had better tell me at once.' She paused, but Thomas held his tongue. 'I don't suppose you want to kill me.'

'God forbid,' said Thomas.

'But you will. What must everybody think of me in the city when they find that it is put off. Poor mamma has been dreadful, quite dreadful! And here is Arabella now laid up on a bed of sickness.' This, too, was indiscreet. Camilla should have said nothing about her sister's sickness.

'I have been so sorry to hear about dear Bella,' said Mr Gibson.

'I don't suppose she's very bad,' said Camilla, 'but of course we all feel it. Of course we're upset. As for me, I bear up; because I've that spirit that I won't give way if it's ever so; but, upon my word, it tries me hard. What is the meaning of it, Thomas?'

But Thomas had nothing to say beyond what he had said before to Mrs French. He was very particular, he said, about money; and certain money matters made it incumbent on him not to marry before the 29th of April. When Camilla suggested to him that as she was to be his wife, she ought to know all about his money matters, he told her that she should some day. When they were married, he would tell her all. Camilla talked a great deal, and said some things that were very severe. Mr Gibson did not enjoy his morning, but he endured the upbraidings of his fair one with more firmness than might perhaps have been expected from him. He left all the talking to Camilla; but when he got up to leave her, the 29th of April had been fixed, with some sort of assent from her, as the day on which she was really to become Mrs Gibson.

When he left the room, he again met Mrs French on the landing-place. She hesitated a moment, waiting to see whether the door would be shut; but the door could not be shut, as Camilla was standing in the entrance. 'Mr Gibson,' said Mrs French, in a voice that was scarcely a whisper, 'would you mind stepping in and seeing poor Bella for a moment?'

'Why she is in bed,' said Camilla.

'Yes she is in bed; but she thinks it would be a comfort to her. She has seen nobody these four days except Mr Martin, and she thinks it would comfort her to have a word or two with Mr Gibson.' Now Mr Gibson was not only going to be Bella's brother-in-law, but he was also a clergyman. Camilla in her heart believed that the half-clerical aspect which her mother had given to the request was false and hypocritical. There were special reasons why Bella should not have wished to see Mr Gibson in her bedroom, at any rate till Mr Gibson had become her brother-in-law. The expression of such a wish at the present moment was almost indecent.

'You'll be there with them?' said Camilla. Mr Gibson blushed up to his ears as he heard the suggestion. 'Of course you'll be there with them, mamma.'

'No, my dear, I think not. I fancy she wishes him to read to her or something of that sort.' Then Mr Gibson, without speaking a word, but still blushing up to his ears, was taken to Arabella's room; and Camilla, flouncing into the drawing-room, banged the door behind her. She had hitherto fought her battle with considerable skill and with great courage, but her very success had made her imprudent. She had become so imperious in the great position which she had reached, that she could not control her temper or wait till her power was confirmed. The banging of that door was heard through the whole house, and every one knew why it was banged.

She threw herself on to a sofa, and then, instantly rising again, paced the room with quick step. Could it be possible that there was treachery? Was it on the cards that that weak, poor creature, Bella, was intriguing once again to defraud her of her husband? There were different things that she now remembered. Arabella, in that moment of bliss in which she had conceived herself to be engaged to Mr Gibson, had discarded her chignon. Then she had resumed it in all its monstrous proportions. Since that it had been lessened by degrees, and brought down, through various interesting but abnormal shapes, to a size which would hardly have drawn forth any anathema from Miss Stanbury. And now, on this very morning, Arabella had put on a clean nightcap, with muslin frills. It is perhaps not unnatural that a sick lady, preparing to receive a clergyman in her bedroom, should put on a clean nightcap; but to suspicious eyes small causes suffice to create alarm. And if there were any such hideous wickedness in the wind, had Arabella any colleague in her villainy? Could it be that the mother was plotting against her daughter's happiness and respectability? Camilla was well aware that her mamma would at first have preferred to give Arabella to Mr Gibson, had the choice in the matter been left to her. But now, when the thing had been settled before all the world, would not such treatment on a mother's part be equal to infanticide? And then as to Mr Gibson himself! Camilla was not prone to think little of her own charms, but she had been unable not to perceive that her lover had become negligent in his personal attentions to her. An accepted lover, who deserves to have been accepted, should devote every hour at his command to his mistress. But Mr Gibson had of late been so chary of his presence at Heavitree, that Camilla could not but have known that he took no delight in coming thither. She had acknowledged this to herself; but she had consoled herself with the reflection that marriage would make this all right. Mr Gibson was not the man to stray from his wife, and she could trust herself to obtain a sufficient hold upon her husband hereafter, partly by the strength of her tongue, partly by the ascendancy of her spirit, and partly, also, by the comforts which she would provide for him. She had not doubted but that it would be all well when they should be married; but how if, even now, there should be no marriage for her? Camilla French had never heard of Creusa and of Jason, but as she paced her mother's drawing-room that morning she was a Medea in spirit. If any plot of that kind should be in the wind, she would do such things that all Devonshire should hear of her wrongs and of her revenge!

In the meantime Mr Gibson was sitting by Arabella's bedside, while Mrs French was trying to make herself busy in her own chamber, next door. There had been a reading of some chapter of the Bible or of some portion of a chapter. And Mr Gibson, as he read, and Arabella, as she listened, had endeavoured to take to their hearts and to make use of the word which they heard. The poor young woman, when she begged her mother to send to her the man who was so dear to her, did so with some half-formed condition that it would be good for her to hear a clergyman read to her. But now the chapter had been read, and the book was back in Mr Gibson's pocket, and he was sitting with his hand on the bed.'she is so very arrogant,' said Bella,' and so domineering.' To this Mr Gibson made no reply. 'I'm sure I have endeavoured to bear it well, though you must have known what I have suffered, Thomas. Nobody can understand it so well as you do.'

'I wish I had never been born,' said Mr Gibson tragically.

'Don't say that, Thomas, because it's wicked.'

'But I do. See all the harm I have done, and yet I did not mean it.'

'You must try and do the best you can now. I am not saying what that should be. I am not dictating to you. You are a man, and, of course, you must judge for yourself. But I will say this. You shouldn't do anything just because it is the easiest. I don't suppose I should live after it. I don't indeed. But that should not signify to you.'

'I don't suppose that any man was ever before in such a terrible position since the world began.'

'It is difficult; I am sure of that, Thomas.'

'And I have meant to be so true. I fancy sometimes that some mysterious agency interferes with the affairs of a man and drives him on and on and on, almost till he doesn't know where it drives him.' As he said this in a voice that was quite sepulchral in its tone, he felt some consolation in the conviction that this mysterious agency could not affect a man without imbuing him with a certain amount of grandeur, very uncomfortable, indeed, in its nature, but still having considerable value as a counterpoise. Pride must bear pain, but pain is recompensed by pride.

'She is so strong, Thomas, that she can put up with anything,' said Arabella, in a whisper.

'Strong yes,' said he, with a shudder 'she is strong enough.'

'And as for love—'

'Don't talk about it,' said he, getting up from his chair. 'Don't talk about it. You will drive me frantic.'

'You know what my feelings are, Thomas; you have always known them. There has been no change since I was the young thing you first knew me.' As she spoke, she just touched his hand with hers; but he did not seem to notice this, sitting with his elbow on the arm of his chair and his forehead on his hand. In reply to what she said to him, he merely shook his head not intending to imply thereby any doubt of the truth of her assertion. 'You have now to make up your mind, and to be bold, Thomas,' continued Arabella.'she says that you are a coward; but I know that you are no coward. I told her so, and she said that I was interfering. Oh that she should be able to tell me that I interfere when I defend you!'

'I must go,' said Mr Gibson, jumping up from his chair. 'I must go. Bella, I cannot stand this any longer. It is too much for me. I will pray that I may decide aright. God bless you!' Then he kissed her brow as she lay in bed, and hurried out of the room.

He had hoped to go from the house without further converse with any of its inmates; for his mind was disturbed, and he longed to be at rest. But he was not allowed to escape so easily. Camilla met him at the dining-room door, and accosted him with a smile. There had been time for much meditation during the last half hour, and Camilla had meditated. 'How do you find her, Thomas?' she asked.

'She seems weak, but I believe she is better. I have been reading to her.'

'Come in, Thomas will you not? It is bad for us to stand talking on the stairs. Dear Thomas, don't let us be so cold to each other.' He had no alternative but to put his arm round her waist, and kiss her, thinking, as he did so, of the mysterious agency which afflicted him. 'Tell me that you love me, Thomas,' she said.

'Of course I love you.' The question is not a pleasant one when put by a lady to a gentleman whose affections towards her are not strong, and it requires a very good actor to produce an efficient answer.

'I hope you do, Thomas. It would be sad, indeed, if you did not. You are not weary of your Camilla are you?'

For a moment there came upon him an idea that he would confess that he was weary of her, but he found at once that such an effort was beyond his powers. 'How can you ask such a question?' he said.

'Because you do not come to me.' Camilla, as she spoke, laid her head upon his shoulder and wept. 'And now you have been five minutes with me and nearly an hour with Bella.'

'She wanted me to read to her,' said Mr Gibson, and he hated himself thoroughly as he said it.

'And now you want to get away as fast as you can,' continued Camilla.

'Because of the morning service,' said Mr Gibson. This was quite true, and yet he hated himself again for saying it. As Camilla knew the truth of the last plea, she was obliged to let him go; but she made him swear before he went that he loved her dearly. 'I think it's all right,' she said to herself as he went down the stairs. 'I don't think he'd dare make it wrong. If he does, o-oh!'

Mr Gibson, as he walked into Exeter, endeavoured to justify his own conduct to himself. There was no moment, he declared to himself, in which he had not endeavoured to do right. Seeing the manner in which he had been placed among these two young women, both of whom had fallen in love with him, how could he have saved himself from vacillation? And by what untoward chance had it come to pass that he had now learned to dislike so vigorously, almost to hate, the one with whom he had been for a moment sufficiently infatuated to think that he loved?

But with all his arguments he did not succeed in justifying to himself his own conduct, and he hated himself.

CHAPTER LXVI. OF A QUARTER OF LAMB

Miss Stanbury, looking out of her parlour window, saw Mr Gibson hurrying towards the cathedral, down the passage which leads from Southernhay into the Close. 'He's just come from Heavitree, I'll be bound,' said Miss Stanbury to Martha, who was behind her.

'Like enough, ma'am.'

'Though they do say that the poor fool of a man has become quite sick of his bargain already.'

'He'll have to be sicker yet, ma'am,' said Martha.

'They were to have been married last week, and nobody ever knew why it was put off. It's my belief he'll never marry her. And she'll be served right, quite right.'

'He must marry her now, ma'am. She's been buying things all over Exeter, as though there was no end of their money.'

'They haven't more than enough to keep body and soul together,' said Miss Stanbury. 'I don't see why I mightn't have gone to service this morning, Martha. It's quite warm now out in the Close.'

'You'd better wait, ma'am, till the east winds is over. She was at Puddock's only the day before yesterday, buying bed-linen, the finest they had, and that wasn't good enough.'

'Psha!' said Miss Stanbury.

'As though Mr Gibson hadn't things of that kind good enough for her,' said Martha.

Then there was silence in the room for awhile. Miss Stanbury was standing at one window, and Martha at the other, watching the people as they passed backwards and forwards, in and out of the Close. Dorothy had now been away at Nuncombe Putney for some weeks, and her aunt felt her loneliness with a heavy sense of weakness. Never had she entertained a companion in the house who had suited her as well as her niece, Dorothy. Dorothy would always listen to her, would always talk to her, would always bear with her. Since Dorothy had gone, various letters had been interchanged between them. Though there had been anger about Brooke Burgess, there had been no absolute rupture; but Miss Stanbury had felt that she could not write and beg her niece to come back to her. She had not sent Dorothy away. Dorothy had chosen to go, because her aunt had bad an opinion of her own as to what was fitting for her heir; and as Miss Stanbury would not give up her opinion, she could not ask her niece to return to her. Such had been her resolution, sternly expressed to herself a dozen times during these solitary weeks; but time and solitude had acted upon her, and she longed for the girl's presence in the house. 'Martha,' she said at last, 'I think I shall get you to go over to Nuncombe Putney.'

'Again, ma'am?'

'Why not again? It's not so far, I suppose, that the journey will hurt you.'

'I don't think it'd hurt me, ma'am, only what good will I do?'

'If you'll go rightly to work, you may do good. Miss Dorothy was a fool to go the way she did, a great fool.'

'She stayed longer than I thought she would, ma'am.'

'I'm not asking you what you thought. I'll tell you what. Do you send Giles to Winslow's, and tell them to send in early to-morrow a nice fore-quarter of lamb. Or it wouldn't hurt you if you went and chose it yourself.'

'It wouldn't hurt me at all, ma'am.'

'You get it nice, not too small, because meat is meat at the price things are now; and how they ever see butcher's meat at all is more than I can understand.'

'People as has to be careful, ma'am, makes a little go a long way.'

'You get it a good size, and take it over in a basket. It won't hurt you, done up clean in a napkin.'

'It won't hurt me at all, ma'am.'

'And you give it to Miss Dorothy with my love. Don't you let 'em think I sent it to my sister-in-law.'

'And is that to be all, ma'am?'

'How do you mean all?'

'Because, ma'am, the railway and the carrier would take it quite ready, and there would be a matter of ten or twelve shillings saved in the journey.'

'Whose affair is that?'

'Not mine, ma'am, of course.'

'I believe you're afraid of the trouble, Martha. Or else you don't like going because they're poor.'

'It ain't fair, ma'am, of you to say so, that it ain't. All I ask is, is that to be all? When I've giv'em the lamb, am I just to come away straight, or am I to say anything? It will look so odd if I'm just to put down the basket and come away without e'er a word.'

'Martha!'

'Yes, ma'am.'

'You're a fool.'

'That's true, too, ma'am.'

'It would be like you to go about in that dummy way, wouldn't it, and you that was so fond of Miss Dorothy.'

'I was fond of her, ma'am.'

'Of course you'll be talking to her and why not? And if she should say anything about returning—'

'Yes, ma'am.'

'You can say that you know her old aunt wouldn't wouldn't refuse to have her back again. You can put it your own way, you know. You needn't make me find words for you.'

'But she won't, ma'am.'

'Won't what?'

'Won't say anything about returning.'

'Yes, she will, Martha, if you talk to her rightly.' The servant didn't reply for a while, but stood looking out of the window. 'You might as well go about the lamb at once, Martha.'

'So I will, ma'am, when I've got it out, all clear.'

'What do you mean by that?'

'Why just this, ma'am. May I tell Miss Dolly straight out that you want her to come back, and that I've been sent to say so?'

'No, Martha.'

'Then how am I to do it, ma'am?'

'Do it out of your own head, just as it comes up at the moment.'

'Out of my own head, ma'am?'

'Yes just as you feel, you know.'

'Just as I feel, ma'am?'

'You understand what I mean, Martha.'

'I'll do my best, ma'am, and I can't say no more. And if you scolds me afterwards, ma'am why, of course, I must put up with it.'

'But I won't scold you, Martha.'

'Then I'll go out to Winslow's about the lamb at once, ma'am.'

'Very nice, and not too small, Martha.'

Martha went out and ordered the lamb, and packed it as desired quite clean in a napkin, and fitted it into the basket, and arranged with Giles Hickbody to carry it down for her early in the morning to the station, so that she might take the first train to Lessborough. It was understood that she was to hire a fly at Lessborough to take her to Nuncombe Putney. Now that she understood the importance of her mission and was aware that the present she took with her was only the customary accompaniment of an ambassadress entrusted with a great mission, Martha said nothing even about the expense. The train started for Lessborough at seven, and as she was descending from her room at six, Miss Stanbury in her flannel dressing-gown stepped out of the door of her own room. 'Just put this in the basket,' said she, handing a note to her servant. 'I thought last night I'd write a word. Just put it in the basket and say nothing about it.' The note which she sent was as follows:

The Close,
8th April, 186—.

My Dear Dorothy

As Martha talks of going over to pay you a visit, I've thought that I'd just get her to take you a quarter of lamb, which is coming in now very nice. I do envy her going to see you, my dear, for I had gotten somehow to love to see your pretty face. I'm getting almost strong again; but Sir Peter, who was here this afternoon, just calling as a friend, was uncivil enough to say that I'm too much of an old woman to go out in the east wind. I told him it didn't much matter for the sooner old women made way for young ones, the better.

I am very desolate and solitary here. But I rather think that women who don't get married are intended to be desolate; and perhaps it is better for them, if they bestow their time and thoughts properly as I hope you do, my dear. A woman with a family of children has almost too many of the cares of this world, to give her mind as she ought to the other. What shall we say then of those who have no such cares, and yet do not walk uprightly? Dear Dorothy, be not such a one. For myself, I acknowledge bitterly the extent of my shortcomings. Much has been given to me; but if much be expected, how shall I answer the demand?

I hope I need not tell you that whenever it may suit you to pay a visit to Exeter, your room will be ready for you, and there will be a warm welcome. Mrs MacHugh always asks after you; and so has Mrs Clifford. I won't tell you what Mrs Clifford said about your colour, because it would make you vain. The Heavitree affair has all been put off; of course you have heard that. Dear, dear, dear! You know what I think, so I need not repeat it.

Give my respects to your mamma and Priscilla, and for yourself, accept the affectionate love of

Your loving old aunt,   JEMIMA STANBURY.

P.S. If Martha should say anything to you, you may feel sure that she knows my mind.

Poor old soul. She felt an almost uncontrollable longing to have her niece back again, and yet she told herself that she was bound not to send a regular invitation, or to suggest an unconditional return. Dorothy had herself decided to take her departure, and if she chose to remain away so it must be. She, Miss Stanbury, could not demean herself by renewing her invitation. She read her letter before she added to it the postscript, and felt that it was too solemn in its tone to suggest to Dorothy that which she wished to suggest. She had been thinking much of her own past life when she wrote those words about the state of an unmarried woman, and was vacillating between two minds—whether it were better for a young woman to look forward to the cares and affections, and perhaps hard usage, of a married life; or to devote herself to the easier and safer course of an old maid's career. But an old maid is nothing if she be not kind and good. She acknowledged that, and, acknowledging it, added the postscript to her letter. What though there was a certain blow to her pride in the writing of it! She did tell herself that, in thus referring her niece to Martha for an expression of her own mind after that conversation which she and Martha had had in the parlour, she was in truth eating her own words. But the postscript was written, and though she took the letter up with her to her own room in order that she might alter the words if she repented of them in the night, the letter was sent as it was written, postscript and all.

She spent the next day with very sober thoughts. When Mrs MacHugh called upon her and told her that there were rumours afloat in Exeter that the marriage between

Camilla French and Mr Gibson would certainly be broken off, in spite of all purchases that had been made, she merely remarked that they were two poor, feckless things, who didn't know their own minds. 'Camilla knows her's plain enough,' said Mrs MacHugh sharply; but even this did not give Miss Stanbury any spirit. She waited, and waited patiently, till Martha should return, thinking of the sweet pink colour which used to come and go in Dorothy's cheeks which she had been wont to observe so frequently, not knowing that she had observed it and loved it.

CHAPTER LXVII. RIVER'S COTTAGE

Three days after Hugh Stanbury's visit to Manchester Street, he wrote a note to Lady Rowley, telling her of the address at which might be found both Trevelyan and his son. As Bozzle had acknowledged, facts are things which may be found out. Hugh had gone to work somewhat after the Bozzlian fashion, and had found out this fact. 'He lives at a place called River's Cottage, at Willesden,' wrote Stanbury. 'If you turn off the Harrow Road to the right, about a mile beyond the cemetery, you will find the cottage on the left hand side of the lane, about a quarter of a mile from the Harrow Road. I believe you can go to Willesden by railway but you had better take a cab from London.' There was much consultation respecting this letter between Lady Rowley and Mrs Trevelyan, and it was decided that it should not be shown to Sir Marmaduke. To see her child was at the present moment the most urgent necessity of the poor mother, and both the ladies felt that Sir Marmaduke in his wrath might probably impede rather than assist her in this desire. If told where he might find Trevelyan, he would probably insist on starting in quest of his son-in-law himself, and the distance between the mother and her child might become greater in consequence, instead of less. There were many consultations; and the upshot of these was, that Lady Rowley and her daughter determined to start for Willesden without saying anything to Sir Marmaduke of the purpose they had in hand. When Emily expressed her conviction that if Trevelyan should be away from home they would probably be able to make their way into the house so as to see the child, Lady Rowley with some hesitation acknowledged that such might be the case. But the child's mother said nothing to her own mother of a scheme which she had half formed of so clinging to her boy that no human power should separate them.

They started in a cab, as advised by Stanbury, and were driven to a point on the road from which a lane led down to Willesden, passing by River's Cottage. They asked as they came along, and met no difficulty in finding their way. At the point on the road indicated, there was a country inn for hay-waggoners, and here Lady Rowley proposed that they should leave their cab, urging that it might be best to call at the cottage in the quietest manner possible; but Mrs Trevelyan, with her scheme in her head for the recapture of their child, begged that the cab might go on and thus they were driven up to the door.

River's Cottage was not a prepossessing abode. It was a new building, of light-coloured bricks, with a door in the middle and one window on each side. Over the door was a stone tablet, bearing the name River's Cottage. There was a little garden between the road and the house, across which there was a straight path to the door. In front of one window was a small shrub, generally called a puzzle-monkey, and in front of the other was a variegated laurel. There were two small morsels of green turf, and a distant view round the corner of the house of a row of cabbage stumps. If Trevelyan were living there, he had certainly come down in the world since the days in which he had occupied the house in Curzon Street. The two ladies got out of the cab, and slowly walked across the little garden. Mrs Trevelyan was dressed in black, and she wore a thick veil.

She had altogether been unable to make up her mind as to what should be her conduct to her husband should she see him. That must be governed by circumstances as they might occur. Her visit was made not to him, but to her boy.

The door was opened before they knocked, and Trevelyan himself was standing in the narrow passage.

Lady Rowley was the first to speak. 'Louis,' she said, 'I have brought your wife to see you.'

'Who told you that I was here?' he asked, still standing in the passage.

'Of course a mother would find out where was her child,' said Lady Rowley.

'You should not have come here without notice,' he said. 'I was careful to let you know the conditions on which you should come.'

'You do not mean that I shall not see my child,' said the mother. 'Oh, Louis, you will let me see him.'

Trevelyan hesitated a moment, still keeping his position firmly in the doorway. By this time an old woman, decently dressed and of comfortable appearance, had taken her place behind him, and behind her was a slip of a girl about fifteen years of age. This was the owner of River's Cottage and her daughter, and all the inhabitants of the cottage were now there, standing in the passage. 'I ought not to let you see him,' said Trevelyan; 'you have intruded upon me in coming here! I had not wished to see you here till you had complied with the order I had given you.' What a meeting between a husband and a wife who had not seen each other now for many months, between a husband and a wife who were still young enough not to have outlived the first impulses of their early love! He still stood there guarding the way, and had not even put out his hand to greet her. He was guarding the way lest she should, without his permission, obtain access to her own child! She had not removed her veil, and now she hardly dared to step over the threshold of her husband's house. At this moment, she perceived that the woman behind was pointing to the room on the left, as the cottage was entered, and Emily at once understood that her boy was there. Then at that moment she heard her son's voice, as, in his solitude, the child began to cry. 'I must go in,' she said; 'I will go in;' and rushing on she tried to push aside her husband. Her mother aided her, nor did Trevelyan attempt to stop her with violence, and in a moment she was kneeling at the foot of a small sofa, with her child in her arms. 'I had not intended to hinder you,' said Trevelyan, 'but I require from you a promise that you will not attempt to remove him.'

'Why should she not take him home with her?' said Lady Rowley.

'Because I will not have it so,' replied Trevelyan. 'Because I choose that it should be understood that I am to be the master of my own affairs.'

Mrs Trevelyan had now thrown aside her bonnet and her veil, and was covering her child with caresses. The poor little fellow, whose mind had been utterly dismayed by the events which had occurred to him since his capture, though he returned her kisses, did so in fear and trembling. And he was still sobbing, rubbing his eyes with his knuckles, and by no means yielding himself with his whole heart to his mother's tenderness as she would have had him do. 'Louey,' she said, whispering to him, 'you know mamma; you haven't forgotten mamma?' He half murmured some little infantine word through his sobs, and then put his cheek up to be pressed against his mother's face. 'Louey will never, never forget his own mamma will he, Louey?' The poor boy had no assurances to give, and could only raise his cheek again to be kissed. In the meantime Lady Rowley and Trevelyan were standing by, not speaking to each other, regarding the scene in silence.

She, Lady Rowley, could see that he was frightfully altered in appearance, even since the day on which she had so lately met him in the City. His cheeks were thin and haggard, and his eyes were deep and very bright, and he moved them quickly from side to side, as though ever suspecting something. He seemed to be smaller in stature, withered, as it were, as though he had melted away. And, though he stood looking upon his wife and child, he was not for a moment still. He would change the posture of his hands and arms, moving them quickly with little surreptitious jerks; and would shuffle his feet upon the floor, almost without altering his position. His clothes hung about him, and his linen was soiled and worn. Lady Rowley noticed this especially, as he had been a man peculiarly given to neatness of apparel. He was the first to speak. 'You have come down here in a cab?' said he.

'Yes, in a cab, from London,' said Lady Rowley.

'Of course you will go back in it? You cannot stay here. There is no accommodation. It is a wretched place, but it suits the boy. As for me, all places are now alike.'

'Louis,' said his wife, springing up from her knees, coming to him, and taking his right hand between both her own, 'you will let me take him with me. I know you will let me take him with me.'

'I cannot do that, Emily; it would be wrong.'

'Wrong to restore a child to his mother? Oh, Louis, think of it, What must my life be without him or you?'

'Don't talk of me. It is too late for that.'

'Not if you will be reasonable, Louis, and listen to me. Oh, heavens, how ill you are!' As she said this she drew nearer to him, so that her face was almost close to his. 'Louis, come back; come back, and let it all be forgotten. It shall be a dream, a horrid dream, and nobody shall speak of it.' He left his hand within hers and stood looking into her face. He was well aware that his life since he had left her had been one long hour of misery. There had been to him no alleviation, no comfort, no consolation. He had not a friend left to him. Even his satellite, the policeman, was becoming weary of him and manifestly suspicious. The woman with whom he was now lodging, and whose resources were infinitely benefited by his payments to her, had already thrown out hints that she was afraid of him. And as he looked at his wife, he knew that he loved her. Everything for him now was hot and dry and poor and bitter. How sweet would it be again to sit with her soft hand in his, to feel her cool brow against his own, to have the comfort of her care, and to hear the music of loving words! The companionship of his wife had once been to him everything in the world; but now, for many months past, he had known no companion. She bade him come to her, and look upon all this trouble as a dream not to be mentioned. Could it be possible that it should be so, and that they might yet be happy together, perhaps in some distant country, where the story of all their misery might not be known? He felt all this truly and with a keen accuracy. If he were mad, he was not all mad. 'I will tell you of nothing that is past,' said she, hanging to him, and coming still nearer to him, and embracing his arm.

Could she have condescended to ask him not to tell her of the past, had it occurred to her so to word her request, she might perhaps have prevailed. But who can say how long the tenderness of his heart would have saved him from further outbreak and whether such prevailing on her part would have been of permanent service? As it was, her words wounded him in that spot of his inner self which was most sensitive, on that spot from whence had come all his fury. A black cloud came upon his brow, and he made an effort to withdraw himself from her grasp. It was necessary to him that she should in some fashion own that he had been right, and now she was promising him that she would not tell him of his fault! He could not thus swallow down all the convictions by which he had fortified himself to bear the misfortunes which he had endured. Had he not quarrelled with every friend he possessed on this score; and should he now stultify himself in all those quarrels by admitting that he had been cruel, unjust, and needlessly jealous? And did not truth demand of him that he should cling to his old assurances? Had she not been disobedient, ill-conditioned, and rebellious? Had she not received the man, both him personally and his letters, after he had explained to her that his honour demanded that it should not be so? How could he come into such terms as those now proposed to him, simply because he longed to enjoy the rich sweetness of her soft hand, to feel the fragrance of her breath, and to quench the heat of his forehead in the cool atmosphere of her beauty? 'Why have you driven me to this by your intercourse with that man?' he said. 'Why, why, why did you do it?'

She was still clinging to him. 'Louis,' she said, 'I am your wife.'

'Yes; you are my wife.'

'And will you still believe such evil of me without any cause?'

'There has been cause horrible cause. You must repent, repent, repent.'

'Heaven help me,' said the woman, falling back from him, and returning to the boy who was now seated in Lady Rowley's lap. 'Mamma, do you speak to him. What can I say? Would he think better of me were I to own myself to have been guilty, when there has been no guilt, no slightest fault? Does he wish me to purchase my child by saying that I am not fit to be his mother?'

'Louis,' said Lady Rowley, 'if any man was ever wrong, mad, madly mistaken, you are so now.'

'Have you come out here to accuse me again, as you did, before in London?' he asked. 'Is that the way in which you and she intend to let the past be, as she says, like a dream? She tells me that I am ill. It is true. I am ill and she is killing me, killing me, by her obstinacy.'

'What would you have me do?' said the wife, again rising from her child.

'Acknowledge your transgressions, and say that you will amend your conduct for the future.'

'Mamma, mamma, what shall I say to him?'

'Who can speak to a man that is beside himself?' replied Lady Rowley.

'I am not so beside myself as yet, Lady Rowley, but that I know how to guard my own honour and to protect my own child. I have told you, Emily, the terms on which you can come back to me. You had better now return to your mother's house; and if you wish again to have a house of your own, and your husband, and your boy, you know by what means you may acquire them. For another week I shall remain here; after that I shall remove far from hence.'

'And where will you go, Louis?'

'As yet I know not. To Italy, I think, or perhaps to America. It matters little where for me.'

'And will Louey be taken with you?'

'Certainly he will go with me. To strive to bring him up so that he may be a happier man than his father is all that there is now left for me in life.' Mrs Trevelyan had now got the boy in her arms, and her mother was seated by her on the sofa. Trevelyan was standing away from them, but so near the door that no sudden motion on their part would enable them to escape with the boy without his interposition. It now again occurred to the mother to carry off her prize in opposition to her husband, but she had no scheme to that effect laid with her mother, and she could not reconcile herself to the idea of a contest with him in which personal violence would be necessary. The woman of the house had, indeed, seemed to sympathise with her, but she could not dare in such a matter to trust to assistance from a stranger. 'I do not wish to be uncourteous,' said Trevelyan, 'but if you have no assurance to give me, you had better leave me.'

Then there came to be a bargaining about time, and the poor woman begged almost on her knees that she might be allowed to take her child upstairs and be with him alone for a few minutes. It seemed to her that she had not seen her boy till she had had him to herself, in absolute privacy, till she had kissed his limbs, and had her hand upon his smooth back, and seen that he was white and clean and bright as he had ever been. And the bargain was made. She was asked to pledge her word that she would not take him out of the house, and she pledged her word, feeling that there was no strength in her for that action which she had meditated. He, knowing that he might still guard the passage at the bottom of the stairs, allowed her to go with the boy to his bedroom, while he remained below with Lady Rowley. A quarter of an hour was allowed to her, and she humbly promised that she would return when that time was expired.

Trevelyan held the door open for her as she went, and kept it open during her absence. There was hardly a word said between him and Lady Rowley, but he paced from the passage into the room and from the room into the passage with his hands behind his back. 'It is cruel,' he said once. 'It is very cruel.'

'It is you that are cruel,' said Lady Rowley.

'Of course, of course. That is natural from you. I expect that from you.' To this she made no answer, and he did not open his lips again.

After a while Mrs Trevelyan called to her mother, and Lady Rowley was allowed to go upstairs. The quarter of an hour was of course greatly stretched, and all the time Trevelyan continued to pace in and out of the room. He was patient, for he did not summon them; but went on pacing backwards and forwards, looking now and again to see that the cab was at its place, that no deceit was being attempted, no second act of kidnapping being perpetrated. At last the two ladies came down the stairs, and the boy was with them and the woman of the house.

'Louis,' said the wife, going quickly up to her husband, 'I will do anything, if you will give me my child.'

'What will you do?'

'Anything; say what you want. He is all the world to me, and I cannot live if he be taken from me.'

'Acknowledge that you have been wrong.'

'But how, in what words, how am I to speak it?'

'Say that you have sinned and that you will sin no more.'

'Sinned, Louis, as the woman did in the Scripture?

'He cannot think that it is so,' said Lady Rowley.

But Trevelyan had not understood her. 'Lady Rowley, I should have fancied that my thoughts at any rate were my own. But this is useless now. The child cannot go with you to-day, nor can you remain here. Go home and think of what I have said. If then you will do as I would have you, you shall return.'

With many embraces, with promises of motherly love, and with prayers for love in return, the poor woman did at last leave the house, and return to the cab. As she went there was a doubt on her own mind whether she should ask to kiss her husband; but he made no sign, and she at last passed out without any mark of tenderness. He stood by the cab as they entered it, and closed the door upon them, and then went slowly back to his room. 'My poor bairn,' he said to the boy; 'my poor bairn.'

'Why for mamma go?' sobbed the child.

'Mamma goes; oh, heaven and earth, why should she go? She goes because her spirit is obstinate, and she will not bend. She is stiff-necked, and will not submit herself. But Louey must love mamma always, and mamma some day will come back to him, and be good to him.'

'Mamma is good always,' said the child. Trevelyan had intended on this very afternoon to have gone up to town to transact business with Bozzle; for he still believed, though the aspect of the man was bitter to him as wormwood, that Bozzle was necessary to him in all his business. And he still made appointments with the man, sometimes at Stony Walk, in the Borough, and sometimes at the tavern in Poulter's Court, even though Bozzle not unfrequently neglected to attend the summons of his employer. And he would go to his banker's and draw out money, and then walk about the crowded lanes of the City, and afterwards return to his desolate lodgings at Willesden, thinking that he had been transacting business and that this business was exacted from him by the unfortunate position of his affairs. But now he gave up his journey. His retreat had been discovered; and there came upon him at once a fear that if he left the house his child would be taken. His landlady told him on this very day that the boy ought to be sent to his mother, and had made him understand that it would not suit her to find a home any longer for one who was so singular in his proceedings. He believed that his child would be given up at once, if he were not there to guard it. He stayed at home, therefore, turning in his mind many schemes. He had told his wife that he should go either to Italy or to America at once; but in doing so he had had no formed plan in his head. He had simply imagined at the moment that such a threat would bring her to submission. But now it became a question whether he would do better than go to America. He suggested to himself that he should go to Canada, and fix himself with his boy on some remote farm, far away from any city; and would then invite his wife to join him if she would. She was too obstinate, as he told himself, ever to yield, unless she should be absolutely softened and brought down to the ground by the loss of her child. What would do this so effectually as the interposition of the broad ocean between him and her? He sat thinking of this for the rest of the day, and Louey was left to the charge of the mistress of River's Cottage.

'Do you think he believes it, mamma?' Mrs Trevelyan said to her mother when they had already made nearly half their journey home in the cab. There had been nothing spoken hitherto between them, except some half-formed words of affection intended for consolation to the young mother in her great affliction.

'He does not know what he believes, dearest.'

'You heard what he said. I was to own that I had sinned.'

'Sinned yes; because you will not obey him like a slave. That is sin to him.'

'But I asked him, mamma. Did you not hear me? I could not say the word plainer but I asked him whether he meant that sin. He must have known, and he would not answer me. And he spoke of my transgression. Mamma, if he believed that, he would not let me come back at all.'

'He did not believe it, Emily.'

'Could he possibly then so accuse me, the mother of his child! If his heart be utterly hard and false towards me, if it is possible that he should be cruel to me with such cruelty as that, still he must love his boy. Why did he not answer me, and say that he did not think it?'

'Simply because his reason has left him.'

'But if he be mad, mamma, ought we to leave him like that? And, then, did you see his eyes, and his face, and his hands? Did you observe how thin he is and his back, how bent? And his clothes, how they were torn and soiled. It cannot be right that he should be left like that.'

'We will tell papa when we get home,' said Lady Rowley, who was herself beginning to be somewhat frightened by what she had seen. It is all very well to declare that a friend is mad when one simply desires to justify one's self in opposition to that friend, but the matter becomes much more serious when evidence of the friend's insanity becomes true and circumstantial. 'I certainly think that a physician should see him,' continued Lady Rowley. On their return home Sir Marmaduke was told of what had occurred, and there was a long family discussion in which it was decided that Lady Milborough should be consulted, as being the oldest friend of Louis Trevelyan himself with whom they were acquainted. Trevelyan had relatives of his own name living in Cornwall; but Mrs Trevelyan herself had never even met one of that branch of the family.

Sir Marmaduke, however, resolved that he himself would go out to see his son-in-law. He too had called Trevelyan mad, but he did not believe that the madness was of such a nature as to interfere with his own duties in punishing the man who had ill used his daughter. He would at any rate see Trevelyan himself; but of this he said nothing either to his wife or to his child.

CHAPTER LXVIII. MAJOR MAGRUDER'S COMMITTEE

Sir Marmaduke could not go out to Willesden on the morning after Lady Rowley's return from River's Cottage, because on that day he was summoned to attend at twelve o'clock before a Committee of the House of Commons, to give his evidence and, the fruit of his experience as to the government of British colonies generally; and as he went down to the House in a cab from Manchester Street he thoroughly wished that his friend Colonel Osborne had not been so efficacious in bringing him home. The task before him was one which he thoroughly disliked, and of which he was afraid. He dreaded the inquisitors before whom he was to appear, and felt that though he was called there to speak as a master of his art of governing, he would in truth be examined as a servant, and probably as a servant who did not know his business. Had his sojourn at home been in other respects happy, he might have been able to balance the advantage against the inquiry, but there was no such balancing for him now. And, moreover, the expense of his own house in Manchester Street was so large that this journey, in a pecuniary point of view, would be of but little service to him. So he went down to the House in an unhappy mood; and when he shook hands in one of the passages with his friend Osborne who was on the Committee, there was very little cordiality in his manner. 'This is the most ungrateful thing I ever knew,' said the Colonel to himself; 'I have almost disgraced myself by having this fellow brought home; and now he quarrels with me because that idiot, his son-in-law, has quarrelled with his wife.' And Colonel Osborne really did feel that he was a martyr to the ingratitude of his friend.

The Committee had been convoked by the House in compliance with the eager desires of a certain ancient pundit of the constitution, who had been for many years a member, and who had been known as a stern critic of our colonial modes of government. To him it certainly seemed that everything that was, was bad as regarded our national dependencies. But this is so usually the state of mind of all parliamentary critics, it is so much a matter of course that the members who take up the army or the navy, guns, India, our relations with Spain, or workhouse management, should find everything to be bad, rotten, and dishonest, that the wrath of the member for Killicrankie against colonial peculation and idleness, was not thought much of in the open House. He had been at the work for years, and the Colonial Office were so used to it that they rather liked him. He had made himself free of the office, and the clerks were always glad to see him. It was understood that he said bitter things in the House—that was Major Magruder's line of business;

but he could be quite pleasant when he was asking questions of a private secretary, or telling the news of the day to a senior clerk. As he was now between seventy and eighty, and had been at the work for at least twenty years, most of those concerned had allowed themselves to think that he would ride his hobby harmlessly to the day of his parliamentary death. But the drop from a house corner will hollow a stone by its constancy, and Major Magruder at last persuaded the House to grant him a Committee of Inquiry. Then there came to be serious faces at the Colonial Office, and all the little pleasantries of a friendly opposition were at an end. It was felt that the battle must now become a real fight, and Secretary and Under-Secretary girded up their loins.

Major Magruder was chairman of his own committee, and being a man of a laborious turn of mind, much given to blue-books, very patient, thoroughly conversant with the House, and imbued with a strong belief in the efficacy of parliamentary questionings to carry a point, if not to elicit a fact, had a happy time of it during this session. He was a man who always attended the House from 4 p.m. to the time of its breaking up, and who never missed a division. The slight additional task of sitting four hours in a committee-room three days a week, was only a delight, the more especially as during those four hours he could occupy the post of Chairman. Those who knew Major Magruder well did not doubt but that the Committee would sit for many weeks, and that the whole theory of colonial government, or rather of imperial control supervising such government, would be tested to the very utmost. Men who had heard the old Major maunder on for years past on his pet subject, hardly knew how much vitality would be found in him when his maundering had succeeded in giving him a committee.

A Governor from one of the greater colonies had already been under question for nearly a week, and was generally thought to have come out of the fire unscathed by the flames of the Major's criticism. This Governor had been a picked man, and he had made it appear that the control of Downing Street was never more harsh and seldom less refreshing and beautifying than a spring shower in April. No other lands under the sun were so blest, in the way of government, as were the colonies with which he had been acquainted; and, as a natural consequence, their devotion and loyalty to the mother country were quite a passion with them. Now the Major had been long of a mind that one or two colonies had better simply be given up to other nations, which were more fully able to look after them than was England, and that three or four more should be allowed to go clear, costing England nothing, and owing England nothing. But the well-chosen Governor who had now been before the Committee, had rather staggered the Major, and things altogether were supposed to be looking up for the Colonial Office.

And now had come the day of Sir Marmaduke's martyrdom. He was first requested, with most urbane politeness, to explain the exact nature of the government which he exercised in the Mandarins. Now it certainly was the case that the manner in which the legislative and executive authorities were intermingled in the affairs of these islands, did create a complication which it was difficult for any man to understand, and very difficult indeed for a man to explain to others. There was a Court of Chancery, so called, which Sir Marmaduke described as a little parliament. When he was asked whether the court exercised legislative or executive functions, he said at first that it exercised both, and then that it exercised neither. He knew that it consisted of nine men, of whom five were appointed by the colony and four by the Crown. Yet he declared that the Crown had the control of the court, which, in fact, was true enough no doubt, as the five open members were not perhaps, all of them, immaculate patriots; but on this matter poor Sir Marmaduke was very obscure. When asked who exercised the patronage of the Crown in nominating the four members, he declared that the four members exercised it themselves. Did he appoint them? No he never appointed anybody himself. He consulted the Court of Chancery for everything. At last it came out that the chief justice of the islands, and three other officers, always sat in the court, but whether it was required by the constitution of the islands that this should be so, Sir Marmaduke did not know. It had worked well; that is to say, everybody had complained of it, but he, Sir Marmaduke, would not recommend any change. What he thought best was that the Colonial Secretary should send out his orders, and that the people in the colonies should mind their business and grow coffee. When asked what would be the effect upon the islands, under his scheme of government, if an incoming Colonial Secretary should change the policy of his predecessor, he said that he didn't think it would matter much if the people did not know anything about it.

In this way the Major had a field day, and poor Sir Marmaduke was much discomfited. There was present on the Committee a young Parliamentary Under-Secretary, who with much attention had studied the subject of the Court of Chancery in the Mandarins, and who had acknowledged to his superiors in the office that it certainly was of all legislative assemblies the most awkward and complicated. He did what he could, by questions judiciously put, to pull Sir Marmaduke through his difficulties; but the unfortunate Governor had more than once lost his temper in answering the chairman; and in his heavy confusion was past the power of any Under-Secretary, let him be ever so clever, to pull him through. Colonel Osborne sat by the while and asked no questions. He had been put on the Committee as a respectable dummy; but there was not a member sitting there who did not know that Sir Marmaduke had been brought home as his friend; and some of them, no doubt, had whispered that this bringing home of Sir Marmaduke was part of the payment made by the Colonel for the smiles of the Governor's daughter. But no one alluded openly to the inefficiency of the evidence given. No one asked why a Governor so incompetent had been sent to them. No one suggested that a job had been done. There are certain things of which opposition members of Parliament complain loudly, and there are certain other things as to which they are silent. The line between these things is well known; and should an ill-conditioned, a pig-headed, an underbred, or an ignorant member not understand this line and transgress it, by asking questions which should not be asked, he is soon put down from the Treasury bench, to the great delight of the whole House.

Sir Marmaduke, after having been questioned for an entire afternoon, left the House with extreme disgust. He was so convinced of his own failure, that he felt that his career as a Colonial Governor must be over. Surely they would never let him go back to his islands after such an exposition as he had made of his own ignorance. He hurried off into a cab, and was ashamed to be seen of men. But the members of the Committee thought little or nothing about it. The Major, and those who sided with him, had been anxious to entrap their witness into contradictions and absurdities, for the furtherance of their own object; and for the furtherance of theirs, the Under-Secretary from the Office and the supporters of Government had endeavoured to defend their man. But, when the affair was over, if no special admiration had been elicited for Sir Marmaduke, neither was there expressed any special reprobation. The Major carried on his Committee over six weeks, and succeeded in having his blue-book printed; but, as a matter of course, nothing further came of it; and the Court of Chancery in the Mandarin Islands still continues to hold its own, and to do its work, in spite of the absurdities displayed in its construction. Major Magruder has had his day of success, and now feels that Othello's occupation is gone. He goes no more to the Colonial Office, lives among his friends on the memories of his Committee, not always to their gratification, and is beginning to think that as his work is done, he may as well resign Killicrankie to some younger politician. Poor Sir Marmaduke remembered his defeat with soreness long after it had been forgotten by all others who had been present, and was astonished when he found that the journals of the day, though they did in some curt fashion report the proceedings of the Committee, never uttered a word of censure against him, as they had not before uttered a word of praise for that pearl of a Governor who had been examined before him.

On the following morning he went to the Colonial Office by appointment, and then he saw the young Irish Under-Secretary whom he had so much dreaded. Nothing could be more civil than was the young Irish Under-Secretary, who told him that he had better of course stay in town till the Committee was over, though it was not probable that he would be wanted again. When the Committee had done its work he would be allowed to remain six weeks on service to prepare for his journey back. If he wanted more time after that he could ask for leave of absence. So Sir

Marmaduke left the Colonial Office with a great weight off his mind, and blessed that young Irish Secretary as he went.

CHAPTER LXIX SIR MARMADUKE AT WILLESDEN

On the next day Sir Marmaduke purposed going to Willesden. He was in great doubt whether or no he would first consult that very eminent man Dr Trite Turbury, as to the possibility, and if possible as to the expediency, of placing Mr Trevelyan under some control. But Sir Marmaduke, though he would repeatedly declare that his son-in-law was mad, did not really believe in this madness. He did not, that is, believe that Trevelyan was so mad as to be fairly exempt from the penalties of responsibility; and he was therefore desirous of speaking his own mind out fully to the man, and, as it were, of having his own personal revenge, before he might be deterred by the interposition of medical advice. He resolved therefore that he would not see Sir Trite Turbury, at any rate till he had come back from Willesden. He also went down in a cab, but he left the cab at the public-house at the corner of the road, and walked to the cottage.

When he asked whether Mr Trevelyan was at home, the woman of the house hesitated and then said that her lodger was out. 'I particularly wish to see him,' said Sir Marmaduke, feeling that the woman was lying to him. 'But he ain't to be seen, sir,' said the woman. 'I know he is at home,' said Sir Marmaduke. But the argument was soon cut short by the appearance of Trevelyan behind the woman's shoulder.

'I am here, Sir Marmaduke Rowley,' said Trevelyan. 'If you wish to see me you may come in. I will not say that you are welcome, but you can come in.' Then the woman retired, and Sir Marmaduke followed Trevelyan into the room in which Lady Rowley and Emily had been received; but the child was not now in the chamber.

'What are these charges that I hear against my daughter?' said Sir Marmaduke, rushing at once into the midst of his indignation.

'I do not know what charges you have heard.'

'You have put her away.'

'In strict accuracy that is not correct, Sir Marmaduke.'

'But she is put away. She is in my house now because you have no house of your own for her. Is not that so? And when I came home she was staying with her uncle, because you had put her away. And what was the meaning of her being sent down into Devonshire? What has she done? I am her father, and I expect to have an answer.'

'You shall have an answer, certainly.'

'And a true one. I will have no hocus-pocus, no humbug, no Jesuitry.'

'Have you come here to insult me, Sir Marmaduke? Because, if so, there shall be an end to this interview at once.'

'There shall not be an end—by G—, no, not till I have heard what is the meaning of all this. Do you know what people are saying of you: that you are mad, and that you must be locked up, and your child taken away from you, and your property?'

'Who are the people that say so? Yourself and, perhaps, Lady Rowley? Does my wife say so? Does she think that I am mad? She did not think so on Thursday, when she prayed that she might be allowed to come back and live with me.'

'And you would not let her come?'

'Pardon me,' said Trevelyan. 'I would wish that she should, come but it must be on certain conditions.'

'What I want to know is why she was turned out of your house?'

'She was not turned out.'

'What has she done that she should be punished?' urged Sir Marmaduke, who was unable to arrange his questions with the happiness which had distinguished Major Magruder. 'I insist upon knowing what it is that you lay to her charge. I am her father, and I have a right to know. She has been barbarously, shamefully ill-used, and by G— I will know.'

'You have come here to bully me, Sir Marmaduke Rowley.'

'I have come here, sir, to do the duty of a parent to his child; to protect my poor girl against the cruelty of a husband who in an unfortunate hour was allowed to take her from her home. I will know the reason why my daughter has been treated as though—as though—as though—'

'Listen to me for a minute,' said Trevelyan.

'I am listening.'

'I will tell you nothing; I will answer you not a word.'

'You will not answer me?'

'Not when you come to me in this fashion. My wife is my wife, and my claim to her is nearer and closer than is yours, who are her father. She is the mother of my child, and the only being in the world except that child whom I love. Do you think that with such motives on my part for tenderness towards her, for loving care, for the most anxious solicitude, that I can be made more anxious, more tender, more loving by coarse epithets from you? I am the most miserable being under the sun because our happiness has been interrupted, and is it likely that such misery should be cured by violent words and gestures? If your heart is wrung for her, so is mine. If she be much to you, she is more to me. She came here the other day, almost as a stranger, and I thought that my heart would have burst beneath its weight of woe. What can you do that can add an ounce to the burden that I bear? You may as well leave me or at least be quiet.'

Sir Marmaduke had stood and listened to him, and he, too, was so struck by the altered appearance of the man that the violence of his indignation was lessened by the pity which he could not suppress. When Trevelyan spoke of his wretchedness, it was impossible not to believe him. He was as wretched a being to look at as it might have been possible to find. His contracted cheeks, and lips always open, and eyes glowing in their sunken caverns, told a tale which even Sir Marmaduke, who was not of nature quick in deciphering such stories, could not fail to read. And then the twitching action of the man's hands, and the restless shuffling of his feet, produced a nervous feeling that if some remedy were not applied quickly, some alleviation given to the misery of the suffering wretch, human power would be strained too far, and the man would break to pieces or else the mind of the man. Sir Marmaduke, during his journey in the cab, had resolved that, old as he was, he would, take this sinner by the throat, this brute who had striven to stain his daughter's name—and would make him there and then acknowledge his own brutality. But it was now very manifest to Sir Marmaduke that there could be no taking by the throat in this case. He could not have brought himself to touch the poor, weak, passionate creature before him. Indeed, even the fury of his words was stayed, and after that last appeal he stormed no more. 'But what is to be the end of it?' he said.

'Who can tell? Who can say? She can tell. She can put an end to it all. She has but to say a word, and I will devote my life to her. But that word must be spoken.' As he said this, he dashed his hand upon the table, and looked up with an air that would have been comic with its assumed magnificence had it not been for the true tragedy of the occasion.

'You had better, at any rate, let her have her child for the present.'

'No, my boy shall go with me. She may go, too, if she pleases, but my boy shall certainly go with me. If I had put her from me, as you said just now, it might have been otherwise. But she shall be as welcome to me as flowers in May, as flowers in May! She shall be as welcome to me as the music of heaven.'

Sir Marmaduke felt that he had nothing more to urge. He had altogether abandoned that idea of having his revenge at the cost of the man's throat, and was quite convinced that reason could have no power with him. He was already thinking that he would go away, straight to his lawyer, so that some step might be taken at once to stop, if possible, the taking away of the boy to America, when the lock of the door was gently turned, and the landlady entered the room.

'You will excuse me, sir,' said the woman, 'but if you be anything to this gentleman—'

'Mrs Fuller, leave the room,' said Trevelyan. 'I and the gentleman are engaged.'

'I see you be engaged, and I do beg pardon. I ain't one as would intrude wilful, and, as for listening, or the likes of that, I scorn it. But if this gentleman be anything to you, Mr Trevelyan—'

'I am his wife's father,' said Sir Marmaduke.

'Like enough. I was thinking perhaps so. His lady was down here on Thursday, as sweet a lady as any gentleman need wish to stretch by his side.'

'Mrs Fuller,' said Trevelyan, marching up towards her, 'I will not have this, and I desire that you will retire from my room.'

But Mrs Fuller escaped round the table, and would not be banished. She got round the table, and came closely opposite to Sir Marmaduke. 'I don't want to say nothing out of my place, sir,' said she, 'but something ought to be done. He ain't fit to be left to hisself, not alone, not as he is at present. He ain't, indeed, and I wouldn't be doing my duty if I didn't say so. He has them sweats at night as'd be enough to kill any man; and he eats nothing, and he don't do nothing; and as for that poor little boy as is now in my own bed upstairs, if it wasn't that I and my Bessy is fond of children, I don't know what would become of that boy.'

Trevelyan, finding it impossible to get rid of her, had stood quietly, while he listened to her.'she has been good to my child,' he said. 'I acknowledge it. As for myself, I have not been well. It is true. But I am told that travel will set me on my feet again. Change of air will do it.' Not long since he had been urging the wretchedness of his own bodily health as a reason why his wife should yield to him; but now, when his sickness was brought as a charge against him, was adduced as a reason why his friends should interfere, and look after him and concern themselves in his affairs, he saw at once that it was necessary that he should make little of his ailments.

'Would it not be best, Trevelyan, that you should come with me to a doctor?' said Sir Marmaduke.

'No no. I have my own doctor. That is, know the course which I should follow. This place, though it is good for the boy, has disagreed with me, and my life has not been altogether pleasant—I may say, by no means pleasant. Troubles have told upon me, but change of air will mend it all.'

'I wish you would come with me, at once, to London. You shall come back, you know. I will not detain you.'

'Thank you no. I will not trouble you'. That will do, Mrs Fuller. You have intended to do your duty, no doubt, and now you can go.' Whereupon Mrs Fuller did go. 'I am obliged for your care, Sir Marmaduke, but I can really do very well without troubling you.'

'You cannot suppose, Trevelyan, that we can allow things to go on like this.'

'And what do you mean to do?'

'Well I shall take advice. I shall go to a lawyer and to a doctor, and perhaps to the Lord Chancellor, and all that kind of thing. We can't let things go on like this.'

'You can do as you please,' said Trevelyan, 'but as you have threatened me, I must ask you to leave me.'

Sir Marmaduke could do no more, and could say no more, and he took his leave, shaking hands with the man, and speaking to him with a courtesy which astonished himself. It was impossible to maintain the strength of his indignation against a poor creature who was so manifestly unable to guide himself. But when he was in London he drove at once to the house of Dr Trite Turbury, and remained there till the doctor returned from his round of visits. According to the great authority, there was much still to be done before even the child could be rescued out of the father's hands. 'I can't act without the lawyers,' said Dr Turbury. But he explained to Sir Marmaduke what steps should be taken in such a matter.

Trevelyan, in the mean time, clearly understanding that hostile measures would now be taken against him, set his mind to work to think how best he might escape at once to America with his boy.

CHAPTER LXX. SHEWING WHAT NORA ROWLEY THOUGHT ABOUT CARRIAGES

Sir Marmaduke, on his return home from Dr Turbury's house, found that he had other domestic troubles on hand over and above those arising from his elder daughter's position. Mr Hugh Stanbury had been in Manchester Street during his absence, and had asked for him, and, finding that he was away from home, had told his story to Lady Rowley. When he had been shown upstairs all the four daughters had been with their mother; but he had said a word or two signifying his desire to speak to Lady Rowley, and the three girls had left the room. In this way it came to pass that he had to plead his cause before Nora's mother and her elder sister. He had pleaded it well, and Lady Rowley's heart had been well disposed towards him; but when she asked of his house and his home, his answer had been hardy more satisfactory than that of Alan-a-Dale. There was little that he could call his own beyond 'The blue vault of heaven.' Had he saved any money? No, not a shilling—that was to say, as he himself expressed it, nothing that could be called money. He had a few pounds by him, just to go on with. What was his income? Well last year he had made four hundred pounds, and this year he hoped to make something more. He thought he could see his way plainly to five hundred a year. Was it permanent; and if not, on what did it depend? He believed it to be as permanent as most other professional incomes, but was obliged to confess that, as regarded the source from whence it was drawn at the present moment, it might be brought to an abrupt end any day by a disagreement between himself and the editor of the *D. R.* Did he think that this was fixed income? He did think that if he and the editor of the *D. R.* were to fall out, he could come across other editors who would gladly employ him. Would he himself feel safe in giving his own sister to a man with such an income? In answer to this question, he started some rather bold doctrines on the subject of matrimony in general, asserting that safety was not desirable, that energy, patience, and mutual confidence would be increased by the excitement of risk, and that in his opinion it behoved young men and young women to come together and get themselves married, even though there might be some not remote danger of distress before them. He admitted that starvation would be disagreeable, especially for children, in the eyes of their parents, but alleged that children as a rule were not starved, and quoted the Scripture to prove that honest laborious men were not to be seen begging their bread in the streets. He was very eloquent, but his eloquence itself was against him. Both Lady Rowley and Mrs

Trevelyan were afraid of such advanced opinions; and, although everything was of course to be left, nominally, to the decision of Sir Marmaduke, they both declared that they could not recommend Sir Marmaduke to consent. Lady Rowley said a word as to the expediency of taking Nora back with her to the Mandarins, pointing out what appeared to her then to be the necessity of taking Mrs Trevelyan with them also; and in saying this she hinted that if Nora were disposed to stand by her engagement, and Mr Stanbury equally so disposed, there might be some possibility of a marriage at a future period. Only, in such case, there must be no correspondence. In answer to this Hugh declared that he regarded such a scheme as being altogether bad. The Mandarins were so very far distant that he might as well be engaged to an angel in heaven. Nora, if she were to go away now, would perhaps never come back again; and if she did come back, would be an old woman, with hollow cheeks. In replying to this proposition, he let fall an opinion that Nora was old enough to judge for herself. He said nothing about her actual age, and did not venture to plead that the young lady had a legal right to do as she liked with herself; but he made it manifest that such an idea was in his mind. In answer to this, Lady Rowley asserted that Nora was a good girl, and would do as her father told her; but she did not venture to assert that Nora would give up her engagement. Lady Rowley at last undertook to speak to Sir Rowley, and to speak also to her daughter. Hugh was asked for his address, and gave that of the office of the *D. R.* He was always to be found there between three and five; and after that, four times a week, in the reporters' gallery of the House of Commons. Then he was at some pains to explain to Lady Rowley that though he attended the reporters' gallery, he did not report himself. It was his duty to write leading political articles, and, to enable him to do so, he attended the debates.

Before he went Mrs Trevelyan thanked him most cordially for the trouble he had taken in procuring for her the address at Willesden, and gave him some account of the journey which she and her mother had made to River's Cottage. He argued with both of them that the unfortunate man must now be regarded as being altogether out of his mind, and something was said as to the great wisdom and experience of Dr Trite Turbury. Then Hugh Stanbury took his leave; and even Lady Rowley bade him adieu with kind cordiality. 'I don't wonder, mamma, that Nora should like him,' said Mrs Trevelyan.

'That is all very well, my dear, and no doubt he is pleasant, and manly, and all that; but really it would be almost like marrying a beggar.'

'For myself,' said Mrs Trevelyan, 'if I could begin life again, I do not think that any temptation would induce me to place myself in a man's power.'

Sir Marmaduke was told of all this on his return home, and he asked many questions as to the nature of Stanbury's work. When it was explained to him, Lady

Rowley repeating as nearly as she could all that Hugh had himself said about it, he expressed his opinion that writing for a penny newspaper was hardly more safe as a source of income than betting on horse races. 'I don't see that it is wrong,' said Mrs Trevelyan.

'I say nothing about wrong. I simply assert that it is uncertain. The very existence of such a periodical must in itself be most insecure.' Sir Marmaduke, amidst the cares of his government at the Mandarins, had, perhaps, had no better opportunity of watching what was going on in the world of letters than had fallen to the lot of Miss Stanbury at Exeter.

'I think your papa is right,' said Lady Rowley.

'Of course I am right. It is out of the question; and so Nora must be told.' He had as yet heard nothing about Mr Glascock. Had that misfortune been communicated to him his cup would indeed have been filled with sorrow to overflowing.

In the evening Nora was closeted with her father. 'Nora, my dear, you must understand, once and for all, that this cannot be,' said Sir Marmaduke. The Governor, when he was not disturbed by outward circumstances, could assume a good deal of personal dignity, and could speak, especially to his children, with an air of indisputable authority.

'What can't be, papa?' said Nora.

Sir Marmaduke perceived at once that there was no indication of obedience in his daughter's voice, and he prepared himself for battle. He conceived himself to be very strong, and thought that his objections were so well founded that no one would deny their truth and that his daughter had not a leg to stand on. 'This, that your mamma tells me of about Mr Stanbury. Do you know, my dear, that he has not a shilling in the world?'

'I know that he has no fortune, papa if you mean that.'

'And no profession either—nothing that can be called a profession. I do not wish to argue it, my dear, because there is no room for argument. The whole thing is preposterous. I cannot but think ill of him for having proposed it to you; for he must have known, must have known, that a young man without an income cannot be accepted as a fitting suitor for a gentleman's daughter. As for yourself, I can only hope that you will get the little idea out of your head very quickly; but mamma will speak to you about that. What I want you to understand from me is this, that there must be an end to it.'

Nora listened to this speech in perfect silence, standing before her father, and waiting patiently till the last word of it should be pronounced. Even when he had finished she still paused before she answered him. 'Papa,' she said at last and hesitated again before she went on.

'Well, my dear.'

'I can not give it up.'

'But you must give it up.'

'No, papa. I would do anything I could for you and mamma, but that is impossible.'

'Why is it impossible?'

'Because I love him so dearly.'

'That is nonsense. That is what all girls say when they choose to run against their parents. I tell you that it shall be given up. I will not have him here. I forbid you to see him. It is quite out of the question that you should marry such a man. I do hope, Nora, that you are not going to add to mamma's difficulties and mine by being obstinate and disobedient.' He paused a moment, and then added, 'I do not think that there is anything more to be said.'

'Papa.'

'My dear, I think you had better say nothing further about it. If you cannot bring yourself at the present moment to promise that there shall be an end of it, you had better hold your tongue. You have heard what I say, and you have heard what mamma says. I do not for a moment suppose that you dream of carrying on a communication with this gentleman in opposition to our wishes.'

'But I do.'

'Do what?'

'Papa, you had better listen to me.' Sir Marmaduke, when he heard this, assumed an air of increased authority, in which he intended that paternal anger should be visible; but he seated himself, and prepared to receive, at any rate, some of the arguments with which Nora intended to bolster up her bad cause. 'I have promised Mr Stanbury that I will be his wife.'

'That is all nonsense.'

'Do listen to me, papa. I have listened to you and you ought to listen to me. I have promised him, and I must keep my promise. I shall keep my promise if he wishes it. There is a time when a girl must be supposed to know what is best for herself, just as there is for a man.'

'I never heard such stuff in all my life. Do you mean that you'll go out and marry him like a beggar, with nothing but what you stand up in, with no friend to be with you, an outcast, thrown off by your mother with your father's curse?'

'Oh, papa, do not say that. You would not curse me. You could not.'

'If you do it at all, that will be the way.'

'That will not be the way, papa. You could not treat me like that.'

'And how are you proposing to treat me?'

'But, papa, in whatever way I do it, I must do it. I do not say today or tomorrow; but it must be the intention and purpose of my life, and I must declare that it is, everywhere. I have made up my mind about it. I am engaged to him, and I shall always say so unless he breaks it. I don't care a bit about fortune. I thought I did once, but I have changed all that.'

'Because this scoundrel has talked sedition to you.'

'He is not a scoundrel, papa, and he has not talked sedition. I don't know what sedition is. I thought it meant treason, and I'm sure he is not a traitor. He has made me love him, and I shall be true to him.'

Hereupon Sir Marmaduke began almost to weep. There came first a half-smothered oath and then a sob, and he walked about the room, and struck the table with his fist, and rubbed his bald head impatiently with his hand. 'Nora,' he said, 'I thought you were so different from this! If I had believed this of you, you never should have come to England with Emily.'

'It is too late for that now, papa.'

'Your mamma always told me that you had such excellent ideas about marriage.'

'So I have, I think,' said she, smiling.

'She always believed that you would make a match that would be a credit to the family.'

'I tried it, papa, the sort of match that you mean. Indeed I was mercenary enough in what I believed to be my views of life. I meant to marry a rich man if I could, and did not think much whether I should love him or not. But when the rich man came—'

'What rich man?'

'I suppose mamma has told you about Mr Glascock.'

'Who is Mr Glascock? I have not heard a word about Mr Glascock.' Then Nora was forced to tell the story, was called upon to tell it with all its aggravating details. By degrees Sir Marmaduke learned that this Mr Glascock, who had desired to be his son-in-law, was in very truth the heir to the Peterborough title and estates, would have been such a son-in-law as almost to compensate, by the brilliance of the connection, for that other unfortunate alliance. He could hardly control his agony when he was made to understand that this embryo peer had in truth been in earnest.

'Do you mean that he went down after you into Devonshire?'

'Yes, papa.'

'And you refused him then a second time?'

'Yes, papa.'

'Why, why, why? You say yourself that you liked him, that you thought that you would accept him.'

'When it came to speaking the word, papa, I found that I could not pretend to love him when I did not love him. I did not care for him, and I liked somebody else so much better! I just told him the plain truth and so he went away.'

The thought of all that he had lost, of all that might so easily have been his, for a time overwhelmed Sir Marmaduke, and drove the very memory of Hugh Stanbury almost out of his head; He could understand that a girl should not marry a man whom she did not like; but he could not understand how any girl should not love such a suitor as was Mr Glascock. And had she accepted this pearl of men, with her position, with her manners and beauty and appearance, such a connection would have been as good as an assured marriage for every one of Sir Marmaduke's numerous daughters. Nora was just the woman to look like a great lady, a lady of high rank such a lady as could almost command men to come and throw themselves at her unmarried sisters' feet. Sir Marmaduke had believed in his daughter Nora, had looked forward to see her do much for the family; and, when the crash had come upon the Trevelyan household, had thought almost as much of her injured prospects as he had of the misfortune of her sister. But now it seemed that more than all the good things of what he had dreamed had been proposed to this unruly girl, in spite of that great crash, and had been rejected! And he saw more than this as he thought. These good things would have been accepted had it not been for this rascal of a penny-a-liner, this friend of that other rascal Trevelyan, who had come in the way of their family to destroy the happiness of them all! Sir Marmaduke, in speaking of Stanbury after this, would constantly call him a penny-a-liner, thinking that the contamination of the penny communicated itself to all transactions of the *Daily Record*.

'You have made your bed for yourself, Nora, and you must lie upon it.'

'Just so, papa.'

'I mean that, as you have refused Mr Glascock's offer, you can never again hope for such an opening in life.'

'Of course I cannot. I am not such a child as to suppose that there are many Mr Glascocks to come and run after me. And if there were ever so many, papa, it would be no good. As you say, I have chosen for myself, and I must put up with it. When I see the carriages going about in the streets, and remember how often shall have to go home in an omnibus, I do think about it a good deal.'

'I'm afraid you will think when it is too late.'

'It isn't that I don't like carriages, papa. I do like them; and pretty dresses, and brooches, and men and women who have nothing to do, and balls, and the opera; but I love this man, and that is more to me than all the rest. I cannot help myself if it were ever so. Papa, you mustn't be angry with me. Pray, pray, pray do not say that horrid word again.'

This was the end of the interview. Sir Marmaduke found that he had nothing further to say. Nora, when she reached her last prayer to her father, referring to that curse with which he had threatened her, was herself in tears, and was leaning on him with her head against his shoulder. Of course he did not say a word which could be understood as sanctioning her engagement with Stanbury. He was as strongly determined as ever that it was his duty to save her from the perils of such a marriage as that. But, nevertheless, he was so far overcome by her as to be softened in his manners towards her. He kissed her as he left her, and told her to go to her mother. Then he went out and thought of it all, and felt as though Paradise had been opened to his child and she had refused to enter the gate.

CHAPTER LXXI. SHEWING WHAT HUGH STANBURY THOUGHT ABOUT THE DUTY OF MAN

In the conference which took place between Sir Marmaduke and his wife after the interview between him and Nora, it was his idea that nothing further should be done at all. 'I don't suppose the man will come here if he be told not,' said Sir Marmaduke, 'and if he does, Nora of course will not see him.' He then suggested that Nora would of course go back with them to the Mandarins, and that when once there she would not be able to see Stanbury any more. 'There must be no correspondence or anything of that sort, and so the thing will die away.' But Lady Rowley declared that this would not quite suffice. Mr Stanbury had made his offer in due form, and must be held to be entitled to an answer. Sir Marmaduke, therefore, wrote the following letter to the 'penny-a-liner,' mitigating the asperity of his language in compliance with his wife's counsels.

> Manchester Street,
> April 20th, 186—.

MY DEAR SIR,

Lady Rowley has told me of your proposal to my daughter Nora; and she has told me also what she learned from you as to your circumstances in life. I need hardly point out to you that no father would be justified in giving his daughter to a gentleman upon so small an income, and upon an income so very insecure.

I am obliged to refuse my consent, and I must therefore ask you to abstain from visiting and from communicating with my daughter.

Yours faithfully,

MARMADUKE ROWLEY.

Hugh Stanbury, Esq.

This letter was directed to Stanbury at the office of the *D. R.*, and Sir Marmaduke, as he wrote the pernicious address, felt himself injured in that he was compelled to write about his daughter to a man so circumstanced. Stanbury, when he got the letter, read it hastily and then threw it aside. He knew what it would contain before he opened it. He had heard enough from Lady Rowley to be aware that Sir Marmaduke would not welcome him as a son-in-law; Indeed, he had never expected such welcome. He was half-ashamed of his own suit because of the lowliness of his position, half-regretful that he should have induced such a girl as

Nora Rowley to give up for his sake her hopes of magnificence and splendour. But Sir Marmaduke's letter did not add anything to this feeling. He read it again, and smiled as he told himself that the father would certainly be very weak in the hands of his daughter. Then he went to work again at his article with a persistent resolve that so small a trifle as such a note should have no effect upon his daily work. 'Of course Sir Marmaduke would refuse his consent. Of course it would be for him, Stanbury, to marry the girl he loved in opposition to her father. Her father indeed! If Nora chose to take him—and as to that he was very doubtful as to Nora's wisdom—but if Nora would take him, what was any father's opposition to him. He wanted nothing from Nora's father. He was not looking for money with his wife, nor for fashion, nor countenance. Such a Bohemian was he that he would be quite satisfied if his girl would walk out to him, and become his wife, with any morning-gown on and with any old hat that might come, readiest to hand. He wanted neither cards, nor breakfast, nor carriages, nor fine clothes. If his Nora should choose to come to him as she was, he having had all previous necessary arrangements duly made, such as calling of banns or procuring of licence, if possible, he thought that a father's opposition would almost add something to the pleasure of the occasion. So he pitched the letter on one side, and went on with his article. And he finished his article; but it may be doubted whether it was completed with the full strength and pith needed for moving the pulses of the national mind as they should be moved by leading articles in the *D. R.* As he was writing he was thinking of Nora and thinking of the letter which Nora's father had sent to him. Trivial as was the letter, he could not keep himself from repeating the words of it to himself. '"Need hardly point out," oh; needn't he? Then why does he? Refusing his consent! I wonder what the old buffers think is the meaning of their consent, when they are speaking of daughters old enough to manage for themselves? Abstain from visiting or communicating with her! But if she visits and communicates with me, what then? I can't force my way into the house, but she can force her way out. Does he imagine that she can be locked up in the nursery or put into the corner?' So he argued with himself, and by such arguments he brought himself to the conviction that it would be well for him to answer Sir Marmaduke's letter. This he did at once before leaving the office of the *D. R.*

250, Fleet Street,
20th April.

My Dear Sir Marmaduke Rowley

'I have just received your letter, and am indeed sorry that its contents should be so little favourable to my hopes. I understand that your objection to me is simply in regard to the smallness and insecurity of my income. On the first point I may say that I have fair hopes that it may be at once increased. As to the second, I believe I may assert that it is as sure at least as the income of other professional men, such as barristers, merchants, and doctors. I cannot promise to say that I will not see your daughter. If she desires me to do so, of course I shall be guided by her views. I wish that I might be allowed an opportunity of seeing you, as think I could reverse or at least mitigate some of the objections which you feel to our marriage.

Yours most faithfully, HUGH STANBURY.

On the next day but one Sir Marmaduke came to him. He was sitting at the office of the *D. R.*, in a very small and dirty room at the back of the house, and Sir Marmaduke found his way thither through a confused crowd of compositors, pressmen, and printers' boys. He thought that he had never before been in a place so foul, so dark, so crowded, and so comfortless. He himself was accustomed to do his work, out in the Islands, with many of the appanages of vice-royalty around him. He had his secretary, and his private secretary, and his inner-room, and his waiting-room; and not unfrequently he had the honour of a dusky sentinel walking before the door through which he was to be approached. He had an idea that all gentlemen at their work had comfortable appurtenances around them such as carpets, dispatch-boxes, unlimited stationery, easy chairs for temporary leisure, big table-space, and a small world of books around them to give at least a look of erudition to their pursuits. There was nothing of the kind in the miserably dark room occupied 'by Stanbury. He was sitting at a wretched little table on which there was nothing but a morsel of blotting paper, a small ink-bottle, and the paper on which he was scribbling. There was no carpet there, and no dispatch box, and the only book in the room was a little dog's-eared dictionary.'Sir Marmaduke, I am so much obliged to you for coming,' said Hugh. 'I fear you will find this place a little rough, but we shall be all alone.'

'The place, Mr Stanbury, will not signify, I think'

'Not in the least—if you don't mind it. I got your letter, you know, Sir Marmaduke.'

'And I have had your reply. I have come to you because you have expressed a wish for an interview, but I do not see that it will do any good.'

'You are very kind for coming, indeed, Sir Marmaduke, very kind. I thought I might explain something to you about my income.'

'Can you tell me that you have any permanent income?'

'It goes on regularly from month to month;' Sir Marmaduke did not feel the slightest respect for an income that was paid monthly. According to his ideas, a gentleman's income should be paid quarterly, or perhaps half-yearly. According to his view, a monthly salary was only one degree better than weekly wages 'and I suppose that is permanence,' said Hugh Stanbury.

'I cannot say that I so regard it.'

'A barrister gets his, you know, very irregularly. There is no saying when he may have it.'

'But a barrister's profession is recognised as a profession among gentlemen, Mr Stanbury.'

'And is not ours recognised? Which of us, barristers or men of literature, have the most effect on the world at large? Who is most thought of in London, Sir Marmaduke, the Lord Chancellor or the Editor of the *Jupiter*?'

'The Lord Chancellor a great deal,' said Sir Marmaduke, quite dismayed by the audacity of the question.

'By no means, Sir Marmaduke,' said Stanbury, throwing out his hand before him so as to give the energy of action to his words. 'He has the higher rank. I will admit that.'

'I should think so,' said Sir Marmaduke.

'And the larger income.'

'Very much larger, I should say,' said Sir Marmaduke, with a smile.

'And he wears a wig.'

'Yes he wears a wig,' said Sir Marmaduke, hardly knowing in what spirit to accept this assertion.

'And nobody cares one brass button for him or his opinions,' said Stanbury, bringing down his hand heavily on the little table for the sake of emphasis.

'What, sir?'

'If you'll think of it, it is so.'

'Nobody cares for the Lord Chancellor!' It certainly is the fact that gentlemen living in the Mandarin Islands do think more of the Lord Chancellor, and the Lord Mayor, and the Lord-Lieutenant, and the Lord Chamberlain, than they whose spheres of life bring them into closer contact with those august functionaries. 'I presume, Mr Stanbury, that a connection with a penny newspaper makes such opinions as these almost a necessity.'

'Quite a necessity, Sir Marmaduke. No man can hold his own in print, now-a-days, unless he can see the difference between tinsel and gold.'

'And the Lord Chancellor, of course, is tinsel.'

'I do not say so. He may be a great lawyer and very useful. But his lordship, and his wig, and his woolsack, are tinsel in comparison with the real power possessed by the editor of a leading newspaper. If the Lord Chancellor were to go to bed for a month, would he be much missed?'

'I don't know, sir. I'm not in the secrets of the Cabinet. I should think he would.'

'About as much as my grandmother; but if the Editor of the *Jupiter* were to be taken ill, it would work quite a commotion. For myself I should be glad on public grounds because I don't like his mode of business. But it would have an effect because he is a leading man.'

'I don't see what all this leads to, Mr Stanbury.'

'Only to this, that we who write for the press think that our calling is recognised, and must be recognised, as a profession. Talk of permanence, Sir Marmaduke; are not the newspapers permanent? Do not they come out regularly every day, and more of them, and still more of them, are always coming out? You do not expect a collapse among them.'

'There will be plenty of newspapers, I do not doubt more than plenty, perhaps.'

'Somebody must write them, and the writers will be paid.'

'Anybody could write the most of them, I should say.'

'I wish you would try, Sir Marmaduke. Just try your hand at a leading article to-night, and read it yourself tomorrow morning.'

'I've a great deal too much to do, Mr Stanbury.'

'Just so. You have, no doubt, the affairs of your Government to look to. We are all so apt to ignore the work of our neighbours! It seems to me that I could go over and govern the Mandarins without the slightest trouble in the world. But, no doubt, I am mistaken, just as you are about writing for the newspapers.'

'I do not know,' said Sir Marmaduke, rising from his chair with dignity, 'that I called here to discuss such matters as these. As it happens, you, Mr Stanbury, are not the Governor of the Mandarins, and I have not the honour to write for the columns of the penny newspaper with which you are associated. It is therefore useless to discuss what either of us might do in the position held by the other.'

'Altogether useless, Sir Marmaduke, except just for the fun of the thing.'

'I do not see the fun, Mr Stanbury. I came here, at your request, to hear what you might have to urge against the decision which I expressed to you in reference to my daughter. As it seems that you have nothing to urge, I will not take up your time further.'

'But I have a great deal to urge, and have urged a great deal.'

'Have you, indeed?'

'You have complained that my work is not permanent. I have shewn that it is so permanent that there is no possibility of its coming to an end. There must be newspapers, and the people trained to write them must be employed. I have been at it now about two years. You know what I earn. Could I have got so far in so short a time as a lawyer, a doctor, a clergyman, a soldier, a sailor, a Government clerk, or in any of those employments which you choose to call professions? I think that is urging a great deal. I think it is urging everything.'

'Very well, Mr Stanbury. I have listened to you, and in a certain degree I admire your your your zeal and ingenuity, shall I say.'

'I didn't mean to call for admiration, Sir Marmaduke; but suppose you say good sense and discrimination.'

'Let that pass. You must permit me to remark that your position is not such as to justify me in trusting my daughter to your care. As my mind on that matter is quite made up, as is that also of Lady Rowley, I must ask you to give me your promise that your suit to my daughter shall be discontinued.'

'What does she say about it, Sir Marmaduke?'

'What she has said to me has been for my ears, and not for yours.'

'What I say is for her ears and for yours, and for her mother's ears, and for the ears of any who may choose to hear it. I will never give up my suit to your daughter till I am forced to do so, by a full conviction given me up. It is best to be plain, Sir Marmaduke, of course.'

'I do not understand this, Mr Stanbury.'

'I mean to be quite clear.'

'I have always thought that when a gentleman was told by the head of a family that he could not be made welcome in that family, it was considered to be the duty of that gentleman, as a gentleman, to abandon his vain pursuit. I have been brought up with that idea.'

'And I, Sir Marmaduke, have been brought up in the idea that when a man has won the affections of a woman, it is the duty of that man, as a man, to stick to her through thick and thin; and I mean to do my duty, according to my idea.'

'Then, sir, I have nothing further to say, but to take my leave. I must only caution you not to enter my doors.' As the passages were dark and intricate, it was necessary that Stanbury should shew Sir Marmaduke out, and this he did in silence. When they parted each of them lifted his hat, and not a word more was said.

That same night there was a note put into Nora's hands as she was following her mother out of one of the theatres. In the confusion she did not even see the messenger who had handed it to her. Her sister Lucy saw that she had taken the note, and questioned her about it afterwards with discretion, however, and in privacy. This was the note:

DEAREST LOVE,

I have seen your father, who is stern after the manner of fathers. What granite equals a parent's flinty bosom! For myself, I do not prefer clandestine arrangements and rope-ladders; and you, dear, have nothing of the Lydia about you. But I do like my own way, and like it especially when you are at the end of the path. It is quite out of the question that you should go back to those islands. I think I am justified in already assuming enough of the husband to declare that such going back must not be held for a moment in question. My proposition is that you should authorise me to make such arrangements as may be needed, in regard to licence, banns, or whatever else, and that you should then simply walk from the house to the church and marry me. You are of age, and can do as you please. Neither your father nor mother can have any right to stop you. I do not doubt but that your mother would accompany you, if she were fully satisfied of your purpose. Write to me to the *D. R.*

Your own, ever and ever, and always,   H. S.

I shall try and get this given to you as you leave the theatre. If it should fall into other hands, I don't much care. I'm not in the least ashamed of what I am doing; and I hope that you are not.

CHAPTER LXXII. THE DELIVERY OF THE LAMB

It is hoped that a certain quarter of lamb will not have been forgotten—a quarter of lamb that was sent as a peace-offering from Exeter to Nuncombe Putney by the hands of Miss Stanbury's Martha, not with purposes of corruption, not intended to buy back the allegiance of Dorothy, folded delicately and temptingly in one of the best table napkins, with no idea of bribery, but sent as presents used to be sent of old in the trains of great ambassadors as signs of friendship and marks of true respect. Miss Stanbury was, no doubt, most anxious that her niece should return to her, but was not, herself, low spirited enough to conceive that a quarter of lamb could be efficacious in procuring such return. If it might be that Dorothy's heart could be touched by mention of the weariness of her aunt's solitary life; and if, therefore, she would return, it would be very well; but it could not be well unless the offer should come from Dorothy herself. All of which Martha had been made to understand by her mistress, considerable ingenuity having been exercised in the matter on each side.

On her arrival at Lessboro', Martha had hired a fly, and been driven out to Nuncombe Putney; but she felt, she knew not why, a dislike to be taken in her carriage to the door of the cottage; and was put down in the middle of the village, from whence she walked out to Mrs Stanbury's abode, with the basket upon her arm. It was a good half mile, and the lamb was heavy, for Miss Stanbury had suggested that a bottle of sherry should be put in under the napkin and Martha was becoming tired of her burden, when whom should she see on the road before her but Brooke Burgess! As she said herself afterwards, it immediately occurred to her, 'that all the fat was in the fire.' Here had this young man come down, passing through Exeter without even a visit to Miss Stanbury, and had clandestinely sought out the young woman whom he wasn't to marry; and here was the young woman herself flying in her aunt's face, when one scratch of a pen might ruin them both! Martha entertained a sacred, awful, overcoming feeling about her mistress's will. That she was to have something herself she supposed, and her anxiety was not on that score; but she had heard so much about it, had realised so fully the great power which Miss Stanbury possessed, and had had her own feelings so rudely invaded by alterations in Miss Stanbury's plans, that she had come to entertain an idea that all persons around her should continually bear that will in their memory. Hugh had undoubtedly been her favourite, and, could Martha have dictated the will herself, she would still have made Hugh the heir; but she had realised the resolution of her mistress so far as to confess that the bulk of the property was to go back to a Burgess. But there were very many Burgesses; and here was the one who had been selected, flying in the very face of the testatrix! What was to be done? Were she to go back and not tell her mistress that she had seen Brooke Burgess at Nuncombe, then, should the fact be found out, would the devoted anger of Miss Stanbury fall upon her own head? It would be absolutely necessary that she should tell the story, let the consequences be what they might; but the consequences, probably, would be very dreadful. 'Mr Brooke, that is not you?' she said, as she came up to him, putting her basket down in the middle of the dusty road.

'Then who can it be?' said Brooke, giving her his hand to shake.

'But what do bring you here, Mr Brooke? Goodness me, what will missus say?'

'I shall make that all straight. I'm going back to Exeter tomorrow.' Then there were many questions and many answers. He was sojourning at Mrs Crocket's, and had been there for the last two days. 'Dear, dear, dear,' she said over and over again. 'Deary me, deary me!' and then she asked him whether it was 'all along of Miss Dorothy' that he had come. Of course, it was all along of Miss Dorothy. Brooke made no secret about it. He had come down to see Dorothy's mother and sister, and to say a bit of his own mind about future affairs and to see the beauties of the country. When he talked about the beauties of the country, Martha looked at him as the people of Lessboro' and Nuncombe Putney should have looked at Colonel Osborne, when he talked of the church porch at Cockchaffington. 'Beauties of the countries, Mr Brooke you ought to be ashamed of yourself!' said Martha.

'But I ain't the least in the world,' said Brooke.

Then Martha took up her basket, and went on to the cottage, which had been close in sight during their conversation in the road. She felt angry with Dorothy. In such matters a woman is always angry with the woman who has probably been quite passive, and rarely with the man, who is ever the real transgressor. Having a man down after her at Nuncombe Putney! It had never struck Martha as very horrible that Brooke Burgess should fall in love with Dorothy in the city, but this meeting, in the remoteness of the country, out of sight even of the village, was almost indecent; and all, too, with Miss Stanbury's will just, as one might say, on the balance! Dorothy ought to have buried herself rather than have allowed Brooke to see her at Nuncombe Putney; and Dorothy's mother and Priscilla must be worse. She trudged on, however, with her lamb, and soon found herself in the presence of the three ladies.

'What Martha!' said Dorothy.

'Yes, miss, here I am. I'd have been here half-an-hour ago a'most, if I hadn't been stopped on the road.'

'And who stopped you?' asked Priscilla.

'Why Mr Brooke, of course.'

'And what did Mr Brooke say to you?' asked Dorothy.

Martha perceived at once that Dorothy was quite radiant. She told her mistress that she had never seen Miss Dorothy look half so comely before. 'Laws, ma'am, she brightened up and speckled about, till it did your heart good to see her in spite of all.' But this was some time afterwards.

'He didn't say very much,' replied Martha, gravely. 'But I've got very much to tell you,' continued Dorothy. 'I'm engaged to be married to Mr Brooke, and you must congratulate me. It is settled now, and mamma and my sister know all about it.'

Martha, when she was thus asked directly for congratulation, hardly knew at once how to express herself. Being fully aware of Miss Stanbury's objection to the marriage, she could not venture to express her approbation of it. It was very improper, in Martha's mind, that any young woman should have a follower, when the 'missus' didn't approve of it. She understood well enough that, in that matter of followers, privileges are allowed to young ladies which are not accorded to maid servants. A young lady may do things, have young men to walk and talk with them, to dance with them and embrace them, and perhaps even more than this, when for half so much a young woman would be turned into the streets without a character. Martha knew all this, and knew also that Miss Dorothy, though her mother lived in a very little cottage, was not altogether debarred, in the matter of followers, from the privileges of a lady. But yet Miss Dorothy's position was so very peculiar!

Look at that will or, rather, at that embryo will, which might be made any day, which now probably would be made, and which might affect them both so terribly! People who have not got money should not fly in the face of those who have. Such at least was Martha's opinion very strongly. How could she congratulate Miss Dorothy under the existing circumstances. 'I do hope you will be happy, miss, that you knows,' said Martha, in her difficulty. 'And now, ma'am, miss, I mean,' she added, correcting herself, in obedience to Miss Stanbury's direct orders about the present 'missus has just sent me over with a bit of lamb, and a letter as is here in the basket, and to ask how you is and the other ladies.'

'We are very much obliged,' said Mrs Stanbury, who had not understood the point of Martha's speech.

'My sister is, I'm sure,' said Priscilla, who had understood it.

Dorothy had taken the letter, and had gone aside with it, and was reading it very carefully. It touched her nearly, and there had come tears into both her eyes, as she dwelt upon it. There was something in her aunt's allusion to the condition of unmarried women which came home to her especially. She knew her aunt's past history, and now she knew, or hoped that she knew, something of her own future destiny. Her aunt was desolate, whereas upon her the world smiled, most benignly. Brooke had just informed her that he intended to make her his wife as speedily as possible, with her aunt's consent if possible, but if not, then without it. He had ridiculed the idea of his being stopped by Miss Stanbury's threats, and had said all this in such fashion that even Priscilla herself had only listened and obeyed. He had spoken not a word of his own income, and none of them had dreamed even of asking him a question. He had been as a god in the little cottage, and all of them had been ready to fall down and worship him. Mrs Stanbury had not known how to treat him with sufficient deference, and, at the same time, with sufficient affection. He had kissed them all round, and Priscilla had felt an elation which was hardly intelligible to herself. Dorothy, who was so much honoured, had come to enjoy a status in her mother's estimation very different from that which she had previously possessed, and had grown to be quite beautiful in her mother's eyes.

There was once a family of three ancient maiden ladies, much respected and loved in the town in which they lived. Their manners of life were well known among their friends, and excited no surprise; but a stranger to the locality once asked of the elder why Miss Matilda, the younger, always went first out of the room? 'Matilda once had an offer of marriage,' said the dear simple old lady, who had never been so graced, and who felt that such an episode in life was quite sufficient to bestow brevet rank. It was believed by Mrs Stanbury that Dorothy's honours would be carried further than those of Miss Matilda, but there was much of the same feeling in the bosom of the mother towards the fortunate daughter, who, in the eyes of a man, had seemed goodly enough to be his wife.

With this swelling happiness round her heart, Dorothy read her aunt's letter, and was infinitely softened. 'I had gotten somehow to love to see your pretty face.' Dorothy had thought little enough of her own beauty, but she liked being told by her aunt that her face had been found to be pretty. 'I am very desolate and solitary here,' her aunt said; and then had come those words about the state of maiden women and then those other words, about women's duties, and her aunt's prayer on her behalf. 'Dear Dorothy, be not such a one.' She held the letter to her lips and to her bosom, and could hardly continue its perusal because of her tears. Such prayers from the aged addressed to the young are generally held in light esteem, but this adjuration was valued by the girl to whom it was addressed. She put together the invitation or rather the permission accorded to her, to make a visit to Exeter and the intimation in the postscript that Martha knew her mistress's mind; and then she returned to the sitting-room, in which Martha was still seated with her mother, and took the old servant apart. 'Martha,' she said, 'is my aunt happy now?'

'Well, miss.'

'She is strong again; is she not?'

'Sir Peter says she is getting well; and Mr Martin; but Mr Martin isn't much account.'

'She eats and drinks again?'

'Pretty well not as it used to be, you know, miss. I tell her she ought to go somewheres but she don't like moving nohow. She never did. I tell her if she'd go to Dawlish just for a week. But she don't think there's a bed fit to sleep on, nowhere, except just her own.'

'She would go if Sir Peter told her.'

'She says that these movings are newfangled fashions, and that the air didn't use to want changing for folk when she was young. I heard her tell Sir Peter herself, that if she couldn't live at Exeter, she would die there. She won't go nowheres, Miss Dorothy. She ain't careful to live.'

'Tell me something, Martha; will you?'

'What is it, Miss Dorothy?'

'Be a dear good woman now, and tell me true. Would she be better if I were with her?'

'She don't like being alone, miss. I don't know nobody as does.'

'But now, about Mr Brooke, you know.'

'Yes; Mr Brooke! That's it.'

'Of course, Martha, I love him better than anything in all the world. I can't tell you how it was, but I think I loved him the very first moment I saw him.'

'Dear, dear, dear!'

'I couldn't help it, Martha but it's no good talking about it, for of course I shan't try to help it now. Only this, that I would do anything in the world for my aunt except that.'

'But she don't like it, Miss Dorothy. That is the truth, you know.'

'It can't be helped now, Martha; and of course she'll be told at once. Shall I go and tell her? I'd go today if you think she would like it.'

'And Mr Brooke?'

'He is to go tomorrow.'

'And will you leave him here?'

'Why not? Nobody will hurt him. I don't mind a bit about having him with me now. But I can tell you this. When he went away from us once, it made me very unhappy. Would Aunt Stanbury be glad to see me, Martha?'

Martha's reserve was at last broken down, and she expressed herself in strong language. There was nothing on earth her mistress wanted so much as to have her favourite niece back again. Martha acknowledged that there were great difficulties about Brooke Burgess, and she did not see her way clearly through them. Dorothy declared her purpose of telling her aunt boldly at once. Martha shook her head, admiring the honesty and courage, but doubting the result. She understood better than did any one else the peculiarity of mind which made her mistress specially anxious that none of the Stanbury family should enjoy any portion of the Burgess money, beyond that which she herself had saved out of the income. There had been moments in which Martha had hoped that this prejudice might be overcome in favour of Hugh; but it had become stronger as the old woman grew to be older and more feeble, and it was believed now to be settled as Fate. 'She'd sooner give it all to old Barty over the way,' Martha had once said, 'than let it go to her own kith and kin. And if she do hate any human creature, she do hate Barty Burgess.' She assented, however, to Dorothy's proposal; and, though Mrs Stanbury and Priscilla were astounded by the precipitancy of the measure, they did not attempt to oppose it.

'And what am I to do?' said Brooke, when he was told.

'You'll come tomorrow, of course,' said Dorothy.

'But it may be that the two of us together will be too many for the dear old lunatic.'

'You shan't call her a lunatic, Brooke. She isn't so much a lunatic as you are, to run counter to her, and disobey her, and all that kind of thing.'

'And how about yourself?'

'How can I help it, Brooke? It is you that say it must be so.'

'Of course it must. Who is to be stayed from doing what is reasonable because an old woman has a bee on her bonnet. I don't believe in people's wills.'

'She can do what she likes about it, Brooke.'

'Of course she can, and of course she will. What I mean is that it never pays to do this or that because somebody may alter his will, or may make a will, or may not make a will. You become a slave for life, and then your dead tyrant leaves you a mourning-ring, and grins at you out of his grave. All the same she'll kick up a row, I fancy, and you'll have to bear the worst of it.'

'I'll tell her the truth; and if she be very angry, I'll just come home again. But I think I'll come home tomorrow any way, so that I'll pass you on the road. That will be best. She won't want us both together. Only then, Brooke, I shan't see you again.'

'Not till June.'

'And is it to be really in June?'

'You say you don't like May.'

'You are such a goose, Brooke. It will be May almost tomorrow. I shall be such a poor wife for you, Brooke. As for getting my things ready, I shall not bring hardly any things at all. Have you thought what it is to take a body so very poor?'

'I own I haven't thought as much about it, Dolly, as I ought to have done, perhaps.'

'It is too late now, Brooke.'

'I suppose it is.'

'Quite too late. A week ago I could have borne it. I had almost got myself to think that it would be better that I should bear it. But you have come, and banished all the virtue out of my head. I am ashamed of myself, because I am so unworthy; but I would put up with that shame rather than lose you now. Brooke, Brooke, I will so try to be good to you!'

In the afternoon Martha and Dorothy started together for Exeter, Brooke and Priscilla accompanying them as far as Mrs Crocket's, where the Lessboro' fly was awaiting them. Dorothy said little or nothing during the walk, nor, indeed, was she very communicative during the journey into Exeter. She was going to her aunt, instigated simply by the affection of her full heart; but she was going with a tale in her mouth which she knew would be very unwelcome. She could not save herself from feeling that, in having accepted Brooke, and in having not only accepted him but even fixed the day for her marriage, she had been ungrateful to her aunt. Had it not been for her aunt's kindness and hospitality, she would never have seen Brooke Burgess. And as she had been under her aunt's care at Exeter, she doubted whether she had not been guilty of some great fault in falling in love with this man, in opposition as it were to express orders. Should her aunt still declare that she would in no way countenance the marriage, that she would still oppose it and use her influence with Brooke to break it off, then would Dorothy return on the morrow to her mother's cottage at Nuncombe Putney, so that her lover might be free to act with her aunt as he might think fit. And should he yield, she would endeavour, she would struggle hard, to think that he was still acting for the best. 'I must tell her myself, Martha,' said Dorothy, as they came near to Exeter.

'Certainly, miss, only you'll do it tonight.'

'Yes at once. As soon after I get there as possible.'

CHAPTER LXXIII. DOROTHY RETURNS TO EXETER

Miss Stanbury perfectly understood that Martha was to come back by the train reaching Exeter at 7 p.m., and that she might be expected in the Close about a quarter-of-an-hour after that time. She had been nervous and anxious all day, so much so that Mr Martin had told her that she must be very careful. 'That's all very well,' the old woman had said, 'but you haven't got any medicine for my complaint, Mr Martin.' The apothecary had assured her that the worst of her complaint was in the east wind, and had gone away begging her to be very careful. 'It is not God's breezes that are hard to any one,' the old lady had said to herself 'but our own hearts.' After her lonely dinner she had fidgeted about the room, and had rung twice for the girl, not knowing what order to give when the servant came to her. She was very anxious about her tea, but would not have it brought to her till after Martha should have arrived. She was half-minded to order that a second cup and saucer should be placed there, but she had not the courage to face the disappointment which would fall upon her, should the cup and saucer stand there for no purpose. And yet, should she come, how nice it would be to shew her girl that her old aunt had been ready for her. Thrice she went to the window after the cathedral clock had struck seven, to see whether her ambassador was returning. From her window there was only one very short space of pathway on which she could have seen her and, as it happened, there came the ring at the door, and no ambassador had as yet been viewed. Miss Stanbury was immediately off her seat, and out upon the landing. 'Here we are again, Miss Dorothy,' said Martha. Then Miss Stanbury could not restrain herself but descended the stairs, moving as she had never moved since she had first been ill. 'My bairn,' she said; 'my dearest bairn! I thought that perhaps it might be so. Jane, another tea-cup and saucer up-stairs.' What a pity that she had not ordered it before! 'And get a hot cake, Jane. You will be ever so hungry, my darling, after your journey.'

'Are you glad to see me, Aunt Stanbury?' said Dorothy.

'Glad, my pretty one!' Then she put up her hands, and smoothed down the girl's cheeks, and kissed her, and patted Martha on the back, and scolded her at the same time for not bringing Miss Dorothy from the station in a cab. 'And what is the meaning of that little bag?' she said. 'You shall go back for the rest yourself, Martha, because it is your own fault.' Martha knew that all this was pleasant enough, but then her mistress's moods would sometimes be changed so suddenly!

How would it be when Miss Stanbury knew that Brooke Burgess had been left behind at Nuncombe Putney?

'You see I didn't stay to eat any of the lamb,' said Dorothy, smiling.

'You shall have a calf instead, my dear,' said Miss Stanbury, 'because you are a returned prodigal.'

All this was very pleasant, and Miss Stanbury was so happy dispensing her tea, and the hot cake, and the clotted cream, and was so intent upon her little methods of caressing and petting her niece, that Dorothy had no heart to tell her story while the plates and cups were still upon the table. She had not, perhaps, cared much for the hot cake, having such a weight upon her mind, but she had seemed to care, understanding well that she might so best conduce to her aunt's comfort. Miss Stanbury was a woman who could not bear that the good things which she had provided for a guest should not be enjoyed. She could taste with a friend's palate, and drink with a friend's throat. But when debarred these vicarious pleasures by what seemed to her to be the caprice of her guests, she would be offended. It had been one of the original sins of Camilla and Arabella French that they would declare at her tea-table that they had dined late and could not eat tea-cake. Dorothy knew all this and did her duty, but with a heavy heart. There was the story to be told, and she had promised Martha that it should be told tonight. She was quite aware, too, independently of her promise, that it was necessary that it should be told tonight. It was very sad very grievous that the dear old lady's happiness should be disturbed so soon; but it must be done. When the tea-things were being taken away her aunt was still purring round her, and saying gentle, loving words. Dorothy bore it as well as she could bore it well, smiling and kissing her aunt's hand, and uttering now and then some word of affection. But the thing had to be done; and as soon as the room was quiet for a moment, she jumped up from her chair and began. 'Aunt Stanbury, I must tell you something at once. Who, do you think, is at Nuncombe Putney?'

'Not Brooke Burgess?'

'Yes, he is. He is there now, and is to be here with you tomorrow.'

The whole colour and character of Miss Stanbury's face was changed in a moment. She had been still purring up to the moment in which this communication had been made to her. Her gratification had come to her from the idea that her pet had come back to her from love of her as in very truth had been the case; but now it seemed that Dorothy had returned to ask for a great favour for herself. And she reflected at once that Brooke had passed through Exeter without seeing her. If he was determined to marry without reference to her, he might at any rate have had the grace to come to her and say so. She, in the fulness of her heart, had written words of affection to Dorothy, and both Dorothy and Brooke had at once taken advantage of her expressions for their own purposes. Such was her reading of the story of the day. 'He need not trouble himself to come here now,' she said.

'Dear aunt, do not say that.'

'I do say it. He need not trouble himself to come now. When I said that I should be glad to see you, I did not intend that you should meet Mr Burgess under my roof. I did not wish to have you both together.'

'How could I help coming, when you wrote to me like that?'

'It is very well, but he need not come. He knows the way from Nuncombe to London without stopping at Exeter.'

'Aunt Stanbury, you must let me tell it you all.'

'There is no more to tell, I should think.'

'But there is more. You knew what he thought about me, and what he wished.'

'He is his own master, my dear and you are your own mistress.'

'If you speak to me like that you will kill me, Aunt Stanbury. I did not think of coming, only when Martha brought your dear letter I could not help it. But he was coming. He meant to come tomorrow, and he will. Of course he must defend himself, if you are angry with him.'

'He need not defend himself at all.'

'I told them, and I told him, that I would only stay one night if you did not wish that we should be here together. You must see him, Aunt Stanbury. You would not refuse to see him.'

'If you please, my dear, you must allow me to judge whom I will see.'

After that the discussion ceased between them for awhile, and Miss Stanbury left the room that she might hold a consultation with Martha. Dorothy went up to her chamber, and saw that everything had been prepared for her with most scrupulous care. Nothing could be whiter, neater, cleaner, nicer than was everything that surrounded her. She had perceived while living under her aunt's roof, how, gradually, small delicate feminine comforts had been increased for her. Martha had been told that Miss Dorothy ought to have this, and that Miss Dorothy ought to have that; till at last she, who had hitherto known nothing of the small luxuries that come from an easy income, had felt ashamed of the prettinesses that had been added to her. Now she could see at once that infinite care had been used to make her room bright and smiling only in the hope that she would return. As soon as she saw it all, she sat down on her bed and burst out into tears. Was it not hard upon her that she should be forced into such ingratitude! Every comfort prepared for her was a coal of hot fire upon her head. And yet, what had she done that she ought not to have done? Was it unreasonable that she should have loved this man, when they two were brought together? And had she even dared to think of him otherwise than as an acquaintance till he had compelled her to confess her love? And after that had she not tried to separate herself from him, so that they two, her aunt and her lover, might be divided by no quarrel? Had not Priscilla told her that she was right in all that she was doing? Nevertheless, in spite of all this, she could not refrain from accusing herself of ingratitude towards her aunt. And she began to think it would have been better for her now to have remained at home, and have allowed Brooke to come alone to Exeter than to have obeyed the impulse which had arisen from the receipt of her aunt's letter. When she went down again she found herself alone in the room, and she was beginning to think that it was intended that she should go to bed without again seeing her aunt; but at last Miss Stanbury came to her, with a sad countenance, but without that look of wrath which Dorothy knew so well. 'My dear,' she said, 'it will be better that Mr Burgess should go up to London tomorrow. I will see him, of course, if he chooses to come, and Martha shall meet him at the station and explain it. If you do not mind, I would prefer that you should not meet him here.'

'I meant only to stay one night, aunt.'

'That is nonsense. If I am to part with either of you, I will part with him. You are dearer to me than he is. Dorothy, you do not know how dear to me you are.'

Dorothy immediately fell on her knees at her aunt's feet, and hid her face in her aunt's lap. Miss Stanbury twined round her fingers the soft hair, which she loved so well because it was a grace given by God and not bought out of a shop, and caressed the girl's head, and muttered something that was intended for a prayer. 'If he will let me, aunt, I will give him up,' said Dorothy, looking up into her aunt's face. 'If he will say that I may, though I shall love him always, he may go.'

'He is his own master,' said Miss Stanbury. 'Of course he is his own master.'

'Will you let me return tomorrow just for a few days and then you can talk to him as you please. I did not mean to come to stay. I wished him good-bye because I knew that I should not meet him here.'

'You always talk of going away, Dorothy, as soon as ever you are in the house. You are always threatening me.'

'I will come again, the moment you tell me. If he goes in the morning, I will be here the same evening. And I will write to him, Aunt Stanbury, and tell him that he is quite free, quite free, quite free.'

Miss Stanbury made no reply to this, but sat, still playing with her niece's hair. 'I think I will go to bed,' she said at last. 'It is past ten. You need not go to Nuncombe, Dorothy. Martha shall meet him, and he can see me here. But I do not wish him to stay in the house. You can go over and call on Mrs MacHugh. Mrs MacHugh will take it well of you that you should call on her.' Dorothy made no further opposition to this arrangement, but kissed her aunt, and went to her chamber.

How was it all to be for her? For the last two days she had been radiant with new happiness. Everything had seemed to be settled. Her lover, in his high-handed way, had declared that in no important crisis of life would he allow himself to be driven out of his way by the fear of what an old woman might do in her will. When Dorothy assured him that not for worlds would she, though she loved him dearly, injure his material prospects, he had thrown it all aside, after a grand fashion, that had really made the girl think that all Miss Stanbury's money was as nothing to his love for her. She and Priscilla and her mother had been carried away so entirely by Brooke's oratory as to feel for the time that the difficulties were entirely conquered. But now the aspect of things was so different! Whatever Brooke might owe to Miss Stanbury, she, Dorothy, owed her aunt everything. She would immolate herself if Brooke would only let her. She did not quite understand her aunt's stubborn opposition; but she knew that there was some great cause for her aunt's feeling on the matter. There had been a promise made, or an oath sworn, that the property of the Burgess family should not go into the hands of any Stanbury. Dorothy told herself that, were she married, she would be a Stanbury no longer, that her aunt would still comply with the obligation she had fixed for herself; but, nevertheless, she was ready to believe that her aunt might be right. Her aunt had always declared that it should be so; and Dorothy, knowing this, confessed to herself that she should have kept her heart under better control. Thinking of these things, she went to the table where paper and ink and pens had all been prepared for her so prettily, and began her letter to Brooke. 'Dearest, dearest Brooke.' But then she thought that this was not a fair keeping of her promise, and she began again. 'My dear Brooke.' The letter, however, did not get itself written that night. It was almost impossible for her to write it. 'I think it will be better for you,' she had tried to say, 'to be guided by my aunt.' But how could she say this when she did not believe it? It was her wish to make him understand that she would never think ill of him, for a moment, if he would make up his mind to abandon her—but she could not find the words to express herself, and she went, at last, to bed, leaving the half-covered paper upon the table.

She went to bed, and cried herself to sleep. It had been so sweet to have a lover, a man of her own, to whom she could say what she pleased, from whom she had a right to ask for counsel and protection, a man who delighted to be near her, and to make much of her. In comparison with her old mode of living, her old ideas of life, her life with such a lover was passed in an Elysium. She had entered from barren lands into so rich a paradise! But there is no paradise, as she now found, without apples which must be eaten, and which lead to sorrow. She regretted in this hour that she had ever seen Brooke Burgess. After all, with her aunt's love and care for her, with her mother and sister near her, with the respect of those who knew her, why should the lands have been barren, even had there been no entrance for her into that Elysium? And did it not all result in this, that the Elysium to be desired should not be here; that the paradise, without the apples, must be waited for till beyond the grave? It is when things go badly with us here, and for most of us only then, that we think that we can see through the dark clouds into the joys of heaven. But at last she slept, and in her dreams Brooke was sitting with her in Niddon Park with his arm tight clasped round her waist.

She slept so soundly, that when a step crept silently into her room, and when a light was held for awhile over her face, neither the step nor the light awakened her. She was lying with her head back upon the pillow, and her arm hung by the bedside, and her lips were open, and her loose hair was spread upon the pillow. The person who stood there with the light thought that there never had been a fairer sight. Everything there was so pure, so sweet, so good! She was one whose only selfish happiness could come to her from the belief that others loved her. The step had been very soft, and even the breath of the intruder was not allowed to pass heavily into the air, but the light of the candle shone upon the eyelids of the sleeper, and she moved her head restlessly on the pillow. 'Dorothy, are you awake? Can you speak to me?'

Then the disturbed girl gradually opened her eyes and gazed upwards, and raised herself in her bed, and sat wondering. 'Is anything the matter, aunt?' she said.

'Only the vagaries of an old woman, my pet, of an old woman who cannot sleep in her bed.'

'But what is it, aunt?'

'Kiss me, dearest.' Then, with something of slumber still about her, Dorothy raised herself in her bed, and placed her arm on her aunt's shoulder and embraced her. 'And now for my news,' said Miss Stanbury.

'What news, aunt? It isn't morning yet; is it?'

'No it is not morning. You shall sleep again presently. I have thought of it, and you shall be Brooke's wife, and I will have it here, and we will all be friends.'

'What!'

'You will like that—will you not?'

'And you will not quarrel with him? What am I to say? What am I to do?' She was, in truth, awake now, and, not knowing what she did, she jumped out of bed, and stood holding her aunt by the arm.

'It is not a dream,' said Miss Stanbury.

'Are you sure that it is not a dream? And may he come here tomorrow?'

'Of course he will come tomorrow.'

'And may I see him, Aunt Stanbury?'

'Not if you go home, my dear.'

'But I won't go home. And will you tell him? Oh dear, oh dear! Aunt Stanbury, I do not think that I believe it yet.'

'You will catch cold, my dear, if you stay there trying to believe it. You have nothing on. Get into bed and believe it there. You will have time to think of it before the morning.' Then Miss Stanbury went back to her own chamber, and Dorothy was left alone to realise her bliss.

She thought of all her life for the last twelve months, of the first invitation to Exeter, and the doubts of the family as to its acceptance, of her arrival and of her own doubts as to the possibility of her remaining, of Mr Gibson's courtship and her aunt's disappointment, of Brooke's coming, of her love and of his, and then of her departure back to Nuncombe. After that had come the triumph of Brooke's visit, and then the terrible sadness of her aunt's displeasure. But now everything was good and glorious. She did not care for money herself. She thought that she never could care much for being rich. But had she made Brooke poor by marrying him, that must always have been to her matter of regret, if not of remorse. But now it was all to be smooth and sweet. Now a paradise was to be opened to her, with no apples which she might not eat, no apples which might not, but still must, be eaten. She thought that it would be impossible that she should sleep again that night; but she did sleep, and dreamed that Brooke was holding her in Niddon Park, tighter than ever.

When the morning came she trembled as she walked down into the parlour. Might it not still be possible that it was all a dream? or what if her aunt should again have changed her purpose? But the first moment of her aunt's presence told her that there was nothing to fear. 'How did you sleep, Dorothy?' said the old lady.

'Dear aunt, I do not know. Was it all sleep?'

'What shall we say to Brooke when he comes?'

'You shall tell him.'

'No, dearest, you must tell him. And you must say to him that if he is not good to my girl, and does not love her always, and cling to her, and keep her from harm, and be in truth her loving husband, I will hold him to be the most ungrateful of human beings.' And before Brooke came, she spoke again. 'I wonder whether he thinks you as pretty as I do, Dolly?'

'He never said that he thought me pretty at all.'

'Did he not? Then he shall say so, or he shall not have you. It was your looks won me first, Dolly, like an old fool as I am. It is so pleasant to have a little nature after such a deal of artifice.' In which latter remarks it was quite understood that Miss Stanbury was alluding to her enemies at Heavitree.

CHAPTER LXXIV. THE LIONESS AROUSED

Brooke Burgess had been to Exeter and had gone, for he only remained there one night, and everything was apparently settled. It was not exactly told through Exeter that Miss Stanbury's heir was to be allowed to marry Miss Stanbury's niece; but Martha knew it, and Giles Hickbody guessed it, and Dorothy was allowed to tell her mother and sister, and Brooke himself, in his own careless way, had mentioned the matter to his uncle Barty. As Miss Stanbury had also told the secret in confidence to Mrs MacHugh, it cannot be said that it was altogether well kept. Four days after Brooke's departure the news reached the Frenches at Heavitree. It was whispered to Camilla by one of the shopmen with whom she was still arranging her marriage trousseau, and was repeated by her to her mother and sister with some additions which were not intended to be good-natured. 'He gets her and the money together as a bargain of course,' said Camilla. 'I only hope the money won't be found too dear.'

'Perhaps he won't get it after all,' said Arabella.

'That would be cruel,' replied Camilla. 'I don't think that even Miss Stanbury is so false as that.'

Things were going very badly at Heavitree. There was war there, almost everlastingly, though such little playful conversations as the above shewed that there might be an occasional lull in the battle. Mr Gibson was not doing his duty. That was clear enough. Even Mrs French, when she was appealed to with almost frantic energy by her younger daughter, could not but acknowledge that he was very remiss as a lover. And Camilla, in her fury, was very imprudent. That very frantic energy which induced her to appeal to her mother was, in itself, proof of her imprudence. She knew that she was foolish, but she could not control her passion. Twice had she detected Arabella in receiving notes from Mr Gibson, which she did not see, and of which it had been intended that she should know nothing. And once, when she spent a night away at Ottery St. Mary with a friend, a visit which was specially prefatory to marriage, and made in reference to bridesmaids' dresses, Arabella had had—so at least Camilla was made to believe—a secret meeting with Mr Gibson in some of the lanes which lead down from Heavitree to the Topsham road.

'I happened to meet him, and spoke two words to him,' said Arabella. 'Would you have me cut him?'

'I'll tell you what it is, Bella, if there is any underhand game going on that I don't understand, all Exeter shall be on fire before you shall carry it out.'

Bella made no answer to this, but shrugged her shoulders. Camilla was almost at a loss to guess what might be the truth. Would not any sister, so accused on such an occasion, rebut the accusation with awful wrath? But Arabella simply shrugged her shoulders, and went her way. It was now the 16th of April, and there wanted but one short fortnight to their marriage. The man had not the courage to jilt her! She felt sure that he had not heart enough to do a deed of such audacity. And her sister, too, was weak and a coward, and would lack the power to stand on her legs and declare herself to be the perpetrator of such villany. Her mother, as she knew well, would always have preferred that her elder daughter should be the bride; but her mother was not the woman to have the hardihood, now, in the eleventh hour, to favour such an intrigue. Let her wish be what it might, she would not be strong enough to carry through the accomplishment of it. They would all know that that threat of hers of setting Exeter on fire would be carried out after some fashion that would not be inadequate to the occasion. A sister, a mother, a promised lover, all false—all so damnably, cruelly false! It was impossible. No history, no novel of most sensational interest, no wonderful villany that had ever been wrought into prose or poetry, would have been equal to this. It was impossible. She told herself so a score of times a day. And yet the circumstances were so terribly suspicious! Mr Gibson's conduct as a lover was simply disgraceful to him as a man and a clergyman. He was full of excuses, which she knew to be false. He would never come near her if he could help it. When he was with her, he was as cold as an archbishop both in word and in action. Nothing would tempt him to any outward manifestation of affection. He would talk of nothing but the poor women of St. Peter-cum-Pumpkin in the city, and the fraudulent idleness of a certain colleague in the cathedral services, who was always shirking his work. He made her no presents. He never walked with her. He was always gloomy, and he had indeed so behaved himself in public that people were beginning to talk of 'poor Mr Gibson.' And yet he could meet Arabella on the sly in the lanes, and send notes to her by the green-grocer's boy! Poor Mr Gibson indeed! Let her once get him well over the 29th of April, and the people of Exeter might talk about poor Mr Gibson if they pleased. And Bella's conduct was more wonderful almost than that of Mr Gibson. With all her cowardice, she still held up her head, held it perhaps a little higher than was usual with her. And when that grievous accusation was made against her—made and repeated—an accusation the very thought and sound of which would almost have annihilated her had there been a decent feeling in her bosom, she would simply shrug her shoulders and walk away. 'Camilla,' she had once said, 'you will drive that man mad before you have done.' 'What is it to you how I drive him?' Camilla had answered in her fury. Then Arabella had again shrugged her shoulders and walked away. Between Camilla and her mother, too, there had come to be an almost internecine quarrel on a collateral point. Camilla was still carrying on a vast arrangement which she called the preparation of her trousseau, but which both Mrs French and Bella regarded as a spoliation of the domestic nest, for the proud purposes of one of the younger birds. And this had grown so fearfully that in two different places Mrs French had found herself compelled to request that no further articles might be supplied to Miss Camilla. The bride elect had rebelled, alleging that as no fortune was to be provided for her, she had a right to take with her such things as she could carry away in her trunks and boxes. Money could be had at the bank, she said; and, after all, what were fifty pounds more or less on such an occasion as this? And then she went into a calculation to prove that her mother and sister would be made so much richer by her absence, and that she was doing so much for them by her marriage, that nothing could be more mean in them than that they should hesitate to supply her with such things as she desired to make her entrance into Mr Gibson's house respectable. But Mrs French was obdurate, and Mr Gibson was desired to speak to her. Mr Gibson, in fear and trembling, told her that she ought to repress her spirit of extravagance, and Camilla at once foresaw that he would avail himself of this plea against her should he find it possible at any time to avail himself of any plea. She became ferocious, and, turning upon him, told him to mind his own business. Was it not all for him that she was doing it? 'She was not,' she said, 'disposed to submit to any control in such matters from him till he had assumed his legal right to it by standing with her before the altar.' It came, however, to be known all over Exeter that Miss Camilla's expenditure had been checked, and that, in spite of the joys naturally incidental to a wedding, things were not going well with the ladies at Heavitree.

At last the blow came. Camilla was aware that on a certain morning her mother had been to Mr Gibson's house, and had held a long conference with him. She could learn nothing of what took place there, for at that moment she had taken upon herself to place herself on non-speaking terms with her mother in consequence of those disgraceful orders which had been given to the tradesmen. But Bella had not been at Mr Gibson's house at the time, and Camilla, though she presumed that her own conduct had been discussed in a manner very injurious to herself, did not believe that any step was being then arranged which would be positively antagonistic to her own views. The day fixed was now so very near that there could, she felt, be no escape for the victim. But she was wrong.

Mr Gibson had been found by Mrs French in a very excited state on that occasion. He had wept, and pulled his hair, and torn open his waistcoat, had spoken of himself as a wretch, pleading, however, at the same time, that he was more sinned against than sinning, had paced about the room with his hands dashing against his brows, and at last had flung himself prostrate on the ground. The meaning of it all was that he had tried very hard, and had found at last that 'he couldn't do it.' 'I am ready to submit,' said he, 'to any verdict that you may pronounce against me, but I should deceive you and deceive her if I didn't say at once that I can't do it.' He went on to explain that since he had unfortunately entered into his present engagement with Camilla, of whose position he spoke in quite a touching manner, and since he had found what was the condition of his own heart and feelings, he had consulted a friend who, if any merely human being was capable of advising, might be implicitly trusted for advice in such a matter, and that this friend had told him that he was bound to give up the marriage, let the consequences to himself or to others be what they might. 'Although the skies should fall on me, I cannot stand at the hymeneal altar with a lie in my mouth,' said Mr Gibson immediately upon his rising from his prostrate condition on the floor. In such a position as this a mother's fury would surely be very great! But Mrs French was hardly furious. She cried, and begged him to think better of it, and assured him that Camilla, when she should be calmed down by matrimony, would not be so bad as she seemed, but she was not furious. 'The truth is, Mr Gibson,' she said through her tears, 'that, after all, you like Bella best.' Mr Gibson owned that he did like Bella best, and although no bargain was made between them then and there—and such making of a bargain then and there would hardly have been practicable—it was understood that Mrs French would not proceed to extremities if Mr Gibson would still make himself forthcoming as a husband for the advantage of one of the daughters of the family.

So far Mr Gibson had progressed towards a partial liberation from his thraldom with a considerable amount of courage; but he was well aware that the great act of daring still remained to be done. He had suggested to Mrs French that she should settle the matter with Camilla, but this Mrs French had altogether declined to do. It must, she said, come from himself. If she were to do it, she must sympathise with her child; and such sympathy would be obstructive of the future arrangements which were still to be made. 'She always knew that I liked Bella best,' said Mr Gibson still sobbing, still tearing his hair, still pacing the room with his waistcoat torn open. 'I would not advise you to tell her that,' said Mrs French. Then Mrs French went home, and early on the following morning it was thought good by Arabella that she also should pay a visit at Ottery St. Mary's. 'Good-bye, Cammy,' said Arabella as she went. 'Bella,' said Camilla, 'I wonder whether you are a serpent. I do not think you can be so base a serpent as that.' 'I declare, Cammy, you do say such odd things that no one can understand what you mean.' And so she went.

On that morning Mr Gibson was walking at an early hour along the road from Exeter to Cowley, contemplating his position and striving to arrange his plans.

What was he to do, and how was he to do it? He was prepared to throw up his living, to abandon the cathedral, to leave the diocese, to make any sacrifice rather than take Camilla to his bosom. Within the last six weeks he had learned to regard her with almost a holy horror. He could not understand by what miracle of self-neglect he had fallen into so perilous an abyss. He had long known Camilla's temper. But in those days in which he had been beaten like a shuttlecock between the Stanburys and the Frenches, he had lost his head and had done he knew not what. 'Those whom the God chooses to destroy, he first maddens,' said Mr Gibson to himself of himself, throwing himself back upon early erudition and pagan philosophy. Then he looked across to the river Exe, and thought that there was hardly water enough there to cover the multiplicity of his sorrows.

But something must be done. He had proceeded so far in forming a resolution, as he reached St. David's Church on his return homewards. His sagacious friend had told him that as soon as he had altered his mind, he was bound to let the lady know of it without delay. 'You must remember,' said the sagacious friend, 'that you will owe her much very much.' Mr Gibson was perplexed in his mind when he reflected how much he might possibly be made to owe her if she should decide on appealing to a jury of her countrymen for justice. But anything would be better than his home at St. Peter's-cum-Pumpkin with Camilla sitting opposite to him as his wife. Were there not distant lands in which a clergyman, unfortunate but still energetic, might find work to do? Was there not all America? And were there not Australia, New Zealand, Natal, all open to him? Would not a missionary career among the Chinese be better for him than St. Peter's-cum-Pumpkin with Camilla French for his wife? By the time he had reached home his mind was made up. He would write a letter to Camilla at once; and he would marry Arabella at once on any day that might be fixed on condition that Camilla would submit to her defeat without legal redress. If legal redress should be demanded, he would put in evidence the fact that her own mother had been compelled to caution the tradesmen of the city in regard to her extravagance.

He did write his letter in an agony of spirit. 'I sit down, Camilla, with a sad heart and a reluctant hand,' he said, 'to communicate to you a fatal truth. But truth should be made to prevail, and there is nothing in man so cowardly, so detrimental, and so unmanly as its concealment. I have looked into myself, and have inquired of myself, and have assured myself, that were I to become your husband, I should not make you happy. It would be of no use for me now to dilate on the reasons which have convinced me, but I am convinced, and I consider it my duty to inform you so at once. I have been closeted with your mother, and have made her understand that it is so.

I have not a word to say in my own justification but this: that I am sure I am acting honestly in telling you the truth. I would not wish to say a word animadverting on yourself. If there must be blame in this matter, I am willing to take it all on my own shoulders. But things have been done of late, and words have been spoken, and habits have displayed themselves, which would not, I am sure, conduce to our mutual comfort in this world, or to our assistance to each other in our struggles to reach the happiness of the world to come.

I think that you will agree with me, Camilla, that when a man or a woman has fallen into such a mistake as that which I have now made, it is best that it should be acknowledged. I know well that such a change of arrangements as that which I now propose will be regarded most unfavourably. But will not anything be better than the binding of a matrimonial knot which cannot be again unloosed, and which we should both regret?

I do not know that I need add anything further. What can I add further? Only this, that I am inflexible. Having resolved to take this step and to bear the evil things that may be said of me, for your happiness and for my own tranquillity, I shall not now relinquish my resolution. I do not ask you to forgive me. I doubt much whether I shall ever be quite able to forgive myself. The mistake which I have made is one which should not have been committed. I do not ask you to forgive me; but I do ask you to pray that I may be forgiven.

Yours, with feelings of the truest friendship,   THOMAS GIBSON.'

The letter had been very difficult, but he was rather proud of it than otherwise when it was completed. He had felt that he was writing a letter which not improbably might become public property. It was necessary that he should be firm, that he should accuse himself a little in order that he might excuse himself much, and that he should hint at causes which might justify the rupture, though he should so veil them as not to appear to defend his own delinquency by ungenerous counter-accusation. When he had completed the letter, he thought that he had done all this rather well, and he sent the despatch off to Heavitree by the clerk of St. Peter's Church, with something of that feeling of expressible relief which attends the final conquest over some fatal and all but insuperable misfortune. He thought that he was sure now that he would not have to marry Camilla on the 29th of the month and there would probably be a period of some hours before he would be called upon to hear or read Camilla's reply.

Camilla was alone when she received the letter, but she rushed at once to her mother. 'There,' said she; 'there I knew that it was coming!' Mrs French took the paper into her hands and gasped, and gazed at her daughter without speaking. 'You knew of it, mother.'

'Yesterday when he told me, I knew of it.'

'And Bella knows it.'

'Not a word of it.'

'She does. I am sure she does. But it is all nothing. I will not accept it. He cannot treat me so. I will drag him there, but he shall come.'

'You can't make him, my dear.'

'I will make him. And you would help me, mamma, if you had any spirit. What, a fortnight before the time, when the things are all bought! Look at the presents that have been sent! Mamma, he doesn't know me. And he never would have done it, if it had not been for Bella, never. She had better take care, or there shall be such a tragedy that nobody ever heard the like. If she thinks that she is going to be that man's wife she is mistaken.' Then there was a pause for a moment.

'Mamma,' she said, 'I shall go to him at once. I do not care in the least what anybody may say. I shall go to him at once.' Mrs French felt that at this moment it was best that she should be silent.

CHAPTER LXXV. THE ROWLEYS GO OVER THE ALPS

By the thirteenth of May the Rowley family had established itself in Florence, purposing to remain either there or at the baths of Lucca till the end of June, at which time it was thought that Sir Marmaduke should begin to make preparations for his journey back to the Islands. Their future prospects were not altogether settled. It was not decided whether Lady Rowley should at once return with him, whether Mrs Trevelyan should return with him, nor was it settled among them what should be the fate of Nora Rowley. Nora Rowley was quite resolved herself that she would not go back to the Islands, and had said as much to her mother. Lady Rowley had not repeated this to Sir Marmaduke, and was herself in doubt as to what might best be done. Girls are understood by their mothers better than they are by their fathers. Lady Rowley was beginning to be aware that Nora's obstinacy was too strong to be overcome by mere words, and that other steps must be taken if she were to be weaned from her pernicious passion for Hugh Stanbury. Mr Glascock was still in Florence. Might she not be cured by further overtures from Mr Glascock? The chance of securing such a son-in-law was so important, so valuable, that no trouble was too great to be incurred, even though the probability of success might not be great.

It must not, however, be supposed that Lady Rowley carried off all the family to Italy, including Sir Marmaduke, simply in chase of Mr Glascock. Anxious as she was on the subject, she was too proud, and also too well-conditioned, to have suggested to herself such a journey with such an object. Trevelyan had escaped from Willesden with the child, and they had heard again through Stanbury that he had returned to Italy. They had all agreed that it would be well that they should leave London for awhile, and see something of the continent; and when it was told to them that little Louis was probably in Florence, that alone was reason enough for them to go thither. They would go to the city till the heat was too great and the mosquitoes too powerful, and then they would visit the baths of Lucca for a month. This was their plan of action, and the cause for their plan; but Lady Rowley found herself able to weave into it another little plan of her own, of which she said nothing to anybody. She was not running after Mr Glascock; but if Mr Glascock should choose to run after them or her, who could say that any harm had been done?

Nora had answered that proposition of her lover's to walk out of the house in Manchester Street, and get married at the next church, in a most discreet manner. She had declared that she would be true and firm, but that she did not wish to draw upon herself the displeasure of her father and mother. She did not, she said, look upon a clandestine marriage as a happy resource. But this she added at the end of a long and very sensible letter: she intended to abide by her engagement, and she did not intend to go back to the Mandarins. She did not say what alternative she would choose in the event of her being unable to obtain her father's consent before his return. She did not suggest what was to become of her when Sir Marmaduke's leave of absence should be expired. But her statement that she would not go back to the islands was certainly made with more substantial vigour, though, perhaps, with less of reasoning, than any other of the propositions made in her letter. Then, in her postscript, she told him that they were all going to Italy. 'Papa and mamma think that we ought to follow poor Mr Trevelyan. The lawyer says that nothing can be done while he is away with the boy. We are therefore all going to start to Florence. The journey is delightful. I will not say whose presence will be wanting to make it perfect.'

Before they started there came a letter to Nora from Dorothy, which shall be given entire, because it will tell the reader more of Dorothy's happiness than would be learned from any other mode of narrative.

> The Close,
> Thursday.

DEAREST NORA,

I have just had a letter from Hugh, and that makes me feel that I should like to write to you. Dear Hugh has told me all about it, and I do so hope that things may come right and that we may be sisters. He is so good that I do not wonder that you should love him. He has been the best son and the best brother in the world, and everybody speaks well of him except my dear aunt, who is prejudiced because she does not like newspapers. I need not praise him to you, for I dare say you think quite as well of him as I do. I cannot tell you all the beautiful things he says about you, but I dare say he has told them to you himself.

I seem to know you so well because Priscilla has talked about you so often. She says that she knew that you and my brother were fond of each other because you growled at each other when you were together at the Clock House, and never had any civil words to say before people. I don't know whether growling is a sign of love, but Hugh does growl sometimes when he is most affectionate. He growls at me, and I understand him, and I like to be growled at. I wonder whether you like him to growl at you.

And now I must tell you something about myself because if you are to be my sister you ought to know it all. I also am going to be married to a man whom I love oh, so dearly! His name is Mr Brooke Burgess, and he is a great friend of my aunt's. At first she did not like our being engaged, because of some family reason—but she has got over that, and nothing can be kinder and nicer than she is. We are to be married here, some day in June, the 11th I think it will be. How I do wish you could have been here to be my bridesmaid. It would have been so nice to have had Hugh's sweetheart with me. He is a friend of Hugh's, and no doubt you will hear all about him. The worst of it is that we must live in London, because my husband as will be—you see I call him mine already— is in an office there. And so poor Aunt Stanbury will be left all alone. It will be very sad, and she is so wedded to Exeter that I fear we shall not get her up to London.

I would describe Mr Burgess to you, only I do not suppose you would care to hear about him. He is not so tall as Hugh, but he is a great deal better looking. With you two the good looks are to be with the wife; but, with us, with the husband. Perhaps you think Hugh is handsome. We used to declare that he was the ugliest boy in the country. I don't suppose it makes very much difference. Brooke is handsome, but I don't think I should like him the less if he were ever so ugly.

Do you remember hearing about the Miss Frenches when you were in Devonshire? There has come up such a terrible affair about them. A Mr Gibson, a clergyman, was going to marry the younger; but has changed his mind and wants to take the elder. I think he was in love with her first.' Dorothy did not say a word about the little intermediate stage of attachment to herself. 'All this is making a great noise in the city, and some people think he should be punished severely. It seems to me that a gentleman ought not to make such a mistake; but if he does, he ought to own it. I hope they will let him marry the eider one. Aunt Stanbury says it all comes from their wearing chignons. I wish you knew Aunt Stanbury, because she is so good. Perhaps you wear a chignon. I think Priscilla said that you did. It must not be large, if you come to see Aunt Stanbury.

Pray write to me and believe that I hope to be your most affectionate sister,

DOROTHY STANBURY.

P.S. I am so happy, and I do so hope that you will be the same.

This was received only a day before the departure of the Rowleys for Italy, and was answered by a short note promising that Nora would write to her correspondent from Florence.

There could be no doubt that Trevelyan had started with his boy, fearing the result of the medical or legal interference with his affairs which was about to be made at Sir Marmaduke's instance. He had written a few words to his wife, neither commencing nor ending his note after any usual fashion, telling her that he thought it expedient to travel, that he had secured the services of a nurse for the little boy, and that during his absence a certain income would, as heretofore, be paid to her. He said nothing as to his probable return, or as to her future life; nor was there anything to indicate whither he was going. Stanbury, however, had learned from the faithless and frightened Bozzle that Trevelyan's letters were to be sent after him to Florence. Mr Bozzle, in giving this information, had acknowledged that his employer was 'becoming no longer quite himself under his troubles,' and had expressed his opinion that he ought to be 'looked after.' Bozzle had made his money; and now, with a grain of humanity mixed with many grains of faithlessness, reconciled it to himself to tell his master's secrets to his master's enemies. What would a counsel be able to say about his conduct in a court of law? That was the question which Bozzle was always asking himself as to his own business. That he should be abused by a barrister to a jury, and exposed as a spy and a fiend, was, he thought, a matter of course. To be so abused was a part of his profession. But it was expedient for him in all cases to secure some loop-hole of apparent duty by which he might in part escape from such censures. He was untrue to his employer now, because he thought that his employer ought to be 'looked after.' He did, no doubt, take a five-pound note from Hugh Stanbury; but then it was necessary that he should live. He must be paid for his time. In this way Trevelyan started for Florence, and within a week afterwards the Rowleys were upon his track.

Nothing had been said by Sir Marmaduke to Nora as to her lover since that stormy interview in which both father and daughter had expressed their opinions very strongly, and very little had been said by Lady Rowley. Lady Rowley had spoken more than once of Nora's return to the Mandarins, and had once alluded to it as a certainty. 'But I do not know that I shall go back,' Nora had said. 'My dear,' the mother had replied, 'unless you are married, I suppose your home must be with your parents.' Nora, having made her protest, did not think it necessary to persevere, and so the matter was dropped. It was known, however, that they must all come back to London before they started for their seat of government, and therefore the subject did not at present assume its difficult aspect. There was a tacit understanding among them that everything should be done to make the journey pleasant to the young mother who was in search of her son; and, in addition to this, Lady Rowley had her own little understanding, which was very tacit indeed, that in Mr Glascock might be found an escape from one of their great family difficulties.

'You had better take this, papa,' Mrs Trevelyan had said, when she received from the office of Mr Bideawhile a cheque payable to her order for the money sent to her by her husband's direction.

'I do not want the man's money,' said Sir Marmaduke. 'But you are going to this place for my sake, papa and it is right that he should bear the expense for his own wife. And, papa, you must remember always that though his mind is distracted on this horrible business, he is not a bad man. No one is more liberal or more just about money.' Sir Marmaduke's feelings on the matter were very much the same as those which had troubled Mr Outhouse, and he, personally, refused to touch the money; but his daughter paid her own share of the expenses of the journey.

They travelled at their ease, stopping at Paris, and at Geneva, and at Milan. Lady Rowley thought that she was taken very fast, because she was allowed to sleep only two nights at each of these places, and Sir Rowley himself thought that he had achieved something of a Hannibalian enterprise in taking five ladies and two maids over the Simplon and down into the plains of Lombardy, with nobody to protect him but a single courier. He had been a little nervous about it, being unaccustomed to European travelling, and had not at first realised the fact that the journey is to be made with less trouble than one from the Marble Arch to Mile End. 'My dears,' he said to his younger daughters, as they were rattling round the steep downward twists and turns of the great road, 'you must sit quite still on these descents, or you do not know where you may go. The least thing would overset us.' But Lucy and Sophy soon knew better, and became so intimate with the mountain, under the friendly guidance of their courier, that before the plains were reached, they were in and out, and here and there, and up and down, as though they had been bred among the valleys of the pass. There would come a ringing laugh from some rock above their head, and Lady Rowley looking up would see their dresses fluttering on a pinnacle which appeared to her to be fit only for a bird; and there would be the courier behind them, with two parasols, and a shawl, and a cloak, and an eye-glass, and a fine pair of grizzled whiskers. They made an Alpine club of their own, refusing to admit their father because he would not climb up a rock, and Nora thought of the letters about it which she would write to her lover, only that she had determined that she would not write to him at all without telling her mother, and Mrs Trevelyan would for moments almost forget that she had been robbed of her child.

From Milan they went on to Florence, and though they were by that time quite at home in Italy, and had become critical judges of Italian inns and Italian railways, they did not find that journey to be quite so pleasant. There is a romance to us still in the name of Italy which a near view of many details in the country fails to realise. Shall we say that a journey through Lombardy is about as interesting as one through the flats of Cambridgeshire and the fens of Norfolk? And the station of Bologna is not an interesting spot in which to spend an hour or two, although it may be conceded that provisions may be had there much better than any that can be procured at our own railway stations. From thence they went, still by rail, over the Apennines, and unfortunately slept during the whole time. The courier had assured them that if they would only look out they would see the castles of which they had read in novels; but the day had been very hot, and Sir Marmaduke had been cross, and Lady Rowley had been weary, and so not a castle was seen. 'Pistoia, me lady, this,' said the courier opening the door 'to stop half an hour.' 'Oh, why was it not Florence?' Another hour and a half! So they all went to sleep again, and were very tired when they reached the beautiful city.

During the next day they rested at their inn, and sauntered through the Duomo, and broke their necks looking up at the inimitable glories of the campanile. Such a one as Sir Marmaduke had of course not come to Florence without introductions. The Foreign Office is always very civil to its next-door neighbours of the colonies, civil and cordial, though perhaps a little patronising. A minister is a bigger man than a governor; and the smallest of the diplomatic fry are greater swells than even secretaries in quite important dependencies. The attache, though he be unpaid, dwells in a capital, and flirts with a countess. The governor's right-hand man is confined to an island, and dances with a planter's daughter. The distinction is quite understood, but is not incompatible with much excellent good feeling on the part of the superior department. Sir Marmaduke had come to Florence fairly provided with passports to Florentine society, and had been mentioned in more than one letter as the distinguished Governor of the Mandarins, who had been called home from his seat of government on a special mission of great importance. On the second day he went out to call at the embassy and to leave his cards. 'Have you been able to learn whether he is here?' asked Lady Rowley of her husband in a whisper, as soon as they were alone.

'Who, Trevelyan?'

I did not suppose you could learn about him, because he would be hiding himself. But is Mr Glascock here?'

'I forgot to ask,' said Sir Marmaduke.

Lady Rowley did not reproach him. It is impossible that any father should altogether share a mother's anxiety in regard to the marriage of their daughters. But what a thing it would be! Lady Rowley thought that she could compound for all misfortunes in other respects, if she could have a daughter married to the future Lord Peterborough. She had been told in England that he was faultless not very clever, not very active, not likely to be very famous; but, as a husband, simply faultless. He was very rich, very good-natured, easily managed, more likely to be proud of his wife than of himself, addicted to no jealousies, afflicted by no vices, so respectable in every way that he was sure to become great as an English nobleman by the very weight of his virtues. And it had been represented also to Lady Rowley that this paragon among men had been passionately attached to her daughter! Perhaps she magnified a little the romance of the story; but it seemed to her that this greatly endowed lover had rushed away from his country in despair, because her daughter Nora would not smile upon him. Now they were, as she hoped, in the same city with him. But it was indispensable to her success that she should not seem to be running after him. To Nora, not a word had been said of the prospect of meeting Mr Glascock at Florence. Hardly more than a word had been said to her sister Emily, and that under injunction of strictest secrecy. It must be made to appear to all the world that other motives had brought them to Florence as, indeed, other motives had brought them. Not for worlds would Lady Rowley have run after a man for her daughter; but still, still—still, seeing that the man was himself so unutterably in love with her girl, seeing that he was so fully justified by his position to be in love with any girl, seeing that such a maximum of happiness would be the result of such a marriage, she did feel that, even for his sake, she must be doing a good thing to bring them together! Something, though not much of all this, she had been obliged to explain to Sir Marmaduke and yet he had not taken the trouble to inquire whether Mr Glascock was in Florence!

On the third day after their arrival, the wife of the British minister came to call upon Lady Rowley, and the wife of the British minister was good-natured, easy-mannered, and very much given to conversation. She preferred talking to listening, and in the course of a quarter of an hour had told Lady Rowley a good deal about Florence; but she had not mentioned Mr Glascock's name. It would have been so pleasant if the requisite information could have been obtained without the asking of any direct question on the subject! But Lady Rowley, who from many years' practice of similar, though perhaps less distinguished, courtesies on her part, knew well the first symptom of the coming end of her guest's visit, found that the minister's wife was about to take her departure without an allusion to Mr Glascock. And yet the names had been mentioned of so many English residents in Florence, who neither in wealth, rank, or virtue, were competent to hold a candle to that phœnix! She was forced, therefore, to pluck up courage, and to ask the question. 'Have you had a Mr Glascock here this spring?' said Lady Rowley.

'What Lord Peterborough's son? Oh, dear, yes. Such a singular being!'

Lady Rowley thought that she could perceive that her phœnix had not made himself agreeable at the embassy. It might perhaps be that he had buried himself away from society because of his love. 'And is here now?' asked Lady Rowley.

'I cannot say at all. He is sometimes here and sometimes with his father at Naples. But when here, he lives chiefly with the Americans. They say he is going to marry an American girl their minister's niece. There are three of-them, I think, and he is to take the eldest.' Lady Rowley asked no more questions, and let her august visitor go, almost without another word.

CHAPTER LXXVI. 'WE SHALL BE SO POOR'

Mr Glascock at that moment was not only in Florence, but was occupying rooms in the very hotel in which the Rowleys were staying. Lady Rowley, when she heard that he was engaged to marry an American lady, became suddenly very sick at heart sick with a sickness that almost went beyond her heart. She felt ill, and was glad to be alone. The rumour might be untrue. Such rumours generally are untrue. But then, as Lady Rowley knew very well, they generally have some foundation in truth. Mr Glascock, if he were not actually engaged to the American girl, had probably been flirting with her and, if so, where was that picture which Lady Rowley had been painting for herself of a love-lorn swain to be brought back to the pleasures and occupations of the world only by the girl of whom he was enamoured? But still she would not quite give up the project. Mr Glascock, if he was in Italy, would no doubt see by the newspapers that Sir Marmaduke and his family were in Florence and would probably come to them. Then, if Nora would only behave herself, the American girl might still be conquered.

During two or three days after this nothing was seen or heard of Mr Glascock. Had Lady Rowley thought of mentioning the name to the waiter at the hotel, she would have learned that he was living in the next passage; but it did not occur to her to seek information in that fashion. Nor did she ask direct questions in other quarters about Mr Glascock himself. She did, however, make inquiry about Americans living in Florence, especially about the American Minister and, before a week had passed overhead, had been introduced to the Spaldings. Mrs Spalding was very civil, and invited Lady Rowley and all the girls and Sir Marmaduke to come to her on her 'Fridays.' She received her friends every Friday, and would continue to do so till the middle of June. She had nieces who would, she said, be so happy to make the acquaintance of the Miss Rowleys.

By this time the picture galleries, the churches, and the palaces in Florence had nearly all been visited. Poor Lady Rowley had dragged herself wearily from sight to sight, hoping always to meet with Mr Glascock, ignorant of the fact that residents in a town do not pass their mornings habitually in looking after pictures. During this time inquiries were being made, through the police, respecting Trevelyan; and Sir Marmaduke had obtained information that an English gentleman, with a little boy, had gone on to Siena, and had located himself there. There seemed to be but little doubt that this was Trevelyan, though nothing had been learned with certainty as to the gentleman's name. It had been decided that Sir Marmaduke, with his courier and Mrs Trevelyan, should go on to Siena, and endeavour to come upon the fugitive, and they had taken their departure on a certain morning. On that same day Lady Rowley was walking with Nora and one of the other girls through the hall of the hotel, when they were met in full face by Mr Glascock! Lady Rowley and Lucy were in front, and they, of course, did not know the man. Nora had seen him at once, and in her confusion hardly knew how to bear herself. Mr Glascock was passing by her without recognising her had passed her mother and sister, and had so far gone on, that Nora had determined to make no sign, when he chanced to look up and see who it was that was so close to him. 'Miss Rowley,' he said, 'who thought of meeting you in Florence!' Lady Rowley, of course, turned round, and there was an introduction. Poor Nora, though she knew nothing of her mother's schemes, was confused and ill at ease. Mr Glascock was very civil, but at the same time rather cold. Lady Rowley was all smiles and courtesy. She had, she said, heard his name from her daughters, and was very happy to make his acquaintance. Lucy looked on somewhat astonished to find that the lover whom her sister had been blamed for rejecting, and who was spoken of with so many encomiums, was so old a man. Mr Glascock asked after Mrs Trevelyan; and Lady Rowley, in a low, melancholy whisper, told him that they were now all in Florence, in the hope of meeting Mr Trevelyan. 'You have heard the sad story, I know, Mr Glascock, and therefore I do not mind telling you.' Mr Glascock acknowledged that he did know the story, and informed her that he had seen Mr Trevelyan in Florence within the last ten days. This was so interesting, that, at Lady Rowley's request, he went with them up to their rooms, and in this way the acquaintance was made. It turned out that Mr Glascock had spoken to Mr Trevelyan, and that Trevelyan had told him that he meant for the present to take up his residence in some small Italian town. 'And how was he looking, Mr Glascock?'

'Very ill, Lady Rowley, very ill, indeed.'

'Do not tell her so, Mr Glascock. She has gone now with her father to Siena. We think that he is there, with the boy or, at least, that he may be heard of there. And you you are living here?' Mr Glascock said that he was living between Naples and Florence, going occasionally to Naples, a place that he hated, to see his father, and coming back at intervals to the capital. Nora sat by, and hardly spoke a word. She was nicely dressed, with an exquisite little bonnet, which had been bought as they came through Paris; and Lady Rowley, with natural pride, felt that if he was ever in love with her child, that love must come back upon him now. American girls, she had been told, were hard, and dry, and sharp, and angular. She had seen some at the Mandarins, with whom she thought it must be impossible that any Englishman should be in love. There never, surely, had been an American girl like her Nora. 'Are you fond of pictures, Mr Glascock?' she asked. Mr Glascock was not very fond of pictures, and thought that he was rather tired of them. What was he fond of? Of sitting at home and doing nothing. That was his reply, at least; and a very unsatisfactory reply it was, as Lady Rowley could hardly propose that they should come and sit and do nothing with him. Could he have been lured into churches or galleries, Nora might have been once more thrown into his company. Then Lady Rowley took courage, and asked him whether he knew the Spaldings. They were going to Mrs Spalding's that very evening, she and her daughters. Mr Glascock replied that he did know the Spaldings, and that he also should be at their house. Lady Rowley thought that she discovered something like a blush about his cheekbones and brow, as he made his answer. Then he left them, giving his hand to Nora as he went but there was nothing in his manner to justify the slightest hope.

'I don't think he is nice at all,' said Lucy.

'Don't be so foolish, Lucy,' said Lady Rowley angrily.

'I think he is very nice,' said Nora. 'He was only talking nonsense when he said that he liked to sit still and do nothing. He is not at all an idle man; at least I am told so.'

'But he is as old as Methuselah,' said Lucy.

'He is between thirty and forty,' said Lady Rowley.

'Of course we know that from the peerage.' Lady Rowley, however, was wrong. Had she consulted the peerage, she would have seen that Mr Glascock was over forty.

Nora, as soon as she was alone and could think about it all, felt quite sure that Mr Glascock would never make her another offer. This ought not to have caused her any sorrow, as she was very well aware that she would not accept him, should he do so. Yet, perhaps, there was a moment of some feeling akin to disappointment. Of course she would not have accepted him. How could she? Her faith was so plighted to Hugh Stanbury that she would be a by-word among women for ever, were she to be so false. And, as she told herself, she had not the slightest feeling of affection for Mr Glascock. It was quite out of the question, and a matter simply for speculation. Nevertheless it would have been a very grand thing to be Lady Peterborough, and she almost regretted that she had a heart in her bosom.

She had become fully aware during that interview that her mother still entertained hopes, and almost suspected that Lady Rowley had known something of Mr Glascock's residence in Florence. She had seen that her mother had met Mr Glascock almost as though some such meeting had been expected, and had spoken to him almost as though she had expected to have to speak to him. Would it not be better that she should at once make her mother understand that all this could be of no avail? If she were to declare plainly that nothing could bring about such a marriage, would not her mother desist? She almost made up her mind to do so; but as her mother said nothing to her before they started for Mr Spalding's house, neither did she say anything to her mother. She did not wish to have angry words if they could be avoided, and she felt that there might be anger and unpleasant words were she to insist upon her devotion to Hugh Stanbury while this rich prize was in sight. If her mother should speak to her, then, indeed, she would declare her own settled purpose; but she would do nothing to accelerate the evil hour.

There were but few people in Mrs Spalding's drawing-room when they were announced, and Mr Glascock was not among them. Miss Wallachia Petrie was there, and in the confusion of the introduction was presumed by Lady Rowley to be one of the nieces introduced. She had been distinctly told that Mr Glascock was to marry the eldest, and this lady was certainly older than the other two. In this way Lady Rowley decided that Miss Wallachia Petrie was her daughter's hated rival, and she certainly was much surprised at the gentleman's taste. But there is nothing nothing in the way of an absurd matrimonial engagement into which a man will not allow himself to be entrapped by pique. Nora would have a great deal to answer for, Lady Rowley thought, if the unfortunate man should be driven by her cruelty to marry such a woman as this one now before her.

It happened that Lady Rowley soon found herself seated by Miss Petrie, and she at once commenced her questionings. She intended to be very discreet, but the subject was too near her heart to allow her to be altogether silent. 'I believe you know Mr Glascock?' she said.

'Yes,' said Wallachia, 'I do know him.' Now the peculiar nasal twang which our cousins over the water have learned to use, and which has grown out of a certain national instinct which coerces them to express themselves with self-assertion—let the reader go into his closet and talk through his nose for awhile with steady attention to the effect which his own voice will have, and he will find that this theory is correct—this intonation, which is so peculiar among intelligent Americans, had been adopted *con amore*, and, as it were, taken to her bosom by Miss Petrie. Her ears had taught themselves to feel that there could be no vitality in speech without it, and that all utterance unsustained by such tone was effeminate, vapid, useless, unpersuasive, unmusical and English. It was a complaint frequently made by her against her friends Caroline and Olivia that they debased their voices, and taught themselves the puling British mode of speech. 'I do know the gentleman,' said Wallachia, and Lady Rowley shuddered. Could it be that such a woman as this was to reign over Monkhams, and become the future Lady Peterborough?

'He told me that he is acquainted with the family,' said Lady Rowley. 'He is staying at our hotel, and my daughter knew him very well when he was living in London.'

'I dare say. I believe that in London the titled aristocrats do hang pretty much together.' It had never occurred to poor Lady Rowley, since the day in which her husband had been made a knight, at the advice of the Colonial Minister, in order that the inhabitants of some island might be gratified by the opportunity of using the title, that she and her children had thereby become aristocrats. Were her daughter Nora to marry Mr Glascock, Nora would become an aristocrat or would, rather, be ennobled, all which Lady Rowley understood perfectly.

'I don't know that London society is very exclusive in that respect,' said Lady Rowley.

'I guess you are pretty particular,' said Miss Petrie, 'and it seems to me you don't have much regard to intellect or erudition but fix things up straight according to birth and money.'

'I hope we are not quite so bad as that,' said Lady Rowley. 'I do not know London well myself, as I have passed my life in very distant places.'

'The distant places are, in my estimation, the best. The further the mind is removed from the contamination incidental to the centres of long-established luxury, the more chance it has of developing itself according to the intention of the Creator, when he bestowed his gifts of intellect upon us.' Lady Rowley, when she heard this eloquence, could hardly believe that such a man as Mr Glascock should really be intent upon marrying such a lady as this who was sitting next to her.

In the meantime, Nora and the real rival were together, and they also were talking of Mr Glascock. Caroline Spalding had said that Mr Glascock had spoken to her of Nora Rowley, and Nora acknowledged that there had been some acquaintance between them in London. 'Almost more than that, I should have thought,' said Miss Spalding, 'if one might judge by his manner of speaking of you.'

'He is a little given to be enthusiastic,' said Nora, laughing.

'The least so of all mankind, I should have said. You must know he is very intimate in this house. It begun in this way. Olivia and I were travelling together, and there was a difficulty, as we say in our country when three or four gentlemen shoot each other. Then there came up Mr Glascock and another gentleman. By-the-bye, the other gentleman was your brother-in-law.'

'Poor Mr Trevelyan!'

'He is very ill, is he not?'

'We think so. My sister is with us, you know. That is to say, she is at Siena today.'

'I have heard about him, and it is so sad. Mr Glascock knows him. As I said, they were travelling together, when Mr Glascock came to our assistance. Since that, we have seen him very frequently. I don't think he is enthusiastic except when he talks of you.'

'I ought to be very proud,' said Nora.

'I think you ought, as Mr Glascock is a man whose good opinion is certainly worth having. Here he is. Mr Glascock, I hope your ears are tingling. They ought to do so, because we are saying all manner of fine things about you.'

'I could not be well spoken of by two on whose good word I should set a higher value,' said he.

'And whose do you value the most?' said Caroline.

'I must first know whose eulogium will run the highest.'

Then Nora answered him. 'Mr Glascock, other people may praise you louder than I can do, but no one will ever do so with more sincerity.' There was a pretty earnestness about her as she spoke, which Lady Rowley ought to have heard. Mr Glascock bowed, and Miss Spalding smiled, and Nora blushed.

'If you are not overwhelmed now,' said Miss Spalding, 'you must be so used to flattery, that it has no longer any effect upon you. You must be like a drunkard, to whom wine is as water, and who thinks that brandy is not strong enough.'

'I think I had better go away,' said Mr Glascock, 'for fear the brandy should be watered by degrees.' And so he left them.

Nora had become quite aware, without much process of thinking about it, that her former lover and this American young lady were very intimate with each other. The tone of the conversation had shewn that it was so and, then, how had it come to pass that Mr Glascock had spoken to this American girl about her, Nora Rowley? It was evident that he had spoken of her with warmth, and had done so in a manner to impress his hearer. For a minute or two they sat together in silence after Mr Glascock had left them, but neither of them stirred. Then Caroline Spalding turned suddenly upon Nora, and took her by the hand. 'I must tell you something,' said she, 'only it must be a secret for awhile.'

'I will not repeat it.'

'Thank you, dear. I am engaged to him as his wife. He asked me this very afternoon, and nobody knows it but my aunt. When I had accepted him, he told me all the story about you. He had very often spoken of you before, and I had guessed how it must have been. He wears his heart so open for those whom he loves, that there is nothing concealed. He had seen you just before he came to me. But perhaps I am wrong to tell you that now. He ought to have been thinking of you again at such a time.'

'I did not want him to think of me again.'

'Of course you did not. Of course I am joking. You might have been his wife if you wished it. He has told me all that. And he especially wants us to be friends. Is there anything to prevent it?'

'On my part? Oh, dear, no except that you will be such grand folk, and we shall be so poor.'

'We!' said Caroline, laughing. 'I am so glad that there is a "we."'

CHAPTER LXXVII. THE FUTURE LADY PETERBOROUGH

'If you have not sold yourself for British gold, and for British acres, and for British rank, I have nothing to say against it,' said Miss Wallachia Petrie that same evening to her friend Caroline Spalding.

'You know that I have not sold myself, as you call it,' said Caroline. There had been a long friendship between these two ladies, and the younger one knew that it behoved her to bear a good deal from the elder. Miss Petrie was honest, clever, and in earnest. We in England are not usually favourably disposed to women who take a pride in a certain antagonism to men in general, and who are anxious to shew the world that they can get on very well without male assistance; but there are many such in America who have noble aspirations, good intellects, much energy, and who are by no means unworthy of friendship. The hope in regard to all such women—the hope entertained not by themselves, but by those who are solicitous for them—is that they will be cured at last by a husband and half-a-dozen children. In regard to Wallachia Petrie there was not, perhaps, much ground for such hope. She was so positively wedded to women's rights in general, and to her own rights in particular, that it was improbable that she should ever succumb to any man, and where would be the man brave enough to make the effort? From circumstances Caroline Spalding had been the beloved of her heart since Caroline Spalding was a very little girl; and she had hoped that Caroline would through life have borne arms along with her in that contest which she was determined to wage against man, and which she always waged with the greatest animosity against men of the British race. She hated rank; she hated riches; she hated monarchy and with a true woman's instinct in battle, felt that she had a specially strong point against Englishmen, in that they submitted themselves to dominion from a woman monarch.

And now the chosen friend of her youth, the friend who had copied out all her poetry, who had learned by heart all her sonnets, who had, as she thought, reciprocated all her ideas, was going to be married and to be married to an English lord! She had seen that it was coming for some time, and had spoken out very plainly, hoping that she might still save the brand from the burning. Now the evil was done; and Caroline Spalding, when she told her news, knew well that she would have to bear some heavy reproaches.

'How many of us are there who never know whether we sell ourselves or not?' said Wallachia. 'The senator who longs for office, and who votes this way instead of that in order that he may get it, thinks that he is voting honestly. The minister who calls himself a teacher of God's word, thinks that it is God's word that he preaches when he strains his lungs to fill his church. The question is this, Caroline would you have loved the same man had he come to you with a woodman's axe in his hand or a clerk's quill behind his ear? I guess not.'

'As to the woodman's axe, Wally, it is very well in theory; but—'

'Things good in theory, Caroline, will be good also when practised. You may be sure of that. We dislike theory simply because our intelligences are higher than our wills. But we will let that pass.'

'Pray let it pass, Wally. Do not preach me sermons tonight. I am so happy, and you ought to wish me joy.'

'If wishing you joy would get you joy, I would wish it you while I lived. I cannot be happy that you should be taken from us whither I shall never see you again.'

'But you are to come to us. I have told him so, and it is settled.'

'No, dear; I shall not do that. What should I be in the glittering halls of an English baron? Could there be any visiting less fitting, any admixture less appropriate? Could I who have held up my voice in the Music Hall of Lacedæmon amidst the glories of the West, in the great and free State of Illinois, against the corruption of an English aristocracy, could I, who have been listened to by two thousand of my countrywomen and men while I spurned the unmanly, inhuman errors of primogeniture, could I, think you, hold my tongue beneath the roof of a feudal lord!' Caroline Spalding knew that her friend could not hold her tongue, and hesitated to answer. There had been that fatal triumph of a lecture on the joint rights of men and women, and it had rendered poor Wallachia Petrie unfit for ordinary society.

'You might come there without talking politics, Wally,' said Caroline.

'No, Caroline; no. I will go into the house of no man in which the free expression of my opinion is debarred me. I will not sit even at your table with a muzzled tongue. When you are gone, Caroline, I shall devote myself to what, after all, must be the work of my life, and I shall finish the biographical history of our great hero in verse which I hope may at least be not ephemeral. From month to month I shall send you what I do, and you will not refuse me your friendly criticism and, perhaps, some slight meed of approbation because you are dwelling beneath the shade of a throne. Oh, Caroline, let it not be a upas tree!'

The Miss Petries of the world have this advantage, an advantage which rarely if ever falls to the lot of a man, that they are never convinced of error. Men, let them be ever so much devoted to their closets, let them keep their work ever so closely veiled from public scrutiny, still find themselves subjected to criticism, and under the necessity of either defending themselves or of succumbing. If, indeed, a man neither speaks, nor writes, if he be dumb as regards opinion, he passes simply as one of the crowd, and is in the way neither of convincing nor of being convinced; but a woman may speak, and almost write, as she likes, without danger of being wounded by sustained conflict. Who would have the courage to begin with such a one as Miss Petrie, and endeavour to prove to her that she is wrong from the beginning. A little word of half-dissent, a smile, a shrug, and an ambiguous compliment which is misunderstood, are all the forms of argument which can be used against her. Wallachia Petrie, in her heart of hearts, conceived that she had fairly discussed her great projects from year to year with indomitable eloquence and unanswerable truth and that none of her opponents had had a leg to stand upon. And this she believed because the chivalry of men had given to her sex that protection against which her life was one continued protest.

'Here he is,' said Caroline, as Mr Glascock came up to them. 'Try and say a civil word to him, if he speaks about it. Though he is to be a lord, still he is a man and a brother.'

'Caroline,' said the stern monitress, 'you are already learning to laugh at principles which have been dear to you since you left your mother's breast. Alas, how true it is, "You cannot touch pitch and not be defiled."'

The further progress of these friendly and feminine amenities was stopped by the presence of the gentleman who had occasioned them. 'Miss Petrie,' said the hero of the hour, 'Caroline was to tell you of my good fortune, and no doubt she has done so.'

'I cannot wait to hear the pretty things he has to say,' said Caroline, 'and I must look after my aunt's guests. There is poor Signor Buonarosci without a soul to say a syllable to him, and I must go and use my ten Italian words.'

'You are about to take with you to your old country, Mr Glascock,' said Miss Petrie, 'one of the brightest stars in our young American firmament.' There could be no doubt, from the tone of Miss Petrie's voice, that she now regarded this star, however bright, as one of a sort which is subjected to falling.

'I am going to take a very nice young woman,' said Mr Glascock.

'I hate that word woman, sir, uttered with the halfhidden sneer which always accompanies its expression from the mouth of a man.'

'Sneer, Miss Petrie!'

'I quite allow that it is involuntary, and not analysed or understood by yourselves. If you speak of a dog, you intend to do so with affection, but there is always contempt mixed with it. The so-called chivalry of man to woman is all begotten in the same spirit. I want no favour, but I claim to be your equal.'

'I thought that American ladies were generally somewhat exacting as to those privileges which chivalry gives them.'

'It is true, sir, that the only rank we know in our country is in that precedence which man gives to woman. Whether we maintain that, or whether we abandon it, we do not intend to purchase it at the price of an acknowledgment of intellectual inferiority. For myself, I hate chivalry—what you call chivalry. I can carry my own chair, and I claim the right to carry it whithersoever I may please.'

Mr Glascock remained with her for some time, but made no opportunity for giving that invitation to Monkhams of which Caroline had spoken. As he said afterwards, he found it impossible to expect her to attend to any subject so trivial; and when, afterwards, Caroline told him, with some slight mirth, the capability of which on such a subject was coming to her with her new ideas of life, that, though he was partly saved as a man and a brother, still he was partly the reverse as a feudal lord, he began to reflect that Wallachia Petrie would be a guest with whom he would find it very difficult to make things go pleasantly at Monkhams.

'Does she not bully you horribly?' he asked.

'Of course she bullies me,' Caroline answered; 'and I cannot expect you to understand as yet how it is that I love her and like her; but I do. If I were in distress tomorrow, she would give everything she has in the world to put me right.'

'So would I,' said he.

'Ah, you, that is a matter of course. That is your business now. And she would give everything she has in the world to set the world right. Would you do that?'

'It would depend on the amount of my faith. If I could believe in the result, I suppose I should do it.'

'She would do it on the slightest hope that such giving would have any tendency that way. Her philanthropy is all real. Of course she is a bore to you.'

'I am very patient.'

'I hope I shall find you so always. And, of course, she is ridiculous in your eyes. I have learned to see it, and to regret it; but I shall never cease to love her.'

'I have not the slightest objection. Her lessons will come from over the water, and mine will come from where shall I say? over the table. If I can't talk her down with so much advantage on my side, I ought to be made a woman's-right man myself.'

Poor Lady Rowley had watched Miss Petrie and Mr Glascock during those moments that they had been together, and had half believed the rumour, and had half doubted, thinking in the moments of her belief that Mr Glascock must be mad, and in the moments of unbelief that the rumours had been set afloat by the English Minister's wife with the express intention of turning Mr Glascock into ridicule. It had never occurred to her to doubt that Wallachia was the eldest of that family of nieces. Could it be possible that a man who had known her Nora, who had undoubtedly loved her Nora, who had travelled all the way from London to Nuncombe Putney to ask Nora to be his wife, should within twelve months of that time have resolved to marry a woman whom he must have selected simply as being the most opposite to Nora of any female human being that he could find? It was not credible to her; and if it were not true, there might still be a hope. Nora had met him, and had spoken to him, and it had seemed that for a moment or two they had spoken as friends. Lady Rowley, when talking to Mrs Spalding, had watched them closely; and she had seen that Nora's eyes had been bright, and that there had been something between them which was pleasant. Suddenly she found herself close to Wallachia, and thought that she would trust herself to a word.

'Have you been long in Florence?' asked Lady Rowley in her softest voice.

'A pretty considerable time, ma'am, that is, since the fall began.'

What a voice; what an accent; and what words! Was there a man living with sufficient courage to take this woman to England, and shew her to the world as Lady Peterborough?

'Are you going to remain in Italy for the summer?' continued Lady Rowley.

'I guess I shall or, perhaps, locate myself in the purer atmosphere of the Swiss mountains.'

'Switzerland in summer must certainly be much pleasanter.'

'I was thinking at the moment of the political atmosphere,' said Miss Petrie; 'for although, certainly, much has been done in this country in the way of striking off shackles and treading sceptres under foot, still, Lady Rowley, there remains here that pernicious thing—a king. The feeling of the dominion of a single man and that of a single woman is, for aught I know, worse with me, so clouds the air, that the breath I breathe fails to fill my lungs.' Wallachia, as she said this, put forth her hand, and raised her chin, and extended her arm. She paused, feeling that justice demanded that Lady Rowley should have a right of reply. But Lady Rowley had not a word to say, and Wallachia Petrie went on. 'I cannot adapt my body to the sweet savours and the soft luxuries of the outer world with any comfort to my inner self, while the circumstances of the society around me are oppressive to my spirit. When our war was raging all around me I was light-spirited as the lark that mounts through the morning sky.'

'I should have thought it was very dreadful,' said Lady Rowley.

'Full of dread, of awe, and of horror, were those fiery days of indiscriminate slaughter; but they were not days of desolation, because hope was always there by our side. There was a hope in which the soul could trust, and the trusting soul is ever light and buoyant.'

'I dare say it is,' said Lady Rowley.

'But apathy, and serfdom, and kinghood, and dominion, drain the fountain of its living springs, and the soul becomes like the plummet of lead, whose only tendency is to hide itself in subaqueous mud and unsavoury slush.'

Subaqueous mud and unsavoury slush! Lady Rowley repeated the words to herself as she made good her escape, and again expressed to herself her conviction that it could not possibly be so. The 'subaqueous mud and unsavoury slush,' with all that had gone before it about the soul, was altogether unintelligible to her; but she knew that it was American buncombe of a high order of eloquence, and she told herself again and again that it could not be so. She continued to keep her eyes upon Mr Glascock, and soon saw him again talking to Nora. It was hardly possible, she thought, that Nora should speak to him with so much animation, or he to her, unless there was some feeling between them which, if properly handled, might lead to a renewal of the old tenderness. She went up to Nora, having collected the other girls, and said that the carriage was then waiting for them. Mr Glascock immediately offered Lady Rowley his arm, and took her down to the hall. Could it be that she was leaning upon a future son-in-law? There was something in the thought which made her lay her weight upon him with a freedom which she would not otherwise have used. Oh! that her Nora should live to be Lady Peterborough! We are apt to abuse mothers for wanting high husbands for their daughters but can there be any point in which the true maternal instinct can shew itself with more affectionate enthusiasm? This poor mother wanted nothing for herself from Mr Glascock. She knew very well that it was her fate to go back to the Mandarins, and probably to die there. She knew also that such men as Mr Glascock, when they marry beneath themselves in rank and fortune, will not ordinarily trouble themselves much with their mothers-in-law. There was nothing desired for herself. Were such a match accomplished, she might, perhaps, indulge herself in talking among the planters' wives of her daughter's coronet; but at the present moment there was no idea even of this in her mind. It was of Nora herself, and of Nora's sisters, that she was thinking, for them that she was plotting that the one might be rich and splendid, and the others have some path opened for them to riches and splendour. Husband-hunting mothers may be injudicious; but surely they are maternal and unselfish. Mr Glascock put her into the carriage, and squeezed her hand and then he squeezed Nora's hand. She saw it, and was sure of it. 'I am so glad you are going to be happy,' Nora had said to him before this. 'As far as I have seen her, I like her so much.' 'If you do not come and visit her in her own house, I shall think you have no spirit of friendship,' he said. 'I will,' Nora had replied 'I will.' This had been said just as Lady Rowley was coming to them, and on this understanding, on this footing, Mr Glascock had pressed her hand.

As she went home, Lady Rowley's mind was full of doubt as to the course which it was best that she should follow with her daughter. She was not unaware how great was the difficulty before her. Hugh Stanbury's name had not been mentioned since they left London, but at that time Nora was obstinately bent on throwing herself away upon the 'penny-a-liner.' She had never been brought to acknowledge that such a marriage would be even inappropriate, and had withstood gallantly the expression of her father's displeasure. But with such a spirit as Nora's, it might be easier to prevail by silence than by many words. Lady Rowley was quite sure of this: that it would be far better to say nothing further of Hugh Stanbury. Let the cure come, if it might be possible, from absence and from her daughter's good sense. The only question was whether it would be wise to say any word about Mr Glascock. In the carriage she was not only forbearing but flattering in her manner to Nora. She caressed her girl's hand and spoke to her as mothers know how to speak when they want to make much of their girls, and to have it understood that those girls are behaving as girls should behave. There was to be nobody to meet them tonight, as it had been arranged that Sir Marmaduke and Mrs Trevelyan should sleep at Siena. Hardly a word had been spoken in the carriage; but upstairs, in their drawing-room, there came a moment in which Lucy and Sophie had left them, and Nora was alone with her mother. Lady Rowley almost knew that it would be most prudent to be silent; but a word spoken in season, how good it is! And the thing was so near to her that she could not hold her peace. 'I must say, Nora,' she began, 'that I do like your Mr Glascock.'

'He is not my Mr Glascock, mamma,' said Nora, smiling.

'You know what I mean, dear.' Lady Rowley had not intended to utter a word that should appear like pressure on her daughter at this moment. She had felt how imprudent it would be to do so. But now Nora seemed to be leading the way herself to such discourse. 'Of course, he is not your Mr Glascock. You cannot eat your cake and have it, nor can you throw it away and have it.'

'I have thrown my cake away altogether, and certainly I cannot have it.' She was still smiling as she spoke, and seemed to be quite merry at the idea of regarding Mr Glascock as the cake which she had declined to eat.

'I can see one thing quite plainly, dear.'

'What is that, mamma?'

'That in spite of what you have done, you can still have your cake whenever you choose to take it.'

'Why, mamma, he is engaged to be married!'

'Mr Glascock?'

'Yes, Mr Glascock. It's quite settled. Is it not sad?'

'To whom is he engaged?' Lady Rowley's solemnity as she asked this question was piteous to behold.

'To Miss Spalding Caroline Spalding.'

'The eldest of those nieces?'

'Yes—the eldest.'

'I cannot believe it.'

'Mamma, they both told me so. I have sworn an eternal friendship with her already.'

'I did not see you speaking to her.'

'But I did talk to her a great deal.'

'And he is really going to marry that dreadful woman?'

'Dreadful, mamma!'

'Perfectly awful! She talked to me in a way that I have read about in books, but which I did not before believe to be possible. Do you mean that he is going to be married to that hideous old maid, that bell-clapper?'

'Oh, mamma, what slander! I think her so pretty.'

'Pretty!'

'Very pretty. And, mamma, ought I not to be happy that he should have been able to make himself so happy? It was quite, quite, quite impossible that I should have been his wife. I have thought about it ever so much, and I am so glad of it! I think she is just the girl that is fit for him.'

Lady Rowley took her candle and went to bed, professing to herself that she could not understand it. But what did it signify? It was, at any rate, certain now that the man had put himself out of Nora's reach, and if he chose to marry a republican virago, with a red nose, it could now make no difference to Nora. Lady Rowley almost felt a touch of satisfaction in reflecting on the future misery of his married life.

CHAPTER LXXVIII. CASALUNGA

Sir Marmaduke had been told at the Florence post-office that he would no doubt be able to hear tidings of Trevelyan, and to learn his address, from the officials in the post-office at Siena. At Florence he had been introduced to some gentleman who was certainly of importance, a superintendent who had clerks under him and who was a big man. This person had been very courteous to him, and he had gone to Siena thinking that he would find it easy to obtain Trevelyan's address or to learn that there was no such person there. But at Siena he and his courier together could obtain no information. They rambled about the huge cathedral and the picturesque market-place of that quaint old city for the whole day, and on the next morning after breakfast they returned to Florence. They had learned nothing. The young man at the post-office had simply protested that he knew nothing of the name of Trevelyan. If letters should come addressed to such a name, he would keep them till they were called for; but, to the best of his knowledge, he had never seen or heard the name. At the guard-house of the gendarmerie they could not, or would not, give him any information, and Sir Marmaduke came back with an impression that everybody at Siena was ignorant, idiotic, and brutal. Mrs Trevelyan was so dispirited as to be ill, and both Sir Marmaduke and Lady Rowley were disposed to think that the world was all against them. 'You have no conception of the sort of woman that man is going to marry,' said Lady Rowley.

'What man?'

'Mr Glascock! A horrid American female, as old almost as I am, who talks through her nose, and preaches sermons about the rights of women. It is incredible! And Nora might have had him just for lifting up her hand.' But Sir Marmaduke could not interest himself much about Mr Glascock. When he had been told that his daughter had refused the heir to a great estate and a peerage, it had been matter of regret; but he had looked upon the affair as done, and cared nothing now though Mr Glascock should marry a transatlantic Xantippe. He was angry with Nora because by her obstinacy she was adding to the general perplexities of the family, but he could not make comparisons on Mr Glascock's behalf between her and Miss Spalding as his wife was doing, either mentally or aloud, from hour to hour. 'I suppose it 'is too late now,' said Lady Rowley, shaking her head.

'Of course it is too late. The man must marry whom he pleases. I am beginning to wonder that anybody should ever want to get married. I am indeed.'

'But what are the girls to do?'

'I don't know what anybody is to do. Here is a man as mad as a March hare, and yet nobody can touch him. If it was not for the child, I should advise Emily to put him out of her head altogether.'

But though Sir Marmaduke could not bring himself to take any interest in Mr Glascock's affairs, and would not ask a single question respecting the fearful American female whom this unfortunate man was about to translate to the position of an English peeress, yet circumstances so fell out that before three days were over he and Mr Glascock were thrown together in very intimate relations. Sir Marmaduke had learned that Mr Glascock was the only Englishman in Florence to whom Trevelyan had been known, and that he was the only person with whom Trevelyan had been seen to speak while passing through the city. In his despair, therefore, Sir Marmaduke had gone to Mr Glascock, and it was soon arranged that the two gentlemen should renew the search at Siena together, without having with them either Mrs Trevelyan or the courier. Mr Glascock knew the ways of the people better than did Sir Marmaduke, and could speak the language. He obtained a passport to the good offices of the police at Siena, and went prepared to demand rather than to ask for assistance. They started very early, before breakfast, and on arriving at Siena at about noon, first employed themselves in recruiting exhausted nature. By the time that they had both declared that the hotel at Siena was the very worst in all Italy, and that a breakfast without eatable butter was not to be considered a breakfast at all, they had become so intimate that Mr Glascock spoke of his own intended marriage. He must have done this with the conviction on his mind that Nora Rowley would have told her mother of his former intention, and that Lady Rowley would have told Sir Marmaduke; but he did not feel it to be incumbent on himself to say anything on that subject. He had nothing to excuse. He had behaved fairly and honourably. It was not to be expected that he should remain unmarried for ever for the sake of a girl who had twice refused him. 'Of course there are very many in England,' he said, 'who will think me foolish to marry a girl from another country.'

'It is done every day,' said Sir Marmaduke.

'No doubt it is. I admit, however, that I ought to be more careful than some other persons. There is a title and an estate to be perpetuated, and I cannot, perhaps, be justified in taking quite so much liberty as some other men may do; but I think I have chosen a woman born to have a high position, and who will make her own way in any society in which she may be placed.'

'I have no doubt she will,' said Sir Marmaduke, who had still sounding in his ears the alarming description which his wife had given him of this infatuated man's proposed bride. But he would have been bound to say as much had Mr Glascock intended to marry as lowly as did King Cophetua.

'She is highly educated, gentle-mannered, as sweetly soft as any English girl I ever met, and very pretty. You have met her, I think.'

'I do not remember that I have observed her.'

'She is too young for me, perhaps,' said Mr Glascock; 'but that is a fault on the right side.' Sir Marmaduke, as he wiped his beard after his breakfast, remembered what his wife had told him about the lady's age. But it was nothing to him.'she is four-and-twenty, I think,' said Mr Glascock. If Mr Glascock chose to believe that his intended wife was four-and-twenty instead of something over forty, that was nothing to Sir Marmaduke.

'The very best age in the world,' said he.

They had sent for an officer of the police, and before they had been three hours in Siena they had been told that Trevelyan lived about seven miles from the town, in a small and very remote country house, which he had hired for twelve months from one of the city hospitals. He had hired it furnished, and had purchased a horse and small carriage from a man in the town. To this man they went, and it soon became evident to them that he of whom they were in search was living at this house, which was called Casalunga, and was not, as the police officer told them, on the way to any place. They must leave Siena by the road for Rome, take a turn to the left about a mile beyond the city gate, and continue on along the country lane till they saw a certain round hill to the right. On the top of that round hill was Casalunga. As the country about Siena all lies in round hills, this was no adequate description, but it was suggested that the country people would know all about it. They got a small open carriage in the market-place, and were driven out. Their driver knew nothing of Casalunga, and simply went whither he was told. But by the aid of the country people they got along over the unmade lanes, and in little more than an hour were told, at the bottom of the hill, that they must now walk up to Casalunga. Though the hill was round-topped, and no more than a hill, still the ascent at last was very steep, and was paved with stones set edgeway in a manner that could hardly have been intended to accommodate wheels. When Mr Glascock asserted that the signor who lived there had a carriage of his own, the driver suggested that he must keep it at the bottom of the hill. It was clearly not his intention to attempt to drive up the ascent, and Sir Marmaduke and Mr Glascock were therefore obliged to walk. It was now in the latter half of May, and there was a blazing Italian sky over their heads. Mr Glascock was acclimated to Italian skies, and did not much mind the work; but Sir Marmaduke, who never did much in walking, declared that Italy was infinitely hotter than the Mandarins, and could hardly make his way as far as the house door.

It seemed to both of them to be a most singular abode for such a man as Trevelyan. At the top of the hill there was a huge entrance through a wooden gateway, which seemed to have been constructed with the intention of defying any intruders not provided with warlike ammunition. The gates were, indeed, open at the period of their visit, but it must be supposed that they were intended to be closed at any rate at night. Immediately on the right, as they entered through the gates, there was a large barn, in which two men were coopering wine vats. From thence a path led slanting to the house, of which the door was shut, and all the front windows blocked with shutters. The house was very long, and only of one story for a portion of its length. Over that end at which the door was placed there were upper rooms, and there must have been space enough for a large family with many domestics. There was nothing round or near the residence which could be called a garden, so that its look of desolation was extreme. There were various large barns and outhouses, as though it had been intended by the builder that corn and hay and cattle should be kept there; but it seemed now that there was nothing there except the empty vats at which the two men were coopering. Had the Englishmen gone farther into the granary, they would have seen that there were wine-presses stored away in the dark corners.

They stopped and looked at the men, and the men halted for a moment from their work and looked at them; but the men spoke never a word. Mr Glascock then asked after Mr Trevelyan, and one of the coopers pointed to the house. Then they crossed over to the door, and Mr Glascock finding there neither knocker nor bell, first tapped with his knuckles, and then struck with his stick. But no one came. There was not a sound in the house, and no shutter was removed. 'I don't believe that there is a soul here,' said Sir Marmaduke.

'We'll not give it up till we've seen it all at any rate,' said Mr Glascock. And so they went round to the other front.

On this side of the house the tilled ground, either ploughed or dug with the spade, came up to the very windows. There was hardly even a particle of grass to be seen. A short way down the hill there were rows of olive trees, standing in prim order and at regular distances, from which hung the vines that made the coopering of the vats necessary. Olives and vines have pretty names, and call up associations of landscape beauty. But here they were in no way beautiful. The ground beneath them was turned up, and brown, and arid, so that there was not a blade of grass to be seen. On some furrows the maize or Indian corn was sprouting, and there were patches of growth of other kinds, each patch closely marked by its own straight lines; and there were narrow paths, so constructed as to take as little room as possible. But all that had been done had been done for economy, and nothing for beauty. The occupiers of Casalunga had thought more of the produce of their land than of picturesque or attractive appearance.

The sun was blazing fiercely hot, hotter on this side, Sir Marmaduke thought, even than on the other; and there was not a wavelet of a cloud in the sky. A balcony ran the whole length of the house, and under this Sir Marmaduke took shelter at once, leaning with his back against the wall. 'There is not a soul here at all,' said he.

'The men in the barn told us that there was,' said Mr Glascock; 'and, at any rate, we will try the windows.' So saying, he walked along the front of the house, Sir Marmaduke following him slowly, till they came to a door, the upper half of which was glazed, and through which they looked into one of the rooms. Two or three of the other windows in this frontage of the house came down to the ground, and were made for egress and ingress; but they had all been closed with shutters, as though the house was deserted. But they now looked into a room which contained some signs of habitation. There was a small table with a marble top, on which lay two or three books, and there were two arm-chairs in the room, with gilded arms and legs, and a morsel of carpet, and a clock on, a shelf over a stove, and a rocking-horse. 'The boy is here, you may be sure,' said Mr Glascock. 'The rocking-horse makes that certain. But how are we to get at any one!'

'I never saw such a place for an Englishman to come and live in before,' said Sir Marmaduke. 'What on earth can he do here all day!' As he spoke the door of the room was opened, and there was Trevelyan standing before them, looking at them through the window. He wore an old red English dressing-gown, which came down to his feet, and a small braided Italian cap on his head. His beard had been allowed to grow, and he had neither collar nor cravat. His trousers were unbraced, and he shuffled in with a pair of slippers, which would hardly cling to his feet. He was paler and still thinner than when he had been visited at Willesden, and his eyes seemed to be larger, and shone almost with a brighter brilliancy.

Mr Glascock tried to open the door, but found that it was closed. 'Sir Marmaduke and I have come to visit you,' said Mr Glascock, aloud. 'Is there any means by which we can get into the house?' Trevelyan stood still and stared at them. 'We knocked at the front door, but nobody came,' continued Mr Glascock. 'I suppose this is the way you usually go in and out.'

'He does not mean to let us in,' whispered Sir Marmaduke.

'Can you open this door,' said Mr Glascock, 'or shall we go round again?' Trevelyan had stood still contemplating them, but at last came forward and put back the bolt. 'That is all right,' said Mr Glascock, entering. 'I am sure you will be glad to see Sir Marmaduke.'

'I should be glad to see him or you, if I could entertain you,' said Trevelyan. His voice was harsh and hard, and his words were uttered with a certain amount of intended grandeur. 'Any of the family would be welcome were it not—'

'Were it not what?' asked Mr Glascock.

'It can be nothing to you, sir, what troubles I have here. This is my own abode, in which I had flattered myself that I could be free from intruders. I do not want visitors. I am sorry that you should have had trouble in coming here, but I do not want visitors. I am very sorry that I have nothing that I can offer you, Mr Glascock.'

'Emily is in Florence,' said Sir Marmaduke.

'Who brought her? Did I tell her to come? Let her go back to her home. I have come here to be free from her, and I mean to be free. If she wants my money, let her take it.'

'She wants her child,' said Mr Glascock.

'He is my child,' said Trevelyan, 'and my right to him is better than hers. Let her try it in a court of law, and she shall see. Why did she deceive me with that man? Why has she driven me to this? Look here, Mr Glascock my whole life is spent in this seclusion, and it is her fault.'

'Your wife is innocent of all fault, Trevelyan,' said Mr Glascock.

'Any woman can say as much as that and all women do say it. Yet what are they worth?'

'Do you mean, sir, to take away your wife's character?' said Sir Marmaduke, coming up in wrath. 'Remember that she is my daughter, and that there are things which flesh and blood cannot stand.'

'She is my wife, sir, and that is ten times more. Do you think that you would do more for her than I would do, drink more of Esill? You had better go away, Sir Marmaduke. You can do no good by coming here and talking of your daughter. I would have given the world to save her but she would not be saved.'

'You are a slanderer!' said Sir Marmaduke, in his wrath.

Mr Glascock turned round to the father, and tried to quiet him. It was so manifest to him that the balance of the poor man's mind was gone, that it seemed to him to be ridiculous to upbraid the sufferer. He was such a piteous sight to behold, that it was almost impossible to feel indignation against him. 'You cannot wonder,' said Mr Glascock, advancing close to the master of the house, 'that the mother should want to see her only child. You do not wish that your wife should be the most wretched woman in the world.'

'Am not I the most wretched of men? Can anything be more wretched than this? Is her life worse than mine? And whose fault was it? Had I any friend to whom she objected? Was I untrue to her in a single thought?'

'If you say that she was untrue, it is a falsehood,' said Sir Marmaduke.

'You allow yourself a liberty of expression, sir, because you are my wife's father,' said Trevelyan, 'which you would not dare to take in other circumstances.'

'I say that it is a false calumny, a lie! And I would say so to any man on earth who should dare to slander my child's name.'

'Your child, sir! She is my wife, my wife, my wife!' Trevelyan, as he spoke, advanced close up to his father-in-law; and at last hissed out his words, with his lips close to Sir Marmaduke's face. 'Your right in her is gone, sir. She is mine, mine, mine! And you see the way in which she has treated me, Mr Glascock. Everything I had was hers; but the words of a grey-haired sinner were sweeter to her than all my love. I wonder whether you think that it is a pleasant thing for such a one as I to come out here and live in such a place as this? I have not a friend, a companion, hardly a book. There is nothing that I can eat or drink! I do not stir out of the house, and I am ill, very ill! Look at me. See what she has brought me to! Mr Glascock, on my honour as a man, I never wronged her in a thought or a word.'

Mr Glascock had come to think that his best chance of doing any good was to get Trevelyan into conversation with himself, free from the interruption of Sir Marmaduke. The father of the injured woman could not bring himself to endure the hard words that were spoken of his daughter. During this last speech he had broken out once or twice; but Trevelyan, not heeding him, had clung to Mr Glascock's arm. 'Sir Marmaduke,' said he, 'would you not like to see the boy?'

'He shall not see the boy,' said Trevelyan. 'You may see him. He shall not. What is he that he should have control over me?'

'This is the most fearful thing I ever heard of,' said Sir Marmaduke. 'What are we to do with him?'

Mr Glascock whispered a few words to Sir Marmaduke, and then declared that he was ready to be taken to the child. 'And he will remain here?' asked Trevelyan.. A pledge was then given by Sir Marmaduke that he would not force his way farther into the house, and the two other men left the chamber together. Sir Marmaduke, as he paced up and down the room alone, perspiring at every pore, thoroughly uncomfortable and ill at ease, thought of all the hard positions of which he had ever read, and that his was harder than them all. Here was a man married to his daughter, in possession of his daughter's child, manifestly mad, and yet he could do nothing to him! He was about to return to the seat of his government, and he must leave his own child in this madman's power! Of course, his daughter could not go with him, leaving her child in this madman's hands. He had been told that even were he to attempt to prove the man to be mad in Italy, the process would be slow; and, before it could be well commenced, Trevelyan would be off with the child elsewhere. There never was an embarrassment, thought Sir Marmaduke, out of which it was so impossible to find a clear way.

In the meantime, Mr Glascock and Trevelyan were visiting the child. It was evident that the father, let him be ever so mad, had discerned the expediency of allowing some one to see that his son was alive and in health. Mr Glascock did not know much of children, and could only say afterwards that the boy was silent and very melancholy, but clean, and apparently well. It appeared that he was taken out daily by his father in the cool hours of the morning, and that his father hardly left him from the time that he was taken up till he was put to bed. But Mr Glascock's desire was to see Trevelyan alone, and this he did after they had left the boy. 'And now, Trevelyan,' he said, 'what do you mean to do?'

'To do?'

'In what way do you propose to live? I want you to be reasonable with me.'

'They do not treat me reasonably.'

'Are you going to measure your own conduct by that of other people? In the first place, you should go back to England. What good can you do here?' Trevelyan shook his head, but remained silent. 'You cannot like this life.'

'No, indeed. But whither can I go now that I shall like to live?'

'Why not home?'

'I have no home.'

'Why not go back to England? Ask your wife to join you, and return with her. She would go at a word.' The poor wretch again shook his head. 'I hope you think that I speak as your friend,' said Mr Glascock.

'I believe you do.'

'I will say nothing of any imprudence; but you cannot believe that she has been untrue to you?' Trevelyan would say nothing to this, but stood silent waiting for Mr Glascock to continue. 'Let her come back to you here; and then, as soon as you can arrange it, go to your own home.'

'Shall I tell you something?' said Trevelyan.

'What is it?'

He came up close to Mr Glascock, and put his hand upon his visitor's shoulder. 'I will tell you what she would do at once. I dare say that she would come to me. I dare say that she would go with me. I am sure she would. And directly she got me there, she would say that I was mad! She my wife, would do it! He, that furious, ignorant old man below, tried to do it before. His wife said that I was mad.' He paused a moment, as though waiting for a reply; but Mr Glascock had none to make. It had not been his object, in the advice which he had given, to entrap the poor fellow by a snare, and to induce him so to act that he should deliver himself up to keepers; but he was well aware that wherever Trevelyan might be, it would be desirable that he should be placed for awhile in the charge of some physician. He could not bring himself at the spur of the moment to repudiate the idea by which Trevelyan was actuated. 'Perhaps you think that she would be right?' said Trevelyan.

'I am quite sure that she would do nothing that is not for the best,' said Mr Glascock.

'I can see it all. I will not go back to England, Mr Glascock. I intend to travel. I shall probably leave this and go to to to Greece, perhaps. It is a healthy place, this, and I like it for that reason; but I shall not stay here. If my wife likes to travel with me, she can come. But to England I will not go.'

'You will let the child go to his mother?'

'Certainly not. If she wants to see the child, he is here. If she will come without her father she shall see him. She shall not take him from hence. Nor shall she return to live with me, without full acknowledgment of her fault, and promises of an amended life. I know what I am saying, Mr Glascock, and have thought of these things perhaps more than you have done. I am obliged to you for coming to me; but now, if you please, I would prefer to be alone.'

Mr Glascock, seeing that nothing further could be done, joined Sir Marmaduke, and the two walked down to their carriage at the bottom of the hill. Mr Glascock, as he went, declared his conviction that the unfortunate man was altogether mad, and that it would be necessary to obtain some interference on the part of the authorities for the protection of the child. How this could be done, or whether it could be done in time to intercept a further flight on the part of Trevelyan, Mr Glascock could not say. It was his idea that Mrs Trevelyan should herself go out to Casalunga, and try the force of her own persuasion.

'I believe that he would murder her,' said Sir Marmaduke.

'He would not do that. There is a glimmer of sense in all his madness, which will keep him from any actual violence.'

CHAPTER LXXIX. 'I CAN SLEEP ON THE BOARDS'

Three days after this there came another carriage to the bottom of the hill on which Casalunga stood, and a lady got out of it all alone. It was Emily Trevelyan, and she had come thither from Siena in quest of her husband and her child. On the previous day Sir Marmaduke's courier had been at the house with a note from the wife to the husband, and had returned with an answer, in which Mrs Trevelyan was told that, if she would come quite alone, she should see her child. Sir Marmaduke had been averse to any further intercourse with the man, other than what might be made in accordance with medical advice, and, if possible, with government authority. Lady Rowley had assented to her daughter's wish, but had suggested that she should at least be allowed to go also at any rate, as far as the bottom of the hill. But Emily had been very firm, and Mr Glascock had supported her. He was confident that the man would do no harm to her, and he was indisposed to believe that any interference on the part of the Italian Government could be procured in such a case with sufficient celerity to be of use. He still thought it might be possible that the wife might prevail over the husband, or the mother over the father. Sir Marmaduke was at last obliged to yield, and Mrs Trevelyan went to Siena with no other companion but the courier. From Siena she made the journey quite alone; and having learned the circumstances of the house from Mr Glascock, she got out of the carriage, and walked up the hill. There were still the two men coopering at the vats, but she did not stay to speak to them. She went through the big gates, and along the slanting path to the door, not doubting of her way, for Mr Glascock had described it all to her, making a small plan of the premises, and even explaining to her the position of the room in which her boy and her husband slept. She found the door open, and an Italian maid-servant at once welcomed her to the house, and assured her that the signor would be with her immediately. She was sure that the girl knew that she was the boy's mother, and was almost tempted to ask questions at once as to the state of the household; but her knowledge of Italian was slight, and she felt that she was so utterly a stranger in the land that she could dare to trust no one. Though the heat was great, her face was covered with a thick veil. Her dress was black, from head to foot, and she was as a woman who mourned for her husband. She was led into the room which her father had been allowed to enter through the window; and here she sat, in her husband's house, feeling that in no position in the world could she be more utterly separated from the interests of all around her. In a few minutes the door was opened, and her husband was with her,

Anthony Trollope

bringing the boy in his hand. He had dressed himself with some care; but it may be doubted whether the garments which he wore did not make him appear thinner even and more haggard than he had looked to be in his old dressing-gown. He had not shaved himself, but his long hair was brushed back from his forehead, after a fashion quaint and very foreign to his former ideas of dress. His wife had not expected that her child would come to her at once, had thought that some entreaties would be necessary, some obedience perhaps exacted from her, before she would be allowed to see him; and now her heart was softened, and she was grateful to her husband. But she could not speak to him till she had had the boy in her arms. She tore off her bonnet, and then clinging to the child, covered him with kisses. 'Louey, my darling! Louey; you remember mamma?' The child pressed himself close to his mother's bosom, but spoke never a word. He was cowed and overcome, not only by the incidents of the moment, but by the terrible melancholy of his whole life. He had been taught to understand, without actual spoken lessons, that he was to live with his father, and that the former woman-given happinesses of his life were at an end. In this second visit from his mother he did not forget her. He recognised the luxury of her love; but it did not occur to him even to hope that she might have come to rescue him from the evil of his days. Trevelyan was standing by, the while, looking on; but he did not speak till she addressed him.

'I am so thankful to you for bringing him to me,' she said.

'I told you that you should see him,' he said. 'Perhaps it might have been better that I should have sent him by a servant; but there are circumstances which make me fear to let him out of my sight.'

'Do you think that I did not wish to see you also? Louis, why do you do me so much wrong? Why do you treat me with such cruelty?' Then she threw her arms round his neck, and before he could repulse her before he could reflect whether it would be well that he should repulse her or not she had covered his brow and cheeks and lips with kisses. 'Louis,' she said; 'Louis, speak to me!'

'It is hard to speak sometimes,' he said.

'You love me, Louis?'

'Yes I love you. But I am afraid of you!'

'What is it that you fear? I would give my life for you, if you would only come back to me and let me feel that you believed me to be true.' He shook his head, and began to think while she still clung to him. He was quite sure that her father and mother had intended to bring a mad doctor down upon him, and he knew that his wife was in her mother's hands. Should he yield to her now, should he make her any promise, might not the result be that he would be shut up in dark rooms, robbed of his liberty, robbed of what he loved better than his liberty, his power as a man. She would thus get the better of him and take the child, and the world would say that in this contest between him and her he had been the sinning one, and she the one against whom the sin had been done. It was the chief object of his mind, the one thing for which he was eager, that this should never come to pass. Let it once be conceded to him from all sides that he had been right, and then she might do with him almost as she willed. He knew well that he was ill. When he thought of his child, he would tell himself that he was dying. He was at some moments of his miserable existence fearfully anxious to come to terms with his wife, in order that at his death his boy might not be without a protector. Were he to die, then it would be better that his child should be with its mother. In his happy days, immediately after his marriage, he had made a will, in which he had left his entire property to his wife for her life, providing for its subsequent descent to his child or children. It had never even occurred to his poor shattered brain that it would be well for him to alter his will. Had he really believed that his wife had betrayed him, doubtless he would have done so. He would have hated her, have distrusted her altogether, and have believed her to be an evil thing. He had no such belief. But in his desire to achieve empire, and in the sorrows which had come upon him in his unsuccessful struggle, his mind had wavered so frequently, that his spoken words were no true indicators of his thoughts; and in all his arguments he failed to express either his convictions or his desires. When he would say something stronger than he intended, and it would be put to him by his wife, by her father or mother, or by some friend of hers, whether he did believe that she had been untrue to him, he would recoil from the answer which his heart would dictate, lest he should seem to make an acknowledgment that might weaken the ground upon which he stood. Then he would satisfy his own conscience by assuring himself that he had never accused her of such sin. She was still clinging to him now as his mind was working after this fashion. 'Louis,' she said, 'let it all be as though there had been nothing.'

'How can that be, my dear?'

'Not to others, but to us it can be so. There shall be no word spoken of the past.' Again he shook his head. 'Will it not be best that there should be no word spoken?'

'"Forgiveness may be spoken with the tongue,"' he said, beginning to quote from a poem which had formerly been frequent in his hands.

'Cannot there be real forgiveness between you and me, between husband and wife who, in truth, love each other? Do you think that I would tell you of it again?' He felt that in all that she said there was an assumption that she had been right, and that he had been wrong. She was promising to forgive. She was undertaking to forget. She was willing to take him back to the warmth of her love, and the comfort of her kindness but was not asking to be taken back. This was what he could not and would not endure. He had determined that if she behaved well to him, he would not be harsh to her, and he was struggling to keep up to his resolve. He would accuse her of nothing if he could help it. But he could not say a word that would even imply that she need forget that she should forgive. It was for him to forgive and he was willing to do it, if she would accept forgiveness: 'I will never speak a word, Louis,' she said, laying her head upon his shoulder.

'Your heart is still hardened,' he replied slowly.

'Hard to you?'

'And your mind is dark. You do not see what you have done. In our religion, Emily, forgiveness is sure, not after penitence, but with repentance.'

'What does that mean?'

'It means this, that though I would welcome you back to my arms with joy, I cannot do so, till you have confessed your fault.'

'What fault, Louis? If I have made you unhappy, I do, indeed, grieve that it has been so.'

'It is of no use,' said he. 'I cannot talk about it. Do you suppose that it does not tear me to the very soul to think of it?'

'What is it that you think, Louis?' As she had been travelling thither, she had determined that she would say anything that he wished her to say, make any admission that might satisfy him. That she could be happy again as other women are happy, she did not expect; but if it could be conceded between them that bygones should be bygones, she might live with him and do her duty, and, at least, have her child with her.

Her father had told her that her husband was mad; but she was willing to put up with his madness on such terms as these. What could her husband do to her in his madness that he could not do also to the child? 'Tell me what you want me to say, and I will say it,' she said.

'You have sinned against me,' he said, raising her head gently from his shoulder.

'Never!' she exclaimed. 'As God is my judge, I never have!' As she said this, she retreated and took the sobbing boy again into her arms.

He was at once placed upon his guard, telling himself that he saw the necessity of holding by his child. How could he tell? Might there not be policemen down from Florence, ready round the house, to seize the boy and carry him away. Though all his remaining life should be a torment to him, though infinite plagues should be poured upon his head, though he should die like a dog, alone, unfriended, and in despair, while he was fighting this battle of his, he would not give way. 'That is sufficient,' he said. 'Louey must return now to his own chamber.'

'I may go with him?'

'No, Emily. You cannot go with him now. I will thank you to release him, that I may take him.' She still held the little fellow closely pressed in her arms. 'Do not reward me for my courtesy by further disobedience,' he said.

'You will let me come again?' To this he made no reply. 'Tell me that I may come again.'

'I do not think that I shall remain here long.'

'And I may not stay now?'

'That would be impossible. There is no accommodation for you.'

'I could sleep on the boards beside his cot,' said Mrs Trevelyan.

'That is my place,' he replied. 'You may know that he is not disregarded. With my own hands I tend him every morning. I take him out myself. I feed him myself. He says his prayers to me. He learns from me, and can say his letters nicely. You need not fear for him. No mother was ever more tender with her child than I am with him.' Then he gently withdrew the boy from her arms, and she let her child go, lest he should learn to know that there was a quarrel between his father and his mother. 'If you will excuse me,' he said, 'I will not come down to you again today. My servant will see you to your carriage.'

So he left her; and she, with an Italian girl at her heels, got into her vehicle, and was taken back to Siena. There she passed the night alone at the inn, and on the next morning returned to Florence by the railway.

CHAPTER LXXX. 'WILL THEY DESPISE HIM?'

Gradually the news of the intended marriage between Mr Glascock and Miss Spalding spread itself over Florence, and people talked about it with that energy which subjects of such moment certainly deserve. That Caroline Spalding had achieved a very great triumph, was, of course, the verdict of all men and of all women; and I fear that there was a corresponding feeling that poor Mr Glascock had been triumphed over, and, as it were, subjugated. In some respects he had been remiss in his duties as a bachelor visitor to Florence, as a visitor to Florence who had manifestly been much in want of a wife. He had not given other girls a fair chance, but had thrown himself down at the feet of this American female in the weakest possible manner. And then it got about the town that he had been refused over and over again by Nora Rowley. It is too probable that Lady Rowley in her despair and dismay had been indiscreet, and had told secrets which should never have been mentioned by her. And the wife of the English minister, who had some grudges of her own, lifted her eyebrows and shook her head and declared that all the Glascocks at home would be outraged to the last degree. 'My dear Lady Rowley,' she said, 'I don't know whether it won't become a question with them whether they should issue a commission *de lunatico*.' Lady Rowley did not know what a commission *de lunatico* meant, but was quite willing to regard poor Mr Glascock as a lunatic. 'And there is poor Lord Peterborough at Naples just at death's door,' continued the British Ministers wife. In this she was perhaps nearly correct; but as Lord Peterborough had now been in the same condition for many months, as his mind had altogether gone, and as the doctor declared that he might live in his present condition for a year, or for years, it could not fairly be said that Mr Glascock was acting without due filial feeling in engaging himself to marry a young lady. 'And she such a creature!' said Lady Rowley, with emphasis. This the British Minister's wife noticed simply by shaking her head. Caroline Spalding was undoubtedly a pretty girl; but, as the British Minister's wife said afterwards, it was not surprising that poor Lady Rowley should be nearly out of her mind.

This had occurred a full week after the evening spent at Mr Spalding's house; and even yet Lady Rowley had never been put right as to that mistake of hers about Wallachia Petrie. That other trouble of hers, and her eldest daughter's journey to Siena, had prevented them from going out; and though the matter had often been discussed between Lady Rowley and Nora, there had not as yet come between them any proper explanation. Nora would declare that the future bride was very pretty and very delightful; and Lady Rowley would throw up her hands in despair and protest that her daughter was insane. 'Why should he not marry whom he likes, mamma?' Nora once said, almost with indignation.

'Because he will disgrace his family.'

'I cannot understand what you mean, mamma. They are, at any rate, as good as we are. Mr Spalding stands quite as high as papa does.'

'She is an American,' said Lady Rowley.

'And her family might say that he is an Englishman,' said Nora.

'My dear, if you do not understand the incongruity between an English peer and a Yankee female, I cannot help you. I suppose it is because you have been brought up within the limited society of a small colony. If so, it is not your fault. But I had hoped you had been in Europe long enough to have learned what was what. Do you think, my dear, that she will look well when she is presented to her Majesty as Lord Peterborough's wife?'

'Splendid,' said Nora.'she has just the brow for a coronet.'

'Heavens and earth!' said Lady Rowley, throwing up her hands. 'And you believe that he will be proud of her in England?'

'I am sure he will.'

'My belief is that he will leave her behind him, or that they will settle somewhere in the wilds of America—out in Mexico, or Massachusetts, or the Rocky Mountains. I do not think that he will have the courage to shew her in London.'

The marriage was to take place in the Protestant church at Florence early in June, and then the bride and bridegroom were to go over the Alps, and to remain there subject to tidings as to the health of the old man at Naples. Mr Glascock had thrown up his seat in Parliament, some month or two ago, knowing that he could not get back to his duties during the present session, and feeling that he would shortly be called upon to sit in the other House. He was thus free to use his time and to fix his days as he pleased; and it was certainly clear to those who knew him, that he was not ashamed of his American bride. He spent much of his time at the Spaldings' house, and was always to be seen with them in the Casino and at the Opera. Mrs Spalding, the aunt, was, of course, in great glory. A triumphant, happy, or even simply a splendid marriage, for the rising girl of a family is a great glory to the maternal mind. Mrs Spalding could not but be aware that the very air around her seemed to breathe congratulations into her ears. Her friends spoke to her, even on indifferent subjects, as though everything was going well with her, better with her than with anybody else; and there came upon her in these days a dangerous feeling, that in spite of all the preachings of the preachers, the next world might perhaps be not so very much better than this. She was, in fact, the reverse of the medal of which poor Lady Rowley filled the obverse. And the American Minister was certainly an inch taller than before, and made longer speeches, being much more regardless of interruption. Olivia was delighted at her sister's success, and heard with rapture the description of Monkhams, which came to her second-hand through her sister. It was already settled that she was to spend her next Christmas at Monkhams, and perhaps there might be an idea in her mind that there were other eldest sons of old lords who would like American brides. Everything around Caroline Spalding was pleasant except the words of Wallachia Petrie.

Everything around her was pleasant till there came to her a touch of a suspicion that the marriage which Mr Glascock was going to make would be detrimental to her intended husband in his own country. There were many in Florence who were saying this besides the wife of the English Minister and Lady Rowley. Of course Caroline Spalding herself was the last to hear it, and to her the idea was brought by Wallachia Petrie. 'I wish I could think you would make yourself happy, or him,' Wallachia had said, croaking.

'Why should I fail to make him happy?'

'Because you are not of the same blood, or race, or manners as himself. They say that he is very wealthy in his own country, and that those who live around him will look coldly on you.'

'So that he does not look coldly, I do not care how others may look,' said Caroline proudly.

'But when he finds that he has injured himself by such a marriage in the estimation of all his friends, how will it be then?'

This set Caroline Spalding thinking of what she was doing. She began to realise the feeling that perhaps she might not be a fit bride for an English lord's son, and in her agony she came to Nora Rowley for counsel. After all, how little was it that she knew of the home and the country to which she was to be carried! She might not, perhaps, get adequate advice from Nora, but she would probably learn something on which she could act. There was no one else among the English at Florence to whom she could speak with freedom. When she mentioned her fears to her aunt, her aunt of course laughed at her. Mrs Spalding told her that Mr Glascock might be presumed to know his own business best, and that she, as an American lady of high standing—the niece of a minister!—was a fitting match for any Englishman, let him be ever so much a lord. But Caroline was not comforted by this, and in her suspense she went to Nora Rowley. She wrote a line to Nora, and when she called at the hotel, was taken up to her friend's bedroom. She found great difficulty in telling her story, but she did tell it. 'Miss Rowley,' she said, 'if this is a silly thing that he is going to do, I am bound to save him from his own folly. You know your own country better than I do. Will they think that he has disgraced himself?'

'Certainly not that,' said Nora.

'Shall I be a load round his neck? Miss Rowley, for my own sake I would not endure such a position as that, not even though I love him. But for his sake! Think of that. If I find that people think ill of him because of me!'

'No one will think ill of him.'

'Is it esteemed needful that such a one as he should marry a woman of his own rank. I can bear to end it all now; but I shall not be able to bear his humiliation, and my own despair, if I find that I have injured him. Tell me plainly, is it a marriage that he should not make?' Nora paused for a while before she answered, and as she sat silent the other girl watched her face carefully. Nora on being thus consulted, was very careful that her tongue should utter nothing that was not her true opinion as best she knew how to express it. Her sympathy would have prompted her to give such an answer as would at once have made Caroline happy in her mind. She would have been delighted to have been able to declare that these doubts were utterly groundless, and this hesitation needless. But she conceived that she owed it as a duty from one woman to another to speak the truth as she conceived it on so momentous an occasion, and she was not sure but that Mr Glascock would be considered by his friends in England to be doing badly in marrying an American girl. What she did not remember was this that her very hesitation was in fact an answer, and such an answer as she was most unwilling to give. 'I see that it would be so,' said Caroline Spalding.

'No, not that.'

'What then? Will they despise him and me?'

'No one who knows you can despise you. No one who sees you can fail to admire you.' Nora, as she said this, thought of her mother, but told herself at once that in this matter her mother's judgment had been altogether destroyed by her disappointment. 'What I think will take place will be this. His family, when first they hear of it, will be sorry.'

'Then,' said Caroline, 'I will put an end to it.'

'You can't do that, dear. You are engaged, and you haven't a right. I am engaged to a man, and all my friends object to it. But I shan't put an end to it. I don't think I have a right. I shall not do it any way, however.'

'But if it were for his good?'

'It couldn't be for his good. He and I have got to go along together somehow.'

'You wouldn't hurt him,' said Caroline.

'I won't if I can help it, but he has got to take me along with him any how; and Mr Glascock has got to take you. If I were you, I shouldn't ask any more questions.'

'It isn't the same. You said that you were to be poor, but he is very rich. And I am beginning to understand that these titles of yours are something like kings' crowns. The man who has to wear them can't do just as he pleases with them. Noblesse oblige. I can see the meaning of that, even when the obligation itself is trumpery in its nature. If it is a man's duty to marry a Talbot because he's a Howard, I suppose he ought to do his duty.' After a pause she went on again. 'I do believe that I have made a mistake. It seemed to be absurd at the first to think of it, but I do believe it now. Even what you say to me makes me think it.'

'At any rate you can't go back,' said Nora enthusiastically.

'I will try.'

'Go to himself and ask him. You must leave him to decide it at last. I don't see how a girl when she is engaged, is to throw a man over unless he consents. Of course you can throw yourself into the Arno.'

'And get the water into my shoes, for it wouldn't do much more at present.'

'And you can jilt him,' said Nora.

'It would not be jilting him.'

'He must decide that. If he so regards it, it will be so. I advise you to think no more about it; but if you speak to anybody it should be to him.' This was at last the result of Nora's wisdom, and then the two girls descended together to the room in which Lady Rowley was sitting with her other daughters. Lady Rowley was very careful in asking after Miss Spalding's sister, and Miss Spalding assured her that Olivia was quite well. Then Lady Rowley made some inquiry about Olivia and Mr Glascock, and Miss Spalding assured her that no two persons were ever such allies, and that she believed that they were together at this moment investigating some old church. Lady Rowley simpered, and declared that nothing could be more proper, and expressed a hope that Olivia would like England. Caroline Spalding, having still in her mind the trouble that had brought her to Nora, had not much to say about this. 'If she goes again to England I am sure she will like it,' replied Miss Spalding.

'But of course she is going,' said Lady Rowley.

'Of course she will some day, and of course she'll like it,' said Miss Spalding. 'We both of us have been there already.'

'But I mean Monkhams,' said Lady Rowley, still simpering.

'I declare I believe mamma thinks that your sister is to be married to Mr Glascock!' said Lucy.

'And so she is, isn't she?' said Lady Rowley.

'Oh, mamma!' said Nora, jumping up. 'It is Caroline, this one, this one, this one,' and Nora took her friend by the arm as she spoke 'it is this one that is to be Mrs Glascock.'

'It is a most natural mistake to make,' said Caroline. Lady Rowley became very red in the face, and was unhappy. 'I declare,' she said, 'that they told me it was your elder sister.'

'But I have no elder sister,' said Caroline, laughing. 'Of course she is oldest,' said Nora 'and looks to be so, ever so much. Don't you, Miss Spalding?'

'I have always supposed so.'

'I don't understand it at all,' said Lady Rowley, who had no image before her mind's eye but that of Wallachia Petrie, and who was beginning to feel that she had disgraced her own judgment by the criticisms she had expressed everywhere as to Mr Glascock's bride. 'I don't understand it at all. Do you mean that both your sisters are younger than you, Miss Spalding?'

'I have only got one, Lady Rowley.'

'Mamma, you are thinking of Miss Petrie,' said Nora, clapping both her hands together.

'I mean the lady that wears the black bugles.'

'Of course you do, Miss Petrie. Mamma has all along thought that Mr Glascock was going to carry away with him the republican Browning!'

'Oh, mamma, how can you have made such a blunder!' said Sophie Rowley. 'Mamma does make such delicious blunders.'

'Sophie, my dear, that is not a proper way of speaking.'

'But, dear mamma, don't you?'

'If somebody has told me wrong, that has not been my fault,' said Lady Rowley.

The poor woman was so evidently disconcerted that Caroline Spalding was quite unhappy.

'My dear Lady Rowley, there has been no fault. And why shouldn't it have been so. Wallachia is so clever, that it is the most natural thing in the world to have thought.'

'I cannot say that I agree with you there,' said Lady Rowley, somewhat recovering herself.

'You must know the whole truth now,' said Nora, turning to her friend, 'and you must not be angry with us if we laugh a little at your poetess. Mamma has been frantic with Mr Glascock because he has been going to marry—whom shall I say—her edition of you. She has sworn that he must be insane. When we have sworn how beautiful you were, and how nice, and how jolly, and all the rest of it she has sworn that you were at least a hundred and that you had a red nose. You must admit that Miss Petrie has a red nose.'

'Is that a sin?'

'Not at all in the woman who has it; but in the man who is going to marry it, yes. Can't you see how we have all been at cross-purposes, and what mamma has been thinking and saying of poor Mr Glascock? You mustn't repeat it, of course; but we have had such a battle here about it. We thought that mamma had lost her eyes and her ears and her knowledge of things in general. And now it has all come out! You won't be angry?'

'Why should I be angry?'

'Miss Spalding,' said Lady Rowley, 'I am really unhappy at what has occurred, and I hope that there may be nothing more said about it. I am quite sure that somebody told me wrong, or I should not have fallen into such an error. I beg your pardon and Mr Glascock's!'

'Beg Mr Glascock's pardon, certainly,' said Lucy.

Miss Spalding looked very pretty, smiled very gracefully, and coming up to Lady Rowley to say good-bye, kissed her on her cheeks. This overcame the spirit of the disappointed mother, and Lady Rowley never said another word against Caroline Spalding or her marriage. 'Now, mamma, what do you think of her?' said Nora, as soon as Caroline was gone.

'Was it odd, my dear, that I should be astonished at his wanting to marry that other woman?'

'But, mamma, when we told you that she was young and pretty and bright!'

'I thought that you were all demented. I did indeed. I still think it a pity that he should take an American. I think that Miss Spalding is very nice, but there are English girls quite as nice-looking as her.' After that there was not another word said by Lady Rowley against Caroline Spalding.

Nora, when she thought of it all that night, felt that she had hardly spoken to Miss Spalding as she should have spoken as to the treatment in England which would be accorded to Mr Glascock's wife. She became aware of the effect which her own hesitation must have had, and thought that it was her duty to endeavour to remove it. Perhaps, too, the conversion of her mother had some effect in making her feel that she had been wrong in supposing that there would be any difficulty in Caroline's position in England. She had heard so much adverse criticism from her mother that she had doubted in spite of her own convictions; but now it had come to light that Lady Rowley's criticisms had all come from a most absurd blunder. 'Only fancy;' she said to herself 'Miss Petrie coming out as Lady Peterborough! Poor mamma!' And then she thought of the reception which would be given to Caroline, and of the place the future Lady Peterborough would fill in the world, and of the glories of Monkhams! Resolving that she would do her best to counteract any evil which she might have done, she seated herself at her desk, and wrote the following letter to Miss Spalding:

Thursday morning.

MY DEAR CAROLINE,

I am sure you will let me call you so, as had you not felt towards me like a friend, you would not have come to me today and told me of your doubts. I think that I did not answer you as I ought to have done when you spoke to me. I did not like to say anything off-hand, and in that way I misled you. I feel quite sure that you will encounter nothing in England as Mr Glascock's wife to make you uncomfortable, and that he will have nothing to repent. Of course Englishmen generally marry Englishwomen; and, perhaps, there may be some people who will think that such a prize should not be lost to their countrywomen. But that will be all. Mr Glascock commands such universal respect that his wife will certainly be respected, and I do not suppose that anything will ever come in your way that can possibly make you feel that he is looked down upon. I hope you will understand what I mean.

As for your changing now, that is quite impossible. If I were you, I would not say a word about it to any living being; but just go on straight forward in your own way, and take the good the gods provide you, as the poet says to the king in the ode. And I think the gods have provided for you very well and for him.

I do hope that I may see you sometimes. I cannot explain to you how very much out of your line "we" shall be, for of course there is a "we." People are more separated with us than they are, I suppose, with you. And my "we" is a very poor man, who works hard at writing in a dingy newspaper office, and we shall live in a garret and have brown sugar in our tea, and eat hashed mutton. And I shall have nothing a year to buy my clothes with. Still I mean to do it; and I don't mean to be long before I do do it. When a girl has made up her mind to be married, she had better go on with it at once, and take it all afterwards as it may come. Nevertheless, perhaps, we may see each other somewhere, and I may be able to introduce you to the dearest, honestest, very best, and most affectionate man in the world. And he is very, very clever.

Yours very affectionately, NORA ROWLEY.

CHAPTER LXXXI. MR GLASCOCK IS MASTER

Caroline Spalding, when she received Nora's letter, was not disposed to give much weight to it. She declared to herself that the girl's unpremeditated expression of opinion was worth more than her studied words. But she was not the less grateful or the less loving towards her new friend. She thought how nice it would be to have Nora at that splendid abode in England of which she had heard so much, but she thought also that in that splendid abode she herself ought never to have part or share. If it were the case that this were an unfitting match, it was clearly her duty to decide that there should be no marriage. Nora had been quite right in bidding her speak to Mr Glascock himself, and to Mr Glascock she would go. But it was very difficult for her to determine on the manner in which she would discuss the subject with him. She thought that she could be firm if her mind were once made up. She believed that perhaps she was by nature more firm than he. In all their intercourse together he had ever yielded to her; and though she had been always pleased and grateful, there had grown upon her an idea that he was perhaps too easy, that he was a man as to whom it was necessary that they who loved him should see that he was not led away by weakness into folly. But she would want to learn something from him before her decision was finally reached, and in this she foresaw a great difficulty. In her trouble she went to her usual counsellor, the Republican Browning. In such an emergency she could hardly have done worse. 'Wally,' she said, 'we talk about England, and Italy, and France, as though we knew all about them; but how hard it is to realise the difference between one's own country and others.'

'We can at least learn a great deal that is satisfactory,' said Wallachia. 'About one out of every five Italians can read a book, about two out of every five Englishmen can read a book. Out of every five New Englanders four and four-fifths can read a book. I guess that is knowing a good deal.'

'I don't mean in statistics.'

'I cannot conceive how you are to learn anything about any country except by statistics. I have just discovered that the number of illegitimate children—'

'Oh, Wally, I can't talk about that—not now, at least. What I cannot realise is this, what sort of a life it is that they will lead at Monkhams.'

'Plenty to eat and drink, I guess; and you'll always have to go around in fine clothes.'

'And that will be all?'

'No not all. There will be carriages and horses, and all manner of people there who won't care much about you. If he is firm, very firm, if he have that firmness which one does not often meet, even in an American man, he will be able, after a while, to give you a position as an English woman of rank.' It is to be feared that Wallachia Petrie had been made aware of Caroline's idea as to Mr Glascock's want of purpose.

'And that will be all?'

'If you have a baby, they'll let you go and see it two or three times a day. I don't suppose you will be allowed to nurse it, because they never do in England. You have read what the Saturday Review says. In every other respect the Saturday Review has been the falsest of all false periodicals, but I guess it has been pretty true in what it has said about English women.'

'I wish I knew more about it really.'

'When a man has to leap through a window in the dark, Caroline, of course he doubts whether the feather bed said to be below will be soft enough for him.'

'I shouldn't fear the leap for myself, if it wouldn't hurt him. Do you think it possible that society can be so formed that a man should lose caste because he doesn't marry just one of his own set?'

'It has been so all over the world, my dear. If like to like is to be true anywhere, it should be true in marriage.'

'Yes but with a difference. He and I are like to like. We come of the same race, we speak the same language, we worship the same God, we have the same ideas of culture and of pleasures. The difference is one that is not patent to the eye or to the ear. It is a difference of accidental incident, not of nature or of acquirement.'

'I guess you would find, Caroline, that a jury of English matrons sworn to try you fairly, would not find you to be entitled to come among them as one of themselves.'

'And how will that affect him?'

'Less powerfully than many others, because he is not impassioned. He is, perhaps, lethargic.'

'No, Wally, he is not lethargic.'

'If you ask me I must speak. It would harass some men almost to death; it will not do so with him. He would probably find his happiness best in leaving his old country and coming among your people.'

The idea of Mr Glascock, the future Lord Peterborough, leaving England, abandoning Monkhams, deserting his duty in the House of Lords, and going away to live in an American town, in order that he might escape the miseries which his wife had brought upon him in his own country, was more than Caroline could bear. She knew that, at any rate, it would not come to that. The lord of Monkhams would live at Monkhams, though the heavens should fall in regard to domestic comforts. It was clear to Caroline that Wallachia Petrie had in truth never brought home to her own imagination the position of an English peer. 'I don't think you understand the people at all,' she said angrily.

'You think that you can understand them better because you are engaged to this man!' said Miss Petrie, with well-pronounced irony. 'You have found generally that when the sun shines in your eyes your sight is improved by it! You think that the love-talk of a few weeks gives clearer instruction than the laborious reading of many volumes and thoughtful converse with thinking persons! I hope that you may find it so, Caroline.' So saying Wallachia Petrie walked off in great dudgeon.

Miss Petrie, not having learned from her many volumes and her much converse with thoughtful persons to read human nature aright, was convinced by this conversation that her friend Caroline was blind to all results, and was determined to go on with this dangerous marriage, having the rays of that sun of Monkhams so full upon her eyes that she could not see at all. She was specially indignant at finding that her own words had no effect. But, unfortunately, her words had had much effect; and Caroline, though she had contested her points, had done so only with the intention of producing her Mentor's admonitions. Of course it was out of the question that Mr Glascock should go and live in Providence, Rhode Island, from which thriving town Caroline Spalding had come; but, because that was impossible, it was not the less probable that he might be degraded and made miserable in his own home. That suggested jury of British matrons was a frightful conclave to contemplate, and Caroline was disposed to believe that the verdict given in reference to herself would be adverse to her. So she sat and meditated, and spoke not a word further to any one on the subject till she was alone with the man that she loved.

Mr Spalding at this time inhabited the ground floor of a large palace in the city, from which there was access to a garden, which at this period of the year was green, bright, and shady, and which, as being in the centre of a city, was large and luxurious. From one end of the house there projected a covered terrace, or loggia, in which there were chairs and tables, sculptured ornaments, busts, and old monumental relics let into the wall in profusion. It was half chamber and half garden, such an adjunct to a house as in our climate would give only an idea of cold, rheumatism, and a false romance, but under an Italian sky is a luxury daily to be enjoyed during most months of the year. Here Mr Glascock and Caroline had passed many hours and here they were now seated, late in the evening, while all others of the family were away. As far as regarded the rooms occupied by the American Minister, they had the house and garden to themselves, and there never could come a time more appropriate for the saying of a thing difficult to be said. Mr Glascock had heard from his father's physician, and had said that it was nearly certain now that he need not go down to Naples again before his marriage. Caroline was trembling, not knowing how to speak, not knowing how to begin but resolved that the thing should be done. 'He will never know you, Carry,' said Mr Glascock. 'It is, perhaps, hardly a sorrow to me, but it is a regret.'

'It would have been a sorrow, perhaps, to him had he been able to know me,' said she, taking the opportunity of rushing at her subject.

'Why so? Of all human beings he was the softest-hearted.'

'Not softer-hearted than you, Charles. But soft hearts have to be hardened.'

'What do you mean? Am I becoming obdurate?'

'I am, Charles,' she said. 'I have got something to say to you. What will your uncles and aunts and your mother's relations say of me when they see me at Monkhams?'

'They will swear to me that you are charming; and then when my back is turned they'll pick you to pieces a little among themselves. I believe that is the way of the world, and I don't suppose that we are to do better than others.'

'And if you had married an English girl, a Lady Augusta Somebody, would they pick her to pieces?'

'I guess they would, as you say.'

'Just the same?'

'I don't think anybody escapes, as far as I can see. But that won't prevent their becoming your bosom friends in a few weeks' time.'

'No one will say that you have been wrong to marry an American girl?'

'Now, Carry, what is the meaning of all this?'

'Do you know any man in your position who ever did marry an American girl, any man of your rank in England?' Mr Glascock began to think of the case, and could not at the moment remember any instance. 'Charles, I do not think you ought to be the first.'

'And yet somebody must be first, if the thing is ever to be done, and I am too old to wait on the chance of being the second.'

She felt that at the rate she was now progressing she would only run from one little suggestion to another, and that he, either wilfully or in sheer simplicity, would take such suggestions simply as jokes; and she was aware that she lacked the skill to bring the conversation round gradually to the point which she was bound to reach. She must make another dash, let it be ever so sudden. Her mode of doing so would be crude, ugly, almost vulgar, she feared; but she would attain her object and say what she had to say. When once she had warmed herself with the heat which argument would produce, then, she was pretty sure, she would find herself at least as strong as he. 'I don't know that the thing ought to be done at all,' she said. During the last moment or two he had put his arm round her waist; and she, not choosing to bid him desist from embracing her, but unwilling in her present mood to be embraced, got up and stood before him. 'I have thought, and thought, and thought, and feel that it should not be done. In marriage, like should go to like.' She despised herself for using Wallachia's words, but they fitted in so usefully, that she could not refrain from them. 'I was wrong not to know it before, but it is better to know it now, than not to have known it till too late. Everything that I hear and see tells me that it would be so. If you were simply an Englishman, I would go anywhere with you; but I am not fit to be the wife of an English lord. The time would come when I should be a disgrace to you, and then I should die.'

'I think I should go near dying myself,' said he, 'if you were a disgrace to me.' He had not risen from his chair, and sat calmly looking up into her face.

'We have made a mistake, and let us unmake it,' she continued. 'I will always be your friend. I will correspond with you. I will come and see your wife.'

'That will be very kind!'

'Charles, if you laugh at me, I shall be angry with you. It is right that you should look to your future life, as it is right that I should do so also. Do you think that I am joking? Do you suppose that I do not mean it?'

'You have taken an extra dose this morning of Wallachia Petrie, and of course you mean it.'

'If you think that I am speaking her mind and not my own, you do not know me.'

'And what is it you propose?' he said, still keeping his seat and looking calmly up into her face.

'Simply that our engagement should be over.'

'And why?'

'Because it is not a fitting one for you to have made. I did not understand it before, but now I do. It will not be good for you to marry an American girl. It will not add to your happiness, and may destroy it. I have learned, at last, to know how much higher is your position than mine.'

'And I am to be supposed to know nothing about it?'

'Your fault is only this that you have been too generous. I can be generous also.'

'Now, look here, Caroline, you must not be angry with me if on such a subject I speak plainly. You must not even be angry if I laugh a little.'

'Pray do not laugh at me! not now.'

'I must a little, Carry. Why am I supposed to be so ignorant of what concerns my own happiness and my own duties? If you will not sit down, I will get up, and we will take a turn together.' He rose from his seat, but they did not leave the covered terrace. They moved on to the extremity, and then he stood hemming her in against a marble table in the corner. 'In making this rather wild proposition, have you considered me at all?'

'I have endeavoured to consider you, and you only.'

'And how have you done it? By the aid of some misty, far-fetched ideas respecting English society, for which you have no basis except your own dreams, and by the fantasies of a rabid enthusiast.'

'She is not rabid,' said Caroline earnestly; 'other people think just the same.'

'My dear, there is only one person whose thinking on this subject is of any avail, and I am that person. Of course, I can't drag you into church to be married, but practically you can not help yourself from being taken there now. As there need be no question about our marriage which is a thing as good as done—'

'It is not done at all,' said Caroline.

'I feel quite satisfied you will not jilt me, and as I shall insist on having the ceremony performed, I choose to regard it as a certainty. Passing that by, then, I will go on to the results. My uncles, and aunts, and cousins, and the people you talk of, were very reasonable folk when I last saw them, and quite sufficiently alive to the fact that they had to regard me as the head of their family. I do not doubt that we shall find them equally reasonable when we get home; but should they be changed, should there be any sign shewn that my choice of a wife had occasioned displeasure, such displeasure would not affect you.'

'But it would affect you.'

'Not at all. In my own house I am master, and I mean to continue to be so. You will be mistress there, and the only fear touching such a position is that it may be recognised by others too strongly. You have nothing to fear, Carry.'

'It is of you I am thinking.'

'Nor have I. What if some old women, or even some young women, should turn up their noses at the wife I have chosen, because she has not been chosen from among their own countrywomen, is that to be a cause of suffering to us? Can not we rise above that, lasting as it would do for a few weeks, a month or two perhaps, say a year, till my Caroline shall have made herself known? I think that we are strong enough to live down a trouble so light.' He had come close to her as he was speaking, and had again put his arm round her waist.

She tried to escape from his embrace, not with persistency, not with the strength which always suffices for a woman when the embrace is in truth a thing to be avoided, but clutching at his fingers with hers, pressing them rather than loosening their grasp. 'No, Carry,' he continued; 'we have got to go through with it now, and we will try and make the best of it. You may trust me that we shall not find it difficult—not, at least, on the ground of your present fears. I can bear a heavier burden than you will bring upon me.'

'I know that I ought to prove to you that I am right,' she said, still struggling with his hand.

'And I know that you can prove nothing of the kind. Dearest, it is fixed between us now, and do not let us be so silly as to raise imaginary difficulties. Of course you would have to marry me, even if there were cause for such fears. If there were any great cause, still the game would be worth the candle. There could be no going back, let the fear be what it might. But there need be no fear if you will only love me.' She felt that he was altogether too strong for her that she had mistaken his character in supposing that she could be more firm than he. He was so strong that he treated her almost as a child, and yet she loved him infinitely the better for so treating her. Of course, she knew now that her objection, whether true or unsubstantial, could not avail. As he stood with his arm round her, she was powerless to contradict him in anything. She had so far acknowledged this that she no longer struggled with him, but allowed her hand to remain quietly within his. If there was no going back from this bargain that had been made, why, then, there was no need for combating. And when he stooped over her and kissed her lips, she had not a word to say. 'Be good to me,' he said, 'and tell me that I am right.'

'You must be master, I suppose, whether you are right or wrong. A man always thinks himself entitled to his own way.'

'Why, yes. When he has won the battle, he claims his captive. Now, the truth is this, I have won the battle, and your friend, Miss Petrie, has lost it. I hope she will understand that she has been beaten at last out of the field.' As he said this, he heard a step behind them, and turning round saw Wallachia there almost before he could drop his arm.

'I am sorry that I have intruded on you,' she said very grimly.

'Not in the least,' said Mr Glascock. 'Caroline and I have had a little dispute, but we have settled it without coming to blows.'

'I do not suppose that an English gentleman ever absolutely strikes a lady,' said Wallachia Petrie.

'Not except on strong provocation,' said Mr Glascock. 'In reference to wives, a stick is allowed as big as your thumb.'

'I have heard that it is so by the laws of England,' said Wallachia.

'How can you be so ridiculous, Wally!' said Caroline. 'There is nothing that you would not believe.'

'I hope that it may never be true in your case,' said Wallachia.

A couple of days after this Miss Spalding found that it was absolutely necessary that she should explain the circumstances of her position to Nora. She had left Nora with the purpose of performing a very high-minded action, of sacrificing herself for the sake of her lover, of giving up all her golden prospects, and of becoming once again the bosom friend of Wallachia Petrie, with this simple consolation for her future life, that she had refused to marry an English nobleman because the English nobleman's condition was unsuited to her. It would have been an episode in female life in which pride might be taken, but all that was now changed. She had made her little attempt, had made it, as she felt, in a very languid manner, and had found herself treated as a child for doing so. Of course she was happy in her ill success; of course she would have been broken-hearted had she succeeded. But, nevertheless, she was somewhat lowered in her own esteem, and it was necessary that she should acknowledge the truth to the friend whom she had consulted. A day or two had passed before she found herself alone with Nora, but when she did so she confessed her failure at once.

'You told him all, then?' said Nora.

'Oh yes, I told him all. That is, I could not really tell him. When the moment came I had no words.'

'And what did he say?'

'He had words enough. I never knew him to be eloquent before.'

'He can speak out if he likes,' said Nora.

'So I have found with a vengeance. Nobody was ever so put down as I was. Don't you know that there are times when it does not seem to be worth your while to put out your strength against an adversary? So it was with him. He just told me that he was my master, and that I was to do as he bade me.'

'And what did you say?'

'I promised to be a good girl,' said Caroline, 'and not to pretend to have any opinion of my own ever again. And so we kissed, and were friends.'

'I dare say there was a kiss, my dear.'

'Of course there was, and he held me in his arms, and comforted me, and told me how to behave just as you would do a little girl. It's all over now, of course; and if there be a mistake, it is his fault. I feel that all responsibility is gone from myself, and that for all the rest of my life I have to do just what he tells me.'

'And what says the divine Wallachia?'

'Poor Wally! She says nothing, but she thinks that I am a castaway and a recreant. I am a recreant, I know but yet I think that I was right. I know I could not help myself.'

'Of course you were right, my dear,' said the sage Nora. 'If you had the notion in your head, it was wise to get rid of it; but I knew how it would be when you spoke to him.'

'You were not so weak when he came to you.'

'That was altogether another thing. It was not arranged in heaven that I was to become his captive.'

After that Wallachia Petrie never again tried her influence on her former friend, but admitted to herself that the evil was done, and that it could not be remedied. According to her theory of life, Caroline Spalding had been wrong, and weak—had shewn herself to be comfort-loving and luxuriously-minded, had looked to get her happiness from soft effeminate pleasures rather than from rational work and the useful, independent exercise of her own intelligence. In the privacy of her little chamber Wallachia Petrie shed not absolute tears but many tearful thoughts over her friend. It was to her a thing very terrible that the chosen one of her heart should prefer the career of an English lord's wife to that of an American citizeness, with all manner of capability for female voting, female speechmaking, female poetising, and, perhaps, female political action before her. It was a thousand pities! 'You may take a horse to water,' said Wallachia to herself, thinking of the ever-freshly springing fountain of her own mind, at which Caroline Spalding would always have been made welcome freely to quench her thirst 'but you cannot make him drink if he be not athirst.' In the future she would have no friend. Never again would she subject herself to the disgrace of such a failure. But the sacrifice was to be made, and she knew that it was bootless to waste her words further on Caroline Spalding. She left Florence before the wedding, and returned alone to the land of liberty. She wrote a letter to Caroline explaining her conduct, and Caroline Spalding shewed the letter to her husband as one that was both loving and eloquent.

'Very loving and eloquent,' he said. 'But, nevertheless, one does think of sour grapes.'

'There I am sure you wrong her,' said Caroline.

CHAPTER LXXXII. MRS FRENCH'S CARVING KNIFE

During these days there were terrible doings at Exeter. Camilla had sworn that if Mr Gibson did not come to, there should be a tragedy, and it appeared that she was inclined to keep her word. Immediately after the receipt of her letter from Mr Gibson she had had an interview with that gentleman in his lodgings, and had asked him his intentions. He had taken measures to fortify himself against such an attack; but, whatever those measures were, Camilla had broken through them. She had stood before him as he sat in his armchair, and he had been dumb in her presence. It had perhaps been well for him that the eloquence of her indignation had been so great that she had hardly been able to pause a moment for a reply. 'Will you take your letter back again?' she had said. 'I should be wrong to do that,' he had lisped out in reply, 'because it is true. As a Christian minister I could not stand with you at the altar with a lie in my mouth.' In no other way did he attempt to excuse himself but that, twice repeated, filled up all the pause which she made for him.

There never had been such a case before so impudent, so cruel, so gross, so uncalled for, so unmanly, so unnecessary, so unjustifiable, so damnable so sure of eternal condemnation! All this she said to him with loud voice, and clenched fist, and starting eyes regardless utterly of any listeners on the stairs, or of outside passers in the street. In very truth she was moved to a sublimity of indignation. Her low nature became nearly poetic under the wrong inflicted upon her. She was almost tempted to tear him with her hands, and inflict upon him at the moment some terrible vengeance which should be told of for ever in the annals of Exeter. A man so mean as he, so weak, so cowardly, one so little of a hero that he should dare to do it, and dare to sit there before her, and to say that he would do it! 'Your gown shall be torn off your back, Sir, and the very boys of Exeter shall drag you through the gutters!' To this threat he said nothing, but sat mute, hiding his face in his hands. 'And now tell me this, sir, is there anything between you and Bella?' But there was no voice in reply. 'Answer my question, sir. I have a right to ask it.' Still he said not a word. 'Listen to me. Sooner than that you and she should be man and wife, I would stab her! Yes, I would you poor, paltry, lying, cowardly creature!' She remained with him for more than half an hour, and then banged out of the room, flashing back a look of scorn at him as she went. Martha, before that day was over, had learned the whole story from Mr Gibson's cook, and had told her mistress.

'I did not think he had so much spirit in him,' was Miss Stanbury's answer. Throughout Exeter the great wonder arising from the crisis was the amount of spirit which had been displayed by Mr Gibson.

When he was left alone he shook himself, and began to think that if there were danger that such interviews might occur frequently, he had better leave Exeter for good. As he put his hand over his forehead, he declared to himself that a very little more of that kind of thing would kill him. When a couple of hours had passed over his head he shook himself again, and sat down and wrote a letter to his intended mother-in-law.

'I do not mean to complain,' he said, 'God knows I have no right; but I cannot stand a repetition of what has occurred just now. If your younger daughter comes to see me again I must refuse to see her, and shall leave the town. I am ready to make what reparation may be possible for the mistake into which I have fallen.   T. G.'

Mrs French was no doubt much afraid of her younger daughter, but she was less afraid of her than were other people. Familiarity, they say, breeds contempt; and who can be so familiar with a child as its parent? She did not in her heart believe that Camilla would murder anybody, and she fully realised the conviction that, even after all that was come and gone, it would be better that one of her daughters should have a husband than that neither should be so blessed. If only Camilla could be got out of Exeter for a few months how good a thing it would be for them all! She had a brother in Gloucester; if only he could be got to take Camilla for a few months! And then, too, she knew that if the true rights of her two daughters were strictly and impartially examined, Arabella's claim was much stronger than any that Camilla could put forward to the hand of Mr Gibson.

'You must not go there again, Camilla,' the mother said.

'I shall go whenever I please,' replied the fury.

'Now, Camilla, we may as well understand each other. I will not have it done. If I am provoked, I will send to your uncle at Gloucester.' Now the uncle at Gloucester was a timber merchant, a man with protuberant eyes and a great square chin, known to be a very stern man indeed, and not at all afraid of young women.

'What do I care for my uncle? My uncle would take my part.'

'No, he would not. The truth is, Camilla, you interfered with Bella first.'

'Mamma, how dare you say so!'

'You did, my dear. And these are the consequences.'

'And you mean to say that she is to be Mrs Gibson?'

'I say nothing about that. But I do not see why they shouldn't be married if their hearts are inclined to each other.'

'I will die first!'

'Your dying has nothing to do with it, Camilla.'

'And I will kill her!'

'If you speak to me again in that way I will write to your uncle at Gloucester. I have done the best I could for you both, and I will not bear such treatment.'

'And how am I treated?'

'You should not have interfered with your sister.'

'You are all in a conspiracy together,' shouted Camilla, 'you are! There never was anybody so badly treated—never, never, never! What will everybody say of me?'

'They will pity you, if you will be quiet.'

'I don't want to be pitied—I won't be pitied. I wish I could die; and I will die! Anybody else would, at any rate, have had their mother and sister with them!' Then she burst into a flood of real, true, womanly tears.

After this there was a lull at Heavitree for a few days. Camilla did not speak to her sister, but she condescended to hold some intercourse with her mother, and to take her meals at the family table. She did not go out of the house, but she employed herself in her own room, doing no one knew what, with all that new clothing and household gear which was to have been transferred in her train to Mr Gibson's house. Mrs French was somewhat uneasy about the new clothing and household gear, feeling that, in the event of Bella's marriage, at least a considerable portion of it must be transferred to the new bride. But it was impossible at the present moment to open such a subject to Camilla; it would have been as a proposition to a lioness respecting the taking away of her whelps. Nevertheless, the day must soon come in which something must be said about the clothing and household gear. All the property that had been sent into the house at Camilla's orders could not be allowed to remain as Camilla's perquisites, now that Camilla was not to be married. 'Do you know what she is doing, my dear?' said Mrs French to her elder daughter.

'Perhaps she is picking out the marks,' said Bella.

'I don't think she would do that as yet,' said Mrs French.

'She might just as well leave it alone,' said Bella, feeling that one of the two letters would do for her. But neither of them dared to speak to her of her occupation in these first days of her despair.

Mr Gibson in the meantime remained at home, or only left his house to go to the Cathedral or to visit the narrow confines of his little parish. When he was out he felt that everybody looked at him, and it seemed to him that people whispered about him when they saw him at his usual desk in the choir. His friends passed him merely bowing to him, and he was aware that he had done that which would be regarded by every one around him as unpardonable. And yet what ought he to have done? He acknowledged to himself that he had been very foolish, mad, quite demented at the moment when he allowed himself to think it possible that he should marry Camilla French. But having found out how mad he had been at that moment, having satisfied himself that to live with her as his wife would be impossible, was he not right to break the engagement? Could anything be so wicked as marrying a woman whom he hated? Thus he tried to excuse himself; but yet he knew that all the world would condemn him. Life in Exeter would be impossible, if no way to social pardon could be opened for him. He was willing to do anything within bounds in mitigation of his offence. He would give up fifty pounds a year to Camilla for his life or he would marry Bella. Yes; he would marry Bella at once if Camilla would only consent, and give up that idea of stabbing some one. Bella French was not very nice in his eyes; but she was quiet, he thought, and it might be possible to live with her. Nevertheless, he told himself over and over again that the manner in which unmarried men with incomes were set upon by ladies in want of husbands was very disgraceful to the country at large. That mission to Natal which had once been offered to him would have had charms for him now, of which he had not recognised the force when he rejected it.

'Do you think that he ever was really engaged to her?' Dorothy said to her aunt. Dorothy was now living in a seventh heaven of happiness, writing love-letters to Brooke Burgess every other day, and devoting to this occupation a number of hours of which she ought to have been ashamed; making her purchases for her wedding with nothing, however, of the magnificence of a Camilla, but discussing everything with her aunt, who urged her on to extravagances which seemed beyond the scope of her own economical ideas; settling, or trying to settle, little difficulties which perplexed her somewhat, and wondering at her own career. She could not of course be married without the presence of her mother and sister, and her aunt with something of a grim courtesy had intimated that they should be made welcome to the house in the Close for the special occasion. But nothing had been said about Hugh. The wedding was to be in the Cathedral, and Dorothy had a little scheme in her head for meeting her brother among the aisles. He would no doubt come down with Brooke, and nothing perhaps need be said about it to Aunt Stanbury. But still it was a trouble. Her aunt had been so good that Dorothy felt that no step should be taken which would vex the old woman. It was evident enough that when permission had been given for the visit of Mrs Stanbury and Priscilla, Hugh's name had been purposely kept back. There had been no accidental omission. Dorothy, therefore, did not dare to mention it, and yet it was essential for her happiness that he should be there. At the present moment Miss Stanbury's intense interest in the Stanbury wedding was somewhat mitigated by the excitement occasioned by Mr Gibson's refusal to be married. Dorothy was so shocked that she could not bring herself to believe the statement that had reached them through Martha.

'Of course he was engaged to her. We all knew that,' said Miss Stanbury.

'I think there must have been some mistake,' said Dorothy. 'I don't see how he could do it.'

'There is no knowing what people can do, my dear, when they're hard driven. I suppose we shall have a lawsuit now, and he'll have to pay ever so much money. Well, well, well! see what a deal of trouble you might have saved!'

'But, he'd have done the same to me, aunt, only, you know, I never could have taken him. Isn't it better as it is, aunt? Tell me.'

'I suppose young women always think it best when they can get their own ways. An old woman like me has only got to do what she is bid.'

'But this was best, aunt, was it not?'

'My dear, you've had your way, and let that be enough. Poor Camilla French is not allowed to have hers at all. Dear, dear, dear! I didn't think the man would ever have been such a fool to begin with or that he would ever have had the heart to get out of it afterwards.' It astonished Dorothy to find that her aunt was not loud in reprobation of Mr Gibson's very dreadful conduct.

In the meantime Mrs French had written to her brother at Gloucester. The maid-servant, in making Miss Camilla's bed, and in 'putting the room to rights,' as she called it—which description probably was intended to cover the circumstances of an accurate search—had discovered, hidden among some linen, a carving knife! such a knife as is used for the cutting up of fowls; and, after two days' interval, had imparted the discovery to Mrs French. Instant visit was made to the pantry, and it was found that a very aged but unbroken and sharply-pointed weapon was missing. Mrs French at once accused Camilla, and Camilla, after some hesitation, admitted that it might be there. Molly, she said, was a nasty, sly, wicked thing, to go looking in her drawers, and she would never leave anything unlocked again. The knife, she declared, had been taken upstairs, because she had wanted something very sharp to cut the bones of her stays. The knife was given up, but Mrs French thought it best to write to her brother, Mr Crump. She was in great doubt about sundry matters. Had the carving knife really pointed to a domestic tragedy, and if so, what steps ought a poor widow to take with such a daughter? And what ought to be done about Mr Gibson? It ran through Mrs French's mind that unless something were done at once, Mr Gibson would escape scot-free. It was her wish that he should yet become her son-in-law. Poor Bella was entitled to her chance. But if Bella was to be disappointed from fear of carving knives, or for other reasons, then there came the question whether Mr Gibson should not be made to pay in purse for the mischief he had done. With all these thoughts and doubts running through her head, Mrs French wrote to her brother at Gloucester.

There came back an answer from Mr Crump, in which that gentleman expressed a very strong idea that Mr Gibson should be prosecuted for damages with the utmost virulence, and with the least possible delay. No compromise should be accepted. Mr Crump would himself come to Exeter and see the lawyer as soon as he should be told that there was a lawyer to be seen. As to the carving knife, Mr Crump was of opinion that it did not mean anything. Mr Crump was a gentleman who did not believe in strong romance, but who had great trust in all pecuniary claims. The Frenches had always been genteel. The late Captain French had been an officer in the army, and at ordinary times and seasons the Frenches were rather ashamed of the Crump connection. But now the timber merchant might prove himself to be a useful friend.

Mrs French shewed her brother's letter to Bella and poor Bella was again sore-hearted, seeing that nothing was said in it of her claims. 'It will be dreadful scandal to have it all in the papers!' said Bella.

'But what can we do?'

'Anything would be better than that,' said Bella. 'And you don't want to punish Mr Gibson, mamma.'

'But my dear, you see what your uncle says. What can I do, except go to him for advice?'

'Why don't you go to Mr Gibson yourself, mamma?'

But nothing was said to Camilla about Mr Crump—nothing as yet. Camilla did not love Mr Crump, but there was no other house except that of Mr Crump's at Gloucester to which she might be sent, if it could be arranged that Mr Gibson and Bella should be made one. Mrs French took her eldest daughter's advice, and went to Mr Gibson, taking Mr Crump's letter in her pocket. For herself she wanted nothing, but was it not the duty of her whole life to fight for her daughters? Poor woman! If somebody would only have taught her how that duty might best be done, she would have endeavoured to obey the teaching. 'You know I do not want to threaten you,' she said to Mr Gibson; 'but you see what my brother says. Of course I wrote to my brother. What could a poor woman do in such circumstances except write to her brother?'

'If you choose to set the bloodhounds of the law at me, of course you can,' said Mr Gibson.

'I do not want to go to law at all God; knows I do not!' said Mrs French. Then there was a pause. 'Poor dear Bella!' ejaculated Mrs French.

'Dear Bella!' echoed Mr Gibson.

'What do you mean to do about Bella?' asked Mrs French.

'I sometimes think that I had better take poison and have done with it!' said Mr Gibson, feeling himself to be very hard pressed.

CHAPTER LXXXIII. BELLA VICTRIX

Mr Crump arrived at Exeter. Camilla was not told of his coming till the morning of the day on which he arrived; and then the tidings were communicated, because it was necessary that a change should be made in the bed-rooms. She and her sister had separate rooms when there was no visitor with them, but now Mr Crump must be accommodated. There was a long consultation between Bella and Mrs French, but at last it was decided that Bella should sleep with her mother. There would still be too much of the lioness about Camilla to allow of her being regarded as a safe companion through the watches of the night. 'Why is Uncle Jonas coming now?' she asked.

'I thought it better to ask him,' said Mrs French.

After a long pause, Camilla asked another question. 'Does Uncle Jonas mean to see Mr Gibson?'

'I suppose he will,' said Mrs French.

'Then he will see a low, mean fellow: the lowest, meanest fellow that ever was heard of! But that won't make much difference to Uncle Jonas. I wouldn't have him now, if he was to ask me ever so, that I wouldn't!'

Mr Crump came, and kissed his sister and two nieces. The embrace with Camilla was not very affectionate.'so your Joe has been and jilted you?' said Uncle Jonas 'it's like one of them clergymen. They say so many prayers, they think they may do almost anything afterwards. Another man would have had his head punched.'

'The less talk there is about it the better,' said Camilla. On the following day Mr Crump called by appointment on Mr Gibson, and remained closeted with that gentleman for the greater portion of the morning. Camilla knew well that he was going, and went about the house like a perturbed spirit during his absence. There was a look about her that made them all doubt whether she was not, in truth, losing her mind. Her mother more than once went to the pantry to see that the knives were right; and, as regarded that sharp-pointed weapon, was careful to lock it up carefully out of her daughter's way. Mr Crump had declared himself willing to take Camilla back to Gloucester, and had laughed at the obstacles which his niece might, perhaps, throw in the way of such an arrangement. 'She mustn't have much luggage, that is all,' said Mr Crump. For Mr Crump had been made aware of the circumstances of the trousseau. About three o'clock Mr Crump came back from Mr Gibson's, and expressed a desire to be left alone with Camilla. Mrs French was prepared for everything; and Mr Crump soon found himself with his younger niece.

'Camilla, my dear,' said he, 'this has been a bad business.'

'I don't know what business you mean, Uncle Jonas.'

'Yes, you do, my dear, you know. And I hope it won't come too late to prove to you that young women shouldn't be too keen in setting their caps at the gentlemen. It's better for them to be hunted, than to hunt.'

'Uncle Jonas, I will not be insulted.'

'Stick to that, my dear, and you won't get into a scrape again. Now, look here. This man can never be made to marry you, anyhow.'

'I wouldn't touch him with a pair of tongs, if he were kneeling at my feet!'

'That's right; stick to that. Of course, you wouldn't now, after all that has come and gone. No girl with any spirit would.'

'He's a coward and a thief, and he'll be damned for what he has done, some of these days!'

'T-ch, t-ch, t-ch! That isn't a proper way for a young lady to talk. That's cursing and swearing.'

'It isn't cursing and swearing—it's what the Bible says.'

'Then we'll leave him to the Bible. In the meantime, Mr Gibson wants to marry some one else, and that can't hurt you.'

'He may marry whom he likes, but he shan't marry Bella, that's all!'

'It is Bella that he means to marry.'

'Then he won't. I'll forbid the banns. I'll write to the bishop. I'll go to the church and prevent its being done. I'll make such a noise in the town that it can't be done. It's no use your looking at me like that, Uncle Jonas. I've got my own feelings, and he shall never marry Bella. It's what they have been intending all through, and it shan't be done!'

'It will be done.'

'Uncle Jonas, I'll stab her to the heart, and him too, before I'll see it done! Though I were to be killed the next day, I would. Could you bear it?'

'I'm not a young woman. Now, I'll tell you what I want you to do.'

'I'll not do anything.'

'Just pack up your things, and start with me to Gloucester tomorrow.'

'I won't!'

'Then you'll be carried, my dear. I'll write to your aunt, to say that you're coming; and we'll be as jolly as possible when we get you home.'

'I won't go to Gloucester, Uncle Jonas. I won't go away from Exeter. I won't let it be done. She shall never, never, never be that man's wife!'

Nevertheless, on the day but one after this, Camilla French did go to Gloucester. Before she went, however, things had to be done in that house which almost made Mrs French repent that she had sent for so stern an assistant. Camilla was at last told, in so many words, that the things which she had prepared for her own wedding must be given up for the wedding of her sister; and it seemed that this item in the list of her sorrows troubled her almost more than any other. She swore that whither she went there should go the dresses, and the handkerchiefs, and the hats, the bonnets, and the boots. 'Let her have them,' Bella had pleaded. But Mr Crump was inexorable. He had looked into his sister's affairs, and found that she was already in debt. To his practical mind, it was an absurdity that the unmarried sister should keep things that were wholly unnecessary, and that the sister that was to be married should be without things that were needed. There was a big trunk, of which Camilla had the key, but which, unfortunately for her, had been deposited in her mother's room. Upon this she sat, and swore that nothing should move her but a promise that her plunder should remain untouched. But there came this advantage from the terrible question of the wedding raiments, that in her energy to keep possession of them, she gradually abandoned her opposition to her sister's marriage. She had been driven from one point to another till she was compelled at last to stand solely upon her possessions. 'Perhaps we had better let her keep them,' said Mrs French. 'Trash and nonsense!' said Mr Crump. 'If she wants a new frock, let her have it; as for the sheets and tablecloths, you'd better keep them yourself. But Bella must have the rest.'

It was found on the eve of the day on which she was told that she was to depart that she had in truth armed herself with a dagger or clasp knife. She actually displayed it when her uncle told her to come away from the chest on which she was sitting. She declared that she would defend herself there to the last gasp of her life; but of course the knife fell from her hand the first moment that she was touched. 'I did think once that she was going to make a poke at me,' Mr Crump said afterwards; 'but she had screamed herself so weak that she couldn't do it.'

When the morning came, she was taken to the fly and driven to the station without any further serious outbreak. She had even condescended to select certain articles, leaving the rest of the hymeneal wealth behind her. Bella, early on that morning of departure, with great humility, implored her sister to forgive her; but no entreaties could induce Camilla to address one gracious word to the proposed bride. 'You've been cheating me all along!' she said; and that was the last word she spoke to poor Bella.

She went, and the field was once more open to the amorous Vicar of St. Peter's-cum-Pumpkin. It is astonishing how the greatest difficulties will sink away, and become as it were nothing, when they are encountered face to face. It is certain that Mr Gibson's position had been one most trying to the nerves. He had speculated on various modes of escape; a curacy in the north of England would be welcome, or the duties of a missionary in New Zealand, or death. To tell the truth, he had, during the last week or two, contemplated even a return to the dominion of Camilla. That there should ever again be things pleasant for him in Exeter seemed to be quite impossible. And yet, on the evening of the day but one after the departure of Camilla, he was seated almost comfortably with his own Arabella! There is nothing that a man may not do, nothing that he may not achieve, if he have only pluck enough to go through with it.

'You do love me?' Bella said to him. It was natural that she should ask him; but it would have been better perhaps if she had held her tongue. Had she spoken to him about his house, or his income, or the servants, or the duties of his parish church, it would have been easier for him to make a comfortable reply.

'Yes I love you,' he replied; 'of course I love you. We have always been friends, and I hope things will go straight now. I have had a great deal to go through, Bella, and so have you, but God will temper the wind to the shorn lambs.' How was the wind to be tempered for the poor lamb who had gone forth shorn down to the very skin!

Soon after this Mrs French returned to the room, and then there was no more romance. Mrs French had by no means forgiven Mr Gibson all the trouble he had brought into the family, and mixed a certain amount of acrimony with her entertainment of him. She dictated to him, treated him with but scant respect, and did not hesitate to let him understand that he was to be watched very closely till he was actually and absolutely married. The poor man had in truth no further idea of escape. He was aware that he had done that which made it necessary that he should bear a great deal, and that he had no right to resent suspicion. When a day was fixed in June on which he should be married at the church of Heavitree, and it was proposed that he should be married by banns, he had nothing to urge to the contrary. And when it was also suggested to him by one of the prebendaries of the

Cathedral that it might be well for him to change his clerical duties for a period with the vicar of a remote parish in the north of Cornwall so as to be out of the way of remark from those whom he had scandalised by his conduct, he had no objection to make to that arrangement. When Mrs MacHugh met him in the Close, and told him that he was a gay Lothario, he shook his head with a melancholy self-abasement, and passed on without even a feeling of anger. 'When they smite me on the right cheek, I turn unto them my left,' he said to himself, when one of the cathedral vergers remarked to him that after all he was going to be married at last. Even Bella became dominant over him, and assumed with him occasionally the air of one who had been injured.

Bella wrote a touching letter to her sister, a letter that ought to have touched Camilla, begging for forgiveness, and for one word of sisterly love. Camilla answered the letter, but did not send a word of sisterly love. 'According to my way of thinking, you have been a nasty sly thing, and I don't believe you'll ever be happy. As for him, I'll never speak to him again.' That was nearly the whole of her letter. 'You must leave it to time,' said Mrs French wisely;'she'll come round some day.' And then Mrs French thought how bad it would be for her if the daughter who was to be her future companion did not 'come round' some day.

And so it was settled that they should be married in Heavitree Church, Mr Gibson and his first love, and things went on pretty much as though nothing had been done amiss. The gentleman from Cornwall came down to take Mr Gibson's place at St. Peter's-cum-Pumpkin, while his duties in the Cathedral were temporarily divided among the other priest-vicars -with some amount of grumbling on their part. Bella commenced her modest preparations without any of the *éclat* which had attended Camilla's operations, but she felt more certainty of ultimate success than had ever fallen to Camilla's lot. In spite of all that had come and gone, Bella never feared again that Mr Gibson would be untrue to her. In regard to him, it must be doubted whether Nemesis ever fell upon him with a hand sufficiently heavy to punish him for the great sins which he had manifestly committed. He had encountered a bad week or two, and there had been days in which, as has been said, he thought of Natal, of ecclesiastical censures, and even of annihilation; but no real punishment seemed to fall upon him. It may be doubted whether, when the whole arrangement was settled for him, and when he heard that Camilla had yielded to the decrees of Fate, he did not rather flatter himself on being a successful man of intrigue, whether he did not take some glory to himself for his good fortune with women, and pride himself amidst his self-reproaches for the devotion which had been displayed for him by the fair sex in general. It is quite possible that he taught himself to believe that at one time Dorothy Stanbury was devotedly in love with him, and that when he reckoned up his sins she was one of those in regard to whom he accounted himself to have been a sinner. The spirit of intrigue with women, as to which men will flatter themselves, is customarily so vile, so mean, so vapid a reflection of a feeling, so aimless, resultless, and utterly unworthy! Passion exists and has its sway. Vice has its votaries and there is, too, that worn-out longing for vice, 'prurient, yet passionless, cold-studied lewdness', which drags on a feeble continuance with the aid of money. But the commonest folly of man in regard to women is a weak taste for intrigue, with little or nothing on which to feed it a worse than feminine aptitude for male coquetry, which never ascends beyond a desire that somebody shall hint that there is something peculiar; and which is shocked and retreats backwards into its boots when anything like a consequence forces itself on the apprehension. Such men have their glory in their own estimation. We remember how Falstaff flouted the pride of his companion whose victory in the fields of love had been but little glorious. But there are victories going now-a-days so infinitely less glorious, that Falstaff's page was a Lothario, a very Don Juan, in comparison with the heroes whose praises are too often sung by their own lips. There is this recompense: that their defeats are always sung by lips louder than their own. Mr Gibson, when he found that he was to escape apparently unscathed, that people standing respectably before the world absolutely dared to whisper words to him of congratulation on this third attempt at marriage within little more than a year, took pride to himself, and bethought himself that he was a gay deceiver. He believed that he had selected his wife and that he had done so in circumstances of peculiar difficulty! Poor Mr Gibson—we hardly know whether most to pity him, or the unfortunate, poor woman who ultimately became Mrs Gibson.

'And so Bella French is to be the fortunate woman after all,' said Miss Stanbury to her niece.

'It does seem to me to be so odd,' said Dorothy. 'I wonder how he looked when he proposed it.'

'Like a fool, as he always does.'

Dorothy refrained from remarking that Miss Stanbury had not always thought that Mr Gibson looked like a fool, but the idea occurred to her mind. 'I hope they will be happy at last,' she said.

'Pshaw! Such people can't be happy, and can't be unhappy. I don't suppose it much matters which he marries, or whether he marries them both, or neither. They are to be married by banns, they say at Heavitree.'

'I don't see anything bad in that.'

'Only Camilla might step out and forbid them,' said Aunt Stanbury. 'I almost wish she would.'

'She has gone away, aunt, to an uncle who lives at Gloucester.'

'It was well to get her out of the way, no doubt. They'll be married before you now, Dolly.'

'That won't break my heart, aunt.'

'I don't suppose there'll be much of a wedding. They haven't anybody belonging to them, except that uncle at Gloucester.' Then there was a pause. 'I think it is a nice thing for friends to collect together at a wedding,' continued Aunt Stanbury.

'I think it is,' said Dorothy, in the mildest, softest voice.

'I suppose we must make room for that black sheep of a brother of yours, Dolly or else you won't be contented.'

'Dear, dear, dearest aunt!' said Dorothy, falling down on her knees at her aunt's feet.

CHAPTER LXXXIV. SELF-SACRIFICE

Trevelyan, when his wife had left him, sat for hours in silence pondering over his own position and hers. He had taken his child to an upper room, in which was his own bed and the boy's cot, and before he seated himself, he spread out various toys which he had been at pains to purchase for the unhappy little fellow—a regiment of Garibaldian soldiers all with red shirts, and a drum to give the regiment martial spirit, and a soft fluffy Italian ball, and a battledore, and a shuttlecock—instruments enough for juvenile joy, if only there had been a companion with whom the child could use them. But the toys remained where the father had placed them, almost unheeded, and the child sat looking out of the window, melancholy, silent, and repressed. Even the drum did not tempt him to be noisy. Doubtless he did not know why he was wretched, but he was fully conscious of his wretchedness. In the meantime the father sat motionless, in an old worn-out but once handsome leathern arm-chair, with his eyes fixed against the opposite wall, thinking of the wreck of his life.

Thought—deep, correct, continued, and energetic—is quite compatible with madness. At this time Trevelyan's mind was so far unhinged, his ordinary faculties were so greatly impaired, that they who declared him to be mad were justified in their declaration. His condition was such that the happiness and welfare of no human being, not even his own, could safely be entrusted to his keeping. He considered himself to have been so injured by the world, to have been the victim of so cruel a conspiracy among those who ought to have been his friends, that there remained nothing for him but to flee away from them and remain in solitude. But yet, through it all, there was something approaching to a conviction that he had brought his misery upon himself by being unlike to other men; and he declared to himself over and over again that it was better that he should suffer than that others should be punished. When he was alone his reflections respecting his wife were much juster than were his words when he spoke either with her, or to others, of her conduct. He would declare to himself not only that he did not believe her to have been false to him, but that he had never accused her of such crime. He had demanded from her obedience, and she had been disobedient. It had been incumbent upon him, so ran his own ideas, as expressed to himself in these long unspoken soliloquies, to exact obedience, or at least compliance, let the consequences be what they might. She had refused to obey or even to comply, and the consequences were very grievous. But, though he pitied himself with a pity that was feminine, yet he acknowledged to himself that her conduct had been the result of his own moody temperament. Every friend had parted from him. All those to whose counsels he had listened, had counselled him that he was wrong. The whole world was against him. Had he remained in England, the doctors and lawyers among them would doubtless have declared him to be mad. He knew all this, and yet he could not yield. He could not say that he had been wrong. He could not even think that he had been wrong as to the cause of the great quarrel. He was one so miserable and so unfortunate, so he thought, that even in doing right he had fallen into perdition!

He had had two enemies, and between them they had worked his ruin. These were Colonel Osborne and Bozzle. It may be doubted whether he did not hate the latter the more strongly of the two. He knew now that Bozzle had been untrue to him, but his disgust did not spring from that so much as from the feeling that he had defiled himself by dealing with the man. Though he was quite assured that he had been right in his first cause of offence, he knew that he had fallen from bad to worse in every step that he had taken since. Colonel Osborne had marred his happiness by vanity, by wicked intrigue, by a devilish delight in doing mischief; but he, he himself, had consummated the evil by his own folly. Why had he not taken Colonel Osborne by the throat, instead of going to a low-born, vile, mercenary spy for assistance? He hated himself for what he had done, and yet it was impossible that he should yield.

It was impossible that he should yield but it was yet open to him to sacrifice himself. He could not go back to his wife and say that he was wrong; but he could determine that the destruction should fall upon him and not upon her. If he gave up his child and then died—died, alone, without any friend near him, with no word of love in his ears, in that solitary and miserable abode which he had found for himself—then it would at least be acknowledged that he had expiated the injury that he had done. She would have his wealth, his name, his child to comfort her and would be troubled no longer by demands for that obedience which she had sworn at the altar to give him, and which she had since declined to render to him. Perhaps there was some feeling that the coals of fire would be hot upon her head when she should think how much she had received from him and how little she had done for him. And yet he loved her, with all his heart, and would even yet dream of bliss that might be possible with her had not the terrible hand of irresistible Fate come between them and marred it all. It was only a dream now. It could be no more than a dream. He put out his thin wasted hands and looked at them, and touched the hollowness of his own cheeks, and coughed that he might hear the hacking sound of his own infirmity, and almost took glory in his weakness. It could not be long before the coals of fire would be heaped upon her head.

'Louey,' he said at last, addressing the child who had sat for an hour gazing through the window without stirring a limb or uttering a sound; 'Louey, my boy, would you like to go back to mamma?' The child turned round on the floor, and fixed his eyes on his father's face, but made no immediate reply. 'Louey, dear, come to papa and tell him. Would it be nice to go back to mamma?' And he stretched out his hand to the boy. Louey got up, and approached slowly and stood between his father's knees. 'Tell me, darling, you understand what papa says?'

'*Altro*!' said the boy, who had been long enough among Italian servants to pick up the common words of the language. Of course he would like to go back. How indeed could it be otherwise?

'Then you shall go to her, Louey.'

'To-day, papa?'

'Not today, nor to-morrow.'

'But the day after?'

'That is sufficient. You shall go. It is not so bad with you that one day more need be a sorrow to you. You shall go and then you will never see your father again!' Trevelyan as he said this drew his hands away so as not to touch the child. The little fellow had put out his arm, but seeing his father's angry gesture had made no further attempt at a caress. He feared his father from the bottom of his little heart, and yet was aware that it was his duty to try to love papa. He did not understand the meaning of that last threat, but slunk back, passing his untouched toys, to the window, and there seated himself again, filling his mind with the thought that when two more long long days should have crept by, he should once more go to his mother.

Trevelyan had tried his best to be soft and gentle to his child. All that he had said to his wife of his treatment of the boy had been true to the letter. He had spared no personal trouble, he had done all that he had known how to do, he had exercised all his intelligence to procure amusement for the boy, but Louey had hardly smiled since he had been taken from his mother. And now that he was told that he was to go and never see his father again, the tidings were to him simply tidings of joy. 'There is a curse upon me,' said Trevelyan; 'it is written down in the book of my destiny that nothing shall ever love me!'

He went out from the house, and made his way down by the narrow path through the olives and vines to the bottom of the hill in front of the villa. It was evening now, but the evening was very hot, and though the olive trees stood in long rows, there was no shade. Quite at the bottom of the hill there was a little sluggish muddy brook, along the sides of which the reeds grew thickly and the dragon-flies were playing on the water. There was nothing attractive in the spot, but he was weary, and sat himself down on the dry hard bank which had been made by repeated clearing of mud from the bottom of the little rivulet. He sat watching the dragon-flies as they made their short flights in the warm air, and told himself that of all God's creatures there was not one to whom less power of disporting itself in God's sun was given than to him. Surely it would be better for him that he should die, than live as he was now living without any of the joys of life. The solitude of Casalunga was intolerable to him, and yet there was no whither that he could go and find society. He could travel if he pleased. He had money at command, and, at any rate as yet, there was no embargo on his personal liberty. But how could he travel alone even if his strength might suffice for the work? There had been moments in which he had thought that he would be happy in the love of his child, that the companionship of an infant would suffice for him if only the infant would love him. But all such dreams as that were over. To repay him for his tenderness, his boy was always dumb before him. Louey would not prattle as he had used to do. He would not even smile, or give back the kisses with which his father had attempted to win him. In mercy to the boy he would send him back to his mother—in mercy to the boy if not to the mother also. It was in vain that he should look for any joy in any quarter. Were he to return to England, they would say that he was mad!

He lay there by the brook-side till the evening was far advanced, and then he arose and slowly returned to the house. The labour of ascending the hill was so great to him that he was forced to pause and hold by the olive trees as he slowly performed his task. The perspiration came in profusion from his pores, and he found himself to be so weak that he must in future regard the brook as being beyond the tether of his daily exercise. Eighteen months ago he had been a strong walker, and the snow-bound paths of Swiss mountains had been a joy to him. He paused as he was slowly dragging himself on, and looked up at the wretched, desolate, comfortless abode which he called his home. Its dreariness was so odious to him that he was half-minded to lay himself down where he was, and let the night air come upon him and do its worst. In such case, however, some Italian doctor would be sent down who would say that he was mad. Above all the things, and to the last, he must save himself from that degradation.

When he had crawled up to the house, he went to his child, and found that the woman had put the boy to bed. Then he was angry with himself in that he himself had not seen to this, and kept up his practice of attending the child to the last. He would, at least, be true to his resolution, and prepare for the boy's return to his mother. Not knowing how otherwise to manage it, he wrote that night the following note to Mr Glascock:

Casalunga,
Thursday night.

My Dear Sir,

Since you last were considerate enough to call upon me I have resolved to take a step in my affairs which, though it will rob me of my only remaining gratification, will tend to lessen the troubles under which Mrs Trevelyan is labouring. If she desires it, as no doubt she does, I will consent to place our boy again in her custody, trusting to her sense of honour to restore him to me should I demand it. In my present unfortunate position I cannot suggest that she should come for the boy. I am unable to support the excitement occasioned by her presence. I will, however, deliver up my darling either to you, or to any messenger sent by you whom I can trust. I beg heartily to apologise for the trouble I am giving you, and to subscribe myself yours very faithfully,   Louis Trevelyan

The Hon. C. Glascock.

P.S. It is as well, perhaps, that I should explain that I must decline to receive any visit from Sir Marmaduke Rowley. Sir Marmaduke has insulted me grossly on each occasion on which I have seen him since his return home.'

CHAPTER LXXXV. THE BATHS OF LUCCA

June was now far advanced, and the Rowleys and the Spaldings had removed from Florence to the Baths of Lucca. Mr Glascock had followed in their wake, and the whole party were living at the Baths in one of those hotels in which so many English and Americans are wont to congregate in the early weeks of the Italian summer. The marriage was to take place in the last week of the month; and all the party were to return to Florence for the occasion with the exception of Sir Marmaduke and Mrs Trevelyan. She was altogether unfitted for wedding joys, and her father had promised to bear her company when the others left her. Mr Glascock and Caroline Spalding were to be married in Florence, and were to depart immediately from thence for some of the cooler parts of Switzerland. After that Sir Marmaduke and Lady Rowley were to return to London with their daughters, preparatory to that dreary journey back to the Mandarins; and they had not even yet resolved what they had better do respecting that unfortunate man who was living in seclusion on the hilltop near Siena. They had consulted lawyers and doctors in Florence, but it had seemed that everybody there was afraid of putting the law in force against an Englishman. Doubtless there was a law in respect to the custody of the insane; and it was admitted that if Trevelyan were dangerously mad something could be done; but it seemed that nobody was willing to stir in such a case as that which now existed. Something, it was said, might be done at some future time; but the difficulties were so great that nothing could be done now.

It was very sad, because it was necessary that some decision should be made as to the future residence of Mrs Trevelyan and of Nora. Emily had declared that nothing should induce her to go to the Islands with her father and mother unless her boy went with her. Since her journey to Casalunga she had also expressed her unwillingness to leave her husband. Her heart had been greatly softened towards him, and she had declared that where he remained, there would she remain as near to him as circumstances would admit. It might be that at last her care would be necessary for his comfort. He supplied her with means of living, and she would use these means as well as she might be able in his service.

Then there had arisen the question of Nora's future residence. And there had come troubles and storms in the family. Nora had said that she would not go back to the Mandarins, but had not at first been able to say where or how she would live. She had suggested that she might stay with her sister, but her father had insisted that she could not live on the income supplied by Trevelyan. Then, when pressed hard, she had declared that she intended to live on Hugh Stanbury's income. She would marry him at once with her father's leave, if she could get it, but without it if it needs must be so. Her mother told her that Hugh Stanbury was not himself ready for her; he had not even proposed so hasty a marriage, nor had he any home fitted for her. Lady Rowley, in arguing this, had expressed no assent to the marriage, even as a distant arrangement, but had thought thus to vanquish her daughter by suggesting small but insuperable difficulties. On a sudden, however, Lady Rowley found that all this was turned against her, by an offer that came direct from Mr Glascock. His Caroline, he said, was very anxious that Nora should come to them at Monkhams as soon as they had returned home from Switzerland. They intended to be there by the middle of August, and would hurry there sooner, if there was any immediate difficulty about finding a home for Nora. Mr Glascock said nothing about Hugh Stanbury; but, of course, Lady Rowley understood that Nora had told all her troubles and hopes to Caroline, and that Caroline had told them to her future husband. Lady Rowley, in answer to this, could only say that she would consult her husband.

There was something very grievous in the proposition to Lady Rowley. If Nora had not been self-willed and stiff-necked beyond the usual self-willedness and stiff-neckedness of young women she might have been herself the mistress of Monkhams. It was proposed now that she should go there to wait till a poor man should have got together shillings enough to buy a few chairs and tables, and a bed to lie upon! The thought of this was very bitter. 'I cannot think, Nora, how you could have the heart to go there,' said Lady Rowley.

'I cannot understand why not, mamma. Caroline and I are friends, and surely he and I need not be enemies. He has never injured me; and if he does not take offence, why should I?'

'If you don't see it, I can't help it,' said Lady Rowley.

And then Mrs Spalding's triumph was terrible to Lady Rowley. Mrs Spalding knew nothing of her future son-in-law's former passion, and spoke of her Caroline as having achieved triumphs beyond the reach of other girls. Lady Rowley bore it, never absolutely telling the tale of her daughter's fruitless victory. She was too good at heart to utter the boast but it was very hard to repress it. Upon the whole she would have preferred that Mr Glascock and his bride should not have become the fast friends of herself and her family. There was more of pain than of pleasure in the alliance. But circumstances had been too strong for her. Mr Glascock had been of great use in reference to Trevelyan, and Caroline and Nora had become attached to each other almost on their first acquaintance. Here they were together at the Baths of Lucca, and Nora was to be one of the four bridesmaids. When Sir

Marmaduke was consulted about this visit to Monkhams, he became fretful, and would give no answer. The marriage, he said, was impossible, and Nora was a fool. He could give her no allowance more than would suffice for her clothes, and it was madness for her to think of stopping in England. But he was so full of cares that he could come to no absolute decision on this matter. Nora, however, had come to a very absolute decision.

'Caroline,' she said, 'if you will have me, I will go to Monkhams.'

'Of course we will have you. Has not Charles said how delighted he would be?'

'Oh yes, your Charles,' said Nora laughing.

'He is mine now, dear. You must not expect him to change his mind again. I gave him the chance, you know, and he would not take it. But, Nora, come to Monkhams, and stay as long as it suits. I have talked it all over with him, and we both agree that you shall have a home there. You shall be just like a sister. Olivia is coming too after a bit; but he says there is room for a dozen sisters. Of course it will be all right with Mr Stanbury after a while.' And so it was settled among them that Nora Rowley should find a home at Monkhams, if a home in England should be wanted for her.

It wanted but four days to that fixed for the marriage at Florence, and but six to that on which the Rowleys were to leave Italy for England, when Mr Glascock received Trevelyan's letter. It was brought to him as he was sitting at a late breakfast in the garden of the hotel; and there were present at the moment not only all the Spalding family, but the Rowleys also. Sir Marmaduke was there and Lady Rowley, and the three unmarried daughters; but Mrs Trevelyan, as was her wont, had remained alone in her own room. Mr Glascock read the letter, and read it again, without attracting much attention. Caroline, who was of course sitting next to him, had her eyes upon him, and could see that the letter moved him; but she was not curious, and at any rate asked no question. He himself understood fully how great was the offer made, how all-important to the happiness of the poor mother, and he was also aware, or thought that he was aware, how likely it might be that the offer would be retracted. As regarded himself, a journey from the Baths at Lucca to Casalunga and back before his marriage, would be a great infliction on his patience. It was his plan to stay where he was till the day before his marriage, and then to return to Florence with the rest of the party. All this must be altered, and sudden changes must be made, if he decided on going to Siena himself. The weather now was very hot, and such a journey would be most disagreeable to him. Of course he had little schemes in his head, little amatory schemes for prenuptial enjoyment, which, in spite of his mature years, were exceedingly agreeable to him. The chestnut woods round the Baths of Lucca are very pleasant in the early summer, and there were excursions planned in which Caroline would be close by his side, almost already his wife. But, if he did not go, whom could he send? It would be necessary at least that he should consult her, the mother of the child, before any decision was formed.

At last he took Lady Rowley aside, and read to her the letter. She understood at once that it opened almost a heaven of bliss to her daughter, and she understood also how probable it might be that wretched man, with his shaken wits, should change his mind. 'I think I ought to go,' said Mr Glascock. 'But how can you go now?'

'I can go,' said he. 'There is time for it. It need not put off my marriage, to which of course I could not consent. I do not know whom I could send.'

'Moonier could go,' said Lady Rowley, naming the courier.

'Yes he could go. But it might be that he would return without the child, and then we should not forgive ourselves. I will go, Lady Rowley. After all, what does it signify? I am a little old, I sometimes think, for this philandering. You shall take his letter to your daughter, and I will explain it all to Caroline.'

Caroline had not a word to say. She could only kiss him, and promise to make him what amends she could when he came back. 'Of course you are right,' she said. 'Do you think that I would say a word against it, even though the marriage were to be postponed?'

'I should—a good many words. But I will be back in time for that, and will bring the boy with me.'

Mrs Trevelyan, when her husband's letter was read to her, was almost overcome by the feelings which it excited. In her first paroxysm of joy she declared that she would herself go to Siena, not for her child's sake, but for that of her husband. She felt at once that the boy was being given up because of the father's weakness, because he felt himself to be unable to be a protector to his son, and her woman's heart was melted with softness as she thought of the condition of the man to whom she had once given her whole heart. Since then, doubtless, her heart had revolted from him. Since that time there had come hours in which she had almost hated him for his cruelty to her. There had been moments in which she had almost cursed his name because of the aspersion which it had seemed that he had thrown upon her. But this was now forgotten, and she remembered only his weakness. 'Mamma,' she said, 'I will go. It is my duty to go to him.' But Lady Rowley withheld her, explaining that were she to go, the mission might probably fail in its express purpose. 'Let Louey be sent to us first,' said Lady Rowley, 'and then we will see what can be done afterwards.'

And so Mr Glascock started, taking with him a maid-servant who might help him with the charge of the child. It was certainly very hard upon him. In order to have time for his journey to Siena and back, and time also to go out to Casalunga, it was necessary that he should leave the Baths at five in the morning. 'If ever there was a hero of romance, you are he!' said Nora to him.

'The heroes of life are so much better than the heroes of romance,' said Caroline.

'That is a lesson from the lips of the American Browning,' said Mr Glascock. 'Nevertheless, I think I would rather ride a charge against a Paynim knight in Palestine than get up at half-past four in the morning.'

'We will get up too, and give the knight his coffee,' said Nora. They did get up, and saw him off; and when Mr Glascock and Caroline parted with a lover's embrace, Nora stood by as a sister might have done. Let us hope that she remembered that her own time was coming.

There had been a promise given by Nora, when she left London, that she would not correspond with Hugh Stanbury while she was in Italy, and this promise had been kept. It may be remembered that Hugh had made a proposition to his lady-love, that she should walk out of the house one fine morning, and get herself married without any reference to her father's or her mother's wishes. But she had not been willing to take upon herself as yet independence so complete as this would have required. She had assured her lover that she did mean to marry him some day, even though it should be in opposition to her father, but that she thought that the period for filial persuasion was not yet over; and then, in explaining all this to her mother, she had given a promise neither to write nor to receive letters during the short period of her sojourn in Italy. She would be an obedient child for so long but, after that, she must claim the right to fight her own battle. She had told her lover that he must not write; and, of course, she had not written a word herself. But now, when her mother threw it in her teeth that Stanbury would not be ready to marry her, she thought that an unfair advantage was being taken of her and of him. How could he be expected to say that he was ready, deprived as he was of the power of saying anything at all?

'Mamma,' she said, the day before they went to Florence, 'has papa fixed about your leaving England yet? I suppose you'll go now on the last Saturday in July?'

'I suppose we shall, my dear.'

'Has not papa written about the berths?'

'I believe he has, my dear.'

'Because he ought to know who are going. I will not go.

'You will not, Nora. Is that a proper way of speaking?'

'Dear mamma, I mean it to be proper. I hope it is proper. But is it not best that we should understand each other. All my life depends on my going or my staying now. I must decide.'

'After what has passed, you do not, I suppose, mean to live in Mr Glascock's house?'

'Certainly not. I mean to live with with with my husband. Mamma, I promised not to write, and I have not written. And he has not written because I told him not. Therefore, nothing is settled. But it is not fair to throw it in my teeth that nothing is settled.'

'I have thrown nothing in your teeth, Nora.'

'Papa talks sneeringly about chairs and tables. Of course, I know what he is thinking of. As I cannot go with him to the Mandarins, I think I ought to be allowed to look after the chairs and tables.'

'What do you mean, my dear?'

'That you should absolve me from my promise, and let me write to Mr Stanbury. I do not want to be left without a home.'

'You cannot wish to write to a gentleman and ask him to marry you!'

'Why not? We are engaged. I shall not ask him to marry me; that is already settled; but I shall ask him to make arrangements.'

'Your papa will be very angry if you break your word to him.'

'I will write, and show you the letter. Papa may see it, and if he will not let it go, it shall not go. He shall not say that I broke my word. But, mamma, I will not go out to the Islands. I should never get back again, and I should be broken-hearted.' Lady Rowley had nothing to say to this; and Nora went and wrote her letter. 'Dear Hugh,' the letter ran, 'Papa and mamma leave England on the last Saturday in July. I have told mamma that I cannot return with them. Of course, you know why I stay. Mr Glascock is to be married the day after to-morrow, and they have asked me to go with them to Monkhams some time in August. I think I shall do so, unless Emily wants me to remain with her. At any rate, I shall try to be with her till I go there. You will understand why I tell you all this. Papa and mamma know that I am writing. It is only a business letter, and, therefore, I shall say no more, except that I am ever and always yours Nora.' 'There,' she said, handing her letter to her mother, 'I think that ought to be sent. If papa chooses to prevent its going, he can.'

Lady Rowley, when she handed the letter to her husband, recommended that it should be allowed to go to its destination. She admitted that, if they sent it, they would thereby signify their consent to her engagement, and she alleged that Nora was so strong in her will, and that the circumstances of their journey out to the Antipodes were so peculiar, that it was of no avail for them any longer to oppose the match. They could not force their daughter to go with them. 'But I can cast her off from me, if she be disobedient,' said Sir Marmaduke. Lady Rowley, however, had no desire that her daughter should be cast off, and was aware that Sir Marmaduke, when it came to the point of casting off, would be as little inclined to be stern as she was herself. Sir Marmaduke, still hoping that firmness would carry the day, and believing that it behoved him to maintain his parental authority, ended the discussion by keeping possession of the letter, and saying that he would take time to consider the matter. 'What security have we that he will ever marry her, if she does stay?' he asked the next morning. Lady Rowley had no doubt on this score, and protested that her opposition to Hugh Stanbury arose simply from his want of income. 'I should never be justified,' said Sir Marmaduke, 'if I were to go and leave my girl as it were in the hands of a penny-a-liner.' The letter, in the end, was not sent; and Nora and her father hardly spoke to each other as they made their journey back to Florence together.

Emily Trevelyan, before the arrival of that letter from her husband, had determined that she would not leave Italy. It had been her purpose to remain somewhere in the neighbourhood of her husband and child; and to overcome her difficulties or be overcome by them, as circumstances might direct. Now her plans were again changed or, rather, she was now without a plan. She could form no plan till she should again see Mr Glascock. Should her child be restored to her, would it not be her duty to remain near her husband? All this made Nora's line of conduct the more difficult for her. It was acknowledged that she could not remain in Italy. Mrs Trevelyan's position would be most embarrassing; but as all her efforts were to be used towards a reconciliation with her husband, and as his state utterly precluded the idea of a mixed household, of any such a family arrangement as that which had existed in Curzon Street, Nora could not remain with her. Mrs Trevelyan herself had declared that she would not wish it. And, in that case, where was Nora to bestow herself when Sir Marmaduke and Lady Rowley had sailed? Caroline offered to curtail those honeymoon weeks in Switzerland, but it was impossible to listen to an offer so magnanimous and so unreasonable. Nora had a dim romantic idea of sharing Priscilla's bedroom in that small cottage near Nuncombe Putney, of which she had heard, and of there learning lessons in strict economy; but of this she said nothing. The short journey from the Baths of Lucca to Florence was not a pleasant one, and the Rowley family were much disturbed as they looked into the future. Lodgings had now been taken for them, and there was the great additional doubt whether Mrs Trevelyan would find her child there on her arrival.

The Spaldings went one way from the Florence station, and the Rowleys another. The American Minister had returned to the city some days previously, drawn there nominally by pleas of business, but, in truth, by the necessities of the wedding breakfast, and he met them at the station. 'Has Mr Glascock come back?' Nora was the first to ask. Yes he had come. He had been in the city since two o'clock, and had been up at the American Minister's house for half a minute. 'And has he brought the child?' asked Caroline, relieved of doubt on her own account. Mr Spalding did not know; indeed, he had not interested himself quite so intently about Mrs Trevelyan's little boy, as had all those who had just returned from the Baths. Mr Glascock had said nothing to him about the child, and he had not quite understood why such a man should have made a journey to Siena, leaving his sweetheart behind him, just on the eve of his marriage. He hurried his women-kind into their carriage, and they were driven away; and then Sir Marmaduke was driven away with his women-kind. Caroline Spalding had perhaps thought that Mr Glascock might have been there to meet her.

CHAPTER LXXXVI. MR GLASCOCK AS NURSE

A message had been sent by the wires to Trevelyan, to let him know that Mr Glascock was himself coming for the boy. Whether such message would or would not be sent out to Casalunga Mr Glascock had been quite ignorant, but it could, at any rate, do no harm. He did feel it hard as in this hot weather he made the journey, first to Florence, and then on to Siena. What was he to the Rowleys, or to Trevelyan himself, that such a job of work should fall to his lot at such a period of his life? He had been very much in love with Nora, no doubt; but, luckily for him, as he thought, Nora had refused him. As for Trevelyan, Trevelyan had never been his friend. As for Sir Marmaduke, Sir Marmaduke was nothing to him. He was almost angry even with Mrs Trevelyan as he arrived tired, heated, and very dusty, at Siena. It was his purpose to sleep at Siena that night, and to go out to Casalunga early the next morning. If the telegram had not been forwarded, he would send a message on that evening. On inquiry, however, he found that the message had been sent, and that the paper had been put into the Signore's own hand by the Sienese messenger. Then he got into some discourse with the landlord about the strange gentleman at Casalunga. Trevelyan was beginning to become the subject of gossip in the town, and people were saying that the stranger was very strange indeed. The landlord thought that if the Signore had any friends at all, it would be well that such friends should come and look after him. Mr Glascock asked if Mr Trevelyan was ill. It was not only that the Signore was out of health, so the landlord heard, but that he was also somewhat—and then the landlord touched his head. He eat nothing, and went nowhere, and spoke to no one; and the people at the hospital to which Casalunga belonged were beginning to be uneasy about their tenant. Perhaps Mr Glascock had come to take him away. Mr Glascock explained that he had not come to take Mr Trevelyan away but only to take away a little boy that was with him. For this reason he was travelling with a maid-servant, a fact for which Mr Glascock clearly thought it necessary that he should give an intelligible and credible explanation. The landlord seemed to think that the people at the hospital would have been much rejoiced had Mr Glascock intended to take Mr Trevelyan away also.

He started after a very early breakfast, and found himself walking up over the stone ridges to the house between nine and ten in the morning. He himself had sat beside the driver and had put the maid inside the carriage. He had not deemed it wise to take an undivided charge of the boy even from Casalunga to Siena. At the door of the house, as though waiting for him, he found Trevelyan, not dirty as he had been before, but dressed with much appearance of smartness. He had a brocaded cap on his head, and a shirt with a laced front, and a worked waistcoat, and a frockcoat, and coloured bright trowsers. Mr Glascock knew at once that all the clothes which he saw before him had been made for Italian and not for English wear; and could almost have said that they had been bought in Siena and not in Florence. 'I had not intended to impose this labour on you, Mr Glascock,' Trevelyan said, raising his cap to salute his visitor.

'For fear there might be mistakes, I thought it better to come myself,' said Mr Glascock. 'You did not wish to see Sir Marmaduke?'

'Certainly not Sir Marmaduke,' said Trevelyan, with a look of anger that was almost grotesque.

'And you thought it better that Mrs Trevelyan should not come.'

'Yes, I thought it better, but not from any feeling of anger towards her. If I could welcome my wife here, Mr Glascock, without a risk of wrath on her part, I should be very happy to receive her. I love my wife, Mr Glascock. I love her dearly. But there have been misfortunes. Never mind. There is no reason why I should trouble you with them. Let us go in to breakfast. After your drive you will have an appetite.'

Poor Mr Glascock was afraid to decline to sit down to the meal which was prepared for him. He did mutter something about having already eaten, but Trevelyan put this aside with a wave of his hand as he led the way into a spacious room, in which had been set out a table with almost a sumptuous banquet. The room was very bare and comfortless, having neither curtains nor matting, and containing not above half a dozen chairs. But an effort had been made to give it an air of Italian luxury. The windows were thrown open, down to the ground, and the table was decorated with fruits and three or four long-necked bottles. Trevelyan waved with his hand towards an arm-chair, and Mr Glascock had no alternative but to seat himself. He felt that he was sitting down to breakfast with a madman; but if he did not sit down, the madman might perhaps break out into madness. Then Trevelyan went to the door and called aloud for Catarina. 'In these remote places,' said he, 'one has to do without the civilisation of a bell. Perhaps one gains as much in quiet as one loses in comfort.' Then Catarina came with hot meats and fried potatoes, and Mr Glascock was compelled to help himself.

'I am but a bad trencherman myself,' said Trevelyan, 'but I shall lament my misfortune doubly if that should interfere with your appetite.' Then he got up and poured out wine into Mr Glascock's glass. 'They tell me that it comes from the Baron's vineyard,' said Trevelyan, alluding to the wine-farm of Ricasoli, 'and that there is none better in Tuscany. I never was myself a judge of the grape, but this to me is as palatable as any of the costlier French wines. How grand a thing would wine really be, if it could make glad the heart of man. How truly would one worship Bacchus if he could make one's heart to rejoice. But if a man have a real sorrow, wine will not wash it away, not though a man were drowned in it, as Clarence was.'

Mr Glascock hitherto had spoken hardly a word. There was an attempt at joviality about this breakfast or, at any rate, of the usual comfortable luxury of hospitable entertainment which, coming as it did from Trevelyan, almost locked his lips. He had not come there to be jovial or luxurious, but to perform a most melancholy mission; and he had brought with him his saddest looks, and was prepared for a few sad words. Trevelyan's speech, indeed, was sad enough, but Mr Glascock could not take up questions of the worship of Bacchus at half a minute's warning. He eat a morsel, and raised his glass to his lips, and felt himself to be very uncomfortable. It was necessary, however, that he should utter a word. 'Do you not let your little boy come in to breakfast?' he said.

'He is better away,' said Trevelyan gloomily.

'But as we are to travel together,' said Mr Glascock, 'we might as well make acquaintance.'

'You have been a little hurried with me on that score,' said Trevelyan. 'I wrote certainly with a determined mind, but things have changed somewhat since then.'

'You do not mean that you will not send him?'

'You have been somewhat hurried with me, I say. If I remember rightly, I named no time, but spoke of the future. Could I have answered the message which I received from you, I would have postponed your visit for a week or so.'

'Postponed it! Why, I am to be married the day after to-morrow. It was just as much as I was able to do, to come here at all.' Mr Glascock now pushed his chair back from the table, and prepared himself to speak up. 'Your wife expects her child now, and you will ever break her heart by refusing to send him.'

'Nobody thinks of my heart, Mr Glascock.'

'But this is your own offer.'

'Yes, it was my own offer, certainly. I am not going to deny my own words, which have no doubt been preserved in testimony against me.'

'Mr Trevelyan, what do you mean?' Then, when he was on the point of boiling over with passion, Mr Glascock remembered that his companion was not responsible for his expressions. 'I do hope you will let the child go away with me,' he said. 'You cannot conceive the state of his mother's anxiety, and she will send him back at once if you demand it.'

'Is that to be in good faith?'

'Certainly, in good faith. I would lend myself to nothing, Mr Trevelyan, that was not said and done in good faith.'

'She will not break her word, excusing herself, because I am mad?'

'I am sure that there is nothing of the kind in her mind.'

'Perhaps not now; but such things grow. There is no iniquity, no breach of promise, no treason that a woman will not excuse to herself—or a man either—by the comfortable self-assurance that the person to be injured is mad. A hound without a friend is not so cruelly treated. The outlaw, the murderer, the perjurer has surer privileges than the man who is in the way, and to whom his friends can point as being mad!' Mr Glascock knew or thought that he knew that his host in truth was mad, and he could not, therefore, answer this tirade by an assurance that no such idea was likely to prevail. 'Have they told you, I wonder,' continued Trevelyan, 'how it was that, driven to force and an ambuscade for the recovery of my own child, I waylaid my wife and took him from her? I have done nothing to forfeit my right as a man to the control of my own family. I demanded that the boy should be sent to me, and she paid no attention to my words. I was compelled to vindicate my own authority; and then, because I claimed the right which belongs to a father, they said that I was mad! Ay, and they would have proved it, too, had I not fled from my country and hidden myself in this desert. Think of that, Mr Glascock! Now they have followed me here, not out of love for me; and that man whom they call a governor comes and insults me; and my wife promises to be good to me, and says that she will forgive and forget! Can she ever forgive herself her own folly, and the cruelty that has made shipwreck of my life? They can do nothing to me here; but they would entice me home because there they have friends, and can fee doctors with my own money and suborn lawyers, and put me away somewhere in the dark, where I shall be no more heard of among men! As you are a man of honour, Mr Glascock tell me; is it not so?'

'I know nothing of their plans beyond this, that you wrote me word that you would send them the boy.'

'But I know their plans. What you say is true. I did write you word, and I meant it. Mr Glascock, sitting here alone from morning to night, and lying down from night till morning, without companionship, without love, in utter misery, I taught myself to feel that I should think more of her than of myself.'

'If you are so unhappy here, come back yourself with the child. Your wife would desire nothing better.'

'Yes and submit to her, and her father, and her mother. No Mr Glascock; never, never. Let her come to me.'

'But you will not receive her.'

'Let her come in a proper spirit, and I will receive her. She is the wife of my bosom, and I will receive her with joy. But if she is to come to me and tell me that she forgives me—forgives me for the evil that she has done—then, sir, she had better stay away. Mr Glascock, you are going to be married. Believe me no man should submit to be forgiven by his wife. Everything must go astray if that be done. I would rather encounter their mad doctors, one of them after another till they had made me mad; I would encounter anything rather than that. But, sir, you neither eat nor drink, and I fear that my speech disturbs you.'

It was like enough that it may have done so. Trevelyan, as he had been speaking, had walked about the room, going from one extremity to the other with hurried steps, gesticulating with his arms, and every now and then pushing back with his hands the long hair from off his forehead. Mr Glascock was in truth very much disturbed. He had come there with an express object; but, whenever he mentioned the child, the father became almost rabid in his wrath. 'I have done very well, thank you,' said Mr Glascock. 'I will not eat any more, and I believe I must be thinking of going back to Siena.'

'I had hoped you would spend the day with me, Mr Glascock.'

'I am to be married, you see, in two days; and I must be in Florence early to-morrow. I am to meet my wife, as she will be, and the Rowleys, and your wife. Upon my word I can't stay. Won't you just say a word to the young woman and let the boy be got ready?'

'I think not; no, I think not.'

'And am I to have had all this journey for nothing? You will have made a fool of me in writing to me.'

'I intended to be honest, Mr Glascock.'

'Stick to your honesty, and send the boy back to his mother. It will be better for you, Trevelyan.'

'Better for me! Nothing can be better for me. All must be worst. It will be better for me, you say; and you ask me to give up the last drop of cold water wherewith I can touch my parched lips. Even in my hell I had so much left to me of a limpid stream, and you tell me that it will be better for me to pour it away. You may take him, Mr Glascock. The woman will make him ready for you. What matters it whether the fiery furnace be heated seven times, or only six; in either degree the flames are enough! You may take him, you may take him!' So saying, Trevelyan walked out of the window, leaving Mr Glascock seated in his chair. He walked out of the window and went down among the olive trees. He did not go far, however, but stood with his arm round the stem of one of them, playing with the shoots of a vine with his hand. Mr Glascock followed him to the window and stood looking at him for a few moments. But Trevelyan did not turn or move. There he stood gazing at the pale, cloudless, heat-laden, motionless sky, thinking of his own sorrows, and remembering too, doubtless, with the vanity of a madman, that he was probably being watched in his reverie.

Mr Glascock was too practical a man not to make the most of the offer that had been made to him, and he went back among the passages and called for Catarina. Before long he had two or three women with him, including her whom he had brought from Florence, and among them Louey was soon made to appear, dressed for his journey, together with a small trunk in which were his garments. It was quite clear that the order for his departure had been given before that scene at the breakfast-table, and that Trevelyan had not intended to go back on his promise. Nevertheless Mr Glascock thought it might be as well to hurry his departure, and he turned back to say the shortest possible word of farewell to Trevelyan in the garden. But when he got to the window, Trevelyan was not to be found among the olive trees. Mr Glascock walked a few steps down the hill, looking for him, but seeing nothing of him, returned to the house. The elder woman said that her master had not been there, and Mr Glascock started with his charge. Trevelyan was manifestly mad, and it was impossible to treat him as a sane man would have been treated. Nevertheless, Mr Glascock felt much compunction in carrying the child away without a final kiss or word of farewell from its father. But it was not to be so. He had got into the carriage with the child, having the servant seated opposite to him, for he was moved by some undefinable fear which made him determine to keep the boy close to him, and he had not, therefore, returned to the driver's seat when Trevelyan appeared standing by the road-side at the bottom of the hill. 'Would you take him away from me without one word!' said Trevelyan bitterly.

'I went to look for you, but you were gone,' said Mr Glascock.

'No, sir, I was not gone. I am here. It is the last time that I shall ever gladden my eyes with his brightness. Louey, my love, will you come to your father?' Louey did not seem to be particularly willing to leave the carriage, but he made no loud objection when Mr Glascock held him up to the open space above the door. The child had realised the fact that he was to go, and did not believe that his father would stop him now; but he was probably of opinion that the sooner the carriage began to go on the better it would be for him. Mr Glascock, thinking that his father intended to kiss him over the door, held him by his frock; but the doing of this made Trevelyan very angry. 'Am I not to be trusted with my own child in my arms?' said he. 'Give him to me, sir. I begin to doubt now whether I am right to deliver him to you.' Mr Glascock immediately let go his hold of the boy's frock and leaned back in the carriage. 'Louey will tell papa that he loves him before he goes?' said Trevelyan. The poor little fellow murmured something, but it did not please his father, who had him in his arms. 'You are like the rest of them, Louey,' he said; 'because I cannot laugh and be gay, all my love for you is nothing—nothing! You may take him. He is all that I have, all that I have, and I shall never see him again!' So saying he handed the child into the carriage, and sat himself down by the side of the road to watch till the vehicle should be out of sight. As soon as the last speck of it had vanished from his sight, he picked himself up, and dragged his slow footsteps back to the house.

Mr Glascock made sundry attempts to amuse the child, with whom he had to remain all that night at Siena; but his efforts in that line were not very successful. The boy was brisk enough, and happy, and social by nature; but the events, or rather the want of events of the last few months, had so cowed him, that he could not recover his spirits at the bidding of a stranger. 'If I have any of my own,' said Mr Glascock to himself, 'I hope they will be of a more cheerful disposition.'

As we have seen, he did not meet Caroline at the station, thereby incurring his lady-love's displeasure for the period of half-a-minute; but he did meet Mrs Trevelyan almost at the door of Sir Marmaduke's lodgings. 'Yes, Mrs Trevelyan; he is here.'

'How am I ever to thank you for such goodness?' said she. 'And Mr Trevelyan—you saw him?'

'Yes I saw him.'

Before he could answer her further she was upstairs, and had her child in her arms. It seemed to be an age since the boy had been stolen from her in the early spring in that unknown, dingy street near Tottenham Court Road. Twice she had seen her darling since that, twice during his captivity; but on each of these occasions she had seen him as one not belonging to herself, and had seen him under circumstances which had robbed the greeting of almost all its pleasure. But now he was her own again, to take whither she would, to dress and to undress, to feed, to coax, to teach, and to caress. And the child lay up close to her as she hugged him, putting up his little cheek to her chin, and burying himself happily in her embrace. He had not much as yet to say, but she could feel that he was contented.

Mr Glascock had promised to wait for her a few minutes, even at the risk of Caroline's displeasure, and Mrs Trevelyan ran down to him as soon as the first craving of her mother's love was satisfied. Her boy would at any rate be safe with her now, and it was her duty to learn something of her husband. It was more than her duty, if only her services might be of avail to him. 'And you say he was well?' she asked. She had taken Mr Glascock apart, and they were alone together, and he had determined that he would tell her the truth.

'I do not know that he is ill, though he is pale and altered beyond belief.'

'Yes I saw that.'

'I never knew a man so thin and haggard.'

'My poor Louis!'

'But that is not the worst of it.'

'What do you mean, Mr Glascock?'

'I mean that his mind is astray, and that he should not be left alone. There is no knowing what he might do. He is so much more alone there than he would be in England. There is not a soul who could interfere.'

'Do you mean that you think that he is in danger from himself?'

'I would not say so, Mrs Trevelyan; but who can tell? I am sure of this, that he should not be left alone. If it were only because of the misery of his life, he should not be left alone.'

'But what can I do? He would not even see papa.'

'He would see you.'

'But he would not let me guide him in anything. I have been to him twice, and he breaks out as if I were a bad woman.'

'Let him break out. What does it matter?'

'Am I to own to a falsehood, and such a falsehood?'

'Own to anything, and you will conquer him at once. That is what I think. You will excuse what I say, Mrs Trevelyan.'

'Oh, Mr Glascock, you have been such a friend! What should we have done without you!'

'You cannot take to heart the words that come from a disordered reason. In truth, he believes no ill of you.'

'But he says so.'

'It is hard to know what he says. Declare that you will submit to him, and I think that he will be softened towards you. Try to bring him back to his own country. It may be that were he to die there, alone, the memory of his loneliness would be heavy with you in after days.' Then, having so spoken, he rushed off, declaring, with a forced laugh, that Caroline Spalding would never forgive him.

The next day was the day of the wedding, and Emily Trevelyan was left all alone. It was of course out of the question that she should join any party the purport of which was to be festive. Sir Marmaduke went with some grumbling, declaring that wine and severe food in the mornings were sins against the plainest rules of life. And the three Rowley girls went, Nora officiating as one of the bridesmaids. But Mrs Trevelyan was left with her boy, and during the day she was forced to resolve what should be the immediate course of her life. Two days after the wedding her family would return to England. It was open to her to go with them, and to take her boy with her. But a few days since how happy she would have been could she have been made to believe that such a mode of returning would be within her power! But now she felt that she might not return and leave that poor, suffering wretch behind her. As she thought of him she tried to interrogate herself in regard to her feelings. Was it love, or duty, or compassion which stirred her? She had loved him as fondly as any bright young woman loves the man who is to take her away from everything else, and make her a part of his house and of himself. She had loved him as Nora now loved the man whom she worshipped and thought to be a god, doing godlike work in the dingy recesses of the D. R. office. Emily Trevelyan was forced to tell herself that all that was over with her. Her husband had shown himself to be weak, suspicious, unmanly—by no means like a god. She had learned to feel that she could not trust her comfort in his hands, that she could never know what his thoughts of her might be. But still he was her husband, and the father of her child; and though she could not dare to look forward to happiness in living with him, she could understand that no comfort would be possible to her, were she to return to England and to leave him to perish alone at Casalunga. Fate seemed to have intended that her life should be one of misery, and she must bear it as best she might.

The more she thought of it, however, the greater seemed to be her difficulties. What was she to do when her father and mother should have left her? She could not go to Casalunga if her husband would not give her entrance; and if she did go, would it be safe for her to take her boy with her? Were she to remain in Florence she would be hardly nearer to him for any useful purpose than in England; and even should she pitch her tent at Siena, occupying there some desolate set of huge apartments in a deserted palace, of what use could she be to him? Could she stay there if he desired her to go; and was it probable that he would be willing that she should be at Siena while he was living at Casalunga, no more than two leagues distant? How should she begin her work; and if he repulsed her, how should she then continue it?

But during these wedding hours she did make up her mind as to what she would do for the present. She would certainly not leave Italy while her husband remained there. She would for a while keep her rooms in Florence, and there should her boy abide. But from time to time, twice a week perhaps, she would go down to Siena and Casalunga, and there form her plans in accordance with her husband's conduct. She was his wife, and nothing should entirely separate her from him, now that he so sorely wanted her aid.

CHAPTER LXXXVII. MR GLASCOCK'S MARRIAGE COMPLETED

The Glascock marriage was a great affair in Florence so much so, that there were not a few who regarded it as a strengthening of peaceful relations between the United States and the United Kingdom, and who thought that the Alabama claims and the question of naturalisation might now be settled with comparative ease. An English lord was about to marry the niece of an American Minister to a foreign court. The bridegroom was not, indeed, quite a lord as yet, but it was known to all men that he must be a lord in a very short time, and the bride was treated with more than usual bridal honours because she belonged to a legation. She was not, indeed, an ambassador's daughter, but the niece of a daughterless ambassador, and therefore almost as good as a daughter. The wives and daughters of other ambassadors, and the ambassadors themselves, of course, came to the wedding; and as the palace in which Mr Spalding had apartments stood alone, in a garden, with a separate carriage entrance, it seemed for all wedding purposes as though the whole palace were his own. The English Minister came, and his wife, although she had never quite given over turning up her nose at the American bride whom Mr Glascock had chosen for himself. It was such a pity, she said, that such a man as Mr Glascock should marry a young woman from Providence, Rhode Island. Who in England would know anything of Providence, Rhode Island? And it was so expedient, in her estimation, that a man of family should strengthen himself by marrying a woman of family. It was so necessary, she declared, that a man when marrying should remember that his child would have two grandfathers, and would be called upon to account for four great-grandfathers. Nevertheless Mr Glascock was Mr Glascock; and, let him marry whom he would, his wife would be the future Lady Peterborough. Remembering this, the English Minister's wife gave up the point when the thing was really settled, and benignly promised to come to the breakfast with all the secretaries and attaches belonging to the legation, and all the wives and daughters thereof. What may a man not do, and do with *éclat*, if he be heir to a peer and have plenty of money in his pocket?

Mr and Mrs Spalding were covered with glory on the occasion; and perhaps they did not bear their glory as meekly as they should have done. Mrs Spalding laid herself open to some ridicule from the British Minister's wife because of her inability to understand with absolute clearness the condition of her niece's husband in respect to his late and future seat in Parliament, to the fact of his being a commoner and a nobleman at the same time, and to certain information which was conveyed to her, surely in a most unnecessary manner, that if Mr Glascock were to die before his father, her niece would never become Lady Peterborough, although her niece's son, if she had one, would be the future lord. No doubt she blundered, as was most natural; and then the British Minister's wife made the most of the blunders; and when once Mrs Spalding ventured to speak of Caroline as her ladyship, not to the British Minister's wife, but to the sister of one of the secretaries, a story was made out of it which was almost as false as it was ill-natured. Poor Caroline was spoken of as her ladyship backward and forwards among the ladies of the legation in a manner which might have vexed her had she known anything about it; but nevertheless, all the ladies prepared their best flounces to go to the wedding. The time would soon come when she would in truth be a 'ladyship,' and she might be of social use to any one of the ladies in question.

But Mr Spalding was, for the time, the most disturbed of any of the party concerned. He was a tall, thin, clever Republican of the North, very fond of hearing himself talk, and somewhat apt to take advantage of the courtesies of conversation for the purpose of making unpardonable speeches. As long as there was any give and take going on in the *mêlée* of words he would speak quickly and with energy, seizing his chances among others; but the moment he had established his right to the floor, as soon as he had won for himself the position of having his turn at the argument, he would dole out his words with considerable slowness, raise his hand for oratorical effect, and proceed as though Time were annihilated. And he would go further even than this, for fearing by experience the escape of his victims, he would catch a man by the button-hole of his coat, or back him ruthlessly into the corner of a room, and then lay on to him without quarter. Since the affair with Mr Glascock had been settled, he had talked an immensity about England, not absolutely taking honour to himself because of his intended connection with a lord, but making so many references to the aristocratic side of the British constitution as to leave no doubt on the minds of his hearers as to the source of his arguments. In old days, before all this was happening, Mr Spalding, though a courteous man in his personal relations, had constantly spoken of England with the bitter indignation of the ordinary American politician. England must be made to disgorge. England must be made to do justice. England must be taught her place in the world. England must give up her claims. In hot moments he had gone further, and had declared that England must be whipped. He had been specially loud against that aristocracy of England which, according to a figure of speech often used by him, was always feeding on the vitals of the people. But now all this was very much changed. He did not go the length of expressing an opinion that the House of Lords was a valuable institution; but he discussed questions of primogeniture and hereditary legislation, in reference to their fitness for countries which were gradually emerging from feudal systems, with an equanimity, an impartiality, and a perseverance which soon convinced those who listened to him where he had learned his present lessons, and why. 'The conservative nature of your institutions, sir,' he said to poor Sir Marmaduke at the Baths of Lucca a very few days before the marriage, 'has to be studied with great care before its effects can be appreciated in reference to a people who, perhaps, I may be allowed to say, have more in their composition of constitutional reverence than of educated intelligence.' Sir Marmaduke, having suffered before, had endeavoured to bolt; but the American had caught him and pinned him, and the Governor of the Mandarins was impotent in his hands. 'The position of the great peer of Parliament is doubtless very splendid, and may be very useful,' continued Mr Spalding, who was intending to bring round his argument to the evil doings of certain scandalously extravagant young lords, and to offer a suggestion that in such cases a committee of aged and respected peers should sit and decide whether a second son, or some other heir should not be called to the inheritance, both of the title and the property. But Mrs Spalding had seen the sufferings of Sir Marmaduke, and had rescued him. 'Mr Spalding,' she had said, 'it is too late for politics, and Sir Marmaduke has come out here for a holiday.' Then she took her husband by the arm, and led him away helpless.

In spite of these drawbacks to the success, if ought can be said to be a drawback on success of which the successful one is unconscious, the marriage was prepared with great splendour, and everybody who was anybody in Florence was to be present. There were only to be four bridesmaids, Caroline herself having strongly objected to a greater number. As Wallachia Petrie had fled at the first note of preparation for these trivial and unpalatable festivities, another American young lady was found; and the sister of the English secretary of legation, who had so maliciously spread that report about her 'ladyship,' gladly agreed to be the fourth.

As the reader will remember, the whole party from the Baths of Lucca reached Florence only the day before the marriage, and Nora at the station promised to go up to Caroline that same evening. 'Mr Glascock will tell me about the little boy,' said Caroline; 'but I shall be so anxious to hear about your sister.' So Nora crossed the bridge after dinner, and went up to the American Minister's palatial residence. Caroline was then in the loggia, and Mr Glascock was with her; and for a while they talked about Emily Trevelyan and her misfortunes. Mr Glascock was clearly of opinion that Trevelyan would soon be either in an asylum or in his grave. 'I could not bring myself to tell your sister so,' he said; 'but I think your father should be told or your mother. Something should be done to put an end to that fearful residence at Casalunga.' Then by degrees the conversation changed itself to Nora's prospects; and Caroline, with her friend's hand in hers, asked after Hugh Stanbury.

'You will not mind speaking before him will you?' said Caroline, putting her hand on her own lover's arm.

'Not unless he should mind it,' said Nora, smiling.

She had meant nothing beyond a simple reply to her friend's question, but he took her words in a different sense, and blushed as he remembered his visit to Nuncombe Putney.

'He thinks almost more of your happiness than he does of mine,' said Caroline; 'which isn't fair, as I am sure that Mr Stanbury will not reciprocate the attention. And now, dear, when are we to see you?'

'Who on earth can say?'

'I suppose Mr Stanbury would say something, only he is not here.'

'And papa won't send my letter,' said Nora.

'You are sure that you will not go out to the Islands with him?'

'Quite sure,' said Nora. 'I have made up my mind so far as that.'

'And what will your sister do?'

'I think she will stay. I think she will say good-bye to papa and mamma here in Florence.'

'I am quite of opinion that she should not leave her husband alone in Italy,' said Mr Glascock.

'She has not told us with certainty,' said Nora; 'but I feel sure that she will stay. Papa thinks she ought to go with them to London.'

'Your papa seems to have two very intractable daughters,' said Caroline.

'As for me,' declared Nora, solemnly, 'nothing shall make me go back to the Islands unless Mr Stanbury should tell me to do so.'

'And they start at the end of July?'

'On the last Saturday.'

'And what will you do then, Nora?'

'I believe there are casual wards that people go to.'

'Casual wards!' said Caroline.

'Miss Rowley is condescending to poke her fun at you,' said Mr Glascock.

'She is quite welcome, and shall poke as much as she likes; only we must be serious now. If it be necessary, we will get back by the end of July, won't we, Charles?'

'You will do nothing of the kind,' said Nora. 'What! give up your honeymoon to provide me with board and lodgings! How can you suppose that I am so selfish or so helpless? I would go to my aunt, Mrs Outhouse.'

'We know that that wouldn't do,' said Caroline. 'You might as well be in Italy as far as Mr Stanbury is concerned.'

'If Miss Rowley would go to Monkhams, she might wait for us,' suggested Mr Glascock. 'Old Mrs Richards is there; and though of course she would be dull—'

'It is quite unnecessary,' said Nora. 'I shall take a two-pair back in a respectable feminine quarter, like any other young woman who wants such accommodation, and shall wait there till my young man can come and give me his arm to church. That is about the way we shall do it. I am not going to give myself any airs, Mr Glascock, or make any difficulties. Papa is always talking to me about chairs and tables and frying-pans, and I shall practise to do with as few of them as possible. As I am headstrong about having my young man, and I own that I am headstrong about that, I guess I've got to fit myself for that sort of life.' And Nora, as she said this, pronounced her words with something of a nasal twang, imitating certain countrywomen of her friend's.

'I like to hear you joking about it, Nora; because your voice is so cheery and you are so bright when you joke. But, nevertheless, one has to be reasonable, and to look the facts in the face. I don't see how you are to be left in London alone, and you know that your aunt Mrs Outhouse or at any rate your uncle would not receive you except on receiving some strong anti-Stanbury pledge.'

'I certainly shall not give an anti-Stanbury pledge.'

'And, therefore, that is out of the question. You will have a fortnight or three weeks in London, in all the bustle of their departure, and I declare I think that at the last moment you will go with them.'

'Never! unless he says so.'

'I don't see how you are even to meet "him," and talk it over.'

'I'll manage that. My promise not to write lasts only while we are in Italy.'

'I think we had better get back to England, Charles, and take pity on this poor destitute one.'

'If you talk of such a thing I will swear that I will never go to Monkhams. You will find that I shall manage it. It may be that I shall do something very shocking so that all your patronage will hardly be able to bring me round afterwards; but I will do something that will serve my purpose. I have not gone so far as this to be turned back now.' Nora, as she spoke of having 'gone so far,' was looking at Mr Glascock, who was seated in an easy arm-chair close to the girl whom he was to make his wife on the morrow, and she was thinking, no doubt, of the visit which he had made to Nuncombe Putney, and of the first irretrievable step which she had taken when she told him that her love was given to another. That had been her Rubicon. And though there had been periods with her since the passing of it, in which she had felt that she had crossed it in vain, that she had thrown away the splendid security of the other bank without obtaining the perilous object of her ambition, though there had been moments in which she had almost regretted her own courage and noble action, still, having passed the river, there was nothing for her but to go on to Rome. She was not going to be stopped now by the want of a house in which to hide herself for a few weeks. She was without money, except so much as her mother might be able, almost surreptitiously, to give her. She was without friends to help her except these who were now with her, whose friendship had come to her in so singular a mariner, and whose power to aid her at the present moment was cruelly curtailed by their own circumstances. Nothing was settled as to her own marriage. In consequence of the promise that had been extorted from her that she should not correspond with Stanbury, she knew nothing of his present wishes or intention. Her father was so offended by her firmness that he would hardly speak to her. And it was evident to her that her mother, though disposed to yield, was still in hopes that her daughter, in the press and difficulty of the moment, would allow herself to be carried away with the rest of the family to the other side of the world. She knew all this, but she had made up her mind that she would not be carried away. It was not very pleasant, the thought that she would be obliged at last to ask her young man, as she called him, to provide for her; but she would do that and trust herself altogether in his hands sooner than be taken to the Antipodes. 'I can be very resolute if I please, my dear,' she said, looking at Caroline. Mr Glascock almost thought that she must have intended to address him.

They sat there discussing the matter for some time through the long, cool, evening hours, but nothing could be settled further except that Nora would write to her friend as soon as her affairs had begun to shape themselves after her return to England. At last Caroline went into the house, and for a few minutes Mr Glascock was alone with Nora. He had remained, determining that the moment should come, but now that it was there he was for awhile unable to say the words that he wished to utter. At last he spoke. 'Miss Rowley, Caroline is so eager to be your friend.'

'I know she is, and I do love her so dearly. But, without joke, Mr Glascock, there will be as it were a great gulf between us.'

'I do not know that there need be any gulf, great or little. But I did not mean to allude to that. What I want to say is this. My feelings are not a bit less warm or sincere than hers. You know of old that I am not very good at expressing myself.'

'I know nothing of the kind.'

'There is no such gulf as what you speak of. All that is mostly gone by, and a nobleman in England, though he has advantages as a gentleman, is no more than a gentleman. But that has nothing to do with what I am saying now. I shall never forget my journey to Devonshire. I won't pretend to say now that I regret its result.'

'I am quite sure you don't.'

'No; I do not, though I thought then that I should regret it always. But remember this, Miss Rowley that you can never ask me to do anything that I will not, if possible, do for you. You are in some little difficulty now—'

'It will disappear, Mr Glascock. Difficulties always do.'

'But we will do anything that we are wanted to do; and should a certain event take place—'

'It will take place some day.'

'Then I hope that we may be able to make Mr Stanbury and his wife quite at home at Monkhams.' After that he took Nora's hand and kissed it, and at that moment Caroline came back to them.

'Tomorrow, Mr Glascock,' she said, 'you will, I believe, be at liberty to kiss everybody; but today you should be more discreet.'

It was generally admitted among the various legations in Florence that there had not been such a wedding in the City of Flowers since it had become the capital of Italia. Mr Glascock and Miss Spalding were married in the chapel of the legation, a legation chapel on the ground floor having been extemporised for the occasion. This greatly enhanced the pleasantness of the thing, and saved the necessity of matrons and bridesmaids packing themselves and their finery into close fusty carriages. A portion of the guests attended in the chapel, and the remainder, when the ceremony was over, were found strolling about the shady garden. The whole affair of the breakfast was very splendid and lasted some hours. In the midst of this the bride and bridegroom were whisked away with a pair of grey horses to the railway station, and before the last toast of the day had been proposed by the Belgian Councillor of Legation, they were half way up the Apennines on their road to Bologna. Mr Spalding behaved himself like a man on the occasion. Nothing was spared in the way of expense, and when he made that celebrated speech, in which he declared that the republican virtue of the New World had linked itself in a happy alliance with the aristocratic splendour of the Old, and went on with a simile about the lion and the lamb, everybody accepted it with good humour in spite of its being a little too long for the occasion.

'It has gone off very well, mamma; has it not?' said Nora, as she returned home with her mother to her lodgings.

'Yes, my dear; much, I fancy, as these things generally do.'

'I thought it was so nice. And she looked so very well. And he was so pleasant, and so much like a gentleman—not noisy, you know, and yet not too serious.'

'I dare say, my love.'

'It is easy enough, mamma, for a girl to be married, for she has nothing to do but to wear her clothes and look as pretty as she can. And if she cries and has a red nose it is forgiven her. But a man has so difficult a part to play! If he tries to carry himself as though it were not a special occasion, he looks like a fool that way; and if he is very special, he looks like a fool the other way. I thought Mr Glascock did it very well.'

'To tell you the truth, my dear, I did not observe him.'

'I did narrowly. He hadn't tied his cravat at all nicely.'

'How could you think of his cravat, Nora, with such memories as you must have, and such regrets, I cannot understand.'

'Mamma, my memories of Mr Glascock are pleasant memories, and as for regrets, I have not one. Can I regret, mamma, that I did not marry a man whom I did not love and that I rejected him when I knew that I loved another? You cannot mean that, mamma.'

'I know this, that I was thinking all the time how proud I should have been, and how much more fortunate he would have been, had you been standing there instead of that American young woman.' As she said this Lady Rowley burst into tears, and Nora could only answer her mother by embracing her. They were alone together, their party having been too large for one carriage, and Sir Marmaduke having taken his two younger daughters. 'Of course, I feel it,' said Lady Rowley, through her tears. 'It would have been such a position for my child! And that young man without a shilling in the world; and writing in that way, just for bare bread!' Nora had nothing more to say. A feeling that in herself would have been base, was simply affectionate and maternal in her mother. It was impossible that she should make her mother see it as she saw it.

There was but one intervening day and then the Rowleys returned to England. There had been, as it were, a tacit agreement among them that, in spite of all their troubles, their holiday should be a holiday up to the time of the Glascock marriage. Then must commence at once the stern necessity of their return home home, not only to England, but to those antipodean islands from which it was too probable that some of them might never come back. And the difficulties in their way seemed to be almost insuperable. First of all there was to be the parting from Emily Trevelyan. She had determined to remain in Florence, and had written to her husband saying that she would do so, and declaring her willingness to go out to him, or to receive him in Florence at any time and in any manner that he might appoint. She had taken this as a first step, intending to go to Casalunga very shortly, even though she should receive no answer from him. The parting between her and her mother and father and sisters was very bitter. Sir Marmaduke, as he had become estranged from Nora, had grown to be more and more gentle and loving with his eldest daughter, and was nearly overcome at the idea of leaving her in a strange land, with a husband near her, mad, and yet not within her custody. But he could do nothing could hardly say a word toward opposing her. Though her husband was mad, he supplied her with the means of living; and when she said that it was her duty to be near him, her father could not deny it.

The parting came. 'I will return to you the moment you send to me,' were Nora's last words to her sister. 'I don't suppose I shall send,' said Emily. 'I shall try to bear it without assistance.'

Then the journey from Italy to England was made without much gratification or excitement, and the Rowley family again found themselves at Gregg's Hotel.

CHAPTER LXXXVIII. CROPPER AND BURGESS

We must now go back to Exeter and look after Mr Brooke Burgess and Miss Dorothy Stanbury. It is rather hard upon readers that they should be thus hurried from the completion of hymeneals at Florence to the preparations for other hymeneals in Devonshire; but it is the nature of a complex story to be entangled with many weddings towards its close. In this little history there are, we fear, three or four more to come. We will not anticipate by alluding prematurely to Hugh Stanbury's treachery, or death, or the possibility that he after all may turn out to be the real descendant of the true Lord Peterborough and the actual inheritor of the title and estate of Monkhams, nor will we speak of Nora's certain fortitude under either of these emergencies. But the instructed reader must be aware that Camilla French ought to have a husband found for her; that Colonel Osborne should be caught in some matrimonial trap, as how otherwise should he be fitly punished? and that something should be at least attempted for Priscilla Stanbury, who from the first has been intended to be the real heroine of these pages. That Martha should marry Giles Hickbody, and Barty Burgess run away with Mrs MacHugh, is of course evident to the meanest novel-expounding capacity; but the fate of Brooke Burgess and of Dorothy will require to be evolved with some delicacy and much detail.

There was considerable difficulty in fixing the day. In the first place Miss Stanbury was not very well and then she was very fidgety. She must see Brooke again before the day was fixed, and after seeing Brooke she must see her lawyer. 'To have a lot of money to look after is more plague than profit, my dear,' she said to Dorothy one day; 'particularly when you don't quite know what you ought to do with it.' Dorothy had always avoided any conversation with her aunt about money since the first moment in which she had thought of accepting Brooke Burgess as her husband. She knew that her aunt had some feeling which made her averse to the idea that any portion of the property which she had inherited should be enjoyed by a Stanbury after her death, and Dorothy, guided by this knowledge, had almost convinced herself that her love for Brooke was treason either against him or against her aunt. If, by engaging herself to him, she would rob him of his inheritance, how bitter a burden to him would her love have been! If, on the other hand, she should reward her aunt for all that had been done for her by forcing herself, a Stanbury, into a position not intended for her, how base would be her ingratitude! These thoughts had troubled her much, and had always prevented her from answering any of her aunt's chance allusions to the property. For her, things had at last gone very right. She did not quite know how it had come about, but she was engaged to marry the man she loved. And her aunt was, at any rate, reconciled to the marriage. But when Miss Stanbury declared that she did not know what to do about the property, Dorothy could only hold her tongue. She had had plenty to say when it had been suggested to her that the marriage should be put off yet for a short while, and that, in the meantime, Brooke should come again to Exeter. She swore that she did not care for how long it was put off, only that she hoped it might not be put off altogether. And as for Brooke's coming, that, for the present, would be very much nicer than being married out of hand at once. Dorothy, in truth, was not at all in a hurry to be married, but she would have liked to have had her lover always coming and going. Since the courtship had become a thing permitted, she had had the privilege of welcoming him twice at the house in the Close; and that running down to meet him in the little front parlour, and the getting up to make his breakfast for him as he started in the morning, were among the happiest epochs of her life. And then, as soon as ever the breakfast was eaten, and he was gone, she would sit down to write him a letter. Oh, those letters, so beautifully crossed, more than one of which was copied from beginning to end because some word in it was not thought to be sweet enough—what a heaven of happiness they were to her! The writing of the first had disturbed her greatly, and she had almost repented of the privilege before it was ended; but with the first and second the difficulties had disappeared; and, had she not felt somewhat ashamed of the occupation, she could have sat at her desk and written him letters all day. Brooke would answer them, with fair regularity, but in a most cursory manner, sending seven or eight lines in return for two sheets fully crossed; but this did not discompose her in the least. He was worked hard at his office, and had hundreds of other things to do. He, too, could say, so thought Dorothy, more in eight lines than she could put into as many pages.

She was quite happy when she was told that the marriage could not take place till August, but that Brooke must come again in July. Brooke did come in the first week of July, and somewhat horrified Dorothy by declaring to her that Miss Stanbury was unreasonable.

'If I insist upon leaving London so often for a day or two,' said he, 'how am I to get anything like leave of absence when the time comes?' In answer to this Dorothy tried to make him understand that business should not be neglected, and that, as far as she was concerned, she could do very well without that trip abroad which he had proposed for her. 'I'm not going to be done in that way,' said Brooke. 'And now that I am here she has nothing to say to me. I've told her a dozen times that I don't want to know anything about her will, and that I'll take it all for granted. There is something to be settled on you, that she calls her own.'

'She is so generous, Brooke.'

'She is generous enough, but she is very whimsical. She is going to make her whole will over again, and now she wants to send some message to Uncle Barty. I don't know what it is yet, but I am to take it. As far as I can understand, she has sent all the way to London for me, in order that I may take a message across the Close.'

'You talk as though it were very disagreeable, coming to Exeter,' said Dorothy, with a little pout.

'So it is very disagreeable.'

'Oh, Brooke!'

'Very disagreeable if our marriage is to be put off by it. I think it will be so much nicer making love somewhere on the Rhine than having snatches of it here, and talking all the time about wills and tenements and settlements.' As he said this, with his arm round her waist and his face quite close to hers, shewing thereby that he was not altogether averse even to his present privileges, she forgave him.

On that same afternoon, just before the banking hours were over, Brooke went across to the house of Cropper and Burgess, having first been closeted for nearly an hour with his aunt and, as he went, his step was sedate and his air was serious. He found his uncle Barty, and was not very long in delivering his message. It was to this effect, that Miss Stanbury particularly wished to see Mr Bartholomew Burgess on business, at some hour on that afternoon or that evening. Brooke himself had been made acquainted with the subject in regard to which this singular interview was desired; but it was not a part of his duty to communicate any information respecting it. It had been necessary that his consent to certain arrangements should be asked before the invitation to Barty Burgess could be given; but his present mission was confined to an authority to give the invitation.

Old Mr Burgess was much surprised, and was at first disposed to decline the proposition made by the 'old harridan,' as he called her. He had never put any restraint on his language in talking of Miss Stanbury with his nephew, and was not disposed to do so now, because she had taken a new vagary into her head. But there was something in his nephew's manner which at last induced him to discuss the matter rationally.

'And you don't know what it's all about?' said Uncle Barty.

'I can't quite say that. I suppose I do know pretty well. At any rate, I know enough to think that you ought to come. But I must not say what it is.'

'Will it do me or anybody else any good?'

'It can't do you any harm. She won't eat you.'

'But she can abuse me like a pickpocket, and I should return it, and then there would be a scolding match. I always have kept out of her way, and I think I had better do so still.'

Nevertheless Brooke prevailed, or rather the feeling of curiosity which was naturally engendered prevailed. For very, very many years Barty Burgess had never entered or left his own house of business without seeing the door of that in which Miss Stanbury lived, and he had never seen that door without a feeling of detestation for the owner of it. It would, perhaps, have been a more rational feeling on his part had he confined his hatred to the memory of his brother, by whose will Miss Stanbury had been enriched, and he had been, as he thought, impoverished. But there had been a contest, and litigation, and disputes, and contradictions, and a long course of those incidents in life which lead to rancour and ill blood, after the death of the former Brooke Burgess; and, as the result of all this, Miss Stanbury held the property and Barty Burgess held his hatred. He had never been ashamed of it, and had spoken his mind out to all who would hear him. And, to give Miss Stanbury her due, it must be admitted that she had hardly been behind him in the warmth of her expression, of which old Barty was well aware. He hated, and knew that he was hated in return. And he knew, or thought that he knew, that his enemy was not a woman to relent because old age and weakness and the fear of death were coming on her. His enemy, with all her faults, was no coward. It could not be that now at the eleventh hour she should desire to reconcile him by any act of tardy justice, nor did he wish to be reconciled at this, the eleventh hour. His hatred was a pleasant excitement to him. His abuse of Miss Stanbury was a chosen recreation. His unuttered daily curse, as he looked over to her door, was a relief to him. Nevertheless he would go. As Brooke had said, no harm could come of his going. He would go, and at least listen to her proposition.

About seven in the evening his knock was heard at the door. Miss Stanbury was sitting in the small upstairs parlour, dressed in her second best gown, and was prepared with considerable stiffness and state for the occasion. Dorothy was with her, but was desired in a quick voice to hurry away the moment the knock was heard, as though old Barty would have jumped from the hall door into the room at a bound. Dorothy collected herself with a little start, and went without a word. She had heard much of Barty Burgess, but had never spoken to him, and was subject to a feeling of great awe when she would remember that the grim old man of whom she had heard so much evil would soon be her uncle. According to arrangement, Mr Burgess was shewn upstairs by his nephew. Barty Burgess had been born in this very house, but had not been inside the walls of it for more than thirty years. He also was somewhat awed by the occasion, and followed his nephew without a word. Brooke was to remain at hand, so that he might be summoned should he be wanted; but it had been decided by Miss Stanbury that he should not be present at the interview. As soon as her visitor entered the room she rose in a stately way, and curtseyed, propping herself with one hand upon the table as she did so. She looked him full in the face meanwhile, and curtseying a second time, asked him to seat himself in a chair which had been prepared for him. She did it all very well, and it may be surmised that she had rehearsed the little scene, perhaps more than once, when nobody was looking at her. He bowed, and walked round to the chair and seated himself; but finding that he was so placed that he could not see his neighbour's face, he moved his chair. He was not going to fight such a duel as this with the disadvantage of the sun in his eyes.

Hitherto there had hardly been a word spoken. Miss Stanbury had muttered something as she was curtseying, and Barty Burgess had made some return. Then she began: 'Mr Burgess,' she said, 'I am indebted to you for your complaisance in coming here at my request.' To this he bowed again. 'I should not have ventured thus to trouble you were it not that years are dealing more hardly with me than they are with you, and that I could not have ventured to discuss a matter of deep interest otherwise than in my own room.' It was her room now, certainly, by law; but Barty Burgess remembered it when it was his mother's room, and when she used to give them all their meals there now so many, many years ago! He bowed again, and said not a word. He knew well that she could sooner be brought to her point by his silence than by his speech.

She was a long time coming to her point. Before she could do so she was forced to allude to times long past, and to subjects which she found it very difficult to touch without saying that which would either belie herself, or seem to be severe upon him. Though she had prepared herself, she could hardly get the words spoken, and she was greatly impeded by the obstinacy of his silence. But at last her proposition was made to him. She told him that his nephew, Brooke, was about to be married to her niece, Dorothy; and that it was her intention to make Brooke her heir in the bulk of the property which she had received under the will of the late Mr Brooke Burgess. 'Indeed,' she said, 'all that I received at your brother's hands shall go back to your brother's family unimpaired' He only bowed, and would not say a word. Then she went on to say that it had at first been a mater to her of deep regret that Brooke should have set his affections upon her niece, as there had been in her mind a strong desire that none of her own people should enjoy the reversion of the wealth, which she had always regarded as being hers only for the term of her life; but that she had found that the young people had been so much in earnest, and that her own feeling had been so near akin to a prejudice, that she had yielded. When this was said Barty smiled instead of bowing, and Miss Stanbury felt that there might be something worse even than his silence. His smile told her that he believed her to be lying. Nevertheless she went on. She was not fool enough to suppose that the whole nature of the man was to be changed by a few words from her. So she went on. The marriage was a thing fixed, and she was thinking of settlements, and had been talking to lawyers about a new will.

'I do not know that I can help you,' said Barty, finding that a longer pause than usual made some word from him absolutely necessary.

'I am going on to that, and I regret that my story should detain you so long, Mr Burgess' And she did go on. She had, she said, made some saving out of her income. She was not going to trouble Mr Burgess with this matter, only that she might explain to him that what she would at once give to the young couple, and what she would settle on Dorothy after her own death, would all come from such savings, and that such gifts and bequests would not diminish the family property. Barty again smiled as he heard this, and Miss Stanbury in her heart likened him to the devil in person. But still she went on. She was very desirous that Brooke Burgess should come and live at Exeter. His property would be in the town and the neighbourhood. It would be a seemly thing, such was her word, that he should occupy the house that had belonged to his grandfather and his great-grandfather; and then, moreover, she acknowledged that she spoke selfishly; she dreaded the idea of being left alone for the remainder of her own years. Her proposition at last was uttered. It was simply this, that Barty Burgess should give to his nephew, Brooke, his share in the bank.

'I am damned, if I do!' said Barty Burgess, rising up from his chair.

But before he had left the room he had agreed to consider the proposition. Miss Stanbury had of course known that any such suggestion coming from her without an adequate reason assigned, would have been mere idle wind. She was prepared with such adequate reason. If Mr Burgess could see his way to make the proposed transfer of his share of the bank business, she, Miss Stanbury, would hand over to him, for his life, a certain proportion of the Burgess property which lay in the city, the income of which would exceed that drawn by him from the business. Would he, at his time of life, take that for doing nothing which he now got for working hard? That was the meaning of it. And then, too, as far as the portion of the property went, and it extended to the houses owned by Miss Stanbury on the bank side of the Close, it would belong altogether to Barty Burgess for his life. 'It will simply be this, Mr Burgess, that Brooke will be your heir as would be natural.'

'I don't know that it would be at all natural,' said he. 'I should prefer to choose my own heir.'

'No doubt, Mr Burgess, in respect to your own property,' said Miss Stanbury.

At last he said that he would think of it, and consult his partner; and then he got up to take his leave. 'For myself,' said Miss Stanbury, 'I would wish that all animosities might be buried.'

'We can say that they are buried,' said the grim old man 'but nobody will believe us.'

'What matters if we could believe it ourselves?'

'But suppose we didn't. I don't believe that much good can come from talking of such things, Miss Stanbury. You and I have grown too old to swear a friendship. I will think of this thing, and if I find that it can be made to suit without much difficulty, I will perhaps entertain it.' Then the interview was over, and old Barty made his way downstairs, and out of the house. He looked over to the tenements in the Close which were offered to him, every circumstance of each one of which he knew, and felt that he might do worse. Were he to leave the bank, he could not take his entire income with him, and it had been long said of him that he ought to leave it. The Croppers, who were his partners and whom he had never loved, would be glad to welcome in his place one of the old family who would have money; and then the name would be perpetuated in Exeter, which, even to Barty Burgess, was something.

On that night the scheme was divulged to Dorothy, and she was in ecstasies. London had always sounded bleak and distant and terrible to her; and her heart had misgiven her at the idea of leaving her aunt. If only this thing might be arranged! When Brooke spoke the next morning of returning at once to his office, he was rebuked by both the ladies. What was the Ecclesiastical Commission Office to any of them, when matters of such importance were concerned? But Brooke would not be talked out of his prudence. He was very willing to be made a banker at Exeter, and to go to school again and learn banking business; but he would not throw up his occupation in London till he knew that there was another ready for him in the country. One day longer he spent in Exeter, and During that day he was more than once with his uncle. He saw also the Messrs Cropper, and was considerably chilled by the manner in which they at first seemed to entertain the proposition. Indeed, for a couple of hours he thought that the scheme must be abandoned. It was pointed out to him that Mr Barty Burgess's life would probably be short, and that he, Barty, had but a small part of the business at his disposal. But gradually a way to terms was seen, not quite so simple as that which Miss Stanbury had suggested; and Brooke, when he left Exeter, did believe it possible that he, after all, might become the family representative in the old banking-house of the Burgesses.

'And how long will it take, Aunt Stanbury?' Dorothy asked.

'Don't you be impatient, my dear.'

'I am not the least impatient; but of course I want to tell mamma and Priscilla. It will be so nice to live here and not go up to London. Are we to stay here in this very house?'

'Have you not found out yet that Brooke will be likely to have an opinion of his own on such things?'

'But would you wish us to live here, aunt?'

'I hardly know, dear. I am a foolish old woman, and cannot say what I would wish. I cannot bear to be alone.'

'Of course we will stay with you.'

'And yet I should be jealous if I were not mistress of my own house.'

'Of course you will be mistress.'

'I believe, Dolly, that it would be better that I should die. I have come to feel that I can do more good by going out of the world than by remaining in it.' Dorothy hardly answered this in words, but sat close by her aunt, holding the old woman's hand and caressing it, and administering that love of which Miss Stanbury had enjoyed so little during her life and which had become so necessary to her.

The news about the bank arrangements, though kept of course as a great secret, soon became common in Exeter. It was known to be a good thing for the firm in general that Barty Burgess should be removed from his share of the management. He was old-fashioned, unpopular, and very stubborn; and he and a certain Mr Julius Cropper, who was the leading man among the Croppers, had not always been comfortable together. It was at first hinted that old Miss Stanbury had been softened by sudden twinges of conscience, and that she had confessed to some terrible crime in the way of forgery, perjury, or perhaps worse, and had relieved herself at last by making full restitution. But such a rumour as this did not last long or receive wide credence. When it was hinted to such old friends as Sir Peter Mancrudy and Mrs MacHugh, they laughed it to scorn, and it did not exist even in the vague form of an undivulged mystery for above three days. Then it was asserted that old Barty had been found to have no real claim to any share in the bank, and that he was to be turned out at Miss Stanbury's instance that he was to be turned out, and that Brooke had been acknowledged to be the owner of the Burgess share of her business. Then came the fact that old Barty had been bought out, and that the future husband of Miss Stanbury's niece was to be the junior partner. A general feeling prevailed at last that there had been another great battle between Miss Stanbury and old Barty, and that the old maid had prevailed now, as she had done in former days. Before the end of July the papers were in the lawyer's hands, and all the terms had been fixed. Brooke came down again and again, to Dorothy's great delight, and displayed considerable firmness in the management of his own interest. If Fate intended to make him a banker in Exeter instead of a clerk in the Ecclesiastical Commission Office, he would be a banker after a respectable fashion. There was more than one little struggle between him and Mr Julius

Cropper, which ended in accession of respect on the part of Mr Cropper for his new partner. Mr Cropper had thought that the establishment might best be known to the commercial world of the West of England as "Croppers' Bank"; but Broke had been very firm in asserting that if he was to have anything to do with it the old name should be maintained.

'It's to be "Cropper and Burgess," he said to Dorothy one afternoon. 'They fought hard for "Cropper, Cropper, and Burgess" but I wouldn't stand more than one Cropper.'

'Of course not,' said Dorothy, with something almost of scorn in her voice. By this time Dorothy had gone very deeply into banking business.

CHAPTER LXXXIX. 'I WOULDN'T DO IT, IF I WAS YOU'

Miss Stanbury at this time was known all through Exeter to be very much altered from the Miss Stanbury of old or even from the Miss Stanbury of two years since. The Miss Stanbury of old was a stalwart lady who would play her rubber of whist five nights a week, and could hold her own in conversation against the best woman in Exeter, not to speak of her acknowledged superiority over every man in that city. Now she cared little for the glories of debate; and though she still liked her rubber, and could wake herself up to the old fire in the detection of a revoke or the claim for a second trick, her rubbers were few and far between, and she would leave her own house on an evening only when all circumstances were favourable, and with many precautions against wind and water. Some said that she was becoming old, and that she was going out like the snuff of a candle. But Sir Peter Mancrudy declared that she might live for the next fifteen years, if she would only think so herself. 'It was true,' Sir Peter said, 'that in the winter she had been ill, and that there had been danger as to her throat during the east winds of the spring, but those dangers had passed away, and, if she would only exert herself, she might be almost as good a woman as ever she had been.' Sir Peter was not a man of many words, or given to talk frequently of his patients; but it was clearly Sir Peter's opinion that Miss Stanbury's mind was ill at ease. She had become discontented with life, and therefore it was that she cared no longer for the combat of tongues, and had become cold even towards the card-table. It was so in truth; and yet perhaps the lives of few men or women had been more innocent, and few had struggled harder to be just in their dealings and generous in their thoughts.

There was ever present to her mind an idea of failure and a fear lest she had been mistaken in her views throughout her life. No one had ever been more devoted to peculiar opinions, or more strong in the use of language for their expression; and she was so far true to herself, that she would never seem to retreat from the position she had taken. She would still scorn the new fangles of the world around her, and speak of the changes which she saw as all tending to evil. But, through it all, there was an idea present to herself that it could not be God's intention that things should really change for the worse, and that the fault must be in her, because she had been unable to move as others had moved. She would sit thinking of the circumstances of her own life and tell herself that with her everything had failed. She had loved, but had quarrelled with her lover; and her love had come to nothing but barren wealth. She had fought for her wealth and had conquered, and had become hard in the fight, and was conscious of her own hardness. In the early days of her riches and power she had taken her nephew by the hand, and had thrown him away from her because he would not dress himself in her mirror. She had believed herself to be right, and would not, even now, tell herself that she had been wrong; but there were doubts, and qualms of conscience, and an uneasiness because her life had been a failure. Now she was seeking to appease her self-accusations by sacrificing everything for the happiness of her niece and her chosen hero; but as she went on with the work she felt that all would be in vain, unless she could sweep herself altogether from off the scene. She had told herself that if she could bring Brooke to Exeter, his prospects would be made infinitely brighter than they would be in London, and that she in her last days would not be left utterly alone. But as the prospect of her future life came nearer to her, she saw, or thought that she saw, that there was still failure before her. Young people would not want an old woman in the house with them even though the old woman would declare that she would be no more in the house than a tame cat. And she knew herself also too well to believe that she could make herself a tame cat in the home that had so long been subject to her dominion. Would it not be better that she should go away somewhere and die?

'If Mr Brooke is to come here,' Martha said to her one day, 'we ought to begin and make the changes, ma'am'.

'What changes? You are always wanting to make changes'.

'If they was never made till I wanted them they'd never be made, ma'am. But if there is to be a married couple, there should be things proper. Anyways, ma'am, we ought to know oughtn't we?'

The truth of this statement was so evident that Miss Stanbury could not contradict it. But she had not even yet made up her mind. Ideas were running through her head which she knew to be very wild, but of which she could not divest herself. 'Martha,' she said after a while, 'I think I shall go away from this myself.'

'Leave the house, ma'am?' said Martha, awestruck.

'There are other houses in the world, I suppose, in which an old woman can live and die.'

'There is houses, ma'am, of course,'

'And what is the difference between one and another?'

'I wouldn't do it, ma'am, if I was you. I wouldn't do it if it was ever so. Sure the house is big enough for Mr Brooke and Miss Dorothy along with you. I wouldn't go and make such change as that, I wouldn't indeed, ma'am.' Martha spoke out almost with eloquence, so much expression was there in her face. Miss Stanbury said nothing more at the moment, beyond signifying her indisposition to make up her mind to anything at the present moment. Yes the house was big enough as far as rooms were concerned; but how often had she heard that an old woman must always be in the way, if attempting to live with a newly-married couple? If a mother-in-law be unendurable, how much more so one whose connection would be less near? She could keep her own house no doubt, and let them go elsewhere; but what then would come of her old dream, that Burgess, the new banker in the city, should live in the very house that had been inhabited by the Burgesses, the bankers of old? There was certainly only one way out of all these troubles, and that way would be that she should go from them and be at rest.

Her will had now been drawn out and completed for the third or fourth time, and she had made no secret of is contents either with Brooke or Dorothy. The whole estate she left to Brooke, including the houses which were to become his after his uncle's death; and in regard to the property she had made no further stipulation. 'I might have settled it on your children,' she said to him, 'but in doing so I should have settled it on hers. I don't know why an old woman should try to interfere with things after she has gone. I hope you won't squander it, Brooke.'

'I shall be a steady old man by that time,' he said.

'I hope you'll be steady at any rate. But there it is, and God must direct you in the use of it, if He will. It has been a burthen to me; but then I have been a solitary old woman.' Half of what she had saved she proposed to give Dorothy on her marriage, and for doing this arrangements had already been made. There were various other legacies, and the last she announced was one to her nephew, Hugh. 'I have left him a thousand pounds,' she said to Dorothy 'so that he may remember me kindly at last' As to this, however, she exacted a pledge that no intimation of the legacy was to be made to Hugh. Then it was that Dorothy told her aunt that Hugh intended to marry Nora Rowley, one of the ladies who had been at the Clock House during the days in which her mother had lived in grandeur; and then it was also that Dorothy obtained leave to invite Hugh to her own wedding. 'I hope she will be happier than her sister,' Miss Stanbury said, when she heard of the intended marriage.

'It wasn't Mrs Trevelyan's fault, you know, aunt.'

'I say nothing about anybody's fault; but this I do say, that it was a very great misfortune. I fought all that battle with your sister Priscilla, and I don't mean to fight it again, my dear. If Hugh marries the young lady, I hope she will be more happy than her sister. There can be no harm in saying that.'

Dorothy's letter to her brother shall be given, because it will inform the reader of all the arrangements as they were made up to that time, and will convey the Exeter news respecting various persons with whom our story is concerned.

The Close,
July 20, 186—

DEAR HUGH,

The day for my marriage is now fixed, and I wish with all my heart that it was the same with you. Pray give my love to Nora. It seems so odd that, though she was living for a while with mamma at Nuncombe Putney, I never should have seen her yet. I am very glad that Brooke has seen her, and he declares that she is quite magnificently beautiful. Those are his own words.

We are to be married on the 10th of August, a Wednesday, and now comes my great news. Aunt Stanbury says that you are to come and stay in the house. She bids me tell you so with her love; and that you can have a room as long as you like. Of course, you must come. In the first place, you must because you are to give me away, and Brooke wouldn't have me if I wasn't given away properly; and then it will make me so happy that you and Aunt Stanbury should be friends again. You can stay as long as you like, but, of course, you must come the day before the wedding. We are to be married in the Cathedral, and there are to be two clergymen, but I don't yet know who they will be—not Mr Gibson, certainly, as you were good enough to suggest.

Mr Gibson is married to Arabella French, and they have gone away somewhere into Cornwall. Camilla has come back, and I have seen her once. She looked ever so fierce, as though she intended to declare that she didn't mind what anybody may think. They say that she still protests that she never will speak to her sister again.

I was introduced to Mr Barty Burgess the other day. Brooke was here, and we met him in the Close. I hardly knew what he said to me, I was so frightened; but Brooke said that he meant to be civil, and that he is going to send me a present. I have got a quantity of things already, and yesterday Mrs MacHugh sent me such a beautiful cream-jug. If you'll come in time on the 9th, you shall see them all before they are put away.

Mamma and Priscilla are to be here, and they will come on the 9th also. Poor, dear mamma is, I know, terribly flurried about it, and so is Aunt Stanbury. It is so long since they have seen each other. I don't think Priscilla feels it the same way, because she is so brave. Do you remember when it was first proposed that I should come here? I am so glad I came because of Brooke. He will come on the 9th, quite early, and I do so hope you will come with him.

Yours most affectionately,

DOROTHY STANBURY.

Give my best, best love to Nora.

CHAPTER XC. LADY ROWLEY CONQUERED

When the Rowleys were back in London, and began to employ themselves on the terrible work of making ready for their journey to the Islands, Lady Rowley gradually gave way about Hugh Stanbury. She had become aware that Nora would not go back with them unless under an amount of pressure which she would find it impossible to use. And if Nora did not go out to the Islands, what was to become of her unless she married this man? Sir Marmaduke, when all was explained to him, declared that a girl must do what her parents ordered her to do. 'Other girls live with their fathers and mothers, and so must she.' Lady Rowley endeavoured to explain that other girls lived with their fathers and mothers, because they found themselves in established homes from which they are not disposed to run away; but Nora's position was, as she alleged, very different. Nora's home had latterly been with her sister, and it was hardly to be expected that the parental authority should not find itself impaired by the interregnum which had taken place. Sir Marmaduke would not see the thing in the same light, and was disposed to treat his daughter with a high hand. If she would not do as she was bidden, she should no longer be daughter of his. In answer to this Lady Rowley could only repeat her conviction that Nora would not go out to the Mandarins; and that as for disinheriting her, casting her out, cursing her, and the rest, she had no belief in such doings at all. 'On the stage they do such things as that' she said; 'and, perhaps, they used to do it once in reality. But you know that it's out of the question now. Fancy your standing up and cursing at the dear girl, just as we are all starting from Southampton!' Sir Marmaduke knew as well as his wife that it would be impossible, and only muttered something about the 'dear girl' behaving herself with great impropriety.

They were all aware that Nora was not going to leave England, because no berth had been taken for her on board the ship, and because, while the other girls were preparing for their long voyage, no preparations were made for her. Of course she was not going. Sir Marmaduke would probably have given way altogether immediately on his return to London, had he not discussed the matter with his friend Colonel Osborne. It became, of course, his duty to make some inquiry as to the Stanbury family, and he knew that Osborne had visited Mrs Stanbury when he made his unfortunate pilgrimage to the porch of Cockchaffington Church. He told Osborne the whole story of Nora's engagement, telling also that other most heart-breaking tale of her conduct in regard to Mr Glascock, and asked the Colonel what he thought about the Stanburys. Now the Colonel did not hold the Stanburys in high esteem. He had met Hugh, as the reader may perhaps remember, and had had some intercourse with the young man, which had not been quite agreeable to him, on the platform of the railway station at Exeter. And he had also heard something of the ladies at Nuncombe Putney during his short sojourn at the house of Mrs Crocket. 'My belief is, they are beggars,' said Colonel Osborne.

'I suppose so,' said Sir Marmaduke, shaking his head.

'When I went over to call on Emily that time I was at Cockchaffington, you know, when Trevelyan made himself such a d fool, I found the mother and sister living in a decentish house enough; but it wasn't their house.'

'Not their own, you mean?'

'It was a place that Trevelyan had got this young man to take for Emily, and they had merely gone there to be with her. They had been living in a little bit of a cottage; a sort of place that any any ploughman would live in. Just that kind of cottage.'

'Goodness gracious!'

'And they've gone to another just like it so I'm told.'

'And can't he do anything better for them than that?' asked Sir Marmaduke.

'I know nothing about him. I have met him, you know. He used to be with Trevelyan; that was when Nora took a fancy for him, of course. And I saw him once down in Devonshire, when I must say he behaved uncommonly badly, doing all he could to foster Trevelyan's stupid jealousy.'

'He has changed his mind about that, I think.'

'Perhaps he has; but he behaved very badly then. Let him shew up his income; that, I take it, is the question in such a case as this. His father was a clergyman, and therefore I suppose he must be considered to he a gentleman. But has he means to support a wife, and keep up a house in London? If he has not, that is an end to it, I should say.'

But Sir Marmaduke could not see his way to any such end, and, although he still looked black upon Nora, and talked to his wife of his determination to stand no contumacy, and hinted at cursing, disinheriting, and the like, he began to perceive that Nora would have her own way. In his unhappiness he regretted this visit to England, and almost thought that the Mandarins were a pleasanter residence than London. He could do pretty much as he pleased there, and could live quietly, without the trouble which encountered him now on every side.

Nora, immediately on her return to London, had written a note to Hugh, simply telling him of her arrival and begging him to come and see her. 'Mamma,' she said,

'I must see him, and it would be nonsense to say that he must not come here. I have done what I have said I would do, and you ought not to make difficulties.' Lady Rowley declared that Sir Marmaduke would be very angry if Hugh were admitted without his express permission. 'I don't want to do anything in the dark,' continued Nora, 'but of course I must see him. I suppose it will be better that he should come to me than that I should go to him?' Lady Rowley quite understood the threat that was conveyed in this. It would be much better that Hugh should come to the hotel, and that he should be treated then as an accepted lover. She had come to that conclusion. But she was obliged to vacillate for awhile between her husband and her daughter. Hugh came of course, and Sir Marmaduke, by his wife's advice, kept out of the way. Lady Rowley, though she was at home, kept herself also out of the way, remaining above with her two other daughters. Nora thus achieved the glory and happiness of receiving her lover alone.

'My own true girl!' he said, speaking with his arms still round her waist.

'I am true enough; but whether I am your own, that is another question.'

'You mean to be?'

'But papa doesn't mean it. Papa says that you are nobody, and that you haven't got an income; and thinks that I had better go back and be an old maid at the Mandarins.'

'And what do you think yourself, Nora?'

'What do I think? As far as I can understand, young ladies are not allowed to think at all. They have to do what their papas tell them. That will do, Hugh. You can talk without taking hold of me.'

'It is such a time since I have had a hold of you as you call it.'

'It will be much longer before you can do so again, if I go back to the Islands with papa. I shall expect you to be true, you know; and it will be ten years at the least before I can hope to be home again.'

'I don't think you mean to go, Nora.'

'But what am I to do? That idea of yours of walking out to the next church and getting ourselves married sounds very nice and independent, but you know that it is not practicable.'

'On the other hand, I know it is.'

'It is not practicable for me, Hugh. Of all things in the world I don't want to be a Lydia. I won't do anything that anybody shall ever say that your wife ought not to have done. Young women when they are married ought to have their papas' and mammas' consent. I have been thinking about it a great deal for the last month or two, and I have made up my mind to that.'

'What is it all to come to, then?'

'I mean to get papa's consent. That is what it is to come to.'

'And if he is obstinate?'

'I shall coax him round at last. When the time for going comes, he'll yield then.'

'But you will not go with them?' As he asked this he came to her and tried again to take her by the waist; but she retreated from him, and got herself clear from us arm. 'If you are afraid of me, I shall know that you think it possible that we may be parted.'

'I am not a bit afraid of you, Hugh.'

'Nora, I think you ought to tell me something definitely.'

'I think I have been definite enough, sir. You may be sure of this, however I will not go back to the Islands.'

'Give me your hand on that.'

'There is my hand. But, remember, I had told you just as much before. I don't mean to go back. I mean to stay here. I mean—but I do not think I will tell you all the things I mean to do.'

'You mean to be my wife?'

'Certainly, some day, when the difficulty about the chairs and tables can settle itself. The real question now is what am I to do with myself when papa and mamma are gone?'

'Become Mrs H. Stanbury at once. Chairs and tables! You shall have chairs and tables as many as you want. You won't be too proud to live in lodgings for a few months?'

'There must be preliminaries, Hugh even for lodgings, though they may be very slender. Papa goes in less than three weeks now, and mamma has got something else to think of than my marriage garments. And then there are all manner of difficulties, money difficulties and others, out of which I don't see my way yet'. Hugh began to asseverate that it was his business to help her through all money difficulties as well as others; but she soon stopped his eloquence. 'It will be by-and-by, Hugh, and I hope you'll support the burden like a man; but just at present there is a hitch. I shouldn't have come over at all; I should have stayed with Emily in Italy, had I not thought that I was bound to see you.'

'My own darling!'

'When papa goes, I think that I had better go back to her.'

'I'll take you!' said Hugh, picturing to himself all the pleasures of such a tour together, over the Alps.

'No you won't, because that would be improper. When we travel together we must go Darby and Joan fashion, as man and wife. I think I had better go back to Emily, because her position there is so terrible. There must come some end to it, I suppose soon. He will be better, or he will become so bad that that medical interference will be unavoidable. But I do not like that she should be alone. She gave me a home when she had one, and I must always remember that I met you there.' After this there was of course another attempt with Hugh's right arm, which on this occasion was not altogether unsuccessful. And then she told him of her friendship for Mr Glascock's wife, and of her intention at some future time to visit them at Monkhams.

'And see all the glories that might have been your own,' he said.

'And think of the young man who has robbed me of them all! And you are to go there too, so that you may see what you have done. There was a time, Hugh, when I was very nearly pleasing all my friends and shewing myself to be a young lady of high taste and noble fortune and an obedient, good girl.'

'And why didn't you?'

'I thought I would wait just a little longer. Because, because, because— Oh, Hugh, how cross you were to me afterwards when you came down to Nuncombe and would hardly speak to me!'

'And why didn't I speak to you?'

'I don't know. Because you were cross, and surly, and thinking of nothing but your tobacco, I believe. Do you remember how we walked to Liddon, and you hadn't a word for anybody?'

'I remember I wanted you to go down to the river with me, and you wouldn't go.'

'You asked me only once, and I did so long to go with you. Do you remember the rocks in the river? I remember the place as though I saw it now; and how I longed to jump from one stone to another. Hugh, if we are ever married, you must take me there, and let me jump on those stones.'

'You pretended that you could not think of wetting your feet.'

'Of course I pretended, because you were so cross, and so cold. Oh, dear! I wonder whether you will ever know it all.'

'Don't I know it all now?'

'I suppose you do, nearly. There is mighty little of a secret in it, and it is the same thing that is going on always. Only it seems so strange to me that I should ever have loved any one so dearly and that for next to no reason at all. You never made yourself very charming that I know of, did you?'

'I did my best. It wasn't much, I dare say.'

'You did nothing, sir, except just let me fall in love with you. And you were not quite sure that you would let me do that.'

'Nora, I don't think you do understand.'

'I do perfectly. Why were you cross with me, instead of saying one nice word when you were down at Nuncombe? I do understand.'

'Why was it?'

'Because you did not think well enough of me to believe that I would give myself to a man who had no fortune of his own. I know it now, and I knew it then; and therefore I wouldn't dabble in the river with you. But it's all over now, and we'll go and get wet together like dear little children, and Priscilla shall scold us when we come back.'

They were alone in the sitting-room for more than an hour, and Lady Rowley was patient upstairs; as mothers will be patient in such emergencies. Sophie and Lucy had gone out and left her; and there she remained, telling herself, as the weary minutes went by, that as the thing was to be, it was well that the young people should be together. Hugh Stanbury could never be to her what Mr Glascock would have been—a son-in-law to sit and think about, and dream of, and be proud of, whose existence as her son-in-law would in itself have been a happiness to her out in her banishment at the other side of the world; but nevertheless it was natural to her, as a soft-hearted, loving mother with many daughters, that any son-in-law should be dear to her. Now that she had gradually brought herself round to believe in Nora's marriage, she was disposed to make the best of Hugh, to remember that he was certainly a clever man, that he was an honest fellow, and that she had heard of him as a good son and a kind brother, and that he had behaved well in reference to her Emily and Trevelyan. She was quite willing now that Hugh should be happy, and she sat there thinking that the time was very long, but still waiting patiently till she should be summoned. 'You must let me go for mamma for a moment,' Nora said. 'I want you to see her and make yourself a good boy before her. If you are ever to be her son-in-law, you ought to be in her good graces.' Hugh declared that he would do his best, and Nora fetched her mother.

Stanbury found some difficulty in making himself a 'good boy' in Lady Rowley's presence; and Lady Rowley herself, for sometime, felt very strongly the awkwardness of the meeting. She had never formally recognised the young man as her daughter's accepted suitor, and as not yet justified in doing so by any permission from Sir Marmaduke; but, as the young people had been for the last hour or two alone together, with her connivance and sanction, it was indispensable that she should in some way signify her parental adherence to the arrangement. Nora began by talking about Emily, and Trevelyan's condition and mode of living were discussed. Then Lady Rowley said something about their coming journey, and Hugh, with a lucky blunder, spoke of Nora's intended return to Italy. 'We don't know how that may be,' said Lady Rowley. 'Her papa still wishes her to go back with us.'

'Mamma, you know that that is impossible,' said Nora.

'Not impossible, my love.'

'But she will not go back,' said Hugh. 'Lady Rowley, you would not propose to separate us by such a distance as that?'

'It is Sir Marmaduke that you must ask.'

'Mamma, mamma!' exclaimed Nora, rushing to her mother's side, 'it is not papa that we must ask not now. We want you to be our friend. Don't we, Hugh? And, mamma, if you will really be our friend, of course, papa will come round.'

'My dear Nora!'

'You know he will, mamma; and you know that you mean to be good and kind to us. Of course I can't go back to the Islands with you. How could I go so far and leave him behind? He might have half-a-dozen wives before I could get back to him—'

'If you have not more trust in him than that—'

'Long engagements are awful bores,' said Hugh, finding it to be necessary that he also should press forward his argument.

'I can trust him as far as I can see him,' said Nora, 'and therefore I do not want to lose sight of him altogether.'

Lady Rowley of course gave way and embraced her accepted son-in-law. After all it might have been worse. He saw his way clearly, he said, to making six hundred a year, and did not at all doubt that before long he would do better than that. He proposed that they should be married some time in the autumn, but was willing to acknowledge that much must depend on the position of Trevelyan and his wife. He would hold himself ready at any moment, he said, to start to Italy, and would do all that could be done by a brother. Then Lady Rowley gave him her blessing, and kissed him again, and Nora kissed him too, and hung upon him, and did not push him away at all when his arm crept round her waist. And that feeling came upon him which must surely be acknowledged by all engaged young men when they first find themselves encouraged by mammas in the taking of liberties which they have hitherto regarded as mysteries to be hidden, especially from maternal eyes, that feeling of being a fine fat calf decked out with ribbons for a sacrifice.

CHAPTER XCI. FOUR O'CLOCK IN THE MORNING

Another week went by and Sir Marmaduke had even yet not surrendered. He quite understood that Nora was not to go back to the Islands and had visited Mr and Mrs Outhouse at St. Diddulph's in order to secure a home for her there, if it might be possible. Mr Outhouse did not refuse, but gave the permission in such a fashion as to make it almost equal to a refusal. 'He was,' he said, 'much attached to his niece Nora, but he had heard that there was a love affair.' Sir Marmaduke, of course, could not deny the love affair. There was certainly a love affair of which he did not personally approve, as the gentleman had no fixed income and as far as he could understand no fixed profession. 'Such a love affair,' thought Mr Outhouse, 'was a sort of thing that he didn't know how to manage at all. If Nora came to him, was the young man to visit at the house, or was he not?' Then Mrs Outhouse said something as to the necessity of an anti-Stanbury pledge on Nora's part, and Sir Marmaduke found that that scheme must be abandoned. Mrs Trevelyan had written from Florence more than once or twice, and in her last letter had said that she would prefer not to have Nora with her. She was at that time living in lodgings at Siena and had her boy there also. She saw her husband every other day; but nevertheless, according to her statements, her visits to Casalunga were made in opposition to his wishes. He had even expressed a desire that she should leave Siena and return to England. He had once gone so far as to say that if she would do so, he would follow her. But she clearly did not believe him, and in all her letters spoke of him as one whom she could not regard as being under the guidance of reason. She had taken her child with her once or twice to the house, and on the first occasion Trevelyan had made much of his son, had wept over him, and professed that in losing him he had lost his only treasure; but after that he had not noticed the boy, and latterly she had gone alone. She thought that perhaps her visits cheered him, breaking the intensity of his solitude; but he never expressed himself gratified by them, never asked her to remain at the house, never returned with her into Siena, and continually spoke of her return to England as a step which must be taken soon, and the sooner the better. He intended to follow her, he said; and she explained very fully how manifest was his wish that she should go, by the temptation to do so which he thought that he held out by this promise. He had spoken, on every occasion of her presence with him, of Sir Marmaduke's attempt to prove him to be a madman; but declared that he was afraid of no one in England, and would face all the lawyers in Chancery Lane and all the doctors in Savile Row.

Nevertheless, so said Mrs Trevelyan, he would undoubtedly remain at Casalunga till after Sir Marmaduke should have sailed. He was not so mad but that he knew that no one else would be so keen to take steps against him as would Sir Marmaduke. As for his health, her account of him was very sad. 'He seemed,' she said, 'to be withering away.' His hand was mere skin and bone. His hair and beard so covered his thin long cheeks, that there was nothing left of his face but his bright, large, melancholy eyes. His legs had become so frail and weak that they would hardly bear his weight as he walked; and his clothes, though he had taken a fancy to throw aside all that he had brought with him from England, hung so loose about him that they seemed as though they would fall from him. Once she had ventured to send out to him from Siena a doctor to whom she had been recommended in Florence; but he had taken the visit in very bad part, had told the gentleman that he had no need for any medical services, and had been furious with her, because of her offence in having sent such a visitor. He had told her that if ever she ventured to take such a liberty again, he would demand the child back, and refuse her permission inside the gates of Casalunga. 'Don't come, at any rate, till I send for you,' Mrs Trevelyan said in her last letter to her sister. 'Your being here would do no good, and would, I think, make him feel that he was being watched. My hope is, at last, to get him to return with me. If you were here, I think this would be less likely. And then why should you be mixed up with such unutterable sadness and distress more than is essentially necessary? My health stands wonderfully well, though the heat here is very great. It is cooler at Casalunga than in the town, of which I am glad for his sake. He perspires so profusely that it seems to me he cannot stand the waste much longer. I know he will not go to England as long as papa is there, but I hope that he may be induced to do so by slow stages as soon as he knows that papa has gone. Mind you send me a newspaper, so that he may see it stated in print that papa has sailed.'

It followed as one consequence of these letters from Florence that Nora was debarred from the Italian scheme as a mode of passing her time till some house should be open for her reception. She had suggested to Hugh that she might go for a few weeks to Nuncombe Putney, but he had explained to her the nature of his mother's cottage, and had told her that there was no hole there in which she could lay her head. 'There never was such a forlorn young woman,' she said. 'When papa goes I shall literally be without shelter.' There had come a letter from Mrs Glascock, at least it was signed Caroline Glascock, though another name might have been used, dated from Milan, saying that they were hurrying back to Naples even at that season of the year, because Lord Peterborough was dead. 'And she is Lady Peterborough!' said Lady Rowley, unable to repress the expression of the old regrets. 'Of course she is Lady Peterborough, mamma; what else should she be? though she does not so sign herself.' 'We think,' said the American peeress, 'that we shall be at Monkhams before the end of August, and Charles says that you are to come just the same. There will be nobody else there, of course, because of Lord Peterborough's death.' 'I saw it in the paper,' said Sir Marmaduke, 'and quite forgot to mention it.'

That same evening there was a long family discussion about Nora's prospects. They were all together in the gloomy sitting-room at Gregg's Hotel, and Sir Marmaduke had not yielded. The ladies had begun to feel that it would be well not to press him to yield. Practically he had yielded. There was now no question of cursing and of so-called disinheritance. Nora was to remain in England, of course, with the intention of being married to Hugh Stanbury; and the difficulty consisted in the need of an immediate home for her. It wanted now but twelve days to that on which the family were to sail from Southampton, and nothing had been settled. 'If papa will allow me something ever so small, and will trust me, I will live alone in lodgings,' said Nora.

'It is the maddest thing I ever heard,' said Sir Marmaduke.

'Who would take care of you, Nora?' asked Lady Rowley.

'And who would walk about with you?' said Lucy.

'I don't see how it would be possible to live alone like that,' said Sophie.

'Nobody would take care of me, and nobody would walk about with me, and I could live alone very well,' said Nora. 'I don't see why a young woman is to be supposed to be so absolutely helpless as all that comes to. Of course it won't be very nice, but it need not be for long.'

'Why not for long?' asked Sir Marmaduke.

'Not for very long,' said Nora.

'It does not seem to me,' said Sir Marmaduke, after a considerable pause, 'that this gentleman himself is so particularly anxious for the match. I have heard no day named, and no rational proposition made.'

'Papa, that is unfair, most unfair and ungenerous.'

'Nora,' said her mother, 'do not speak in that way to your father.'

'Mamma, it is unfair. Papa accuses Mr Stanbury of being being lukewarm and untrue—of not being in earnest.'

'I would rather that he were not in earnest,' said Sir Marmaduke.

'Mr Stanbury is ready at any time,' continued Nora. 'He would have the banns at once read, and marry me in three weeks if I would let him.'

'Good gracious, Nora!' exclaimed Lady Rowley.

'But I have refused to name any day, or to make any arrangement, because I did not wish to do so before papa had given his consent. That is why things are in this way. If papa will but let me take a room till I can go to Monkhams, I will have everything arranged from there. You can trust Mr Glascock for that, and you can trust her.'

'I suppose your papa will make you some allowance,' said Lady Rowley.

'She is entitled to nothing, as she has refused to go to her proper home,' said Sir Marmaduke.

The conversation, which had now become very disagreeable, was not allowed to go any further. And it was well that it should be interrupted. They all knew that Sir Marmaduke must be brought round by degrees, and that both Nora and Lady Rowley had gone as far as was prudent at present. But all trouble on this head was suddenly ended for this evening by the entrance of the waiter with a telegram. It was addressed to Lady Rowley, and she opened it with trembling hands as ladies always do open telegrams. It was from Emily Trevelyan. 'Louis is much worse. Let somebody come to me. Hugh Stanbury would be the best.'

In a few minutes they were so much disturbed that no one quite knew what should be done at once. Lady Rowley began by declaring that she would go herself. Sir Marmaduke of course pointed out that this was impossible, and suggested that he would send a lawyer. Nora professed herself ready to start immediately on the journey, but was stopped by a proposition from her sister Lucy that in that case Hugh Stanbury would of course go with her. Lady Rowley asked whether Hugh would go, and Nora asserted that he would go immediately as a matter of course. She was sure he would go, let the people at the *D. R.* say what they might. According to her there was always somebody at the call of the editor of the *D. R.* to do the work of anybody else, when anybody else wanted to go away. Sir Marmaduke shook his head, and was very uneasy. He still thought that a lawyer would be best, feeling, no doubt, that if Stanbury's services were used on such an occasion, there must be an end of all opposition to the marriage. But before half-an-hour was over Stanbury was sent for. The boots of the hotel went off in a cab to the office of the *D. R.* with a note from Lady Rowley. 'Dear Mr Stanbury, We have had a telegram from Emily, and want to see you, at once. Please come. We shall sit up and wait for you till you do come, E. R.'

It was very distressing to them because, let the result be what it might, it was all but impossible that Mrs Trevelyan should be with them before they had sailed, and it was quite out of the question that they should now postpone their journey. Were Stanbury to start by the morning train on the following day, he could not reach

Siena till the afternoon of the fourth day; and let the result be what it might when he arrived there, it would be out of the question that Emily Trevelyan should come back quite at once, or that she should travel at the same speed. Of course they might hear again by telegram, and also by letter; but they could not see her, or have any hand in her plans. 'If anything were to happen, she might have come with us,' said Lady Rowley.

'It is out of the question,' said Sir Marmaduke gloomily. 'I could not give up the places I have taken.'

'A few days more would have done it.'

'I don't suppose she would wish to go,' said Nora. 'Of course she would not take Louey there. Why should she? And then I don't suppose he is so ill as that.'

'There is no saying,' said Sir Marmaduke. It was very evident that, whatever might be Sir Marmaduke's opinion, he had no strongly developed wish for his son-in-law's recovery.

They all sat up waiting for Hugh Stanbury till eleven, twelve, one, and two o'clock at night. The 'boots' had returned saying that Mr Stanbury had not been at the office of the newspaper, but that, according to information received, he certainly would be there that night. No other address had been given to the man, and the note had therefore of necessity been left at the office. Sir Marmaduke became very fretful, and was evidently desirous of being liberated from his night watch. But he could not go himself, and shewed his impatience by endeavouring to send the others away. Lady Rowley replied for herself that she should certainly remain in her corner on the sofa all night, if it were necessary; and as she slept very soundly in her corner, her comfort was not much impaired. Nora was pertinacious in refusing to go to bed. 'I should only go to my own room, papa, and remain there,' she said. 'Of course I must speak to him before he goes.' Sophie and Lucy considered that they had as much right to sit up as Nora, and submitted to be called geese and idiots by their father.

Sir Marmaduke had arisen with a snort from a short slumber, and had just sworn that he and everybody else should go to bed, when there came a ring at the front-door bell. The trusty boots had also remained up, and in two minutes Hugh Stanbury was in the room. He had to make his excuses before anything else could be said. When he reached the _D. R._ office between ten and eleven, it was absolutely incumbent on him to write a leading article before he left it. He had been in the reporter's gallery of the House all the evening, and he had come away laden with his article. 'It was certainly better that we should remain up, than that the whole town should be disappointed,' said Sir Marmaduke, with something of a sneer.

'It is so very, very good of you to come,' said Nora. 'Indeed it is,' said Lady Rowley; 'but we were quite sure you would come.' Having kissed and blessed him as her son-in-law, Lady Rowley was now prepared to love him almost as well as though he had been Lord Peterborough.

'Perhaps, Mr Stanbury, we had better shew you this telegram,' said Sir Marmaduke, who had been standing with the scrap of paper in his hand since the ring of the bell had been heard. Hugh took the message and read it. 'I do not know what should have made my daughter mention your name,' continued Sir Marmaduke, 'but as she has done so, and as perhaps the unfortunate invalid himself may have alluded to you, we thought it best to send for you.'

'No doubt it was best, Sir Marmaduke.'

'We are so situated that I cannot go. It is absolutely necessary that we should leave town for Southampton on Friday week. The ship sails on Saturday.'

'I will go as a matter of course,' said Hugh. 'I will start at once, at any time. To tell the truth, when I got Lady Rowley's note, I thought that it was to be so. Trevelyan and I were very intimate at one time, and it may be that he will receive me without displeasure.'

There was much to be discussed, and considerable difficulty in the discussion. This was enhanced, too, by the feeling in the minds of all of them that Hugh and Sir Marmaduke would not meet again probably for many years. Were they to part now on terms of close affection, or were they to part almost as strangers? Had Lucy and Sophie not persistently remained up, Nora would have faced the difficulty, and taken the bull by the horns, and asked her father to sanction her engagement in the presence of her lover. But she could not do it before so many persons, even though the persons were her own nearest relatives. And then there arose another embarrassment. Sir Marmaduke, who had taught himself to believe that Stanbury was so poor as hardly to have the price of a dinner in his pocket although, in fact, our friend Hugh was probably the richer man of the two, said something about defraying the cost of the journey. 'It is taken altogether on our behalf,' said Sir Marmaduke. Hugh became red in the face, looked angry, and muttered a word or two about Trevelyan being the oldest friend he had in the world 'even if there were nothing else.' Sir Marmaduke felt ashamed of himself without cause, indeed, for the offer was natural, said nothing further about it; but appeared to be more stiff and ungainly than ever.

The Bradshaw was had out and consulted, and nearly half an hour was spent in poring over that wondrous volume. It is the fashion to abuse Bradshaw; we speak now especially of Bradshaw the Continental because all the minutest details of the autumn tour, just as the tourist thinks that it may be made, cannot be made patent to him at once without close research amidst crowded figures. After much experience we make bold to say that Bradshaw knows more, and will divulge more in a quarter of an hour, of the properest mode of getting from any city in Europe to any other city more than fifty miles distant, than can be learned in that first city in a single morning with the aid of a courier, a carriage, a pair of horses, and all the temper that any ordinary tourist possesses. The Bradshaw was had out, and it was at last discovered that nothing could be gained in the journey from London to Siena by starting in the morning. Intending as he did to travel through without sleeping on the road, Stanbury could not do better than leave London by the night mail train, and this he determined to do. But when that was arranged, then came the nature of his commission. What was he to do? No commission could be given to him. A telegram should be sent to Emily the next morning to say that he was coming; and then he would hurry on and take his orders from her.

They were all in doubt, terribly in doubt, whether the aggravated malady of which the telegram spoke was malady of the mind or of the body. If of the former nature then the difficulty might be very great indeed; and it would be highly expedient that Stanbury should have some one in Italy to assist him. It was Nora who suggested that he should carry a letter of introduction to Mr Spalding, and it was she who wrote it. Sir Marmaduke had not foregathered very closely with the English Minister, and nothing was said of assistance that should be peculiarly British. Then, at last, about three or four in the morning came the moment for parting. Sir Marmaduke had suggested that Stanbury should dine with them on the next day before he started, but Hugh had declined, alleging that as the day was at his command it must be devoted to the work of providing for his absence. In truth, Sir Marmaduke had given the invitation with a surly voice, and Hugh, though he was ready to go to the North Pole for any others of the family, was at the moment in an aggressive mood of mind towards Sir Marmaduke.

'I will send a message directly I get there,' he said, holding Lady Rowley by the hand, 'and will write fully to you immediately.'

'God bless you, my dear friend!' said Lady Rowley, crying.

'Good night, Sir Marmaduke,' said Hugh.

'Good night, Mr Stanbury.'

Then he gave a hand to the two girls, each of whom, as she took it, sobbed, and looked away from Nora. Nora was standing away from them, by herself, and away from the door, holding on to her chair, and with her hands clasped together. She had prepared nothing, not a word, or an attitude, not a thought, for this farewell. But she had felt that it was coming, and had known that she must trust to him for a cue for her own demeanour. If he could say adieu with a quiet voice, and simply with a touch of the hand, then would she do the same and endeavour to think no worse of him. Nor had he prepared anything; but when the moment came he could not leave her after that fashion. He stood a moment hesitating, not approaching her, and merely called her by her name 'Nora!' For a moment she was still; for a moment she held by her chair; and then she rushed into his arms. He did not much care for her father now, but kissed her hair and her forehead, and held her closely to his bosom. 'My own, own Nora!'

It was necessary that Sir Marmaduke should say something. There was at first a little scene between all the women, during which he arranged his deportment.

'Mr Stanbury,' he said, 'let it be so. I could wish for my child's sake, and also for your own, that your means of living were less precarious.' Hugh accepted this simply as an authority for another embrace, and then he allowed them all to go to bed.

CHAPTER XCII. TREVELYAN DISCOURSES ON LIFE

Stanbury made his journey without pause or hindrance till he reached Florence, and as the train for Siena made it necessary that he should remain there for four or five hours, he went to an inn, and dressed and washed himself, and had a meal, and was then driven to Mr Spalding's house. He found the American Minister at home, and was received with cordiality; but Mr Spalding could tell him little or nothing about Trevelyan. They went up to Mrs Spalding's room, and Hugh was told by her that she had seen Mrs Trevelyan once since her niece's marriage, and that then she had represented her husband as being very feeble. Hugh, in the midst of his troubles, was amused by a second and a third, perhaps by a fourth, reference to 'Lady Peterborough.' Mrs Spalding's latest tidings as to the Trevelyans had been received through 'Lady Peterborough' from Nora Rowley.

'Lady Peterborough' was at the present moment at Naples, but was expected to pass north through Florence in a day or two. They, the Spaldings themselves, were kept in Florence in this very hot weather by this circumstance. They were going up to the Tyrolese mountains for a few weeks as soon as 'Lady Peterborough' should have left them for England. 'Lady Peterborough' would have been so happy to make Mr Stanbury's acquaintance, and to have heard something direct from her friend Nora. Then Mrs Spalding smiled archly, showing thereby that she knew all about Hugh Stanbury and his relation to Nora Rowley. From all which, and in accordance with the teaching which we got alas, now many years ago from a great master on the subject, we must conclude that poor, dear Mrs Spalding was a snob. Nevertheless, with all deference to the memory of that great master, we think that Mrs Spalding's allusions to the success in life achieved by her niece were natural and altogether pardonable; and that reticence on the subject, a calculated determination to abstain from mentioning a triumph which must have been very dear to her, would have betrayed on the whole a condition of mind lower than that which she exhibited. While rank, wealth, and money are held to be good things by all around us, let them be acknowledged as such. It is natural that a mother should be as proud when her daughter marries an Earl's heir as when her son becomes Senior Wrangler; and when we meet a lady in Mrs Spalding's condition who purposely abstains from mentioning the name of her titled daughter, we shall be disposed to judge harshly of the secret workings of that lady's thoughts on the subject. We prefer the exhibition, which we feel to be natural. Mr Spalding got our friend by the button-hole, and was making him a speech on the perilous condition in which Mrs Trevelyan was placed; but Stanbury, urged by the circumstances of his position, pulled out his watch, pleaded the hour, and escaped.

He found Mrs Trevelyan waiting for him at the station at Siena. He would hardly have known her, not from any alteration that was physically personal to herself, not that she had become older in face, or thin, or grey, or sickly, but that the trouble of her life had robbed her for the time of that brightness of apparel, of that pride of feminine gear, of that sheen of high-bred womanly bearing with which our wives and daughters are so careful to invest themselves. She knew herself to be a wretched woman, whose work in life was now to watch over a poor prostrate wretch, and who had thrown behind her all ideas of grace and beauty. It was not quickly that this condition had come upon her. She had been unhappy at Nuncombe Putney; but unhappiness had not then told upon the outward woman. She had been more wretched still at St. Diddulph's, and all the outward circumstances of life in her uncle's parsonage had been very wearisome to her; but she had striven against it all, and the sheen and outward brightness had still been there. After that her child had been taken from her, and the days which she had passed in Manchester Street had been very grievous, but even yet she had not given way. It was not till her child had been brought back to her, and she had seen the life which her husband was living, and that her anger—hot anger—had changed to pity, and that with pity love had returned; it was not till this point had come in her sad life that her dress became always black and sombre, that a veil habitually covered her face, that a bonnet took the place of the jaunty hat that she had worn, and that the prettinesses of her life were lain aside. 'It is very good of you to come,' she said; 'very good, I hardly knew what to do, I was so wretched. On the day that I sent he was so bad that I was obliged to do something.' Stanbury, of course, inquired after Trevelyan's health, as they were being driven up to Mrs Trevelyan's lodgings. On the day on which she had sent the telegram her husband had again been furiously angry with her. She had interfered, or had endeavoured to interfere, in some arrangements as to his health and comfort, and he had turned upon her with an order that the child should be at once sent back to him, and that she should immediately quit Siena. 'When I said that Louey could not be sent—and who could send a child into such keeping?—he told me that I was the basest liar that ever broke a promise, and the vilest traitor that had ever returned evil for good. I was never to come to him again, never; and the gate of the house would be closed against me if I appeared there.'

On the next day she had gone again, however, and had seen him, and had visited him on every day since. Nothing further had been said about the child, and he had now become almost too weak for violent anger. 'I told him you were coming, and though he would not say so, I think he is glad of it. He expects you tomorrow.'

'I will go this evening, if he will let me.'

'Not to-night. I think he goes to bed almost as the sun sets. I am never there myself after four or five in the afternoon. I told him that you should be there tomorrow alone. I have hired a little carriage, and you can take it. He said specially that I was not to come with you. Papa goes certainly on next Saturday?' It was a Saturday now, this day on which Stanbury had arrived at Siena.

'He leaves town on Friday.'

'You must make him believe that. Do not tell him suddenly, but bring it in by degrees. He thinks that I am deceiving him. He would go back if he knew that papa were gone.'

They spent a long evening together, and Stanbury learned all that Mrs Trevelyan could tell him of her husband's state. There was no doubt, she said, that his reason was affected; but she thought the state of his mind was diseased in a ratio the reverse of that of his body, and that when he was weakest in health, then were his ideas the most clear and rational. He never now mentioned Colonel Osborne's name, but would refer to the affairs of the last two years as though they had been governed by an inexorable Fate which had utterly destroyed his happiness without any fault on his part. 'You may be sure,' she said, 'that I never accuse him. Even when he says terrible things of me, which he does, I never excuse myself. I do not think I should answer a word if he called me the vilest thing on earth.' Before they parted for the night many questions were of course asked about Nora, and Hugh described the condition in which he and she stood to each other. 'Papa has consented, then?'

'Yes, at four o'clock in the morning, just as I was leaving them.'

'And when is it to be?'

'Nothing has been settled, and I do not as yet know where she will go to when they leave London. I think she will visit Monkhams when the Glascock people return to England.'

'What an episode in life to go and see the place, when it might all now have been hers!'

'I suppose I ought to feel dreadfully ashamed of myself for having marred such promotion,' said Hugh.

'Nora is such a singular girl, so firm, so headstrong, so good, and so self-reliant, that she will do as well with a poor man as she would have done with a rich. Shall I confess to you that I did wish that she should accept Mr Glascock, and that I pressed it on her very strongly? You will not be angry with me?'

'I am only the more proud of her and of myself.'

'When she was told of all that he had to give in the way of wealth and rank, she took the bit between her teeth and would not be turned an inch. Of course she was in love.'

'I hope she may never regret it, that is all.'

'She must change her nature first. Everything she sees at Monkhams will make her stronger in her choice. With all her girlish ways, she is like a rock; nothing can move her.'

Early on the next morning Hugh started alone for Casalunga, having first, however, seen Mrs Trevelyan. He took out with him certain little things for the sick man's table as to which, however, he was cautioned to say not a word to the sick man himself. And it was arranged that he should endeavour to fix a day for Trevelyan's return to England. That was to be the one object in view. 'If we could get him to England,' she said, 'he and I would, at any rate, be together, and gradually he would be taught to submit himself to advice.' Before ten in the morning, Stanbury was walking up the hill to the house, and wondering at the dreary, hot, hopeless desolation of the spot. It seemed to him that no one could live alone in such a place, in such weather, without being driven to madness. The soil was parched and dusty, as though no drop of rain had fallen there for months. The lizards, glancing in and out of the broken walls, added to the appearance of heat. The vegetation itself was of a faded yellowish green, as though the glare of the sun had taken the fresh colour out of it. There was a noise of grasshoppers and a hum of flies in the air, hardly audible, but all giving evidence of the heat. Not a human voice was to be heard, nor the sound of a human foot, and there was no shelter; but the sun blazed down full upon everything. He took off his hat, and rubbed his head with his handkerchief as he struck the door with his stick. Oh God, to what misery had a little folly brought two human beings who had had every blessing that the world could give within their reach!

In a few minutes he was conducted through the house, and found Trevelyan seated in a chair under the verandah which looked down upon the olive trees. He did not even get up from his seat, but put out his left hand and welcomed his old friend. 'Stanbury,' he said, 'I am glad to see you for auld lang syne's sake. When I found out this retreat, I did not mean to have friends round me here. I wanted to try what solitude was and, by heaven, I've tried it!' He was dressed in a bright Italian dressing-gown, or woollen paletot—Italian, as having been bought in Italy, though, doubtless, it had come from France—and on his feet he had green worked slippers, and on his head a brocaded cap. He had made but little other preparation for his friend in the way of dressing. His long dishevelled hair came down over his neck, and his beard covered his face. Beneath his dressing-gown he had on a night-shirt and drawers, and was as dirty in appearance as he was gaudy in colours.'sit down and let us two moralise,' he said. 'I spend my life here doing nothing, nothing, nothing; while 'you cudgel your brain from day to day to mislead the British public. Which of us two is taking the nearest road to the devil?'

Stanbury seated himself in a second arm-chair, which there was there in the verandah, and looked as carefully as he dared to do at his friend. There could be no mistake as to the restless gleam of that eye. And then the affected air of ease, and the would-be cynicism, and the pretence of false motives, all told the same story. 'They used to tell us,' said Stanbury, 'that idleness is the root of all evil.'

'They have been telling us since the world began so many lies, that I for one have determined never to believe anything again. Labour leads to greed, and greed to selfishness, and selfishness to treachery, and treachery straight to the devil, straight to the devil. Ha, my friend, all your leading articles won't lead you out of that. What's the news? Who's alive? Who dead? Who in? Who out? What think you of a man who has not seen a newspaper for two months; and who holds no conversation with the world further than is needed for the cooking of his *polenta* and the cooling of his modest wine-flask?'

'You see your wife sometimes,' said Stanbury.

'My wife! Now, my friend, let us drop that subject. Of all topics of talk it is the most distressing to man in general, and I own that I am no exception to the lot. Wives, Stanbury, are an evil, more or less necessary to humanity, and I own to being one who has not escaped. The world must be populated, though for what reason one does not see. I have helped to the extent of one male bantling; and if you are one who consider population desirable, I will express my regret that I should have done no more.'

It was very difficult to force Trevelyan out of this humour, and it was not till Stanbury had risen apparently to take his leave that he found it possible to say a word as to his mission there. 'Don't you think you would be happier at home?' he asked.

'Where is my home, Sir Knight of the midnight pen?'

'England is your home, Trevelyan.'

'No, sir; England was my home once; but I have taken the liberty accorded to me by my Creator of choosing a new country. Italy is now my nation, and Casalunga is my home.'

'Every tie you have in the world is in England.'

'I have no tie, sir, no tie anywhere. It has been my study to untie all the ties; and, by Jove, I have succeeded. Look at me here. I have got rid of the trammels pretty well haven't I? have unshackled myself, and thrown off the paddings, and the wrappings, and the swaddling clothes. I have got rid of the conventionalities, and can look Nature straight in the face. I don't even want the *Daily Record*, Stanbury think of that!'

Stanbury paced the length of the terrace, and then stopped for a moment down under the blaze of the sun, in order that he might think how to address this philosopher. 'Have you heard,' he said at last, 'that I am going to marry your sister-in-law, Nora Rowley?'

'Then there will be two more full-grown fools in the world certainly, and probably an infinity of young fools coming afterwards. Excuse me, Stanbury, but this solitude is apt to make one plain-spoken.'

'I got Sir Marmaduke's sanction the day before I left.'

'Then you got the sanction of an illiterate, ignorant, self-sufficient, and most contemptible old man; and much good may it do you.'

'Let him be what he may, I was glad to have it. Most probably I shall never see him again. He sails from Southampton for the Mandarins on this day week.'

'He does, does he? May the devil sail along with him! that is all I say. And does my much respected and ever-to-be-beloved mother-in-law sail with him?'

'They all return together except Nora.'

'Who remains to comfort you? I hope you may be comforted that is all. Don't be too particular. Let her choose her own friends, and go her own gait, and have her own way, and do you be blind and deaf and dumb and properly submissive; and it may be that she'll give you your breakfast and dinner in your own house so long as your hours don't interfere with her pleasures. If she should even urge you beside yourself by her vanity, folly, and disobedience, so that at last you are driven to express your feeling, no doubt she will come to you after a while and tell you with the sweetest condescension that she forgives you. When she has been out of your house for a twelvemonth or more, she will offer to come back to you, and to forget everything on condition that you will do exactly as she bids you for the future.'

This attempt at satire, so fatuous, so plain, so false, together with the would-be jaunty manner of the speaker, who, however, failed repeatedly in his utterances from sheer physical exhaustion, was excessively painful to Stanbury. What can one do at any time with a madman? 'I mentioned my marriage,' said he, 'to prove my right to have an additional interest in your wife's happiness.'

'You are quite welcome, whether you marry the other one or not, welcome to take any interest you please. I have got beyond all that, Stanbury, yes, by Jove, a long way beyond all that.'

'You have not got beyond loving your wife, and your child, Trevelyan?'

'Upon my word, yes I think I have. There may be a grain of weakness left, you know. But what have you to do with my love for my wife?'

'I was thinking more just now of her love for you. There she is at Siena. You cannot mean that she should remain there?'

'Certainly not. What the deuce is there to keep her there?'

'Come with her then to England.'

'Why should I go to England with her? Because you bid me, or because she wishes it, or simply because England is the most damnable, puritanical, God-forgotten, and stupid country on the face of the globe? I know no other reason for going to England. Will you take a glass of wine, Stanbury?' Hugh declined the offer. 'You will excuse me,' continued Trevelyan; 'I always take a glass of wine at this hour.' Then he rose from his chair, and helped himself from a cupboard that was near at hand. Stanbury, watching him as he filled his glass, could see that his legs were hardly strong enough to carry him. And Stanbury saw, moreover, that the unfortunate man took two glasses out of the bottle. 'Go to England indeed. I do not think much of this country; but it is, at any rate, better than England.'

Hugh perceived that he could do nothing more on the present occasion. Having heard so much of Trevelyan's debility, he had been astonished to hear the man speak with so much volubility and attempts at high-flown spirit. Before he had taken the wine he had almost sunk into his chair, but still he had continued to speak with the same fluent would-be cynicism. 'I will come and see you again,' said Hugh, getting up to take his departure.

'You might as well save your trouble, Stanbury; but you can come if you please, you know. If you should find yourself locked out, you won't be angry. A hermit such as I am must assume privileges.'

'I won't be angry,' said Hugh, good humouredly.

'I can smell what you are come about,' said Trevelyan. 'You and my wife want to take me away from here among you, and I think it best to stay here. I don't want much for myself, and why should I not live here? My wife can remain at Siena if she pleases, or she can go to England if she pleases. She must give me the same liberty, the same liberty, the same liberty.' After this he fell a-coughing violently, and Stanbury thought it better to leave him. He had been at Casalunga about two hours, and did not seem as yet to have done any good. He had been astonished both by Trevelyan's weakness, and by his strength; by his folly, and by his sharpness. Hitherto he could see no way for his future sister-in-law out of her troubles.

When he was with her at Siena, he described what had taken place with all the accuracy in his power. 'He has intermittent days,' said Emily. 'To-morrow he will be in quite another frame of mind—melancholy, silent perhaps, and self-reproachful. We will both go tomorrow, and we shall find probably that he has forgotten altogether what has passed to-day between you and him.'

So their plans for the morrow were formed.

CHAPTER XCIII. 'SAY THAT YOU FORGIVE ME'

On the following day, again early in the morning, Mrs Trevelyan and Stanbury were driven out to Casalunga. The country people along the road knew the carriage well, and the lady who occupied it, and would say that the English wife was going to see her mad husband. Mrs Trevelyan knew that these words were common in the people's mouths, and explained to her companion how necessary it would be to use these rumours, to aid her in putting some restraint over her husband even in this country, should they fail in their effort to take him to England. She saw the doctor in Siena constantly, and had learned from him how such steps might be taken. The measure proposed would be slow, difficult, inefficient, and very hard to set aside, if once taken, but still it might be indispensable that something should be done. 'He would be so much worse off here than he would be at home,' she said, 'if we could only make him understand that it would be so.' Then Stanbury asked about the wine. It seemed that of late Trevelyan had taken to drink freely, but only of the wine of the country. But the wine of the country in these parts is sufficiently stimulating, and Mrs Trevelyan acknowledged that hence had arisen a further cause of fear.

They walked up the hill together, and Mrs Trevelyan, now well knowing the ways of the place, went round at once to the front terrace. There he was, seated in his arm-chair, dressed in the same way as yesterday, dirty, dishevelled, and gaudy with various colours; but Stanbury could see at once that his mood had greatly changed. He rose slowly, dragging himself up out of his chair, as they came up to him, but shewing as he did so, and perhaps somewhat assuming, the impotency of querulous sickness. His wife went to him, and took him by the hand, and placed him back in his chair. He was weak, he said, and had not slept, and suffered from the heat; and then he begged her to give him wine. This she did, half filling for him a tumbler, of which he swallowed the contents greedily. 'You see me very poorly, Stanbury, very poorly,' he said, seeming to ignore all that had taken place on the previous day.

'You want change of climate, old fellow,' said Stanbury.

'Change of everything; I want change of everything,' he said. 'If I could have a new body and a new mind, and a new soul!'

'The mind and soul, dear, will do well enough, if you will let us look after the body,' said his wife, seating herself on a stool near his feet. Stanbury, who had settled beforehand how he would conduct himself, took out a cigar and lighted it and then they sat together silent, or nearly silent, for half an hour. She had said that if Hugh would do so, Trevelyan would soon become used to the presence of his old friend, and it seemed that he had already done so. More than once, when he coughed, his wife fetched him some drink in a cup, which he took from her without a word. And Stanbury the while went on smoking in silence.

'You have heard, Louis,' she said at last, 'that, after all, Nora and Mr Stanbury are going to be married?'

'Ah yes; I think I was told of it. I hope you may be happy, Stanbury, happier than I have been.' This was unfortunate, but neither of the visitors winced, or said a word.

'It will be a pity that papa and mamma cannot be present at the wedding,' said Mrs Trevelyan.

'If I had to do it again, I should not regret your father's absence; I must say that. He has been my enemy. Yes, Stanbury, my enemy. I don't care who hears me say so. I am obliged to stay here, because that man would swear every shilling I have away from me if I were in England. He would strive to do so, and the struggle in my state of health would be too much for me.'

'But Sir Marmaduke sails from Southampton this very week,' said Stanbury.

'I don't know. He is always sailing, and always coming back again. I never asked him for a shilling in my life, and yet he has treated me as though I were his bitterest enemy.'

'He will trouble you no more now, Louis,' said Mrs Trevelyan.

'He cannot trouble you again. He will have left England before you can possibly reach it.'

'He will have left other traitors behind him, though none as bad as himself,' said Trevelyan.

Stanbury, when his cigar was finished, rose and left the husband and wife together on the terrace. There was little enough to be seen at Casalunga, but he strolled about looking at the place. He went into the huge granary, and then down among the olive trees, and up into the sheds which had been built for beasts. He stood and teased the lizards, and listened to the hum of the insects, and wiping away the perspiration which rose to his brow even as he was standing. And all the while he was thinking what he would do next, or what say next, with the view of getting Trevelyan away from the place. Hitherto he had been very tender with him, contradicting him in nothing, taking from him good humouredly any absurd insult which he chose to offer, pressing upon him none of the evil which he had himself occasioned, saying to him no word that could hurt either his pride or his comfort. But he could not see that this would be efficacious for the purpose desired. He had come thither to help Nora's sister in her terrible distress, and he must take upon himself to make some plan for giving this aid. When he had thought of all this and made his plan, he sauntered back round the house on to the terrace. She was still there, sitting at her husband's feet, and holding one of his hands in hers. It was well that the wife should be tender, but he doubted whether tenderness would suffice.

'Trevelyan,' he said, 'you know why I have come over here?'

'I suppose she told you to come,' said Trevelyan.

'Well; yes; she did tell me. I came to try and get you back to England. If you remain here, the climate and solitude together will kill you.'

'As for the climate, I like it, and as for the solitude, I have got used even to that.'

'And then there is another thing,' said Stanbury.

'What is that?' asked Trevelyan, starting.

'You are not safe here.'

'How not safe?'

'She could not tell you, but I must.' His wife was still holding his hand, and he did not at once attempt to withdraw it; but he raised himself in his chair, and fixed his eyes fiercely on Stanbury. 'They will not let you remain here quietly,' said Stanbury.

'Who will not?'

'The Italians. They are already saying that you are not fit to be alone; and if once they get you into their hands under some Italian medical board, perhaps into some Italian asylum, it might be years before you could get out, if ever. I have come to tell you what the danger is. I do not know whether you will believe me.'

'Is it so?' he said, turning to his wife.

'I believe it is, Louis.'

'And who has told them? Who has been putting them up to it?' Now his hand had been withdrawn. 'My God, am I to be followed here too with such persecution as this?'

'Nobody has told them, but people have eyes.'

'Liar, traitor, fiend! it is you!' he said, turning upon his wife.

'Louis, as I hope for mercy, I have said not a word to any one that could injure you.'

'Trevelyan, do not be so unjust, and so foolish,' said Stanbury. 'It is not her doing. Do you suppose that you can live here like this and give rise to no remarks? Do you think that people's eyes are not open, and that their tongues will not speak? I tell you, you are in danger here.'

'What am I to do? Where am I to go? Can not they let me stay till I die? Whom am I hurting here? She may have all my money, if she wants it. She has got my child.'

'I want nothing, Louis, but to take you where you may be safe and well.'

'Why are you afraid of going to England?' Stanbury asked.

'Because they have threatened to put me in a mad-house.'

'Nobody ever thought of so treating you,' said his wife.

'Your father did and your mother. They told me so.'

'Look here, Trevelyan. Sir Marmaduke and Lady Rowley are gone. They will have sailed, at least, before we can reach England. Whatever may have been either their wishes or their power, they can do nothing now. Here something would be done very soon; you may take my word for that. If you will return with me and your wife, you shall choose your own place of abode. Is not that so, Emily?'

'He shall choose everything. His boy will be with him, and I will be with him, and he shall be contradicted in nothing. If he only knew my heart towards him!'

'You hear what she says, Trevelyan?'

'Yes; I hear her.'

'And you believe her?'

'I'm not so sure of that, Stanbury; how should you like to be locked up in a madhouse and grin through the bars till your heart was broken. It would not take long with me, I know.'

'You shall never be locked up, never be touched,' said his wife.

'I am very harmless here,' he said, almost crying; 'very harmless. I do not think anybody here will touch me,' he added afterwards. 'And there are other places. There are other places. My God, that I should be driven about the world like this!' The conference was ended by his saying that he would take two days to think of it, and by his then desiring that they would both leave him. They did so, and descended the hill together, knowing that he was watching them, that he would watch them till they were out of sight from the gate for, as Mrs Trevelyan said, he never came down the hill now, knowing that the labour of ascending it was too much for him. When they were at the carriage they were met by one of the women of the house, and strict injunctions were given to her by Mrs Trevelyan to send on word to Siena if the Signore should prepare to move. 'He cannot go far without my knowing it,' said she, 'because he draws his money in Siena, and lately I have taken to him what he wants. He has not enough with him for a long journey.' For Stanbury had suggested that he might be off to seek another residence in another country, and that they would find Casalunga vacant when they reached it on the following Tuesday. But he told himself almost immediately, not caring to express such an opinion to Emily, that Trevelyan would hardly have strength even to prepare for such a journey by himself.

On the intervening day, the Monday, Stanbury had no occupation whatever, and he thought that since he was born no day had ever been so long. Siena contains many monuments of interest, and much that is valuable in art, having had a school of painting of its own, and still retaining in its public gallery specimens of its school, of which as a city it is justly proud. There are palaces there to be beaten for gloomy majesty by none in Italy. There is a cathedral which was to have been the largest in the world, and than which few are more worthy of prolonged inspection. The town is old, and quaint, and picturesque, and dirty, and attractive, as it becomes a town in Italy to be. But in July all such charms are thrown away. In July Italy is not a land of charms to an Englishman. Poor Stanbury did wander into the cathedral, and finding it the coolest place in the town, went to sleep on a stone step. He was awoke by the voice of the priests as they began to chant the vespers. The good-natured Italians had let him sleep, and would have let him sleep till the doors were closed for the night. At five he dined with Mrs Trevelyan, and then endeavoured to while away the evening thinking of Nora with a pipe in his mouth. He was standing in this way at the hotel gateway, when, on a sudden, all Siena was made alive by the clatter of an open carriage and four on its way through the town to the railway. On looking up, Stanbury saw Lord Peterborough in the carriage with a lady whom he did not doubt to be Lord Peterborough's wife. He himself had not been recognised, but he slowly followed the carriage to the railway station. After the Italian fashion, the arrival was three-quarters of an hour before the proper time, and Stanbury had full opportunity of learning their news and telling his own. They were coming up from Rome, and thought it preferable to take the route by Siena than to use the railway through the Maremma; and they intended to reach Florence that night.

'And do you think he is really mad?' asked Lady Peterborough.

'He is undoubtedly so mad as to be unfit to manage anything for himself, but he is not in such a condition that any one would wish to see him put into confinement. If he were raving mad there would be less difficulty, though there might be more distress.'

A great deal was said about Nora, and both Lord Peterborough and his wife insisted that the marriage should take place at Monkhams. 'We shall be home now in less than three weeks,' said Caroline, 'and she must come to us at once. But I will write to her from Florence, and tell her how we saw you smoking your pipe under the archway. Not that my husband knew you in the least.'

'Upon my word no,' said the husband, 'one didn't expect to find you here. Goodbye. I hope you may succeed in getting him home. I went to him once, but could do very little.' Then the train started, and Stanbury went back to Mrs Trevelyan.

On the next day Stanbury went out to Casalunga alone. He had calculated, on leaving England, that if any good might be done at Siena it could be done in three days, and that he would have been able to start on his return on the Wednesday morning or on Wednesday evening at the latest. But now there did not seem to be any chance of that, and he hardly knew how to guess when he might get away. He had sent a telegram to Lady Rowley after his first visit, in which he had simply said that things were not at all changed at Casalunga, and he had written to Nora each day since his arrival. His stay was prolonged at great expense and inconvenience to himself; and yet it was impossible that he should go and leave his work half finished. As he walked up the hill to the house he felt very angry with Trevelyan, and prepared himself to use hard words and dreadful threats. But at the very moment of his entrance on the terrace, Trevelyan professed himself ready to go to England. 'That's right, old fellow,' said Hugh. 'I am so glad.' But in expressing his joy he had hardly noticed Trevelyan's voice and appearance.

'I might as well go,' he said. 'It matters little where I am, or whether they say that I am mad or sane.'

'When we have you over there, nobody shall say a word that is disagreeable.'

'I only hope that you may not have the trouble of burying me on the road. You don't know, Stanbury, how ill I am. I cannot eat. If I were at the bottom of that hill, I could no more walk up it than I could fly. I cannot sleep, and at night my bed is wet through with perspiration. I can remember nothing nothing but what I ought to forget.'

'We'll put you on your legs again when we get you to your own climate.'

'I shall be a poor traveller a poor traveller; but I will do my best.'

When would he start? That was the next question. Trevelyan asked for a week, and Stanbury brought him down at last to three days. They would go to Florence by the evening train on Friday, and sleep there. Emily should come out and assist him to arrange his things on the morrow. Having finished so much of his business, Stanbury returned to Siena. They both feared that he might be found on the next day to have departed from his intention; but no such idea seemed to have occurred to him. He gave instructions as to the notice to be served on the agent from the Hospital as to his house, and allowed Emily to go among his things and make preparations for the journey. He did not say much to her; and when she attempted, with a soft half-uttered word, to assure him that the threat of Italian interference, which had come from Stanbury, had not reached Stanbury from her, he simply shook his head sadly. She could not understand whether he did not believe her, or whether he simply wished that the subject should be dropped. She could elicit no sign of affection from him, nor would he willingly accept such from her, but he allowed her to prepare for the journey, and never hinted that his purpose might again be liable to change. On the Friday, Emily with her child, and Hugh with all their baggage, travelled out on the road to Casalunga, thinking it better that there should be no halt in the town on their return. At Casalunga, Hugh went up the hill with the driver, leaving Mrs Trevelyan in the carriage. He had been out at the house before in the morning, and had given all necessary orders, but still at the last moment he thought that there might be failure. But Trevelyan was ready, having dressed himself up with a laced shirt, and changed his dressing-gown for a blue frock-coat, and his brocaded cap for a Paris hat, very pointed before and behind, and closely turned up at the sides. But Stanbury did not in the least care for his friend's dress. 'Take my arm,' he said, 'and we will go down, fair and easy. Emily would not come up because of the heat.' He suffered himself to be led, or almost carried down the hill; and three women, and the coachman, and an old countryman who worked on the farm, followed with the luggage. It took about an hour and a half to pack the things; but at last they were all packed, and corded, and bound together with sticks, as though it were intended that they should travel in that form to Moscow. Trevelyan the meanwhile sat on a chair which had been brought out for him from one of the cottages, and his wife stood beside him with her boy. 'Now then we are ready,' said Stanbury. And in that way they bade farewell to Casalunga. Trevelyan sat speechless in the carriage, and would not even notice the child. He seemed to be half dreaming and to fix his eyes on vacancy. 'He appears to think of nothing now,' Emily said that evening to Stanbury. But who can tell how busy and how troubled are the thoughts of a madman!

They had now succeeded in their object of inducing their patient to return with them to England; but what were they to do with him when they had reached home with him? They rested only a night at Florence; but they found their fellow-traveller so weary, that they were unable to get beyond Bologna on the second day. Many questions were asked of him as to where he himself would wish to take up his residence in England; but it was found almost impossible to get an answer. Once he suggested that he would like to go back to Mrs Fuller's cottage at

Willesden, from whence they concluded that he would wish to live somewhere out of London. On his first day's journey he was moody and silent, wilfully assuming the airs of a much-injured person. He spoke hardly at all, and would notice nothing that was said to him by his wife. He declared once that he regarded Stanbury as his keeper, and endeavoured to be disagreeable and sullenly combative; but on the second day, he was too weak for this, and accepted, without remonstrance, the attentions that were paid to him. At Bologna they rested a day, and from thence both Stanbury and Mrs Trevelyan wrote to Nora. They did not know where she might be now staying, but the letters, by agreement, were addressed to Gregg's Hotel. It was suggested that lodgings, or, if possible, a small furnished house, should be taken in the neighbourhood of Mortlake, Richmond, or Teddington, and that a telegram as well as letter should be sent to them at the Paris hotel. As they could not travel quick, there might be time enough for them in this way to know whither they should go on their reaching London.

They stayed a day at Bologna, and then they went on again to Turin, over the mountains to Chambery, thence to Dijon, and on to Paris. At Chambery they remained a couple of days, fancying that the air there was cool, and that the delay would be salutary to the sick man. At Turin, finding that they wanted further assistance, they had hired a courier, and at last Trevelyan allowed himself to be carried in and out of the carriages and up and down the hotel stairs almost as though he were a child. The delay was terribly grievous to Stanbury, and Mrs Trevelyan, perceiving this more than once, begged him to leave them, and to allow her to finish the journey with the aid of the courier. But this he could not do. He wrote letters to his friends at the *D. R.* office, explaining his position as well as he could, and suggesting that this and that able assistant should enlighten the British people on this and that subject, which would in the course of nature, as arranged at the *D. R.* office, have fallen into his hands. He and Mrs Trevelyan became as brother and sister to each other on their way home as, indeed, it was natural that they should do. Were they doing right or wrong in this journey that they were taking? They could not conceal from themselves that the labour was almost more than the poor wretch could endure; and that it might be, as he himself had suggested, that they would be called on to bury him on the road. But that residence at Casalunga had been so terrible, the circumstances of it, including the solitude, sickness, madness, and habits of life of the wretched hermit, had been so dangerous, the probability of interference on the part of some native authority so great, and the chance of the house being left in Trevelyan's possession so small, that it had seemed to him that they had no other alternative; and yet, how would it be if they were killing him by the toil of travelling? From Chambery, they made the journey to Paris in two days, and during that time Trevelyan hardly opened his mouth. He slept much, and ate better than he had done in the hotter climate on the other side of the Alps.

They found a telegram at Paris, which simply contained the promise of a letter for the next day. It had been sent by Nora, before she had gone out on her search. But it contained one morsel of strange information; 'Lady Milborough is going with me.' On the next day they got a letter, saying that a cottage had been taken, furnished, between Richmond and Twickenham. Lady Milborough had known of the cottage, and everything would be ready then. Nora would herself meet them at the station in London, if they would, as she proposed, stay a night at Dover. They were to address to her at Lady Milborough's house, in Eccleston Square. In that case, she would have a carriage for them at the Victoria Station, and would go down with them at once to the cottage.

There were to be two days more of weary travelling, and then they were to be at home again. She and he would have a house together as husband and wife, and the curse of their separation would, at any rate, be over. Her mind towards him had changed altogether since the days in which she had been so indignant, because he had set a policeman to watch over her. All feeling of anger was over with her now. There is nothing that a woman will not forgive a man, when he is weaker than she is herself.

The journey was made first to Dover, and then to London. Once, as they were making their way through the Kentish hop-fields, he put out his hand feebly, and touched hers. They had the carriage to themselves, and she was down on her knees before him instantly. 'Oh, Louis! Oh, Louis! say that you forgive me!' What could a woman do more than that in her mercy to a man?

'Yes yes; yes,' he said; 'but do not talk now; I am so tired.'

CHAPTER XCIV. A REAL CHRISTIAN

In the meantime the Rowleys were gone. On the Monday after the departure of Stanbury for Italy, Lady Rowley had begun to look the difficulty about Nora in the face, and to feel that she must do something towards providing the poor girl with a temporary home. Everybody had now agreed that she was to marry Hugh Stanbury as soon as Hugh Stanbury could be ready, and it was not to be thought of that she should be left out in the world as one in disgrace or under a cloud. But what was to be done? Sir Marmaduke was quite incapable of suggesting anything. He would make her an allowance, and leave her a small sum of ready money, but as to residence, he could only suggest again and again that she should be sent to Mrs Outhouse. Now Lady Rowley was herself not very fond of Mrs Outhouse, and she was aware that Nora herself was almost as averse to St. Diddulph's as she was to the Mandarins. Nora already knew that she had the game in her own hands. Once when in her presence her father suggested the near relationship and prudent character and intense respectability of Mrs Outhouse, Nora, who was sitting behind Sir Marmaduke, shook her head at her mother, and Lady Rowley knew that Nora would not go to St. Diddulph's. This was the last occasion on which that proposition was discussed.

Throughout all the Trevelyan troubles Lady Milborough had continued to shew a friendly anxiety on behalf of Emily Trevelyan. She had called once or twice on Lady Rowley, and Lady Rowley had of course returned the visits. She had been forward in expressing her belief that in truth the wife had been but little if at all to blame, and had won her way with Lady Rowley, though she had never been a favourite with either of Lady Rowley's daughters. Now, in her difficulty, Lady Rowley went to Lady Milborough, and returned with an invitation that Nora should come to Eccleston Square, either till such time as she might think fit to go to Monkhams, or till Mrs Trevelyan should have returned, and should be desirous of having her sister with her. When Nora first heard of this she almost screamed with surprise, and, if the truth must be told, with disappointment also.

'She never liked me, mamma.'

'Then she is so much more good-natured.'

'But I don't want to go to her merely because she is good-natured enough to receive a person she dislikes. I know she is very good. I know she would sacrifice herself for anything she thought right. But, mamma, she is such a bore!'

But Lady Rowley would not be talked down, even by Nora, in this fashion. Nora was somewhat touched with an idea that it would be a fine independent thing to live alone, if it were only for a week or two, just because other young ladies never lived alone. Perhaps there was some half-formed notion in her mind that permission to do so was part of the reward due to her for having refused to marry a lord. Stanbury was in some respects a Bohemian, and it would become her, she thought, to have a little practice herself in the Bohemian line. She had, indeed, declined a Bohemian marriage, feeling strongly averse to encounter the loud displeasure of her father and mother; but as long as everything was quite proper, as long as there should be no running away, or subjection of her name to scandal, she considered that a little independence would be useful and agreeable. She had looked forward to sitting up at night alone by a single tallow candle, to stretching a beefsteak so as to last her for two days' dinners, and perhaps to making her own bed. Now, there would not be the slightest touch of romance in a visit to Lady Milborough's house in Eccleston Square, at the end of July. Lady Rowley, however, was of a different opinion, and spoke her mind plainly. 'Nora, my dear, don't be a fool. A young lady like you can't go and live in lodgings by herself. All manner of things would be said. And this is such a very kind offer! You must accept it for Hugh's sake. I have already said that you would accept it.'

'But she will be going out of town.'

'She will stay till you can go to Monkhams if Emily is not back before then. She knows all about Emily's affairs; and if she does come back, which I doubt, poor thing, Lady Milborough and you will be able to judge whether you should go to her.' So it was settled, and Nora's Bohemian Castle in the Air fell into shatters.

The few remaining days before the departure to Southampton passed quickly, but yet sadly. Sir Marmaduke had come to England expecting pleasure and with that undefined idea which men so employed always have on their return home that something will turn up which will make their going back to that same banishment unnecessary. What Governor of Hong-Kong, what Minister to Bogota, what General of the Forces at the Gold Coast, ever left the scene of his official or military labours without a hope, which was almost an expectation, that a grateful country would do something better for him before the period of his return should have arrived? But a grateful country was doing nothing better for Sir Marmaduke, and an ungrateful Secretary of State at the Colonial Office would not extend the term during which he could regard himself as absent on special service. How thankful he had been when first the tidings reached him that he was to come home at the expense of the Crown, and without diminution of his official income! He had now been in England for five months, with a per diem allowance, with his very cabs paid for him, and he was discontented, sullen, and with nothing to comfort him but his official grievance, because he could not be allowed to extend his period of special service more than two months beyond the time at which those special services were in truth ended! There had been a change of Ministry in the last month, and he had thought that a Conservative Secretary of State would have been kinder to him. 'The Duke says I can stay three months with leave of absence and have half my pay stopped. I wonder whether it ever enters into his august mind that even a Colonial Governor must eat and drink.' It was thus he expressed his great grievance to his wife. 'The Duke,' however, had been as inexorable as his predecessor, and Sir Rowley, with his large family, was too wise to remain to the detriment of his pocket. In the meantime the clerks in the office, who had groaned in spirit over the ignorance displayed in his evidence before the committee, were whispering among themselves that he ought not to be sent back to his seat of government at all.

Lady Rowley also was disappointed and unhappy. She had expected so much pleasure from her visit to her daughter, and she had received so little! Emily's condition was very sad, but in her heart of hearts perhaps she groaned more bitterly over all that Nora had lost, than she did over the real sorrows of her elder child. To have had the cup at her lip, and then not to have tasted it! And she had the solace of no communion in this sorrow. She had accepted Hugh Stanbury as her son-in-law, and not for worlds would she now say a word against him to any one. She had already taken him to her heart, and she loved him. But to have had it almost within her grasp to have had a lord, the owner of Monkhams, for her son-in-law! Poor Lady Rowley!

Sophie and Lucy, too, were returning to their distant and dull banishment without any realisation of their probable but unexpressed ambition. They made no complaint, but yet it was hard on them that their sister's misfortune should have prevented them from going almost to a single dance. Poor Sophie and poor Lucy! They must go, and we shall hear no more about them. It was thought well that Nora should not go down with them to Southampton. What good would her going do? 'God bless you, my darling,' said the mother, as she held her child in her arms.

'Good-bye, dear mamma.'

'Give my best love to Hugh, and tell him that I pray him with my last word to be good to you.' Even then she was thinking of Lord Peterborough, but the memory of what might have been was buried deep in her mind.

'Nora, tell me all about it,' said Lucy.

'There will be nothing to tell,' said Nora.

'Tell it all the same,' said Lucy. 'And bring Hugh out to write a book of travels about the Mandarins. Nobody has ever written a book about the Mandarins.' So they parted; and when Sir Marmaduke and his party were taken off in two cabs to the Waterloo Station, Nora was taken in one cab to Eccleston Square.

It may be doubted whether any old lady since the world began ever did a more thoroughly Christian and friendly act that this which was now being done by Lady Milborough. It was the end of July, and she would already have been down in Dorsetshire, but for her devotion to this good deed. For, in truth, what she was doing was not occasioned by any express love for Nora Rowley. Nora Rowley was all very well, but Nora Rowley towards her had been flippant, impatient, and, indeed, not always so civil as a young lady should be to the elderly friends of her married sister. But to Lady Milborough it had seemed to be quite terrible that a young girl should be left alone in the world, without anybody to take care of her. Young ladies, according to her views of life, were fragile plants that wanted much nursing before they could be allowed to be planted out in the gardens of the world as married women. When she heard from Lady Rowley that Nora was engaged to marry Hugh Stanbury, 'You know all about Lord Peterborough, Lady Milborough; but it is no use going back to that now is it? And Mr Stanbury has behaved so exceedingly well in regard to poor Louis,' when Lady Milborough heard this, and heard also that Nora was talking of going to live by herself in lodgings! she swore to herself, like a goodly Christian woman, as she was, that such a thing must not be. Eccleston Square in July and August is not pleasant, unless it be to an inhabitant who is interested in the fag-end of the parliamentary session. Lady Milborough had no interest in politics, had not much interest even in seeing the social season out to its dregs. She ordinarily remained in London till the beginning or middle of July, because the people with whom she lived were in the habit of doing so, but as soon as ever she had fixed the date of her departure, that day to her was a day of release. On this occasion the day had been fixed and it was unfixed, and changed, and postponed, because it was manifest to Lady Milborough that she could do good by remaining for another fortnight. When she made the offer she said nothing of her previous arrangements. 'Lady Rowley, let her come to me. As soon as her friend Lady Peterborough is at Monkhams, she can go there.'

Thus it was that Nora found herself established in Eccleston Square. As she took her place in Lady Milborough's drawing-room, she remembered well a certain day, now two years ago, when she had first heard of the glories of Monkhams in that very house. Lady Milborough, as good-natured then as she was now, had brought Mr Glascock and Nora together, simply because she had heard that the gentleman admired the young lady. Nora, in her pride, had resented this as interference, had felt that the thing had been done, and, though she had valued the admiration of the man, had ridiculed the action of the woman. As she thought of it now she was softened by gratitude. She had not on that occasion been suited with a husband, but she had gained a friend. 'My dear,' said Lady Milborough, as at her request Nora took off her hat, 'I am afraid that the parties are mostly over, that is, those I go to; but we will drive out every day, and the time won't be so very long.'

'It won't be long for me, Lady Milborough, but I cannot but know how terribly I am putting you out.'

'I am never put out, Miss Rowley,' said the old lady, 'as long as I am made to think that what I do is taken in good part.'

'Indeed, indeed it shall be taken in good part,' said Nora 'indeed it shall.' And she swore a solemn silent vow of friendship for the dear old woman.

Then there came letters and telegrams from Chambery, Dijon, and Paris, and the joint expedition in search of the cottage was made to Twickenham. It was astonishing how enthusiastic and how loving the elder and the younger lady were together before the party from Italy had arrived in England. Nora had explained everything about herself; how impossible it had been for her not to love Hugh Stanbury; how essential it had been for her happiness and self-esteem that she should refuse Mr Glascock; how terrible had been the tragedy of her sister's marriage. Lady Milborough spoke of the former subject with none of Lady Rowley's enthusiasm, but still with an evident partiality for her own rank, which almost aroused Nora to indignant eloquence. Lady Milborough was contented to acknowledge that Nora might be right, seeing that her heart was so firmly fixed; but she was clearly of opinion that Mr Glascock, being Mr Glascock, had possessed a better right to the prize in question than could have belonged to any man who had no recognised position in the world. Seeing that her heart had been given away, Nora was no doubt right not to separate her hand from her heart; but Lady Milborough was of opinion that young ladies ought to have their hearts under better control, so that the men entitled to the prizes should get them. It was for the welfare of England at large that the eldest sons of good families should marry the sweetest, prettiest, brightest, and most lovable girls of their age. It is a doctrine on behalf of which very much may be said.

On that other matter, touching Emily Trevelyan, Lady Milborough frankly owned that she had seen early in the day that he was the one most in fault. 'I must say, my dear,' she said, 'that I very greatly dislike your friend, Colonel Osborne.'

'I am sure that he meant not the slightest harm, no more than she did.'

'He was old enough, and ought to have known better. And when the first hint of an uneasiness in the mind of Louis was suggested to him, his feelings as a gentleman should have prompted him to remove himself. Let the suspicion have been ever so absurd, he should have removed himself. Instead of that, he went after her into Devonshire.'

'He went to see other friends, Lady Milborough.'

'I hope it may have been so, I hope it may have been so. But he should have cut off his hand before he rang at the door of the house in which she was living. You will understand, my dear, that I acquit your sister altogether. I did so all through, and said the same to poor Louis when he came to me. But Colonel Osborne should have known better. Why did he write to her? Why did he go to St. Diddulph's? Why did he let it be thought that that she was especially his friend. Oh dear; oh dear; oh dear! I am afraid he is a very bad man.'

'We had known him so long, Lady Milborough.'

'I wish you had never known him at all. Poor Louis! If be had only done what I told him at first, all might have been well. "Go to Naples, with your wife," I said. "Go to Naples." If he had gone to Naples, there would have been no journeys to Siena, no living at Casalunga, no separation. But he didn't seem to see it in the same light. Poor dear Louis. I wish he had gone to Naples when I told him.'

While they were going backwards and forwards, looking at the cottage at Twickenham and trying to make things comfortable there for the sick man, Lady Milborough hinted to Nora that it might be distasteful to Trevelyan, in his present condition, to have even a sister-in-law staying in the house with him. There was a little chamber which Nora had appropriated to herself, and at first it seemed to be taken for granted that she should remain there at least till the 10th of August, on which day Lady Peterborough had signified that she and her husband would be ready to receive their visitor. But Lady Milborough slept on the suggestion, and on the next morning hinted her disapprobation. 'You shall take them down in the carriage, and their luggage can follow in a cab, but the carriage can bring you back. You will see how things are then.'

'Dear Lady Milborough, you would go out of town at once if I left you.'

'And I shall not go out of town if you don't leave me, What difference does it make to an old woman like me? I have got no lover coming to look for me, and all I have to do is to tell my daughter-in-law that I shall not be there for another week or so. Augusta is very glad to have me, but she is the wisest woman in the world, and can get on very well without me.'

'And as I am the silliest, I cannot.'

'You shall put it in that way if you like it, my dear. Girls in your position often do want assistance. I dare say you think me very straight-laced, but I am quite sure Mr Stanbury will be grateful to me. As you are to be married from Monkhams, it will be quite well that you should pass thither through my house as an intermediate resting-place, after leaving your father and mother.' By all which, Lady Milborough intended to express an opinion that the value of the article which Hugh Stanbury would receive at the altar would be enhanced by the distinguished purity of the hands through which it had passed before it came into his possession, in which opinion she was probably right as regarded the price put upon the article by the world at large, though it may perhaps be doubted whether the recipient himself would be of the same opinion.

'I hope you know that I am grateful, whatever he may be,' said Nora, after a pause.

'I think that you take it as it is meant, and that makes me quite comfortable.'

'Lady Milborough, I shall love you for ever and ever. I don't think I ever knew anybody so good as you are or so nice.'

'Then I shall be more than comfortable,' said Lady Milborough. After that there was an embrace, and the thing was settled.

CHAPTER XCV. TREVELYAN BACK IN ENGLAND

Nora, with Lady Milborough's carriage, and Lady Milborough's coach and footman, and with a cab ready for the luggage close behind the carriage, was waiting at the railway station when the party from Dover arrived. She soon saw Hugh upon the platform, and ran to him with her news. They had not a word to say to each other of themselves, so anxious were they both respecting Trevelyan. 'We got a bed-carriage for him at Dover,' said Hugh; 'and I think he has borne the journey pretty well but he feels the heat almost as badly as in Italy. You will hardly know him when you see him.' Then, when the rush of passengers was gone, Trevelyan was brought out by Hugh and the courier, and placed in Lady Milborough's carriage. He just smiled as his eye fell upon Nora, but he did not even put out his hand to greet her.

'I am to go in the carriage with him,' said his wife.

'Of course you are, and so will I and Louey. I think there will be room: it is so large. There is a cab for all the things. Dear Emily, I am so glad to see you.'

'Dearest Nora! I shall be able to speak to you by-and-by, but you must not be angry with me now. How good you have been.'

'Has not she been good? I don't understand about the cottage. It belongs to some friend of hers; and I have not been able to say a word about the rent. It is so nice and looks upon the river. I hope that he will like it.'

'You will be with us?'

'Not just at first. Lady Milborough thinks I had better not, that he will like it better. I will come down almost every day, and will stay if you think he will like it.'

These few words were said while the men were putting Trevelyan into the carriage. And then another arrangement was made. Hugh hired a second cab, in which he and the courier made a part of the procession; and so they all went to Twickenham together. Hugh had not yet learned that he would be rewarded by coming back alone with Nora in the carriage.

The cottage by the River Thames, which, as far as the party knew, was nameless, was certainly very much better than the house on the top of the hill at Casalunga. And now, at last, the wife would sleep once more under the same roof with her husband, and the separation would be over. 'I suppose that is the Thames,' said Trevelyan; and they were nearly the only words he spoke in Nora's hearing that evening. Before she started on her return journey, the two sisters were together for a few minutes, and each told her own budget of news in short, broken fragments. There was not much to tell. 'He is so weak,' said Mrs Trevelyan, 'that he can do literally nothing. He can hardly speak. When we give him wine, he will say a few words, and his mind seems then to be less astray than it was. I have told him just simply that it was all my doing, that I have been in fault all through, and every now and then he will say a word, to shew me that he remembers that I have confessed.'

'My poor Emily!'

'It was better so. What does it all matter? He had suffered so, that I would have said worse than that to give him relief. The pride has gone out of me so, that I do not regard what anybody may say. Of course, it will be said that I went astray, and that he forgave me.'

'Nobody will say that, dearest; nobody. Lady Milborough is quite aware how it all was.'

'What does it signify? There are things in life worse even than a bad name.'

'But he does not think it?'

'Nora, his mind is a mystery to me. I do not know what is in it. Sometimes I fancy that all facts have been forgotten, and that he merely wants the childish gratification of being assured that he is the master. Then, again, there come moments, in which I feel sure that suspicion is lurking within him, that he is remembering the past, and guarding against the future. When he came into this house, a quarter of an hour ago, he was fearful lest there was a mad doctor lurking about to pounce on him. I can see in his eye that he had some such idea. He hardly notices Louey though there was a time, even at Casalunga, when he would not let the child out of his sight.'

'What will you do now?'

'I will try to do my duty, that is all.'

'But you will have a doctor?'

'Of course. He was content to see one in Paris, though he would not let me be present. Hugh saw the gentleman afterwards, and he seemed to think that the body was worse than the mind.' Then Nora told her the name of a doctor whom Lady Milborough had suggested, and took her departure along with Hugh in the carriage.

In spite of all the sorrow that they had witnessed and just left, their journey up to London was very pleasant. Perhaps there is no period so pleasant among all the pleasant periods of love-making as that in which the intimacy between the lovers is so assured, and the coming event so near, as to produce and to endure conversation about the ordinary little matters of life—what can be done with the limited means at their mutual disposal; how that life shall be begun which they are to lead together; what idea each has of the other's duties; what each can do for the other; what each will renounce for the other. There was a true sense of the delight of intimacy in the girl who declared that she had never loved her lover so well as when she told him how many pairs of stockings she had got. It is very sweet to gaze at the stars together; and it is sweet to sit out among the haycocks. The reading of poetry together, out of the same book, with brows all close, and arms all mingled, is very sweet. The pouring out of the whole heart in written words, which the writer knows would be held to be ridiculous by any eyes, and any ears, and any sense, but the eyes and ears and sense of the dear one to whom they are sent, is very sweet; but for the girl who has made a shirt for the man that she loves, there has come a moment in the last stitch of it, sweeter than any that stars, haycocks, poetry, or superlative epithets have produced. Nora Rowley had never as yet been thus useful on behalf of Hugh Stanbury. Had she done so, she might perhaps have been happier even than she was during this journey, but, without the shirt, it was one of the happiest moments of her life. There was nothing now to separate them but their own prudential scruples and of them it must be acknowledged that Hugh Stanbury had very few. According to his shewing, he was as well provided for matrimony as the gentleman in the song, who came out to woo his bride on a rainy night. In live stock he was not so well provided as the Irish gentleman to whom we allude; but in regard to all other provisions for comfortable married life, he had, or at a moment's notice could have, all that was needed. Nora could live just where she pleased—not exactly in Whitehall Gardens or Belgrave Square; but the New Road, Lupus Street, Montague Place, the North Bank, or Kennington Oval, with all their surrounding crescents, terraces, and rows, offered, according to him, a choice so wide, either for lodgings or small houses, that their only embarrassment was in their riches. He had already insured his life for a thousand pounds, and, after paying yearly for that, and providing a certain surplus for saving, five hundred a year was the income on which they were to commence the world. 'Of course, I wish it were five thousand for your sake,' he said; 'and I wish I were a Cabinet Minister, or a duke, or a brewer; but, even in heaven, you know all the angels can't be archangels.' Nora assured him that she would be quite content with virtues simply angelic. 'I hope you like mutton-chops and potatoes; I do,' he said. Then she told him of her ambition about the beef-steak, acknowledging that, as it must now be shared between two, the glorious idea of putting a part of it away in a cupboard must be abandoned. 'I don't believe in beef-steaks,' he said. 'A beef-steak may mean anything. At our club, a beef-steak is a sumptuous and expensive luxury. Now, a mutton-chop means something definite, and must be economical.'

'Then we will have the mutton-chops at home,' said Nora, 'and you shall go to your club for the beef-steak.'

When they reached Eccleston Square, Nora insisted on taking Hugh Stanbury up to Lady Milborough. It was in vain that he pleaded that he had come all the way from Dover on a very dusty day, all the way from Dover, including a journey in a Hansom cab to Twickenham and back, without washing his hands and face. Nora insisted that Lady Milborough was such a dear, good, considerate creature, that she would understand all that, and Hugh was taken into her presence. 'I am delighted to see you, Mr Stanbury,' said the old lady, 'and hope you will think that Nora is in good keeping.'

'She has been telling me how very kind you have been to her. I do not know where she could have bestowed herself if you had not received her.'

'There, Nora I told you he would say so. I won't tell tales, Mr Stanbury; but she had all manner of wild plans which I knew you wouldn't approve. But she is very amiable, and if she will only submit to you as well as she does to me.'

'I don't mean to submit to him at all, Lady Milborough, of course not. I am going to marry for liberty.'

'My dear, what you say, you say in joke; but a great many young women of the present day do, I really believe, go up to the altar and pronounce their marriage vows, with the simple idea that as soon as they have done so, they are to have their own way in everything. And then people complain that young men won't marry! Who can wonder at it?'

'I don't think the young men think much about the obedience,' said Nora.'Some marry for money, and some for love. But I don't think they marry to get a slave.'

'What do you say, Mr Stanbury?' asked the old lady.

'I can only assure you that I shan't marry for money,' said he.

Two or three days after this Nora left her friend in Eccleston Square, and domesticated herself for awhile with her sister. Mrs Trevelyan declared that such an arrangement would be comfortable for her, and that it was very desirable now, as Nora would so soon be beyond her reach. Then Lady Milborough was enabled to go to Dorsetshire, which she did not do, however, till she had presented Nora with the veil which she was to wear on the occasion of her wedding. 'Of course I cannot see it, my dear, as it is to take place at Monkhams; but you must write and tell me the day and I will think of you. And you, when you put on the veil, must think of me.' So they parted, and Nora knew that she had made a friend for life.

When she first took her place in the house at Twickenham as a resident, Trevelyan did not take much notice of her but, after awhile, he would say a few words to her, especially when it might chance that she was with him in her sister's absence. He would speak of dear Emily, and poor Emily, and shake his head slowly, and talk of the pity of it. 'The pity of it, Iago; oh, the pity of it,' he said once. The allusion to her was so terrible that she almost burst out in anger, as she would have done formerly. She almost told him that he had been as wrong throughout as was the jealous husband in the play whose words he quoted, and that his jealousy, if continued, was likely to be as tragical. But she restrained herself, and kept close to her needle, making, let us hope, an auspicious garment for Hugh Stanbury. 'She has seen it now,' he continued; 'she has seen it now.' Still she went on with her hemming in silence. It certainly could not be her duty to upset at a word all that her sister had achieved. 'You know that she has confessed?' he asked.

'Pray, pray do not talk about it, Louis.'

'I think you ought to know,' he said. Then she rose from her seat and left the room. She could not stand it, even though he were mad, even though he were dying!

She went to her sister and repeated what had been said. 'You had better not notice it,' said Emily. 'It is only a proof of what I told you. There are times in which his mind is as active as ever it was, but it is active in so terrible a direction!'

'I cannot sit and hear it. And what am I to say when he asks me a question as he did just now? He said that you had confessed.'

'So I have. Do none confess but the guilty? What is all that we have read about the Inquisition and the old tortures? I have had to learn that torturing has not gone out of the world, that is all.'

'I must go away if he says the same thing to me so again.'

'That is nonsense, Nora. If I can bear it, cannot you? Would you have me drive him into violence again by disputing with him on such a subject?'

'But he may recover and then he will remember what you have said.'

'If he recovers altogether he will suspect nothing. I must take my chance of that. You cannot suppose that I have not thought about it. I have often sworn to myself that though the world should fall around me, nothing should make me acknowledge that I had ever been untrue to my duty as a married woman, either in deed, or word, or thought. I have no doubt that the poor wretches who were tortured in their cells used to make the same resolutions as to their confessions. But yet, when their nails were dragged out of them, they would own to anything. My nails have been dragged out, and I have been willing to confess anything. When he talks of the pity of it, of course I know what he means. There has been something, some remainder of a feeling, which has still kept him from asking me that question. May God, in his mercy, continue to him that feeling!'

'But you would answer truly?'

'How can I say what I might answer when the torturer is at my nails? If you knew how great was the difficulty to get him away from that place in Italy and bring him here; and what it was to feel that one was bound to stay near him, and that yet one was impotent, and to know that even that refuge must soon cease for him, and that he might have gone out and died on the road-side, or have done anything which the momentary strength of madness might have dictated—if you could understand all this, you would not be surprised at my submitting to any degradation which would help to bring him here.'

Stanbury was often down at the cottage, and Nora could discuss the matter better with him than with her sister. And Stanbury could learn more thoroughly from the physician who was now attending Trevelyan what was the state of the sick man, than Emily could do. According to the doctor's idea there was more of ailment in the body than in the mind. He admitted that his patient's thoughts had been forced to dwell on one subject till they had become distorted, untrue, jaundiced, and perhaps mono-maniacal; but he seemed to doubt whether there had ever been a time at which it could have been decided that Trevelyan was so mad as to make it necessary that the law should interfere to take care of him. A man, so argued the doctor, need not be mad because he is jealous, even though his jealousy be ever so absurd. And Trevelyan, in his jealousy, had done nothing cruel, nothing wasteful, nothing infamous. In all this Nora was very little inclined to agree with the doctor, and thought nothing could be more infamous than Trevelyan's conduct at the present moment unless, indeed, he could be screened from infamy by that plea of madness. But then there was more behind. Trevelyan had been so wasted by the kind of life which he had led, and possessed by nature stamina so insufficient to resist such debility, that it was very doubtful whether he would not sink altogether before he could be made to begin to rise. But one thing was clear. He should be contradicted in nothing. If he chose to say that the moon was made of green cheese, let it be conceded to him that the moon was made of green cheese. Should he make any other assertion equally removed from the truth, let it not be contradicted. Who would oppose a man with one foot in the grave?

'Then, Hugh, the sooner I am at Monkhams the better,' said Nora, who had again been subjected to innuendoes which had been unendurable to her. This was on the 7th of August, and it still wanted three days to that on which the journey to Monkhams was to be made.

'He never says anything to me on the subject,' said Hugh.

'Because you have made him afraid of you. I almost think that Emily and the doctor are wrong in their treatment, and that it would be better to stand up to him and tell him the truth.' But the three days passed away, and Nora was not driven to any such vindication of her sister's character towards her sister's husband.

CHAPTER XCVI. MONKHAMS

On the 10th of August Nora Rowley left the cottage by the river-side at Twickenham, and went down to Monkhams. The reader need hardly be told that Hugh brought her up from Twickenham and sent her off in the railway carriage. They agreed that no day could be fixed for their marriage till something further should be known of Trevelyan's state. While he was in his present condition such a marriage could not have been other than very sad. Nora, when she left the cottage, was still very bitter against her brother-in-law, quoting the doctor's opinion as to his sanity, and expressing her own as to his conduct under that supposition.

She also believed that he would rally in health, and was therefore, on that account, less inclined to pity him than was his wife. Emily Trevelyan of course saw more of him than did her sister, and understood better how possible it was that a man might be in such a condition as to be neither mad nor sane—not mad, so that all power over his own actions need be taken from him; nor sane, so that he must be held to be accountable for his words and thoughts. Trevelyan did nothing, and attempted to do nothing, that could injure his wife and child. He submitted himself to medical advice. He did not throw away his money. He had no Bozzle now waiting at his heels. He was generally passive in his wife's hands as to all outward things. He was not violent in rebuke, nor did he often allude to their past unhappiness. But he still maintained, by a word spoken every now and then, that he had been right throughout in his contest with his wife and that his wife had at last acknowledged that it was so. She never contradicted him, and he became bolder and bolder in his assertions, endeavouring on various occasions to obtain some expression of an assent from Nora. But Nora would not assent, and he would scowl at her, saying words, both in her presence and behind her back, which implied that she was his enemy. 'Why not yield to him?' her sister said the day before she went. 'I have yielded, and your doing so cannot make it worse.'

'I can't do it. It would be false. It is better that I should go away. I cannot pretend to agree with him, when I know that his mind is working altogether under a delusion.' When the hour for her departure came, and Hugh was waiting for her, she thought that it would be better that she should go, without seeing Trevelyan. 'There will only be more anger,' she pleaded. But her sister would not be contented that she should leave the house in this fashion, and urged at last, with tears running down her cheeks, that this might possibly be the last interview between them.

'Say a word to him in kindness before you leave us,' said Mrs Trevelyan. Then Nora went up to her brother-in-law's bed-side, and told him that she was going, and expressed a hope that he might be stronger when she returned. And as she did so she put her hand upon the bed-side, intending to press his in token of affection. But his face was turned from her, and he seemed to take no notice of her. 'Louis,' said his wife, 'Nora is going to Monkhams. You will say good-bye to her before she goes?'

'If she be not my enemy, I will,' said he.

'I have never been your enemy, Louis,' said Nora, 'and certainly I am not now.'

'She had better go,' he said. 'It is very little more that I expect of any one in this world, but I will recognise no one as my friend who will not acknowledge that I have been sinned against during the last two years, sinned against cruelly and utterly.' Emily, who was standing at the bed-head, shuddered as she heard this, but made no reply. Nor did Nora speak again, but crept silently out of the room and in half a minute her sister followed her.

'I feared how it would be,' said Nora.

'We can only do our best. God knows that I try to do mine.'

'I do not think you will ever see him again,' said Hugh to her in the train.

'Would you have had me act otherwise? It is not that it would have been a lie. I would not have minded that to ease the shattered feelings of one so infirm and suffering as he. In dealing with mad people I suppose one must be false. But I should have been accusing her; and it may be that he will get well, and it might be that he would then remember what I had said.'

At the station near Monkhams she was met by Lady Peterborough in the carriage. A tall footman in livery came on to the platform to shew her the way and to look after her luggage, and she could not fail to remember that the man might have been her own servant, instead of being the servant of her who now sat in Lord Peterborough's carriage. And when she saw the carriage, and her ladyship's great bay horses, and the glittering harness, and the respectably responsible coachman, and the arms on the panel, she smiled to herself at the sight of these first outward manifestations of the rank and wealth of the man who had once been her lover. There are men who look as though they were the owners of bay horses and responsible coachmen and family blazons, from whose outward personal appearance, demeanour, and tone of voice, one would expect a following of liveries and a magnificence of belongings; but Mr Glascock had by no means been such a man. It had suited his taste to keep these things in abeyance, and to place his pride in the oaks and elms of his park rather than in any of those appanages of grandeur which a man may carry about with him. He could talk of his breed of sheep on an occasion, but he never talked of his horses; and though he knew his position and all its glories as well as any nobleman in England, he was ever inclined to hang back a little in going out of a room, and to bear himself as though he were a small personage in the world. Some perception of all this came across Nora's mind as she saw the equipage, and tried to reflect, at a moment's notice, whether the case might have been different with her, had Mr Glascock worn a little of his tinsel outside when she first met him. Of course she told herself that had he worn it all on the outside, and carried it ever so gracefully, it could have made no difference.

It was very plain, however, that, though Mr Glascock did not like bright feathers for himself, he chose that his wife should wear them. Nothing could be prettier than the way in which Caroline Spalding, whom we first saw as she was about to be stuck into the interior of the diligence at St. Michael, now filled her carriage as Lady Peterborough. The greeting between them was very affectionate, and there was a kiss in the carriage, even though the two pretty hats, perhaps, suffered something. 'We are so glad to have you at last,' said Lady Peterborough. 'Of course we are very quiet; but you won't mind that.' Nora declared that no house could be too quiet for her, and then said something of the melancholy scene which she had just left. 'And no time is fixed for your own marriage? But of course it has not been possible. And why should you be in a hurry? We quite understand that this is to be your home till everything has arranged itself.' There was a drive of four or five miles before they reached the park gates, and nothing could be kinder or more friendly than was the new peeress; but Nora told herself that there was no forgetting that her friend was a peeress. She would not be so ill-conditioned as to suggest to herself that her friend patronised her and, indeed, had she done so, the suggestion would have been false; but she could not rid herself of a certain sensation of external inferiority, and of a feeling that the superiority ought to be on her side, as all this might have been hers only that she had not thought it worth her while to accept it. As these ideas came into her mind, she hated herself for entertaining them; and yet, come they would. While she was talking about her emblematic beef-steak with Hugh, she had no regret, no uneasiness, no conception that any state of life could be better for her than that state in which an emblematic beef-steak was of vital importance; but she could not bring her mind to the same condition of unalloyed purity while sitting with Lady Peterborough in Lord Peterborough's carriage. And for her default in this respect she hated herself.

'This is the beginning of the park,' said her friend.

'And where is the house?'

354   Anthony Trollope

'You can't see the house for ever so far yet; it is two miles off. There is about a mile before you come to the gates, and over a mile afterwards. One has a sort of feeling when one is in that one can't get out, it is so big.' In so speaking, it was Lady Peterborough's special endeavour to state without a boast facts which were indifferent, but which must be stated.

'It is very magnificent,' said Nora. There was in her voice the slightest touch of sarcasm, which she would have given the world not to have uttered, but it had been irrepressible.

Lady Peterborough understood it instantly, and forgave it, not attributing to it more than its true meaning, acknowledging to herself that it was natural. 'Dear Nora,' she said not knowing what to say, blushing as she spoke 'the magnificence is nothing; but the man's love is everything.'

Nora shook herself, and determined that she would behave well. The effort should be made, and the required result should be produced by it. 'The magnificence, as an adjunct, is a great deal,' she said; 'and for his sake, I hope that you enjoy it.'

'Of course I enjoy it.'

'Wallachia's teachings and preachings have all been thrown to the wind, I hope.'

'Not quite all. Poor dear Wally! I got a letter from her the other day, which she began by saying that she would attune her correspondence to my changed condition in life. I understood the reproach so thoroughly! And, when she told me little details of individual men and women, and of things she had seen, and said not a word about the rights of women, or even of politics generally, I felt that I was a degraded creature in her sight. But, though you laugh at her, she did me good and will do good to others. Here we are inside Monkhams, and now you must look at the avenue.'

Nora was now rather proud of herself. She had made the effort, and it had been successful; and she felt that she could speak naturally, and express her thoughts honestly. 'I remember his telling me about the avenue the first time I ever saw him, and here it is. I did not think then that I should ever live to see the glories of Monkhams. Does it go all the way like this to the house?'

'Not quite; where you see the light at the end, the road turns to the right, and the house is just before you. There are great iron gates, and terraces, and wondrous paraphernalia before you get up to the door. I can tell you Monkhams is quite a wonder. I have to shut myself up every Wednesday morning, and hand the house over to Mrs Crutch, the housekeeper, who comes out in a miraculous brown silk gown, to shew it to visitors. On other days, you'll find Mrs Crutch quite civil and useful, but on Wednesdays, she is majestic. Charles always goes off among his sheep on that day, and I shut myself up with a pile of books in a little room. You will have to be imprisoned with me. I do so long to peep at the visitors.'

'And I dare say they want to peep at you.'

'I proposed at first to shew them round myself, but Charles wouldn't let me.'

'It would have broken Mrs Crutch's heart.'

'That's what Charles said. He thinks that Mrs Crutch tells them that I'm locked up somewhere, and that that gives a zest to the search. Some people from Nottingham once did break into old Lady Peterborough's room, and the shew was stopped for a year. There was such a row about it! It prevented Charles coming up for the county. But he wouldn't have got in; and therefore it was lucky, and saved money.'

By this time Nora was quite at her ease; but still there was before her the other difficulty, of meeting Lord Peterborough. They were driven out of the avenue, and round to the right, and through the iron gate, and up to the huge front door. There, upon the top step, was standing Lord Peterborough, with a billycock hat and a very old shooting coat, and nankeen trousers, which were considerably too short for him. It was one of the happinesses of his life to dress just as he pleased as he went about his own place; and it certainly was his pleasure to wear older clothes than any one else in his establishment. 'Miss Rowley,' he said, coming forward to give her a hand out of the carriage, 'I am delighted that you should see Monkhams at last.'

'You see I have kept you to your promise. Caroline has been telling me everything about it; but she is not quite a complete guide as yet. She does not know where the seven oaks are. Do you remember telling me of the seven oaks?'

'Of course I do. They are five miles off at Clatton farm, Carry. I don't think you have been near Clatton yet. We will ride there tomorrow.' And thus Nora Rowley was made at home at Monkhams.

She was made at home, and after a week or two she was very happy. She soon perceived that her host was a perfect gentleman, and as such, a man to be much loved. She had probably never questioned the fact, whether Mr Glascock was a gentleman or not, and now she did not analyse it. It probably never occurred to her, even at the present time, to say to herself that he was certainly that thing, so impossible of definition, and so capable of recognition; but she knew that she had to do with one whose presence was always pleasant to her, whose words and acts towards her extorted her approbation, whose thoughts seemed to her to be always good and manly. Of course she had not loved him, because she had previously known Hugh Stanbury. There could be no comparison between the two men. There was a brightness about Hugh which Lord Peterborough could not rival. Otherwise, except for this reason, it seemed to her to be impossible that any young woman should fail to love Lord Peterborough when asked to do so.

About the middle of September there came a very happy time for her, when Hugh was asked down to shoot partridges, in the doing of which, however, all his brightness did not bring him near in excellence to his host. Lord Peterborough had been shooting partridges all his life, and shot them with a precision which excited Hugh's envy. To own the truth, Stanbury did not shoot well, and was treated rather with scorn by the gamekeeper; but in other respects he spent three or four of the happiest days of his life. He had his work to do, and after the second day over the stubbles, declared that the exigencies of the *D. R.* were too severe to enable him to go out with his gun again; but those rambles about the park with Nora, for which, among the exigencies of the *D. R.*, he did find opportunity, were never to be forgotten.

'Of course I remember that it might have been mine,' she said, sitting with him under an old, hollow, withered sloping stump of an oak, which still, however, had sufficient of a head growing from one edge of the trunk to give them the shade they wanted; 'and if you wish me to own to regrets I will.'

'It would kill me, I think, if you did; and yet I cannot get it out of my head that if it had not been for me your rank and position in life might have been so so suitable to you.'

'No, Hugh; there you're wrong. I have thought about it a good deal, too; and I know very well that the cold beef-steak in the cupboard is the thing for me. Caroline will do very well here. She looks like a peeress, and bears her honours grandly; but they will never harden her. I, too, could have been magnificent with fine feathers. Most birds are equal to so much as that. I fancy that I could have looked the part of the fine English lady, and could have patronised clergymen's wives in the country, could have held my own among my peers in London, and could have kept Mrs Crutch in order; but it would have hardened me, and I should have learned to think that to be a lady of fashion was everything.'

'I do not believe a bit of it.'

'It is better as it is, Hugh for me at least. I had always a sort of conviction that it would be better, though I had a longing to play the other part. Then you came, and you have saved me. Nevertheless, it is very nice, Hugh, to have the oaks to sit under.' Stanbury declared that it was very nice.

But still nothing was settled about the wedding. Trevelyan's condition was so uncertain that it was very difficult to settle anything. Though nothing was said on the subject between Stanbury and Mrs Trevelyan, and nothing written between Nora and her sister, it could not but be remembered that should Trevelyan die, his widow would require a home with them. They were deterred from choosing a house by this reflection, and were deterred from naming a day also by the consideration that were they to do so, Trevelyan's state might still probably prevent it. But this was arranged, that if Trevelyan lived through the winter, or even if he should not live, their marriage should not be postponed beyond the end of March. Till that time Lord Peterborough would remain at Monkhams, and it was understood that Nora's invitation extended to that period.

'If my wife does not get tired of you, I shall not,' Lord Peterborough said to Nora. 'The thing is that when you do go we shall miss you so terribly.' In September, too, there happened another event which took Stanbury to Exeter, and all needful particulars as to that event shall be narrated in the next chapter.

CHAPTER XCVII. MRS BROOKE BURGESS

It may be doubted whether there was a happier young woman in England than Dorothy Stanbury when that September came which was to make her the wife of Mr Brooke Burgess, the new partner in the firm of Cropper and Burgess. Her early aspirations in life had been so low, and of late there had come upon her such a succession of soft showers of success, mingled now and then with slight threatenings of storms which had passed away, that the Close at Exeter seemed to her to have become a very Paradise. Her aunt's temper had sometimes been to her as the threat of a storm, and there had been the Gibson marriage treaty, and the short-lived opposition to the other marriage treaty which had seemed to her to be so very preferable; but everything had gone at last as though she had been Fortune's favourite; and now had come this beautiful arrangement about Cropper and Burgess, which would save her from being carried away to live among strangers in London! When she first became known to us on her coming to Exeter, in compliance with her aunt's suggestion, she was timid, silent, and altogether without self-reliance. Even they who knew her best had never guessed that she possessed a keen sense of humour, a nice appreciation of character, and a quiet reticent wit of her own, under that staid and frightened demeanour. Since her engagement with Brooke Burgess it seemed to those who watched her that her character had become changed, as does that of a flower when it opens itself in its growth. The sweet gifts of nature within became visible, the petals sprang to view, and the leaves spread themselves, and the sweet scent was felt upon the air. Had she remained at Nuncombe, it is probable that none would ever have known her but her sister. It was necessary to this flower that it should be warmed by the sun of life, and strengthened by the breezes of opposition, and filled by the showers of companionship, before it could become aware of its own loveliness. Dorothy was one who, had she remained ever unseen in the retirement of her mother's village cottage, would have lived and died ignorant of even her own capabilities for enjoyment. She had not dreamed that she could win a man's love—had hardly dreamed till she had lived at Exeter that she had love of her own to give back in return. She had not known that she could be firm in her own opinion, that she could laugh herself and cause others to laugh, that she could be a lady and know that other women were not so, that she had good looks of her own and could be very happy when told of them by lips that she loved. The flower that blows the quickest is never the sweetest. The fruit that ripens tardily has ever the finest flavour. It is often the same with men and women. The lad who talks at twenty as men should talk at thirty, has seldom much to say worth the hearing when he is forty; and the girl who at eighteen can shine in society with composure, has generally given over shining before she is a full-grown woman. With Dorothy the scent and beauty of the flower, and the flavour of the fruit, had come late; but the fruit will keep, and the flower will not fall to pieces with the heat of an evening.

'How marvellously your bride has changed since she has been here,' said Mrs MacHugh to Miss Stanbury. 'We thought she couldn't say boo to a goose at first; but she holds her own now among the best of 'em.'

'Of course she does; why shouldn't she? I never knew a Stanbury yet that was a fool.'

They are a wonderful family, of course,' said Mrs MacHugh; 'but I think that of all of them she is the most wonderful. Old Barty said something to her at my house yesterday that wasn't intended to be kind.'

'When did he ever intend to be kind?'

'But he got no change out of her. "The Burgesses have been in Exeter a long time," she said, "and I don't see why we should not get on at any rate as well as those before us." Barty grunted and growled and slunk away. He thought she would shake in her shoes when he spoke to her.'

'He has never been able to make a Stanbury shake in her shoes yet,' said the old lady.

Early in September, Dorothy went to Nuncombe Putney to spend a week with her mother and sister at the cottage. She had insisted on this, though Priscilla had hinted, somewhat unnecessarily, that Dorothy, with her past comforts and her future prospects, would find the accommodation at the cottage very limited. 'I suppose you and I, Pris, can sleep in the same bed, as we always did,' she said, with a tear in each eye. Then Priscilla had felt ashamed of herself, and had bade her come.

'The truth is, Dolly,' said the elder sister, 'that we feel so unlike marrying and giving in marriage at Nuncombe, that I'm afraid you'll lose your brightness and become dowdy, and grim, and misanthropic, as we are. When mamma and I sit down to what we call dinner, I always feel that there is a grace hovering in the air different to that which she says.'

'And what is it, Pris?'

'"Pray, God, don't quite starve us, and let everybody else have indigestion." We don't say it out loud, but there it is; and the spirit of it might damp the orange blossoms.'

She went of course, and the orange blossoms were not damped. She had long walks with her sister round by Niddon and Ridleigh, and even as far distant as Cockchaffington, where much was said about that wicked Colonel as they stood looking at the porch of the church. 'I shall be so happy,' said Dorothy, 'when you and mother come to us. It will be such a joy to me that you should be my guests.'

'But we shall not come.'

'Why not, Priscilla?'

'I know it will be so. Mamma will not care for going, if I do not go.'

'And why should you not come?'

'For a hundred reasons, all of which you know, Dolly. I am stiff, impracticable, ill-conditioned, and very bad at going about visiting. I am always thinking that other people ought to have indigestion, and perhaps I might come to have some such feeling about you and Brooke.'

'I should not be at all afraid of that.'

'I know that my place in the world is here, at Nuncombe Putney. I have a pride about myself, and think that I never did wrong but once when I let mamma go into that odious Clock House. It is a bad pride, and yet I'm proud of it. I hav'n't got a gown fit to go and stay with you, when you become a grand lady in Exeter. I don't doubt you'd give me any sort of gown I wanted.'

'Of course I would. Ain't we sisters, Pris?'

'I shall not be so much your sister as he will be your husband. Besides, I hate to take things. When Hugh sends money, and for mamma's sake it is accepted, I always feel uneasy while it lasts, and think that that plague of an indigestion ought to come upon me also. Do you remember the lamb that came when you went away? It made me so sick.'

'But, Priscilla isn't that morbid?'

'Of course it is. You don't suppose I really think it grand. I am morbid. But I am strong enough to live on, and not get killed by the morbidity. Heaven knows how much more there may be of it forty years, perhaps, and probably the greater portion of that absolutely alone.'

'No, you'll be with us then if it should come.'

'I think not, Dolly. Not to have a hole of my own would be intolerable to me. But, as I was saying, I shall not be unhappy. To enjoy life, as you do, is I suppose out of the question for me. But I have a satisfaction when I get to the end of the quarter and find that there is not half-a-crown due to any one. Things get dearer and dearer, but I have a comfort even in that. I have a feeling that I should like to bring myself to the straw a day.' Of course there were offers made of aid, offers which were rather prayers and plans suggested of what might be done between Brooke and Hugh; but Priscilla declared that all such plans were odious to her. 'Why should you be unhappy about us?' she continued. 'We will come and see you—at least I will—perhaps once in six months, and you shall pay for the railway ticket; only I won't stay, because of the gown.'

'Is not that nonsense, Pris?'

'Just at present it is, because mamma and I have both got new gowns for the wedding. Hugh sent them, and ever so much money to buy bonnets and gloves.'

'He is to be married himself soon down at a place called Monkhams. Nora is staying there.'

'Yes with a lord,' said Priscilla. 'We sha'n't have to go there, at any rate.'

'You liked Nora when she was here?'

'Very much, though I thought her self-willed. But she is not worldly, and she is conscientious. She might have married that lord herself if she would. I do like her. When she comes to you at Exeter, if the wedding gown isn't quite worn out, I shall come and see her. I knew she liked him when she was here, but she never said so.'

'She is very pretty, is she not? He sent me her photograph.'

'She is handsome rather than pretty. I wonder why it is that you two should be married, and so grandly married, and that I shall never, never have any one to love.'

'Oh, Priscilla, do not say that. If I have a child will you not love it?'

'It will be your child, not mine. Do you suppose that I complain. I know that it is right. I know that you ought to be married and I ought not. I know that there is not a man in Devonshire who would take me, or a man in Devonshire whom I would accept. I know that I am quite unfit for any other kind of life than this. I should make any man wretched, and any man would make me wretched. But why is it so? I believe that you would make any man happy.'

'I hope to make Brooke happy.'

'Of course you will, and therefore you deserve it. We'll go home now, dear, and get mamma's things ready for the great day.'

On the afternoon before the great day all the visitors were to come, and during the forenoon old Miss Stanbury was in a great fidget. Luckily for Dorothy, her own preparations were already made, so that she could give her time to her aunt without injury to herself. Miss Stanbury had come to think of herself as though all the reality of her life had passed away from her. Every resolution that she had formed had been broken. She had had the great enemy of her life, Barty Burgess, in the house with her upon terms that were intended to be amicable, and had arranged with him a plan for the division of the family property. Her sister-in-law, whom in the heyday of her strength she had chosen to regard as her enemy, and with whom even as yet there had been no recon, was about to become her guest, as was also Priscilla whom she had ever disliked almost as much as she had respected. She had quarrelled utterly with Hugh in such a manner as to leave no possible chance of a reconciliation, and he also was about to be her guest. And then, as to her chosen heir, she was now assisting him in doing the only thing, as to which she had declared that if he did do it, he should not be her heir. As she went about the house, under an idea that such a multiplicity of persons could not be housed and fed without superhuman exertion, she thought of all this, and could not help confessing to herself that her life had been very vain. It was only when her eyes rested on Dorothy, and she saw how supremely happy was the one person whom she had taken most closely to her heart, that she could feel that she had done anything that should not have been left undone. 'I think I'll sit down now, Dorothy,' she said, 'or I sha'n't be able to be with you tomorrow.'

'Do, aunt. Everything is all ready, and nobody will be here for an hour yet. Nothing can be nicer than the rooms, and nothing ever was done so well before. I'm only thinking how lonely you'll be when we're gone.'

'It'll be only for six weeks.'

'But six weeks is such a long time.'

'What would it have been if he had taken you up to London, my pet? Are you sure your mother wouldn't like a fire in her room, Dorothy?'

'A fire in September, aunt?'

'People live so differently. One never knows.'

'They never have but one fire at Nuncombe, aunt, summer or winter.'

'That's no reason they shouldn't be comfortable here.' However, she did not insist on having the fire lighted.

Mrs Stanbury and Priscilla came first, and the meeting was certainly very uncomfortable. Poor Mrs Stanbury was shy, and could hardly speak a word. Miss Stanbury thought that her visitor was haughty, and, though she endeavoured to be gracious, did it with a struggle. They called each other ma'am, which made Dorothy uneasy. Each of them was so dear to her, that it was a pity that they should glower at each other like enemies. Priscilla was not at all shy; but she was combative, and, as her aunt said of her afterwards, would not keep her prickles in. 'I hope, Priscilla, you like weddings,' said Miss Stanbury to her, not knowing where to find a subject for conversation.

'In the abstract I like them,' said Priscilla. Miss Stanbury did not know what her niece meant by liking weddings in the abstract, and was angry.

'I suppose you do have weddings at Nuncombe Putney sometimes,' she said.

'I hope they do,' said Priscilla, 'but I never saw one. Tomorrow will be my first experience.'

'Your own will come next, my dear,' said Miss Stanbury.

'I think not,' said Priscilla. 'It is quite as likely to be yours, aunt.' This, Miss Stanbury thought, was almost an insult, and she said nothing more on the occasion.

Then came Hugh and the bridegroom. The bridegroom, as a matter of course, was not accommodated in the house, but he was allowed to come there for his tea. He and Hugh had come together; and for Hugh a bedroom had been provided. His aunt had not seen him since he had been turned out of the house, because of his bad practices, and Dorothy had anticipated the meeting between them with alarm. It was, however, much more pleasant than had been that between the ladies. 'Hugh,' she said stiffly, 'I am glad to see you on such an occasion as this.'

'Aunt,' he said, 'I am glad of any occasion that can get me an entrance once more into the dear old house. I am so pleased to see you.' She allowed her hand to remain in his a few moments, and murmured something which was intended to signify her satisfaction. 'I must tell you that I am going to be married myself, to one of the dearest, sweetest, and loveliest girls that ever were seen, and you must congratulate me.'

'I do, I do; and I hope you may be happy.'

'We mean to try to be; and some day you must let me bring her to you, and shew her. I shall not be satisfied, if you do not know my wife.' She told Martha afterwards that she hoped that Mr Hugh had sown his wild oats, and that matrimony would sober him. When, however, Martha remarked that she believed Mr Hugh to be as hardworking a young man as any in London, Miss Stanbury shook her head sorrowfully. Things were being very much changed with her; but not even yet was she to be brought to approve of work done on behalf of a penny newspaper.

On the following morning, at ten o'clock, there was a procession from Miss Stanbury's house into the Cathedral, which was made entirely on foot; indeed, no assistance could have been given by any carriage, for there is a back entrance to the Cathedral, near to the Lady Chapel, exactly opposite Miss Stanbury's house. There were many of the inhabitants of the Close there, to see the procession, and the cathedral bells rang out their peals very merrily. Brooke, the bridegroom, gave his arm to Miss Stanbury, which was, no doubt, very improper, as he should have appeared in the church as coming from some quite different part of the world. Then came the bride, hanging on her brother, then two bridesmaids friends of Dorothy's, living in the town; and, lastly, Priscilla with her mother, for nothing would induce Priscilla to take the part of a bridesmaid. 'You might as well ask an owl to sing to you,' she said. 'And then all the frippery would be thrown away upon me.' But she stood close to Dorothy, and when the ceremony had been performed, was the first, after Brooke, to kiss her.

Everybody acknowledged that the bride was a winsome bride. Mrs MacHugh was at the breakfast, and declared afterwards that Dorothy Burgess, as she then was pleased to call her, was a girl very hard to be understood. 'She came here,' said Mrs MacHugh, 'two years ago, a plain, silent, shy, dowdy young woman, and we all said that Miss Stanbury would be tired of her in a week. There has never come a time in which there was any visible difference in her, and now she is one of our city beauties, with plenty to say to everybody, with a fortune in one pocket and her aunt in the other, and everybody is saying what a fortunate fellow Brooke Burgess is to get her. In a year or two she'll be at the top of everything in the city, and will make her way in the county too.'

The compiler of this history begs to add his opinion to that of 'everybody,' as quoted above by Mrs MacHugh. He thinks that Brooke Burgess was a very fortunate fellow to get his wife.

CHAPTER XCVIII. ACQUITTED

During this time, while Hugh was sitting with his love under the oak trees at Monkhams, and Dorothy was being converted into Mrs Brooke Burgess in Exeter Cathedral, Mrs Trevelyan was living with her husband in the cottage at Twickenham. Her life was dreary enough, and there was but very little of hope in it to make its dreariness supportable. As often happens in periods of sickness, the single friend who could now be of service to the one or to the other was the doctor. He came daily to them, and with that quick growth of confidence which medical kindness always inspires, Trevelyan told to this gentleman all the history of his married life and all that Trevelyan told to him he repeated to Trevelyan's wife. It may therefore be understood that Trevelyan, between them, was treated like a child.

Dr. Nevill had soon been able to tell Mrs Trevelyan that her husband's health had been so shattered as to make it improbable that he should ever again be strong, either in body or in mind. He would not admit, even when treating his patient like a child, that he had ever been mad, and spoke of Sir Marmaduke's threat as unfortunate. 'But what could papa have done?' asked the wife.

'It is often, no doubt, difficult to know what to do: but threats are seldom of avail to bring a man back to reason. Your father was angry with him, and yet declared that he was mad. That in itself was hardly rational. One does not become angry with a madman.'

One does not become angry with a madman; but while a man has power in his hands over others, and when he misuses that power grossly and cruelly, who is there that will not be angry? The misery of the insane more thoroughly excites our pity than any other suffering to which humanity is subject; but it is necessary that the madness should be acknowledged to be madness before the pity can be felt. One can forgive, or, at any rate, make excuses for any injury when it is done; but it is almost beyond human nature to forgive an injury when it is a-doing, let the condition of the doer be what it may. Emily Trevelyan at this time suffered infinitely. She was still willing to yield in all things possible, because her husband was ill, because perhaps he was dying; but she could no longer satisfy herself with thinking that all that she had admitted, all that she was still ready to admit, had been conceded in order that her concessions might tend to soften the afflictions of one whose reason was gone. Dr. Nevill said that her husband was not mad, and indeed Trevelyan seemed now to be so clear in his mind that she could not doubt what the doctor said to her. She could not think that he was mad, and yet he spoke of the last two years as though he had suffered from her almost all that a husband could suffer from a wife's misconduct. She was in doubt about his health. 'He may recover,' the doctor said; 'but he is so weak that the slightest additional ailment would take him off.' At this time Trevelyan could not raise himself from his bed, and was carried, like a child, from one room to another. He could eat nothing solid, and believed himself to be dying. In spite of his weakness, and of his savage memories in regard to the past he treated his wife on all ordinary subjects with consideration. He spoke much of his money, telling her that he had not altered, and would not alter, the will that he had made immediately on his marriage. Under that will all his property would be hers for her life, and would go to their child when she was dead. To her this will was more than just, it was generous in the confidence which it placed in her; and he told his lawyer, in her presence, that, to the best of his judgment, he need not change it. But still there passed hardly a day in which he did not make some allusion to the great wrong which he had endured, throwing in her teeth the confessions which she had made and almost accusing her of that which she certainly never had confessed, even when, in the extremity of her misery at Casalunga, she had thought that it little mattered what she said, so that for the moment he might be appeased. If he died, was he to die in this belief? If he lived, was he to live in this belief? And if he did so believe, was it possible that he should still trust her with his money and with his child?

'Emily,' he said one day, 'it has been a terrible tragedy, has it not?' She did not answer his question, sitting silent as it was her custom to do when he addressed her after such fashion as this. At such times she would not answer him; but she knew that he would press her for an answer. 'I blame him more than I do you,' continued Trevelyan, 'infinitely more. He was a serpent intending to sting me from the first, not knowing perhaps how deep the sting would go.' There was no question in this, and the assertion was one which had been made so often that she could let it pass. 'You are young, Emily, and it may be that you will marry again.

'Never,' she said, with a shudder. It seemed to her then that marriage was so fearful a thing that certainly she could never venture upon it again.

'All I ask of you is, that should you do so, you will be more careful of your husband's honour.'

'Louis,' she said, getting up and standing close to him, 'tell me what it is that you mean.' It was now his turn to remain silent, and hers to demand an answer. 'I have borne much,' she continued, 'because I would not vex you in your illness.'

'You have borne much?'

'Indeed and indeed, yes. What woman has ever borne more!'

'And I?' said he.

'Dear Louis, let us understand each other at last. Of what do you accuse me? Let us, at any rate, know each other's thoughts on this matter, of which each of us is ever thinking.'

'I make no new accusation.'

'I must protest then against your using words which seem to convey accusation. Since marriages were first known upon earth, no woman has ever been truer to her husband than I have been to you.'

'Were you lying to me then at Casalunga when you acknowledged that you had been false to your duties?'

'If I acknowledged that, I did lie. I never said that; but yet I did lie, believing it to be best for you that I should do so. For your honour's sake, for the child's sake, weak as you are, Louis, I must protest that it was so. I have never injured you by deed or thought.'

'And yet you have lied to me! Is a lie no injury—and such a lie! Emily, why did you lie to me! You will tell me tomorrow that you never lied, and never owned that you had lied.'

Though it should kill him, she must tell him the truth now. 'You were very ill at Casalunga,' she said, after a pause.

'But not so ill as I am now. I could breathe that air. I could live there. Had I remained I should have been well now; but what of that?'

'Louis, you were dying there. Pray, pray listen to me. We thought that you were dying; and we knew also that you would be taken from that house.'

'That was my affair. Do you mean that I could not keep a house over my head?' At this moment he was half lying, half sitting, in a large easy chair in the little drawing-room of their cottage, to which he had been carried from the adjoining bed-room. When not excited, he would sit for hours without moving, gazing through the open window, sometimes with some pretext of a book lying within the reach of his hand; but almost without strength to lift it, and certainly without power to read it. But now he had worked himself up to so much energy that he almost raised himself up in his chair, as he turned towards his wife. 'Had I not the world before me, to choose a house in?'

'They would have put you somewhere, and I could not have reached you.'

'In a madhouse, you mean. Yes if you had told them.'

'Will you listen, dear Louis? We knew that it was our duty to bring you home; and as you would not let me come to you, and serve you, and assist you to come here where you are safe unless I owned that you had been right, I said that you had been right.'

'And it was a lie you say now?'

'All that is nothing. I can not go through it; nor should you. There is the only question. You do not think that I have been? I need not say the thing. You do not think that?' As she asked the question, she knelt beside him, and took his hand in hers, and kissed it.'say that you do not think that, and I will never trouble you further about the past.'

'Yes, that is it. You will never trouble me!' She glanced up into his face and saw there the old look which he used to wear when he was at Willesden and at Casalunga; and there had come again the old tone in which he had spoken to her in the bitterness of his wrath, the look and the tone, which had made her sure that he was a madman. 'The craft and subtlety of women passes everything!' he said. 'And so at last I am to tell you that from the beginning it has been my doing. I will never say so, though I should die in refusing to do it.'

After that there was no possibility of further conversation, for there came upon him a fit of coughing, and then he swooned; and in half-an-hour he was in bed, and Dr. Nevill was by his side. 'You must not speak to him at all on this matter,' said the doctor. 'But if he speaks to me?' she asked. 'Let it pass,' said the doctor. 'Let the subject be got rid of with as much ease as you can. He is very ill now, and even this might have killed him.' Nevertheless, though this seemed to be stern, Dr. Nevill was very kind to her, declaring that the hallucination in her husband's mind did not really consist of a belief in her infidelity, but arose from an obstinate determination to yield nothing. 'He does not believe it; but he feels that were he to say as much, his hands would be weakened and yours strengthened.'

'Can he then be in his sane mind?'

'In one sense all misconduct is proof of insanity,' said the doctor. 'In his case the weakness of the mind has been consequent upon the weakness of the body.'

Three days after that Nora visited Twickenham from Monkhams in obedience to a telegram from her sister. 'Louis,' she said, 'had become so much weaker, that she hardly dared to be alone with him. Would Nora come to her?' Nora came of course, and Hugh met her at the station, and brought her with him to the cottage. He asked whether he might see Trevelyan, but was told that it would be better that he should not. He had been almost continually silent since the last dispute which he had with his wife; but he had given little signs that he was always thinking of the manner in which he had been brought home by her from Italy, and of the story she had told him of her mode of inducing him to come. Hugh Stanbury had been her partner in that struggle, and would probably be received, if not with sullen silence, then with some attempt at rebuke. But Hugh did see Dr. Nevill, and learned from him that it was hardly possible that Trevelyan should live many hours. 'He has worn himself out,' said the doctor, 'and there is nothing left in him by which he can lay hold of life again.' Of Nora her brother-in-law took but little notice, and never again referred in her hearing to the great trouble of his life. He said to her a word or two about Monkhams, and asked a question now and again as to Lord Peterborough, whom, however, he always called Mr Glascock; but Hugh Stanbury's name was never mentioned by him. There was a feeling in his mind that at the very last he had been duped in being brought to England, and that Stanbury had assisted in the deception. To his wife he would whisper little petulant regrets for the loss of the comforts of Casalunga, and would speak of the air of Italy and of Italian skies and of the Italian sun, as though he had enjoyed at his Sienese villa all the luxuries which climate can give, and would have enjoyed them still had he been allowed to remain there. To all this she would say nothing. She knew now that he was failing quickly, and there was only one subject on which she either feared or hoped to hear him speak. Before he left her for ever and ever would he tell her that he had not doubted her faith?

She had long discussions with Nora on the matter, as though all the future of her life depended on it. It was in vain that Nora tried to make her understand that if hereafter the spirit of her husband could know anything of the troubles of his mortal life, could ever look back to the things which he had done in the flesh, then would he certainly know the truth, and all suspicion would be at an end. And if not, if there was to be no such retrospect, what did it matter now, for these few last hours before the coil should be shaken off, and all doubt and all sorrow should be at an end? But the wife, who was soon to be a widow, yearned to be acquitted in this world by him to whom her guilt or her innocence had been matter of such vital importance. 'He has never thought it,' said Nora.

'But if he would say so! If he would only look it! It will be all in all to me as long as I live in this world.' And then, though they had determined between themselves in spoken words never to regard him again as one who had been mad, in all their thoughts and actions towards him they treated him as though he were less responsible than an infant. And he was mad mad though every doctor in England had called him sane. Had he not been mad he must have been a fiend or he could not have tortured, as he had done, the woman to whom he owed the closest protection which one human being can give to another.

During these last days and nights she never left him. She had done her duty to him well, at any rate since the time when she had been enabled to come near him in Italy. It may be that in the first days of their quarrel, she had not been regardful, as she should have been, of a husband's will, that she might have escaped this tragedy by submitting herself to the man's wishes, as she had always been ready to submit herself to his words. Had she been able always to keep her neck in the dust under his foot, their married life might have been passed without outward calamity, and it is possible that he might still have lived. But if she erred, surely she had been scourged for her error with scorpions. As she sat at his bedside watching him, she thought of her wasted youth, of her faded beauty, of her shattered happiness, of her fallen hopes. She had still her child, but she felt towards him that she herself was so sad a creature, so sombre, so dark, so necessarily wretched from this time forth till the day of her death, that it would be better for the boy that she should never be with him. There could be nothing left for her but garments dark with woe, eyes red with weeping, hours sad from solitude, thoughts weary with memory. And even yet, if he would only now say that he did not believe her to have been guilty, how great would be the change in her future life!

Then came an evening in which he seemed to be somewhat stronger than he had been. He had taken some refreshment that had been prepared for him, and, stimulated by its strength, had spoken a word or two both to Nora and to his wife. His words had been of no especial interest alluding to some small detail of his own condition, such as are generally the chosen topics of conversation with invalids. But he had been pronounced to be better, and Nora spoke to him cheerfully, when he was taken into the next room by the man who was always at hand to move him. His wife followed him, and soon afterwards returned, and bade Nora good night. She would sit by her husband, and Nora was to go to the room below, that she might receive her lover there. He was expected out that evening, but Mrs Trevelyan said that she would not see him. Hugh came and went, and Nora took herself to her chamber. The hours of the night went on, and Mrs Trevelyan was still sitting by her husband's bed. It was still September, and the weather was very warm. But the windows had been all closed since an hour before sunset. She was sitting there thinking, thinking, thinking. Dr. Nevill had told her that the time now was very near. She was not thinking now how very near it might be, but whether there might yet be time for him to say that one word to her.

'Emily,' he said, in the lowest whisper.

'Darling!' she answered, turning round and touching him with her hand.

'My feet are cold. There are no clothes on them.'

She took a thick shawl and spread it double across the bottom of the bed, and put her hand upon his arm. Though it was clammy with perspiration, it was chill, and she brought the warm clothes up close round his shoulders. 'I can't sleep,' he said. 'If I could sleep, I shouldn't mind.' Then he was silent again, and her thoughts went harping on, still on the same subject. She told herself that if ever that act of justice were to be done for her, it must be done that night. After a while she turned round over him ever so gently, and saw that his large eyes were open and fixed upon the wall.

She was kneeling now on the chair close by the bed-head, and her hand was on the rail of the bedstead supporting her. 'Louis,' she said, ever so softly.

'Well.'

'Can you say one word for your wife, dear, dear, dearest husband?'

'What word?'

'I have not been a harlot to you, have I?'

'What name is that?'

'But what a thing, Louis! Kiss my hand, Louis, if you believe me.' And very gently she laid the tips of her fingers on his lips. For a moment or two she waited, and the kiss did not come. Would he spare her in this the last moment left to him either for justice or for mercy? For a moment or two the bitterness of her despair was almost unendurable. She had time to think that were she once to withdraw her hand, she would be condemned for ever and that it must be withdrawn. But at length the lips moved, and with struggling ear she could hear the sound of the tongue within, and the verdict of the dying man had been given in her favour. He never spoke a word more either to annul it or to enforce it.

Some time after that she crept into Nora's room. 'Nora,' she said, waking the sleeping girl, 'it is all over.'

'Is he dead?'

'It is all over. Mrs Richards is there. It is better than an hour since now. Let me come in.' She got into her sister's bed, and there she told the tale of her tardy triumph. 'He declared to me at last that he trusted me,' she said, almost believing that real words had come from his lips to that effect. Then she fell into a flood of tears, and after a while she also slept.

CHAPTER XCIX. CONCLUSION

At last the maniac was dead, and in his last moments he had made such reparation as was in his power for the evil that he had done. With that slight touch of his dry fevered lips he had made the assertion on which was to depend the future peace and comfort of the woman whom he had so cruelly misused. To her mind the acquittal was perfect; but she never explained to human ears, not even to those of her sister, the manner in which it had been given. Her life, as far as we are concerned with it, has been told. For the rest, it cannot be but that it should be better than that which was passed. If there be any retribution for such sufferings in money, liberty, and outward comfort, such retribution she possessed, for all that had been his, was now hers. He had once suggested what she should do, were she ever to be married again; and she felt that of such a career there could be no possibility. Anything but that! We all know that widows' practices in this matter do not always tally with wives' vows; but, as regards Mrs Trevelyan, we are disposed to think that the promise will be kept. She has her child, and he will give her sufficient interest to make life worth having.

Early in the following spring Hugh Stanbury was married to Nora Rowley in the parish church of Monkhams, at which place by that time Nora found herself to be almost as much at home as she might have been under other circumstances. They had prayed that the marriage might be very private, but when the day arrived there was no very close privacy. The parish church was quite full, there were half-a-dozen bridesmaids, there was a great breakfast, Mrs Crutch had a new brown silk gown given to her, there was a long article in the county gazette, and there were short paragraphs in various metropolitan newspapers. It was generally thought among his compeers that Hugh Stanbury had married into the aristocracy, and that the fact was a triumph for the profession to which he belonged. It shewed what a Bohemian could do, and that men of the press in England might gradually hope to force their way almost anywhere. So great was the name of Monkhams! He and his wife took for themselves a very small house near the Regent's Park, at which they intend to remain until Hugh shall have enabled himself to earn an additional two hundred a-year. Mrs Trevelyan did not come to live with them, but kept the cottage near the river at Twickenham. Hugh Stanbury was very averse to any protracted connection with comforts to be obtained from poor Trevelyan's income, and told Nora that he must hold her to her promise about the beef-steak in the cupboard. It is our opinion that Mr and Mrs Hugh Stanbury will never want for a beef-steak and all comfortable additions until the inhabitants of London shall cease to require newspapers on their breakfast tables.

Brooke and Mrs Brooke established themselves in the house in the Close on their return from their wedding tour, and Brooke at once put himself into intimate relations with the Messrs Croppers, taking his fair share of the bank work. Dorothy was absolutely installed as mistress in her aunt's house with many wonderful ceremonies, with the unlocking of cupboards, the outpouring of stores, the giving up of keys, and with many speeches made to Martha. This was all very painful to Dorothy, who could not bring herself to suppose it possible that she should be the mistress of that house, during her aunt's life. Miss Stanbury, however, of course persevered, speaking of herself as a worn-out old woman, with one foot in the grave, who would soon be carried away and put out of sight. But in a very few days things got back into their places, and Aunt Stanbury had the keys again. 'I knew how it would be, miss,' said Martha to her young mistress, 'and I didn't say nothing, 'cause you understand her so well.'

Mrs Stanbury and Priscilla still live at the cottage, which, however, to Priscilla's great disgust, has been considerably improved and prettily furnished. This was done under the auspices of Hugh, but with funds chiefly supplied from the house of Brooke, Dorothy, and Co. Priscilla comes into Exeter to see her sister, perhaps, every other week, but will never sleep away from home, and very rarely will eat or drink at her sister's table. 'I don't know why, I don't' she said to Dorothy, 'but somehow it puts me out. It delays me in my efforts to come to the straw a day.' Nevertheless, the sisters are dear friends.

I fear that in some previous number a half promise was made that a husband should be found for Camilla French. That half-promise cannot be treated in the manner in which any whole promise certainly would have been handled. There is no husband ready for Cammy French. The reader, however, will be delighted to know that she made up her quarrel with her sister and Mr Gibson, and is now rather fond of being a guest at Mr Gibson's house. On her first return to Exeter after the Gibsons had come back from their little Cornish rustication, Camilla declared that she could not and would not bring herself to endure a certain dress of which Bella was very fond, and as this dress had been bought for Camilla with special reference to the glories of her anticipated married life, this objection was almost natural. But Bella treated it as absurd, and Camilla at last gave way.

It need only further be said that though Giles Hickbody and Martha are not actually married as yet, men and women in their class of life always moving towards marriage with great precaution, it is quite understood that the young people are engaged, and are to be made happy together at some future time.